1001 Dark Nights
Bundle One

Four Novellas
By

Shayla Black
Heather Graham
Liliana Hart
Tina Folsom

EVIL EYE
CONCEPTS

1001 Dark Nights Bundle 1
Print ISBN: 978-1-682305706

Published by Evil Eye Concepts, Incorporated

Sign up for the 1001 Dark Nights Newsletter
and be entered to win a Tiffany Key necklace.

There's a contest every month!

Go to www.1001DarkNights.com to subscribe.

As a bonus, all subscribers will receive a free
1001 Dark Nights story
The First Night
by Lexi Blake & M.J. Rose

Table of Contents

Once upon a time, in the future…

*I was a student fascinated with stories and learning.
I studied philosophy, poetry, history, the occult, and
the art and science of love and magic. I had a vast
library at my father's home and collected thousands
of volumes of fantastic tales.*

*I learned all about ancient races and bygone
times. About myths and legends and dreams of all
people through the millennium. And the more I read
the stronger my imagination grew until I discovered
that I was able to travel into the stories... to actually
become part of them.*

*I wish I could say that I listened to my teacher
and respected my gift, as I ought to have. If I had, I
would not be telling you this tale now.
But I was foolhardy and confused, showing off
with bravery.*

*One afternoon, curious about the myth of the
Arabian Nights, I traveled back to ancient Persia to
see for myself if it was true that every day Shahryar
(Persian: شاه ریار , "king") married a new virgin, and then
sent yesterday's wife to be beheaded. It was written
and I had read, that by the time he met Scheherazade,
the vizier's daughter, he'd killed one thousand
women.*

*Something went wrong with my efforts. I arrived
in the midst of the story and somehow exchanged
places with Scheherazade – a phenomena that had
never occurred before and that still to this day, I
cannot explain.*

*Now I am trapped in that ancient past. I have
taken on Scheherazade's life and the only way I can
protect myself and stay alive is to do what she did to
protect herself and stay alive.*

*Every night the King calls for me and listens as I spin tales.
And when the evening ends and dawn breaks, I stop at a
point that leaves him breathless and yearning for more.
And so the King spares my life for one more day, so that
he might hear the rest of my dark tale.*

*As soon as I finish a story... I begin a new
one... like the one that you, dear reader, have before
you now.*

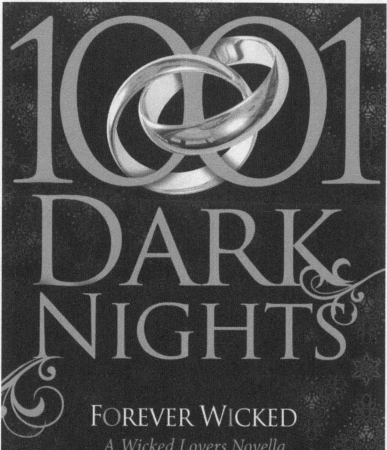

1001 DARK NIGHTS

FOREVER WICKED
A Wicked Lovers Novella

NEW YORK TIMES BESTSELLING AUTHOR

SHAYLA BLACK

Chapter One

"To what do I owe this displeasure?" Jason Denning leaned against the doorjamb and stared at the all-too-familiar face glowering back at him.

This close to Halloween, he wished his visitor was some kid he could hand a piece of candy then send away. Unfortunately, this wasn't someone in a costume.

"Is that any way to talk to your mother?" Samantha Denning-Markham-Lloyd braced her hand against his chest and shoved him out of the way to enter his condo uninvited. The tap-tap-tap of her ever-present stilettos clattered against the hand-scraped hardwood floors and echoed off the high ceilings, resounding through his downtown Dallas loft.

As he followed her across the foyer and into the great room, she picked up his remote and turned off the football game with a dramatic sigh. The TV mounted on the exposed brick wall went dark—sort of like his mood.

"No, really, Mom. I wasn't watching that or anything." He crossed his arms over his chest.

"I haven't seen you in three years, and you'd rather gawk at grown men chasing an oblong ball? Don't you even have a hug for your mother?"

Samantha had barely allowed him to touch her, even when he'd been a little boy. Now, she only ever wanted something from him when her life had gone to hell and she wanted help fixing it. "You mean like we're a warm, well-adjusted family? They usually spend Christmas together. But oh, you didn't show up last year, like we'd planned. Thanks for not calling to let me know you weren't coming. I had a fabulous holiday alone, thanks for asking."

Samantha sighed. "You have your father's sarcastic streak. I could live without it."

"Too bad I can't. Is there a reason you couldn't return my messages? I haven't moved or changed my number for the last few years, so I know you didn't fail to call because you had trouble finding me. I assumed you were too busy with husband number three for your only son."

"I didn't come here for guilt." She waved his words away, and he noticed that her ring finger was currently bare. "Lloyd is long gone. The poor bastard went bankrupt. I couldn't possibly stay."

Jason supposed that whole "for richer or for poorer" thing didn't mean much to Mommy Dearest. "So you dumped him?"

"As it happened, I met another man about the same time. Robert swept me off my feet."

Translation: He had a lot of money and spent a nice chunk on her. "So you left Lloyd for Robert. Beautiful."

"It was," she defended. "We had a fabulous wedding in Fiji. You would have loved it."

Doubtful, but since he hadn't been invited and it sounded like the union was over, his opinion was moot. "Is the divorce final yet?"

"No. He just filed last week." She pursed her artificially plumped lips as much as the injections allowed, looking a bit like a three-year-old in the body of a woman on the downhill slide to sixty. "He met a girl making a music video, of all things."

"A musician?"

"No." She scoffed. "A model strutting around in a bikini and spreading her legs on the hoods of cars for the camera. She convinced him that he still had the libido of a man half his age. Now they're engaged." She gave him a dainty huff. "I kept up my end of our prenuptial, as I have with every husband. I remained a size four. I played the gracious hostess for all his boring business parties. I even gave him the requisite blow job once a week."

Jason winced. "TMI, Mother…"

So Robert had left her—a first for Samantha. She was used to men of all ages falling at her feet and offering her the world. She was usually the trophy. Maybe those days were over.

Jason couldn't tell much difference in his mother's appearance since he'd seen her a few years ago. She stayed in impeccable shape with a personal trainer. A stylist dressed her. She religiously saw an esthetician *and* had a plastic surgeon on speed dial. Most people wouldn't think her more than a day or two above forty.

She fluffed her artificial blonde hair and shot him an impatient stare. "Don't you have anything to say?"

Not really. Though he sensed the incident had broken her ego more than her heart, she still hurt. "Is he refusing to honor the terms of your prenup?"

"No, but..." She paced, looking out over the Dallas skyline all lit up in its evening glory yet not really seeing.

"But?" he prompted. The sooner she said whatever she needed to get off her chest, the sooner she would leave.

"He's thirty-five years older than her. It's ridiculous!"

Jason refrained from pointing out that billionaire Charles Denning had been thirty-two years Samantha's senior when she'd married him. She hadn't believed the age gap ridiculous then. Since his mother had given birth to him six months after she and his father exchanged vows, Jason didn't think his mother had wooed his father away from his first wife of twenty-seven years with her scintillating conversational skills. Pointing that out now would only make her snit worse.

"Do you want a glass of wine?" A few of those usually solved her problems.

She shook her head and unwound her cashmere wrap, then tossed it at him. "It doesn't mix well with my Xanax, and I can't afford the extra calories. I'm looking for another man, one younger than me. I'll show Robert."

His mother sounded bitter. He wasn't surprised. She'd always acted as if the world owed her something.

It was going to be a long evening.

Jason paced to the fridge and grabbed a beer, then tossed himself onto the black leather sofa, peering at the cityscape. He should probably keep his mouth shut. After all, he knew damn well that she hadn't come to him for advice, probably money and sympathy—in that order. But she was all the family he had left. Even if she hadn't been much of a mother, she was his.

"Maybe you should take some time to be alone, consider what you really want in a marriage before you dive into number five. There's a reason things never work out, Mom."

"That's not fair," she shot back. "Your father died on me when you were barely thirteen. I was married to Daniel Markham for over a decade before he got stingy." She sighed. "Lloyd and I had a good five years, then...like I said, he went broke."

"And Robert couldn't keep it in his pants. Got it. I'm just saying that maybe some soul searching wouldn't be all bad before you get involved again," Jason suggested.

She cut him a blue-eyed glare as she perched on the edge of a gray suede chair and crossed her ankles. "What would you know? You've never been married."

Jason froze. He should probably shut up now, but he'd learned a thing or two lately. "Actually, I'm currently married. Have been for almost a year."

With that admission, a familiar weight pressed into his chest, unbearable and suffocating. Anger charged his veins. The constant, nagging pain followed. He shoved it all down and blanked his face.

Samantha reared back, eyes wide with *shock*, as if he'd just said he kept Godzilla as a pet. "*You* married? Why didn't you tell me?"

"I tried. That's what the invitation to spend some family time last Christmas was supposed to be about."

"Oh, well. I didn't know. You didn't invite me to the wedding."

"It was somewhat...impulsive." Because at the time, he'd thought that if he didn't own that woman in every way possible, he would go insane.

Well, he'd slipped a ring on her finger and taken her to bed. Sadly, none of that had kept him from losing his damn mind.

He'd been a stupid bastard.

Samantha's surprise deepened. "You're never impulsive. And you've always expressed utter contempt for marriage."

For years, he had. The not-so-shining examples around him had convinced him that he should never attempt happily ever after. That no one should. But *she* had been different. He'd been right about that. But he'd been so fucking wrong, too. He'd taken a stab at marriage, and the blade had cut him deep.

"Who is she?" Samantha rose to her feet, looking all around. "Where is she?"

Jason dragged in a deep breath and gritted his teeth. "She isn't here."

And she was probably never coming back. The truth fucking hurt.

For once, his mother looked genuinely concerned about him. "So you're separated? Have you started divorce proceedings yet?"

It had crossed his mind…but Jason couldn't make himself call his lawyer. Some senseless part of him kept hoping that if he gave her more time, she would return.

It's been three hundred forty-four days. What are the odds she'll come back to play happy wife?

"No."

"Has she violated her prenup? You *do* have one, right?"

"I do, and she hasn't."

His mother looked around his condo. All sleek black leather, chrome, floor to ceiling windows, and pristine kitchen—without a feminine touch anywhere. Every square inch of the place screamed bachelor pad. Samantha might be a pain in his ass, but she wasn't stupid. She'd know his wife didn't live here and never had.

"How has she not violated the terms of the agreement? You *were* specific, right?"

"I outlined how much money she would receive after every milestone anniversary if we divorced. There's a sunset clause after twenty-five years. There's a division of assets in the event of my death." He shrugged. "Typical stuff, but nothing she violated."

Samantha wagged a finger at him, looking aghast. "Jason Edward Denning, you know better than that. You're a young, good-looking billionaire. You could have any woman you want in any way you desire. Didn't you spell out her duties with regard to the house? The living and sleeping arrangements? The type and amount of sex?"

Jason stifled his anger. He'd wanted her to be a real wife; he hadn't wanted to buy her. "I kept it simple. Unlike your Prince Charming, Robert, I declined to contractually obligate her about how often I wanted oral gratification."

His mother rose and crossed the room, sitting beside him to lay her delicate fingers on his knee. "That's your mistake. You just need to be detailed with her. Surely, if you made yourself clear—"

"I wanted her to *choose* to be with me. She didn't and now she's gone. End of conversation."

Growing up steeped in wealth, he'd seen all sorts of couples marry for reasons that had far more to do with money than devotion. Not that he didn't understand a man's desire for companionship while protecting his assets. But from those interactions, he knew that relationships were a barter, affection bought and paid for. The currency might change, but the concept didn't. Meeting his wife had somehow altered his opinion.

He'd not only appreciated and deeply admired her altruistic, self-sufficient nature, he had married her because of it. Eventually, he'd hoped she would be the mother of his children because she brimmed with honesty and fought for what was right. For her, nothing had been about money, but loyalty and kindness. Caring. He'd trusted her more than he'd ever trusted a female. She put family first. Jason had never imagined the traits he'd once admired so much would bite him in the ass. Or that she'd not only leave him, but deny his most basic rights as her husband and her Dom—to help and protect her—proving that she didn't trust him at all.

Then again, hadn't that been a recurring theme for them?

"Call your attorney," his mother advised. "Maybe you can 'clarify' the terms of the agreement. Then she'll have to sign and recommit or you'll box her into a corner and she will have to leave the marriage first. And in that case, she won't receive anything, right?"

Yes, he could do all that. But she would only hate him for it. For some reason he couldn't fathom, he found that idea intolerable.

Jason slammed his beer on the glass-top table and rose. "I'm going out. If you need a place to stay, there's a guest room at the top of the stairs and to the right. If you need money, there's ten grand on my dresser. You're welcome to either. But if you're here when I come back, my marriage isn't a subject open for discussion—ever."

* * * *

Club Dominion was closed on Sunday nights, but Jason kept a private playroom here and had round-the-clock access to it. The moment he let himself into the dark, still dungeon, he realized it wasn't the room he sought, but the memories.

Quickly making his way down the hall, he pictured his wife as he'd first seen her, arresting a rowdy drunk in the parking lot who'd been harassing females entering. She'd been questioning the club's owner, Mitchell Thorpe. Despite the badge on her chest and the holstered gun at her side, everything about her expression and posture had shouted that she leaned submissive. When she'd looked at him with her soft, dark eyes, Jason's need to possess her had slammed into him like a visceral force. But she'd been gone before he could even learn her name.

The next evening, he'd spotted her out of uniform, entering Dominion with Thorpe, who both escorted and explained. Jason hadn't wasted a second before approaching her. The Dungeon Master had introduced the beauty as Greta. An oddly German name for an obviously Italian girl, but he accepted that she'd chosen a club name as a way to protect her anonymity, especially important since she worked in law enforcement.

They'd talked that first night for hours, mostly about the lifestyle, what she secretly yearned for, what she wanted to understand…and what he would be more than happy to give her.

For over a blissful year, Jason had. Casually at first, of course. He purposely didn't form attachments to others. It wasn't logical when so many merely sought him for his net worth. But from the start, his wife had been different.

Over time, she'd grown from an anxious novice, unsure if she truly wanted to pursue the lifestyle, to an eager, if somewhat willful submissive. During those months, he'd learned her beautiful soul, and their connection had grown. Shockingly, she lacked interest in his money or stature. At first, he'd wondered if her silence on the subject was a ploy to disarm him. Then his infatuation had kicked in, and he'd stopped thinking altogether.

When he'd been foolish enough to make their relationship permanent, everything had gone to hell. Now he had a wound with her name on it. He'd tried to patch and heal it…but he'd never been successful. Since Jason wasn't accustomed to failing, the bleeding bothered him even more.

"Hi, Denning." Thorpe stepped out of the shadows. "It's been weeks since you've darkened these halls. What are you doing here tonight? Not a lot of action."

Thorpe leaned against the wall, his pose seemingly casual. Bullshit. Nothing the man ever did lacked purpose.

Jason shrugged. Thorpe was one of the few who knew he'd married "Greta" and that it hadn't worked out. Thankfully, he'd never asked questions.

Unfortunately, Jason had a hard time maintaining a similar silence. "Have you heard from her?"

Thorpe cocked his head. "Greta is no longer a member here."

That made Jason stiffen and his seeping wound throb. "That's *not* her name. Don't treat me as if I don't know any better. I'm her fucking husband."

"My apologies." Thorpe's tone was smooth and somehow not apologetic at all. "Gia is no longer a member, then."

"She let her fees lapse? I'll pay them."

"No. She called me last month to revoke them. I refunded her the unused portion."

"And it didn't occur to you to call me first?" He tried not to sound like he was seething.

Apparently calling him hadn't occurred to Gia, either. In fact, she had reached out to the club owner before she'd contacted her own husband. More unexpected pain whacked him. Dominion had been his first common thread with her. The place had brought them together. And she had renounced it without a word.

"Gia asked me not to. I respected her privacy, just like I do everyone in this club."

Just then, a petite pixie of a brunette padded through the dungeon with her phone pressed to her ear and a grin on her face. Her tinkling laughter somehow brightened the room. Even from a distance, Jason saw her blue eyes dance with a hint of mischief.

No way Thorpe failed to miss it, either.

"You mean like you're protecting Callie's privacy now?" Jason drawled.

"She's different."

"How?" he questioned. "Unless I miss my guess, she's on the phone with Sean. She accepted his collar months ago, but you're eavesdropping on her conversation like whatever she says or does is still your business."

Thorpe watched the beauty as if he'd forfeit a limb for the chance to touch her. Once, the two of them had been close—not lovers, but certainly more than friends. Jason had no idea what had caused their rift, but clearly the club owner wasn't letting go. And as Callie stole a longing glance at her boss, Jason knew Thorpe's feelings weren't one-sided.

"Listen to me because I'm only going to say this once." Thorpe clenched his jaw. "I protect every woman who passes through those doors, regardless of who or what they require shielding from. Your wife chose this separation. I'm respecting her wishes. I suggest you do the same."

"Do you enjoy the distance between you and Callie these days?" Jason watched the woman end her call with a happy little sigh that left him little doubt she had feelings for Sean. Thorpe looked ready to spit nails. "I don't think so, but you let it happen. That's your choice. Good for you. But I didn't ask for this separation from Gia."

"I understand," Thorpe said.

Regardless of the platitude, the man wasn't going to budge. Thorpe, of all people, should fucking comprehend how agonizing this situation was.

Cursing under his breath, Jason resisted an unusually violent urge and tried and another tactic.

"I can't find my wife. I'm worried about her. She was going through a great deal of personal trauma when we split. She sold her house, disconnected her number. I don't know if she's all right or needs my help. She's my responsibility."

"She's *my* client. I've sworn to protect her privacy. Sorry."

His empty apology nearly yanked the leash off Jason's inner caveman. Maybe being alone for the last eleven and a half months had finally unhinged him. Maybe it was that damn hollow ache gashing his chest and infecting his judgment. Maybe seeing his mother had shown him the future he now stared down. Whatever.

"That's not putting my fears to rest." He gritted between clenched teeth.

"I can't help you."

Jason didn't want to argue with Thorpe. The man was as bendable as steel. But he refused to give up because he wasn't going to heal without seeing Gia again. "Tell me something. What would you do if Callie left Dominion—and you—without warning?"

Thorpe's face tightened as he searched for the right response. "There is no place she can go where I won't find her."

Jason saw his opportunity and seized it. "But what if she disappeared? Wouldn't you goddamn look for her and want to chew the head off of anyone who kept her from you?"

With a sigh, Thorpe sized him up. Resolution crossed his face. "Come into my office and have a drink. We'll talk."

That sounded like as much fun as a lobotomy, but it was progress. Besides, the Dungeon Master had left him little choice.

After trailing the man into his well-appointed office, Jason sat in a cushy leather chair. Thorpe lifted a cut crystal decanter of Scotch from a heavy cabinet and poured him a glass. With a nod, Jason took it.

"Thanks."

After rounding his sizeable desk, Thorpe sank into what could only be called his throne. "Start at the beginning and fill in the blanks for me. Tell me what I'm not seeing in this picture."

In other words, Thorpe would intervene only if he heard the facts and decided the situation warranted his help. Jason didn't particularly like the idea of the other man as judge and jury.

"You know the basics." He really didn't want to air his dirty laundry. He revisited the moments he and Gia had shared enough in his head.

Yes, he could hire a private investigator, but he knew exactly how that would chafe Gia's independent nature. He would find her again, but she'd be too mad to speak to him. If he wanted to locate his wife and have any chance of reconciling with her, he had to play this Thorpe's way.

Leaning back in his seat with a sigh, Jason tried to decide where to start. Not the first big scene he'd set up with "Greta" at Lakeside Park late one night. His wife had exhibitionist urges—and a lot of Catholic good-girl upbringing to overcome. She'd been unable to let go that night, and it had become a disaster.

He'd recovered quickly and staged another scene at Dominion a few days later, more private but still public enough to give her a thrill. Logan Edgington, another member of Dominion, and his wife Tara, at the time an FBI agent in field training, had witnessed his lovely sub stripping down to her skin, exposing her newly waxed pussy, then masturbating for her unknown audience. She'd surrendered to him entirely, giving him every bit of her body for the very first time. Jason still remembered how perfect she felt clinging to him, clutching his cock inside her snug little cunt. He'd suspected even before then that "Greta" was special, but that nooner had sealed the deal.

No sense in spilling those details to the club owner. Because Logan had seen it, the former SEAL had undoubtedly shared it with his buddy Thorpe. Even if Logan hadn't, Thorpe somehow knew most everything that happened under his roof.

Jason swirled the Scotch in his glass. Where to begin? Not the early days of their courtship, but later…when she'd finally trusted him with her real name, when everything between them had become genuine. The beginning of the end.

"Last November, I invited Gia to a benefit dinner for the homeless. It raised money for a shelter and kicked off a coat drive.

She'd seen enough of my life by then to know that we'd be photographed and that people would speculate. At first, she told me that she didn't own a dress fancy enough for a five-thousand-dollar-a-plate dinner. I offered to take care of it. She insisted I take the money I would have spent on her ticket and a dress and donate it because those people needed it far more than she did. She was the first woman I'd ever met who turned down money."

Thorpe sipped his drink. "And that shocked you."

"Completely. I was already infatuated with her. But her selflessness…did something to me." And he'd never recovered.

He swallowed, remembering that he'd driven to her house that night, uninvited, and fucked her like a man possessed. She'd been surprised, but welcoming. Happy, even. The night had been extraordinary, and he'd realized then that he hadn't scened or had sex with anyone else since meeting her. He hadn't wanted to. A first for him.

"The next day, Gia called me because she'd heard on the news that the same foundation would be serving an early Thanksgiving dinner to the homeless downtown and that I would be there helping. She surprised me again by asking if she could come along to lend a hand. When she refused the benefit dinner, I'd wondered if she didn't want to be seen with me and gossiped about. But no. She really just didn't want to take money that would help the needy. Instead of accepting a Versace gown so I could wine and dine her, she offered to donate food, cook, clean—whatever we needed."

Jason had seen Gia's big heart and lost his head. As he'd stood beside her and dished out trays of food to the homeless, he had totally fallen for her. A pressing need to make her utterly his assailed him. He'd been unable to talk himself out of it, so he'd set the wheels in motion.

"Your wife is a good person. I understand the circles you were raised in. A big heart is both very rare and very attractive." Thorpe looked out the open door of his office and spied on Callie, tidying up around the silent dungeon—and sneaking a peek Thorpe's way.

The yearning on the man's face told Jason that he did, in fact, perfectly comprehend.

"The day after Thanksgiving, I took Gia to dinner." He gave a self-deprecating grin. "If I'd been thinking, I would have realized that The Mansion on Turtle Creek wouldn't have been her first choice. I probably also would have chosen a more modest engagement ring, something more her style."

Thorpe looked mildly amused. "How big was it?"

"The center stone was about five carats, cushion cut, set in platinum with another two carats surrounding it. I might have gone overboard."

"Might?" Thorpe raised a brow.

Jason shrugged. "Okay, so I did. My wife isn't a little thing like Callie, but the ring looked huge on her hand. I don't even know if she liked it. She didn't say a word other than 'yes.'"

That had been one of the happiest nights of his life. Gia was the most genuine person he knew, and she made him look at everything in a different light. With her around, he could be more generous and grateful, even optimistic. Other than an isolated childhood, life had been pretty damn good to him. But she'd made everything perfect for that idyllic forty-eight hours.

"You hustled her to Vegas the next day?" Thorpe asked, though he knew the answer.

After keeping her in his bed all night long. "I did. I wasn't going to give her any time to change her mind. By that Saturday afternoon, we were married. We had the penthouse at The Venetian, along with all the room service and champagne we could consume."

And they'd had each other. That incredible night—the only he'd ever spent with her as his wife—was forever etched in his memory. Hands down, it had been the best of his life.

"When did things start to roll downhill? From my vantage point, it looked awfully fast." The Dungeon Master swallowed back the last of his booze, then glanced at Callie as she pranced past his door again.

Thorpe didn't like having emotions for the girl. A hundred bucks said they made him feel somewhere between uncomfortable and unwise. Jason related.

"That Sunday at four a.m., Gia received a call from her father saying that her brother had been killed in the line of duty."

"I heard. He was a cop too, right?"

"Yes. His partner at the time was the only one who witnessed the shooting deep in South Dallas gang turf. He apparently stayed with Tony rather than running the asshole down. None of the other units were willing to come into that neighborhood to back him up and track the thug down. Gia was heartbroken. We rushed home. And that's when things went wrong."

That's when the terrible hemorrhaging had set in.

"She was going through a lot," Thorpe pointed out.

"And like an idiot, I stepped back to give her space because she asked me to." He rubbed at his forehead, where he felt a headache developing. "During that conversation, she admitted that she'd never told her parents about me. She hadn't met my mother either, so I didn't think much of it. I didn't really understand what a big deal family was to her until it was far too late."

"Did she say why she turned you into her dirty little secret?"

"Yes. She's from a family of police officers. Her parents wanted her to marry some guy named Enzo, another cop they'd handpicked for her. He's a member of her church, and she's known him all her life. Gia swore that she married me because she loved me. Whatever that means." Probably not relevant since it hadn't lasted.

"I don't think she's the kind of woman who would lie about her feelings."

"Intentionally, no. I think she liked the fantasy of me better than the reality. When faced with the prospect of telling her family about the guy who wasn't Catholic and didn't have a drop of Italian blood in his veins...not so much." He shook his head. "Until then, I'd never heard that money didn't fix everything."

"Maybe she just needed time to tell them gently."

"I understood why she didn't want to spring the surprise on them the day her brother died, but I thought she'd do it in the next few days. Certainly before the funeral. But she didn't. Instead, she attended without me."

"Ouch."

Jason hated to admit even now the agony that had caused him. He'd needed to lend her support, hold her hand, and be her rock. But she'd turned away from him and anything he might have provided her. Instead, she'd disregarded their vows and elected to do everything for her family alone. In some ways, he'd been proud as hell. He'd been fucking infuriated, too.

"She barely called that first week. Never came to see me. I left her umpteen messages. It didn't take long before she stopped returning them. A week slid into a month. I'm not unfamiliar with the mayor. I asked him to poke around to find out what the hell was wrong. He did some digging, and I learned that Gia was consoling her parents and helping her sister-in-law through an injury of some sort. She was also caring for her nephew and newborn niece."

"She had a lot of people counting on her. Her communication

could have been better, but you can't fault her heart."

"No. However, I can fault her for turning into a one-woman vigilante squad, determined to bring down the gangster who'd killed her brother."

"Yeah, if you discovered that she was gunning for him, you absolutely had to deal with it."

"And I did," Jason confirmed. "As soon as I found out, I called and left her another message, told her that she had twenty-four hours to contact me or there would be hell to pay. I'd had enough. I missed my wife. She hadn't let me lift a finger to help her, goddamn it."

"What did she say?"

"Nothing. A day went by. Then another." He dragged in a deep breath. "She didn't bother to refuse; she just didn't acknowledge me at all."

Thorpe sat up, leaned across the desk. "Seriously?"

"Yep. Instead, she went back into that ghetto and tried to arrest the punk by herself. And he shot at her. I was fucking done."

Thorpe winced. "I don't blame you. What did you do?"

"I reached out to a few people, called in favors, greased palms." Jason shifted in his chair. "I had her put behind a desk. There was no way I was going to stand by and watch her get killed."

"I'm sure that got her attention."

"Oh, she came to see me that night, angrier than hell and itching for a fight. I was dumb enough to give it to her. She threw her ring back at me and stormed out. Hell of an early Christmas present." He smiled grimly and shook his head. "I haven't spoken to her since."

He'd tried. For months, he'd called. Not to apologize. He wasn't going to say that he was sorry for trying to keep her safe, especially after she'd backed him into a corner. But he'd left messages asking her to fucking talk to him, to at least meet him halfway. Nothing. The last time he'd called her, he'd gotten a recording that her number was disconnected. Somewhere between fed up and worried, he'd climbed into the car and driven across the city through rush hour and road construction to her house—only to find that she'd moved out months ago and new owners had taken her place.

Never once had Gia asked for his help. She'd just picked up and carried on with her life as if he didn't matter. No, as if he no longer existed.

Damn it, his chest throbbed again.

"These last months must have been difficult, but you did the right thing. After all, you can't force her to submit if you doesn't want to put herself in your hands."

"Don't I fucking know it." Jason raked a hand through his hair. "Since she apparently wants nothing to do with me, I keep expecting her to file for divorce. I'm surprised she hasn't."

"Why haven't you?"

"Right now, that's not possible since I can't find her." No, that was an excuse—and he knew it. "Even if I could, I'm not ready to quit. We only had twelve hours together as man and wife to decide if we were compatible. I've seen people get divorced quickly, but even that would be a record." Besides, their time together had been damn near perfect. And he had to understand why she'd ended all contact and cut him off at the knees. He might have to give her up eventually, but he refused to do it without a fight.

"I don't know Gia's side of the story," Thorpe admitted. "When she called to revoke her membership, she sounded stressed and upset. I pressed gently, but she wouldn't talk. I'd be violating my own rules if I gave you her current contact information, but I can call and ask if she'd be willing to speak to you." He sighed, sneaking a sideways glance at Callie. "Because if someone left me like that, I wouldn't rest until I had answers."

"Exactly."

Chapter Two

Gia Angelotti sat across from Jason and tried not to visibly shake. Impossible. He always rattled her.

The restaurant she'd chosen for their meeting was loud and public, busy for a Tuesday night. Chatter filled the air, along with the faint notes of mariachi music floating from the overhead speakers. A young Hispanic man set salsa and a bowl of chips on the table between them. She barely noticed because she couldn't do anything except stare at her husband.

God, he looked good. His dark hair appeared recently razor trimmed. His eyes lured her, such an intense crystal blue made even more striking by the two days of stubble and his stark white collar. A charcoal suit coat accommodated his broad shoulders perfectly. Then again, he'd likely had it made to fit him.

Seeing him again kicked her with a bittersweet pang. She'd missed him so much.

Tonight, they had only exchanged clipped pleasantries, and Jason looked through her like a stranger. Maybe she shouldn't have come. But Gia knew she owed him.

A year ago, he would have kissed her breathless, then probably spanked her for the fun of it before commanding her body to stunning ecstasy. She'd always surrendered herself, as if he held some sway over her. As if he alone held the key to her pleasure. But he inflamed more than her flesh. His blazing wit intrigued her. His absolute command of himself and everything around him compelled her. Then last Thanksgiving at the charity dinner for the homeless, Jason had given her intimate glimpses behind his walls, into his compassion. How many billionaires would take the time to serve someone penniless?

As they'd talked, she'd been struck by how few people he seemed to have in his life. He rarely discussed friends and never mentioned family. His lonely solitude had tugged at her heart. Gia ached to help him, heal him because under that stern mien, he had a good heart. When he'd asked her to marry him, she couldn't say anything but yes.

She cleared her throat. "I was surprised when Thorpe called and said you wanted to see me."

For a precious moment, she held her breath. He was going to serve her with divorce papers; she just knew it. That would hurt like hell, but Gia understood. She'd been unable to be a wife to Jason, and he had every right to move on. Maybe she would see their split as a blessing someday…in the very distant future.

She'd been stupid to hope that her fairy tale would end happily ever after. They were from different worlds. What did a sophisticated mogul want with a blue-collar girl who liked pizza and beer and quiet evenings at home? Gia had always thought of Jason as her gorgeous prince. His demeanor might be a little sharp and definitely Dominant, but he had so much to give besides money.

Sadly, no matter how much she loved him and always would, they would never have a happy ending.

"I wanted to talk to you, and you didn't leave me any choice." Anger sharpened his tone.

Gia tried not to wince. She hated disappointing him. "You're right, and I fully accept that responsibility."

He didn't say anything for an uncomfortable minute, just stared expectantly. "Then would you care to explain why my own wife ceased speaking to me?"

The explanation brought up so many painful memories, but he deserved to understand. "I was going through a lot and—"

"I would have been there for you, but you cut me off at the balls. I couldn't help you since you didn't tell me what the fuck was going on."

"My life changed completely, and you didn't sign up for all that. I didn't think it was fair to drag you through my muck. We'd been married for, like, five minutes, so—"

"Five minutes or five decades, we were still married. My number one job was to give you what you needed, and you didn't give me the chance."

She felt his rage thick in the air between them, sizzling across her skin, pulling at her chest. Gia had to fight not to plead with him, to point out that he'd made mistakes, too.

"You're right. Let me explain." She paused, bracing herself to relive the last terrible year. "My sister-in-law, Mila, had given birth to my niece, Bella, just a month before Tony was killed. She was already showing signs of postpartum depression, but the evening after the funeral, she tried to commit suicide by shooting herself in the heart with his gun. Another inch to the right and she'd be dead."

He sat back, his expression shocked before he softened. "I'm sorry. Is she all right now?"

"Better. We covered up her attempted suicide so that she wouldn't lose the kids. She still struggles with depression, so I live with them and try to provide stability. I have since last December."

"I wish you had told me all this."

"I didn't because there was nothing you could have done. You would only have driven yourself crazy trying." His lips tightened, and Gia prayed he would understand. "I had two children under the age of three in my care. My nephew didn't understand why his dad was suddenly gone and his mom wasn't the same. My parents were too grief stricken to handle the demands of two little kids, and my mom isn't as mobile as she used to be. I had to handle everything while still holding down my job. Thank God for daycare. But I needed another pair of hands and I didn't expect you to provide them."

"Why not? You were overwhelmed, and I would have helped you."

"How? I didn't picture you changing diapers and warming bottles for two a.m. feedings."

His expression went from remote to downright chilly. "What had I ever done to make you believe that I'd leave you to deal with everything alone?"

Nothing. Maybe it was unfair, but his playboy image hadn't given her the idea that he was prepared to cope with kids. The one time she'd been to Jason's condo before their marriage, she'd been struck by how spotless—and cold—the place looked. Black, chrome, glass...everything that would show fingerprints. Floating stairs a child could easily tumble down. Walls of windows with a balcony that a curious toddler might be able to scale and fall twenty-four stories to his death. Unfair, perhaps, to judge Jason's ability to take care of children by his condo, but in her mind it had been an indication of his lack of readiness.

"Have you ever even held a baby?" she challenged.

"I could have learned."

True. He was brilliant, and helpless was the last word she'd ever use to describe him.

"Or I could have hired someone qualified to help you. I might not have any experience with kids, but I've got a fortune."

Gia knew that. She'd even thought of asking him for monetary help at the time, but... "I didn't expect you to take on my family crisis. It wasn't your responsibility."

His mouth tightened. "*You* are my responsibility. As your husband, your problems are my problems. Instead of giving them to me, you shut me out and shouldered everything yourself. Stubborn, independent..." He clenched his jaw. "You're making my palm itch."

She hadn't allowed herself to think about how much she'd missed his discipline, his touch. Now, her womb clenched. Her clit throbbed. Her heart ached.

"Who's been taking care of you?" he demanded. "The bags under your eyes suggest you never sleep through the night any more. Your loose clothing tells me you've dropped fifteen pounds you didn't have to lose. Your hair has grown at least three inches, as if you haven't had time to cut it. You have a broken fingernail and a shoe that needs resoling. I'm going to guess your pedicure is months old, as is the wax job on your pussy."

Gia gasped. Jason had always been observant, but his attention to her every detail left her speechless.

He leaned closer, intent. "Stop acting as if I don't know you. I see you. Just like I see that no one has given a shit about you in the last year as I would have."

She couldn't refute him. God knew she'd been horrifically lonely. She'd missed Jason so damn much that sometimes the pangs had been every bit as wracking as the physical ache of withdrawal.

"A million times, I stared at my phone, needing so badly to hear your voice." She'd yearned for his steadiness and calm control to soothe her.

"But you didn't," he bit out.

"Between work and caring for the children, I didn't have anything left to give. I knew that wasn't fair to you. I couldn't take without giving back. Besides…" How did she put this into words that he'd understand? "Some nights, I'd rock Bella to sleep, tuck Tony Jr. in, then spend half the night trying to reach Mila, but she'd just lie pitifully on a mountain of pillows in her bed and stare out the window as if her world had fallen apart, refusing to speak. Guilt crushed me. Why should I have what my heart desired when everyone around me was suffering so much?"

"You felt guilty for wanting to be happy?"

"That's part of it. The other part…" She teared up. "What if I hadn't been in Vegas with you that night? I probably would have heard about the shoot out sooner. He called for backup."

"You weren't on duty that night."

"But maybe I could have gotten there—"

"That's a lot of 'what ifs' and 'mights,' and you'll never know the answer. Stop beating yourself up for failing to prevent what you couldn't foresee."

"I've told myself that logically. But I can't seem to get past the feeling that I let Tony, Mila, my parents, and the kids down." Gia pressed her lips together to hold tears at bay. After nearly a year, she'd hoped the grief would abate, but she still felt her brother's absence every single day.

On the other hand, she'd be lying if she said that missing Jason hadn't compounded her sorrow.

Her husband reached across the table and grabbed her hand. "You've endured a lot this year. If you thought you were saving me, you thought wrong. I would have been there for you. We would have faced it together."

His tender, emphatic words nearly undid her. Tears stung her eyes.

All these months, she'd felt horrible about cutting him from her life, but tried to tell herself she'd done it for his own good. Now… Had she done him a terrible disservice? After all, he'd always seen to her welfare. On their trip to Vegas, he'd treated her like his queen. Maybe he would have stood beside her and found some way to deal with the kids and the chaos. Maybe.

But Jason had betrayed her, too.

The waiter came by and took their drink orders. For a moment, they perused the menus. Gia wasn't hungry. In fact, she hadn't had an appetite all day. Her nerves about this meeting had been eating her up inside. Still, she knew from experience that Jason would insist on feeding her. In the past, he never let her skip a meal. God, she'd missed his exacting care.

By the time she yanked herself from her thoughts, the waiter was setting down their drinks and asking what they'd like to eat. Gia ordered a taco salad, then sipped at her iced tea. Jason frowned and ordered fajitas. After the waiter read back their order, he departed. The sounds around the restaurant nipped at their cocoon, but silence hovered between them.

Gia broke it. "I should have explained everything sooner. I was lost and bottled up. I'm sorry I left you hanging. I was honestly trying to figure out how I could be with you again in some way without my problems swallowing your whole life. Then your phone calls to the brass forced me to ride a desk. After that, I was just furious."

"You weren't communicating, and I needed answers. Once I got them, there was no way I was going to let you put yourself in the path of your brother's killer. I understand you were grieving. You were angry at the world and wanted revenge. You wanted to bring this thug down for your parents and your sense of justice."

Gia sat back. Sometimes, she wondered if Jason knew her at all. Other times, like now, he understood her so perfectly that he scared her.

"As a husband, I was worried. As your Dom, I was giving you hard boundaries the fastest way I could."

"You jeopardized my ability to support my family," she accused.

"I would have taken care of them." He clipped every word insistently.

"But they're my responsibility."

"Don't start that again. We've covered that ground."

"Fine. You blemished my career."

"No." He narrowed his eyes at her. "I brought your actions to light. You made the choice to go after that scumbag all on your own."

"Someone has to. And thanks to you, I'm still stuck behind a desk," she spit, her anger clawing its way up from her belly to her chest.

"You're still alive," he countered, sitting back and crossing his arms.

His stare assessed her, his irritation vibrating in the air between them. How could she be so angry with him at the same time she yearned to fall to her knees and obey his every illicit command?

"And Tony will never have justice. A killer is still on the loose. My brother's children will never really know their father. My parents won't ever be complete again. My sister-in-law doesn't say a word, but I know she's tormented that I haven't caught Ricky Wayman and made him pay for Tony's murder."

Not that Gia had given up. More than once, she'd gone to the thug's crime-ridden neighborhood alone to seek out Ricky. She didn't plan to stop until she brought him in. Confessing that to Jason wouldn't be smart. At this point, she didn't know exactly what his reaction would be, but she didn't think it would be pleasant or accepting.

"What if you got yourself killed? How would your parents take that? What would your sister-in-law do without you?" he challenged.

She couldn't quite meet his gaze. "Since I'm in no danger of being on the streets anytime soon, I guess it's not an issue."

Jason sent her a hard stare. "You're safe."

"I feel useless."

"I would still make those same phone calls again." He grabbed his beer and took a long swallow before setting the bottle far too carefully on the table. "What do you want to happen next? With us, I mean."

Now came the conversation she'd dreaded and feared, but they had to air this out. "I'm assuming you want a divorce."

She hadn't been any sort of wife to him, so that seemed logical.

Instead, he just looked pissed off. "You're assuming?"

"We can't go on this way."

"Finally. Something we agree on." He leaned in again, elbow braced on the table as his stare snared hers. "So I'm going to give you a choice: Spend between now and our anniversary with me—and I mean twenty-four/seven *with* me, in every fucking way I deem. If the twenty-fourth rolls around and you still want a divorce, file. I won't fight you. In fact, I'll not only honor the terms of our prenuptial agreement, but I'll give you the amount stipulated if we'd remained married five years. If you want a divorce now, I'm filing tomorrow, and you get nothing." He raised a brow at her. "Decide."

Gia sucked in a breath at his proposition. "This instant?"

"The offer is only good for the next ten minutes."

She'd always known that Jason played hardball, but she hadn't expected him to use those skills on her. The prince she'd fallen in love with wasn't trying to reconcile with her, but control and punish her.

"So you're trying to coerce me into bed for a little revenge, or do you just want to work me out of your system?"

He shrugged. "My motivation is irrelevant. I merely asked you to make a choice."

Gia's immediate instinct was to tell him to shove his choice up his ass. She couldn't be bought, no matter how rich and powerful he was. On the other hand, her conscience wouldn't allow her to turn her back on him again. Besides, the two hundred fifty thousand dollars he dangled in front of her face could change her entire life. All she had to do was give the man she loved slightly less than three weeks of her time.

It wasn't exactly a nightmare scenario—except for the part where he probably ended up crushing her heart at the end. Maybe she deserved it. Jason might not admit it, but she knew she'd hurt him this past year. If having her under his thumb for a few weeks enabled him to move on after they ended, she owed him that.

"I'll come with you." She'd figure out what to do about work, what to say to her parents, how to make sure Mila and the kids had the help they needed.

A satisfied little smile danced across his lips. "Excellent. Present yourself at my condo tomorrow at precisely six p.m. Arrive wearing no more than three garments and a pair of high heels. Pick whichever three you want, but if I have to peel off more than that before I fuck you, we'll start with punishment."

Shock whiplashed her. He'd always been direct, but his sharp command, followed by the declaration that he intended to take her to bed, both made her mad and frothed up her libido. She hadn't had sex since their wedding night. She hadn't even had energy or privacy for masturbation. Though her long-denied sex drive wasn't at all upset about his demands, her head knew that his proposition was riddled with land mines. Eventually, this would blow up in her face.

Still, she couldn't possibly refuse.

"Fine."

Neither of them said a word more until the waiter set their food down. Even the smell of Jason's sizzling fajitas didn't rouse her appetite for food. Another sort of hunger plagued her. Why should she want him so much when he was being a ruthless bastard? Because she'd always found that side of him hot, and Gia's own excitement now pissed her off.

He thanked the waiter, then turned back to her. "If work presents a problem for the next few weeks, I'll make the necessary phone calls."

"Of course you will," she drawled.

He ignored her jibe. "Does your sister-in-law need a nurse or a nanny during your absence? If so, I'll provide it. I have no desire to leave them in a bind."

Guilt stabbed her. Gia softened. "Thank you. That's generous of you."

"Not at all. I don't want you spending our time together thinking about anyone else."

Of course not. And Jason was used to getting his way.

Gia stifled her guilt. "I'll talk to Mila tonight."

"Whatever she needs so she can manage without you for a few weeks, she'll get. Are we understood?"

The concept wasn't difficult. Jason had bought her until November twenty-fourth, and she'd let him. Though she'd chosen this path of her own free will, it made her feel dirty. "Yes."

He nodded at her. Then the conversation ceased, and he dug into his food. Gia stared at her salad. Her stomach roiled too much to take a bite. She picked at the greens and plucked at the grilled chicken, thinking about tomorrow night. How long would it take him to wholly own her body and heart again? An hour, or could she actually manage to hold out an entire night?

"You're not eating."

"I had a late lunch," she lied.

He set down his fork slowly. "Do you remember what I do to subs who aren't honest with me?"

Orgasm deprivation—hours and hours of it. Her sex tightened. Heat crawled up her cheeks. Even on an olive-skinned Italian girl, the blush would be impossible to miss.

"I see that you do." Jason looked satisfied. "The sensual torture last time will seem minor compared to what I'll do tomorrow night if you don't tell me the truth now."

Gia gritted her teeth. Until tonight, they'd never even had an argument. She'd just willingly fallen under his spell and into his embrace. Trying to resist Jason now was as futile as it was arousing.

"All right, then. I was nervous when I walked in and now I'm sick to my stomach that I let you buy me, even for a few weeks."

With a cynical curl of his lips, he lifted his beer and toasted her. "Everyone has their price, Gia. I just found yours."

Chapter Three

Gia tried to breathe through her nerves as she arrived at Jason's condo the next night. The mountain of lies she'd told her family still scalded her with shame. They wouldn't understand. Mila would tell her not to compromise herself. Her parents would be disappointed that she'd sold her morals and her body, even briefly. Her brother, if he'd been here, would have gone after Jason with cocked fists and a loaded semiautomatic.

Fabricating excuses had been far better for everyone.

As she stepped off the glass elevator that gave her aerial views of the city stretching on forever, she crept into a foyer with a water feature cascading down a glass wall. His door stood to the left. Gripping her suitcase in her hand, she glanced at her phone. Three minutes until six. One hundred eighty seconds to decide how the hell she was going to leave in eighteen days with her sanity and her heart intact. Of course, she'd had nearly twenty-four hours to ruminate on that problem. She'd come up with absolutely nothing.

Gia focused on his imposing black wood and wrought iron door, but couldn't make her feet move. Her belly clamped. Her heart stuttered. She tried to convince herself that she could handle this, but the mental pep talk wasn't working.

To her shock, the door opened suddenly, and Jason stood there in jeans, a long-sleeved jersey knit top in midnight blue, bare feet, and that triumphant hint of a smile she wanted to slap off his face.

"You're on time. Very good." He stepped back to admit her. As she entered with leaden legs, he glanced at her suitcase that had seen better days. "Is that all you brought?"

Had he expected her to bring her whole closet? "You gave me the impression I wasn't going to need many clothes."

"You won't." He shut the door behind her and took her bag. "I don't have many ground rules while you're here. Anything you see in the kitchen you want, take it. Don't leave the building without consulting me. I've got a heated pool on the deck outside our bedroom. There's a full gym downstairs. You're welcome to use either as you'd like. No work while you're here, especially on your brother's case. We'll discuss any family emergencies *together* as they arise. When we're sceneing, you will call me Mr. Denning. Is anything I've said confusing?"

"No." She supposed that since she hadn't seen or knelt for him in nearly a year, he no longer wanted her to call him Master. That was just fine. That slash of pain didn't mean a damn thing.

To avoid staring at him, she eyed his personal space. The expanse of a two-story wall of windows was unbroken by a drape or blind. Then again, why bother? Who could peek in on them this high up?

"Nice shoes." He glanced down at her dressiest T-strap black heels. "What three garments did you choose to wear with them?"

His high-handed attitude made her feel like a piece of merchandise. Gia tried to keep a grip on her temper. Was he punishing her for the last year or was she seeing the real Jason Denning now that he had no reason to woo her?

"Hello to you, too. My day was hectic. How about yours?"

"It dragged by while I counted the hours until I could fuck you again." He pulled his phone from his pocket and glanced at it. "I'm much happier now that my wait is over. And I don't want to hear the attitude again. I've done nothing you haven't agreed to, so don't act as if I've insulted you."

Technically, he was right, and that rubbed Gia completely wrong. "Should I just drop all my clothes here, get to the floor, and spread my legs? Or will I make it up to the bedroom before you're all over me?"

Jason froze. "Do you need to reconsider your decision? The door is right behind you if you'd rather divorce now and forfeit the money."

So cold. Where was the firm but caring Dom she'd fallen for? If she was smart, she'd take him up on this reprieve and walk out the door. But she couldn't afford to. Besides, it wouldn't be the right thing to do. She'd hurt him, so now he meant to hurt her back. An eye for an eye.

"No. I'm staying until the twenty-fourth."

For a silent moment, he let her feel the weight of his anger. "Then act like it or we'll start talking about consequences."

Gia knew she shouldn't mouth off to him again, but she had to ask him one thing. "Would your parents be proud of you right now?"

He shifted his weight and seemed to ponder her question. The conclusion he reached apparently amused him. "My father would. He was an absolute bastard who ate other people for breakfast. My mother would expect it. In fact, just a few days ago she suggested that I take you in hand and be firmer in my expectations. I didn't listen to her much growing up, but I think she might be onto something now."

His answer horrified her, mostly because he appeared dead serious. Nor did he seem to think his behavior was appalling. *Oh god...* She wasn't just in over her head; he'd no doubt drown her before the night was through.

Jason had not only bought her body until their anniversary, he'd bought her soul. She'd sold it to him almost without a fight.

Gia closed her eyes in shame. "I'm wearing a sweater, a bra, and jeans."

"No panties?" he murmured in her ear as he set her suitcase down and began circling her like a shark. She heard the rustle of him around her, felt his body heat across her skin.

"None."

"I'm very pleased. Take everything off."

Her brows drew together as she tensed and tried to find her fortitude. Would it be even harder when she had to spread her legs for him and allow him inside her, knowing he merely wanted revenge? Or would he, like before, overwhelm her with pleasure until she panted and begged? She didn't know which would hurt more.

Slipping out of her shoes, she stepped onto the textured wood. It was solid, comforting, kind of like the floor in her dad's den. Gia focused on that as she peeled her sweater over her head and dropped it to the ground. She tried not to think about what she was doing when she reached behind her and unhooked her bra. Not that the lace covered much, but as she removed what little protection it afforded, cold hit her nipples. They beaded. She refused to believe it had anything to do with Jason's blistering stare.

Slowly, Jason reached out and touched her. Gia started with a little gasp. His ghost of a smile haunted her when he ran his knuckles up the curve of her waist, to the swell of her breast, brushing over the sensitive bead. Against her will, a jolt of desire shivered through her system. Her breath hitched.

"Pretty. Soft," he whispered. "Now lose the jeans so I can see your pussy."

Gia dragged in a shuddering breath, her whole body tense. Why did she resent him and want him so much at the same time? What mystical control did he have over her body? Or did she simply respond because she'd always loved him?

Her fingers shook as she unsnapped her pants. The zipper fell with a subdued hiss. Then she fitted her hands on the waistband and pushed them down her hips. A year ago, they'd been tight. Since then, they'd gotten so big, they fell to her knees with the tiniest shove. She stepped out of them, leaving them piled on the wood beside her sweater.

Gia stood totally bare in front of him, eyes squeezed tightly shut.

Jason took her chin in his grip. "You don't get to escape me by closing your eyes and pretending I'm someone else."

Lashes fluttering, she lifted her lids. "That's not... I wasn't even thinking of another man."

"So this is the sacrificial martyr routine. Perfect," he snapped. "Nothing makes a man feel more wanted than cringing."

Gia clenched her fists. "For the next eighteen days, you can tell me where to be, what to wear, where to sleep, how to kneel, and the way you want me to spread my legs. You do *not* get to tell me how to feel."

He hesitated, his stare taking her in. She wished she could see warmth in his blue eyes—something that made his strict care seem like the safety net it once had. Now it just felt like a blade he held at her throat.

Finally, he stepped back, reaching behind him to grab a fluffy white robe on a coat rack she hadn't noticed. It was too small for him, and it made Gia wonder if he kept it here for his overnight conquests. She tried not to weep at the thought as he slipped it over her shoulders and she rushed to belt it around her waist.

"Go upstairs," he demanded. "At the end of the hall, you'll find our bedroom and someone waiting for you. I'll be up soon."

Someone? He wasn't coming up to push her into bed right this second? Or had he arranged for another person to do his bondage dirty work first? She frowned.

Annoyance tightened his lips. "Problem?"

Whatever awaited her upstairs would allow her precious time to confront her feelings and get them under control. She'd been terrified out of her mind on the job once or twice. She'd buckled down, pushed through, and taken care of business. This required the same strategy.

"None."

Gia swept past him and headed up the stairs. Before they'd married, she would have taunted him with a kiss and a flirty smile. Now, she risked a peek at him over her shoulder and found him watching her, unblinking and resolved.

With a shiver, she raced to the master bedroom and got her first look at his personal space. The soft lights of the recessed cans and the golden glow from a lamp on his nightstand illuminated the room, muting the view of the city. The big dark leather-tufted headboard dominated one wall and lorded over the king-sized bed, covered in white with accents of shimmering taupe. It looked like a sleek hotel room. Except for the two women who stood inside the space, both gorgeous and impeccably groomed.

"Gia?" a blonde in her mid-thirties asked.

"Yes." Were they Jason's lovers? Did he want her to hear their bedroom tales or something?

"I'm Michaela." Her smile broadened, a friendly gesture that surprisingly set her at ease. Then she gestured to the woman beside her. "This is my assistant Stacia."

The very petite, exotic brunette bowed her head in welcome. "Hello."

What was going on? "Nice to meet you."

"If you'll come with me into the bathroom, we'll get started on your hair," said Michaela.

Her hair? Jason wanted her tresses arranged in some fancy do before he tousled her in his big bed? Then again, this was his show. She was here to entertain him.

"Sure."

As they rounded the corner into the modern space, she stopped short. A contemporary oval tub stood alone in the corner of the room on dark slate tile. Views of the city sparkled from the two walls of windows. A double vanity with hideously expensive marble carved out not only the counters but the sinks, all in severe angles. The piece took up half the length of one wall. A massive shower ate up the rest. No curtain or glass partitioned it off. The space was designed to simply walk into, with shower heads to spray a body from every direction, as well as overhead.

In the middle of the large space, Michaela had set up a big leather chair with an ottoman and waved Gia toward it. "Please sit here."

Getting her hair done wasn't exactly like being waterboarded. With a shrug, she eased into the seat.

Immediately, Michaela had her hands in Gia's tresses, fluffing and testing its texture. "Tell me what you'd like to do with your hair. I'd recommend a trim to clean up the ends. We can play with the color if you want. Your dark brown has gold tones. It's pretty, but I can add more warmth, frame your face with some highlights. We can also give you some depth with lowlights."

"He didn't give you specific instructions?" If he'd paid a pair of beauticians to come to his place, she figured that Jason would want to call the shots.

"Just to bring out your natural beauty and make you happy."

That puzzled the hell out of Gia. She'd never been a girly-girl, and highlights would just mean maintenance later that she didn't need to deal with. Her plate was already full. But a free haircut was a free haircut.

"Just a trim, please."

Michaela didn't show her disappointment. "Of course. I'll condition it, too. Now that winter is coming, you'll need a little extra moisture."

Sure. Whatever.

Gia leaned back, lowering her head into one of Jason's sinks as Michaela wet her hair. Stacia approached her with several bottles of nail polish and asked her to pick one for her pedicure. Absently, she picked a peachy-bronze color and sighed as Michaela began to shampoo her. Gia knew she should relax and enjoy the pampering. She hadn't had any in the last year. Instead, the worry that the temporary nanny wouldn't remember to read Tony Jr. a bedtime story distracted her. And the hope that Jason would soon be in a better mood ran a close second.

An hour later, she stared at herself in the mirror, blinking in surprise. With a few snips of the scissors, the brandishing of a blow dryer, and some turns of a curling iron, Michaela had transformed her hair into something beautiful, full of body and shine. Stacia had finished her pedi, and now shaped and buffed her fingernails.

Afterward, she emerged from the bathroom. A baby-doll nightie in a blush color, trimmed with beige lace that would cup her breasts and flirt with her thighs, lay strewn across the bed. A very small thong accompanied it. A pair of new champagne-hued Louboutin stilettos sat on top of their box, their bows glittering, the red soles a bright warning.

"I'm supposed to put all this on?" she asked no one in particular.

"Not yet," Michaela answered, then turned to her assistant.

Gia caught sight of a pot of wax heating as Stacia set up what looked like a wide massage table and covered it with a clean sheet. Her stomach dropped. Jason really meant everything he'd said. He intended to take her to bed. For that, he'd want her waxed. After all, why shouldn't he insist on his money's worth? Remembering how much she'd hurt him and how much she owed him, she eased onto the table, vowing not to give her husband any more of herself than her body.

* * * *

Scrubbing a hand down his face, Jason paced his kitchen. The scents of the savory garlic-herb roasted chicken and vegetables blended with the delicious aroma of yeasty bread. He should be hungry by now. Starved, even. Hell, he couldn't notice a damn thing but the clock ticking, his dick aching, and that wretched pain only Gia could make him feel gouging his chest.

His wife had chosen money. He'd offered her the funds in desperation, never imagining that she'd take them. Rather, he'd clung to the hope that she had agreed to meet him at the Mexican restaurant because she wanted to resume their marriage. In truth, Jason had been worried that Gia had come to seek a divorce. He'd been prepared to talk fast to convince her otherwise. But never had he imagined that she'd actually take him up on his wretched offer and sell herself.

Apparently, she wasn't different from the rest, after all.

The only saving grace to this situation was that his mother had been gone when he'd returned home late Sunday. Not surprisingly, she'd taken the cash on his dresser. Later, she'd texted to say that she had found a new friend while consoling herself at Neiman's. Apparently, the man had invited her to dinner at The French Room. Jason hadn't seen Samantha since. Her new friend must be "entertaining" her. Hell, if the guy had enough money, he'd probably be husband number five.

Finally, the two beauticians he'd hired to take care of Gia's personal needs made their way down the stairs, implements all packaged up in their roller bags. He exchanged a few words with the quiet blonde, but didn't hear a lot beyond the fact that his wife was finished and waiting for him upstairs.

More eager than he wanted to be, Jason paid the women and tipped them amply before he tossed together a dinner tray, added a chilled bottle of wine, and headed up to find his bride.

His heart raced as he reached the closed door. "Gia?"

"Yes."

She didn't sound at all happy. He'd given her more than one opportunity to leave, but she'd taken the mercenary path. He refused to feel sorry for her.

Balancing everything in one hand, he turned the knob and opened the door. As soon as he saw her, he nearly dropped the tray. She looked like his fantasies—only better. Her hair hung in loose waves. One of the women had done something that made her skin glow under the lights. Even her toenails shimmered. When he'd bought the miniscule scrap of lace she now wore, he'd imagined how she would look in it and gotten hard as hell. But seeing her in person? Damn. He could picture her spread out across his sheets, her gaze on him, her arms open as he ripped her thong away to expose her smooth, pouting pussy. The "fuck me" shoes made him want to do exactly that. Jason nearly growled with need. But he'd enjoy the sex more if Gia felt half as eager as he did…and if she'd lie to him and say she loved him, like she used to.

Patience.

If Gia wanted a divorce and she wanted to be paid for her freedom, he planned to make her earn every penny of it first. And if he was very lucky, maybe he'd figure out how to get enough of her and move on.

He set the tray on the dresser, still looking her over. "Beautiful."

She cast her gaze down submissively. Either that or she couldn't bear to look at him. "Thank you."

"I brought us some dinner." He poured the wine, and she took the glass, her expression somewhat guarded. "To…new endings."

Her face closed up entirely. "Hopefully, a quick one."

Jason made a noncommittal sound, repressing his urge to get her naked and flat before he put his stamp on her, hold her in his thrall the way she'd done him. Instead, he forced himself to wait. Gia gulped half her glass as if she needed the liquid courage.

Trying not to grit his teeth, he lifted the lid on the dishes, then pointed at the bed. "Sit."

Slowly, she sat back against a stack of fluffy white pillows and took the plate. "Thank you."

Their gazes met before hers skittered away.

Holding in a curse, Jason gave her a fork. When she grabbed the far end, refusing to even brush his fingers, his lips tightened. If she had a new aversion to touching him, he'd quickly put a stop to it.

Plate in hand, he sat back on the bed against the grouping of pillows, leaning against the headboard beside her. Digging his fork into his rice, he did his best to focus on the food and act as if nothing happening between them bothered him in the least.

"So, you've been dealing with your family. Tell me about the progress you've made in bringing your brother's killer to justice."

Gia tensed. "There hasn't been any. My brother's former partner initially pointed the finger at a thug named Ricky Wayman. A few days later, he recanted and claimed he wasn't sure, but I know better. Patrick was either scared off or paid off. The day before my brother died, he told my dad that he knew Ricky had something big going down and he intended to stop it. Tony died on Ricky's turf, so I know damn well who shot my brother."

"No one has arrested Wayman?"

"They haven't even brought him in for questioning." And that obviously infuriated her.

"Don't the police usually go all out to hunt down a cop killer?"

Something cynical and mad as hell twisted her delicate features. "Usually, yeah. Wayman's got a sick rep and a lot of firepower." Fingers gripping her plate until her knuckles turned white, she drew in an angry breath. "I think the brass is already convinced it's an unwinnable war and it would cost too many lives to bring this one punk to justice. He takes out a lot of other criminals, so…"

"They let him slide." Jason turned her words over in his head, angry on her behalf. Not only did someone as principled as Gia want the badges she worked with to do their jobs and put criminals behind bars, she expected it. She'd been disillusioned by their failure to act.

"Totally," she confirmed, no longer eating.

Jason knew damn well how his wife had been spending her time this past year. Since she hadn't gotten the help she needed from her fellow officers, she'd refused to give up on justice for her brother. "So you've spent all your free time tracking Wayman down yourself and trying to prove his guilt, even after I had you put behind a desk." He sent her a speculative stare. "Your parents don't know, do they?"

With a roll of her eyes, she admitted, "My dad tried to make me promise that I wouldn't go after Wayman alone, but my mom is so grief stricken. I have to try and give her whatever comfort I can. That killer behind bars would help."

Drawing in a deep breath, Jason tried to pull back on his anger. Gia's sense of good and right wouldn't allow her to sit this manhunt out. Funny how the determination and rectitude that had drawn him to her had become the very things he wanted to throttle her for.

"I understand."

Gia hesitated. "You do?"

"It's hard to see people you care for in pain, isn't it?"

She nodded. "Excruciating."

Jason couldn't agree more, and though logic told him that her circumstances shouldn't matter, he couldn't ignore her anguish. "Eat your dinner before it gets cold."

She exhaled and seemed to deflate altogether. "I'm not hungry."

"That isn't a request." He sent her a stern glare.

"Of course it isn't. And people always obey you."

"Generally, yes. I won't apologize for it, especially when it's for your well-being."

And Jason refused to say another word until she'd consumed at least half of the food on her plate, even giving him a low moan at the tastiness of the bread.

When they'd finished, he took her plate and padded downstairs, leaving the dishes in the sink. His maid would be in come morning to take care of the mess.

He pulled the refrigerator open and lifted one large crystal cup, then grabbed a single spoon from the drawer and headed back upstairs, mentally weighing the evening's events.

As he made his way to the bedroom again, he was unpleasantly surprised to find Gia no longer in his bed. After setting the items he held aside, he visually swept the room and sighed in relief. She stood at the window and stared out, looking at the sky lit night and the urban sprawl giving way to suburbia farther north. His wife might be physically in the room with him, but she was really a million miles away.

"What's wrong?"

She jerked back to attention and shook her head. "Nothing. I'm fine."

As she turned to face him, her expression looked neutral, all traces of whatever or whomever she'd been thinking about gone. He held in a snarl of frustration.

"Sit for me."

Dragging her feet, Gia did as he bid, stopping at the edge of the bed. "Naked, I presume? Now that you've done your Domly duty and seen to my needs, you're intending to see to yours, right? Is this the part of the evening where you nail me into the mattress?"

Jason felt his ire rise. Then he caught onto her game. "Trying to make me feel guilty for this arrangement will neither anger nor upset me enough to halt it. I made you an offer. You accepted. End of story."

She gave him a little huff. "I don't understand why you're doing this."

To hear her admit that she had no idea why he might want to spend time with her bugged the hell out of him. It also told him that she'd given up on them already. Somewhere in the back of his head, he'd known that, but it bothered him all the same. "I have my reasons and I'm not obligated to share them. You're my submissive for now—"

"Oh, just say it. I'm your whore and you're getting off on exercising your control over me."

Jason froze. It took everything inside him not to rise to her bait. "If that's how you choose to see the situation, I can't stop you. I merely asked you to sit on the bed. I'm still waiting."

"Fine." She tossed herself onto the mattress and sat against the pillows, crossing her arms over her chest.

"Thank you. Now hold your arms up at your sides."

Her dark eyes flashed suspiciously. She narrowed them as if trying to guess his intent. Finally, she complied, holding them straight out from her shoulders, almost as if opening her arms to him...but not quite.

Jason reached behind his headboard and plucked at a padded wrist cuff, attached to an adjustable chain, then secured it around his wife's wrist.

Gasping, she drilled him with a shocked stare. "What the hell?"

"We are now sceneing. What should you call me?"

"What the hell, Mr. Denning?" she snarled, jerking her free arm down to her side.

He grabbed it again and brought it to the other cuff. Gia fought him, and Jason dug deep for patience. "Give me your wrist or use your safe word. It's divorce."

"You're being a bastard, Mr. Denning."

"Well, we can't all be angels like you. Since opposites attract..." He gave her a tight smile. "In case you're wondering, I'm not offended. Much meaner people have called me names far worse. Are you saying your safe word or giving yourself over to me?"

The fight left Gia. She lifted her hand to him.

"Just to be clear, you're choosing to give your power to me, yes?"

"Yes." She gritted her teeth. "Mr. Denning."

Even though she'd given him the green light grudgingly, satisfaction still rolled through him. For the first time in nearly a year, he would finally have the gratification he'd craved—and he intended to take it. "Excellent."

Wrapping his fingers around her forearm, he aligned her wrist with the cuff and snapped it in place. Now she was beautifully at his mercy.

"Are you uncomfortable physically in any way?" he demanded.

"No."

"Do you have anything you want to say before we get started?"

"No."

"And your safe word is..." he quizzed.

"Divorce." Gia sounded as if she worked hard to shove down her anger.

It couldn't be greater than his own, and he'd get to the bottom of hers when she felt more amenable to conversation. For now, he had something else in mind to remind her once and for all of the way a Dom/sub relationship worked.

"Good." He reached into his nightstand and pulled out a sleep mask. It worked wonders when he needed shut-eye on bright Texas mornings...or when surly little subs needed an attitude adjustment.

When he lifted the mask to her eyes and fitted the Velcro strip behind her head, she gasped. "Jason, no."

"Excuse me?" He injected sharp rebuke into his voice.

"I'm sorry, Mr. Denning..."

Now she sounded breathy and afraid, and he backed down immediately. Cradling her face in his hands, he pressed his lips to her ear. "I'm going to take care of you."

She sucked in a shaky gulp of air. He could almost hear her mentally reviewing the months they'd spent as Master and slave, remembering all the ways he'd seen to her well-being then.

And slowly, her frozen muscles melted a bit. "Thank you."

So she hadn't forgotten the manners he'd taught her when playing with him. He smiled.

As he rose from the bed, Jason stepped back to admire Gia all spread out like a sacrifice, arms wide, innocent lace barely hiding her nipples and pussy from him, eyes covered and breath held, awaiting his pleasure. The sparkling shoes with their five-inch heels elongated her sleek legs. The idea of those shoes in the air while he fucked her turned him on.

With a grimace, he adjusted his hard cock in his jeans and made his way to the dresser to retrieve the goodies he'd left there. Once in hand, he sat on the edge of the bed next to her. God, he couldn't wait for this.

"Open your mouth."

Her breathing caught before the rate of her respiration picked up. Then slowly, she parted her moist, rosy lips. He'd missed kissing her so much, feeding his cock into that mouth and drowning in the warm heaven…

Shit, he had to stay on track.

He lifted the dish and dipped the spoon inside to gather a generous bite. Then he inched it onto her tongue and waited.

As soon as the taste hit her buds, she wrapped her lips around the spoon with a moan that fired his blood and sucked the utensil clean.

"You like that?" A grin tugged at his lips as he scooped up more of the confection for her.

"It's amazing," she hummed, her face lax with pleasure. "You remembered?"

"That chocolate mousse is your favorite, yes. I remember everything."

She tensed. Jason weighed his next options, but he'd done enough cornering and hounding her for the moment. She knew the score. Now was the time to coax her.

He raised the spoon to her lips again and nudged her wider. Gia didn't hesitate, but eagerly took the mousse into her mouth once more. "I think that's the best I've ever had."

Because he'd hunted down a five-star rated chef and paid the man a small fortune to make this just for her. If he was going to coerce her into spending nearly three weeks with him, he had to show her some of the perks. This was a start.

"I think I'd like to try some, too."

Rather than giving her time to ponder his declaration, Jason set the dish and spoon aside, then reached for the buttons holding the baby-doll together between her breasts. One, two, three, they all came undone without a fight. He pushed the sides of the filmy garment apart and exposed the sight he'd been craving since he'd last taken her on their wedding night.

Beauty came in all shapes and sizes, but he was a breast man. And Gia had just about the most beautiful he'd ever seen. Round, firm, on the large side but not disproportionate. Dusky tips surrounded by inch after inch of unblemished olive skin. Just perfect.

As the cool air caressed Gia, her nipples tightened. His mouth watered. With a feral grin, he dipped his finger into the mousse, then rubbed the dark, sugary cream on her distended tip. So the other didn't suffer indifference, he covered it as well.

Gia's small hands curled into fists and she bit her lip, but arched toward him, begging him without a word to ease her ache. Jason gladly complied.

He bent and cradled one breast in his palm, lifting it toward his mouth. The scents of chocolate blended with the succulent musk rising from her skin. As he took one sugary nipple in his mouth, her flavor intoxicated him. She made him dizzy with her sweetness.

Fucking hell, he'd missed Gia. No woman smelled or tasted or affected him the way she did. After nearly two decades of sex for the sake of sex, he knew the difference. And as he laved her peak, licking off every morsel of the chocolate goodness, Jason wondered how he would ever do without her again.

As he sucked on the hard tip of her breast, a whimper slipped from Gia, as if she couldn't hold her reaction in. He refused to let her. She forgot that he knew her body way too well to hide from him. But he'd remind her.

He nipped at the sensitive crest of her breast, then drew on her, sucking hard. She gasped as she tossed her head back with a thump against the headboard. Before she could absorb the pressure of his mouth, he pulled back enough to grip her wet nipple between his thumb and forefinger. As he squeezed, he latched onto the other breast, capturing the hard tip against his tongue and eating off the chocolate while feeling her nipple harden even more.

"Jason…"

His wife's voice sounded somewhere between a moan and a plea. He drank it in, letting the little sigh resonate in his head and swirl together with all the unique things about Gia that left him hungering for her. But he had a point to make now that wasn't about his pleasure—as much as he wished otherwise. Time to remind her exactly who—and what—he was.

Jason pulled back, withdrawing his fingers and lips, removing all stimulation. "Not 'Jason.' Try again."

Her brow furrowed. Her lips pressed together. Gia was confused and frustrated. Clearly, she wanted more pleasure. He withheld. Maybe now she could understand a fraction of what he'd endured for nearly the past year.

"Mr. Denning," she finally gasped out, arching her breasts even closer to him. "Please…"

"Better," he praised before he took her nipples in his mouth again, one after the other, savoring the soft skin of her breasts with his fingertips.

The starch that had stiffened her muscles since she'd walked through his door melted more with every pull of his mouth on the candy-hard crests. He could smell her now. The tang of her arousal filled his nostrils and made his blood boil. Every time he had Gia under his power, she fired him up like no woman ever had. Feeling her now warmed him like the sun after a long, cold winter.

But after what seemed like a thousand freezing seasons without her, he needed more.

With a growl, Jason fitted his hands around the little straps over her hips and ripped her thong away. He lay his palm over her bare pussy, letting her feel the claim he had placed here long ago. Then he ground the heel of his hand in a tight circle, directly over her clit. To his great satisfaction, she spread her legs wider to him, granting him even more access to her secret flesh.

He'd been wrong earlier. His wife didn't just intoxicate him; she held him spellbound.

"Gia, baby, I've missed you," he blurted.

He nearly bit his tongue off. No way should he admit that. The truth gave her power. He had to watch himself, somehow not get lost in her.

With a mewl, she lifted her hips to him. He sank his fingers between the velvety folds of her cunt, dipped his fingers into her wetness, and he caressed her clit. His slow rub had her writhing as he awakened the nerve endings under the hood of her flesh. Then he withdrew.

"I've missed you, too. Don't stop," she begged.

Wondering if she meant that or merely said what she thought he wanted to hear, Jason massaged her clit again, more circular motions that hardened the little bud and had her bucking closer for more. "Tell me who else makes you feel this way."

"No one," she breathed out.

Gia had admitted as much before they married, and he'd hoped the same was still true. "Who else has touched you like this in the last year?"

As he brushed her nerve-laden bundle again, she whimpered. "No one."

"You haven't let anyone pet this pretty pussy since me?" He wanted to hear her admit it again. He ached to believe it.

Jason softened his touch, concentrating the rhythmic cadence exactly where she wanted it, taking her closer and closer to the edge of pleasure.

"No," she gasped out. "Even when I saw you with other women in the newspaper, I couldn't…" Her thighs went taut, and she gyrated, trying to take him deeper. "I couldn't do it."

She thought he'd been unfaithful? That grated on him. It would probably be wise to let her think it, but where his wife was concerned, he had yet to make a damn logical decision.

"I attended benefits and art showings with 'appropriate' dates for one good cause after another. I smiled as photographers snapped pictures. I did *not* take anyone to bed."

Gia turned her head away and tried to draw her legs together to shake off his touch. "You don't have to lie."

"You're right," he agreed. "So why would I bother? Nothing in our prenuptial agreement prevents me from fucking someone else. But I didn't."

Around the edges of the mask, he could see her brows furrow together. "That doesn't make any sense."

"Why?" He ripped the mask away. "Because you think I'm a deceitful playboy who chases one piece of ass after another?"

She blinked, readjusting to the light and focusing on him. "I wouldn't have married you if I thought that."

Jason raised a brow at her. "Do you think I cheated because you're not special enough to inspire fidelity?"

"N-no."

He sat back on his heels. The denial had come out, but he didn't believe it. He wasn't even sure she did.

"Then tell me why you think I've been playing musical beds."

Rolling her shoulders back and crossing her legs, she shut her eyes and refused to meet his gaze. "I assumed you'd moved on with your life."

The way she'd moved on with hers. Damn it. He should probably do the same, but now that he had Gia here, he wasn't convinced he could ever let her go.

Jason grabbed her chin. "Look at me."

Her mouth twisted and her nose reddened as she fought tears. "Can't you just take what you want already?"

So she could hate him for it later? No. She seemed to think he merely saw her as a body to fuck. Or that he didn't care about any pleasure but his own. If they were going to make any progress in the future, he needed to set the record straight now.

Hovering over her, he plunged one hand into her hair and tugged until he captured her gaze and her mouth trembled directly under his. He thrust two fingers into her weeping pussy and prodded her clit with his thumb. As she gasped and her body opened to him again, almost as if against her will, he slammed his lips over the soft velvet of hers and fused their mouths together.

Hell, he couldn't inhale her fast enough, take her deep enough. As he shoved his way into her mouth, sweeping inside for a devouring kiss, Jason reveled in the fact that he touched her, penetrated her. He meant to do it again—frequently—lap at her flavor and drink in her reaction. He'd listen to each little breath and eat up every inch of her surrender over and over until she was completely in his hands and under his control again.

Pumping his fingers in and out of her as he swept through her mouth, Jason waited until an aroused glow suffused his wife, until she held her breath and her legs twitched, until she fought her restraints and kissed him with abandon. Then he jerked away, staring hard at her beautiful flushed face.

"No..." She pleaded with him.

He merely raised a brow at her.

"Mr. Denning," she added hastily. "Please."

Fuck, she was killing him. But this lesson had to take precedence. He might not respect her choice to come here for money, but he refused to let her believe he saw her as a whore.

Shaking his head, he tried not to soften in the face of her entreating stare. "You're my submissive and my wife."

"Yes, but—"

"No," he corrected. "I have not touched another woman since our wedding night. And to set the record straight, if I intended to use you simply for my pleasure, nothing would have stopped me from fucking you right now, especially not the resentment you'd feel afterward. I want you to think about that, *Mrs.* Denning. I'll be back."

Chapter Four

The door shut behind Jason, enclosing Gia in his bedroom by herself. His words hung in the silent room and reverberated through her body. His sudden absence made her feel ridiculously alone, but having him gone didn't stop her body from throbbing for what only he could give her. With her breasts bare and her pussy exposed, she couldn't *not* be aware of her naked vulnerability. Nor could she seem to pry her heart from her throat.

What the hell was going on?

As a police officer, the idea of being restrained in a man's bedroom somewhat against her will should bother her. But Jason had relegated her to a desk because he didn't want her hurt or killed hunting down Tony's killer. Her husband would never physically harm her. On the other hand, he would very likely make her heart bleed—as if she hadn't already been suffering since their separation.

If he hadn't aroused her just now with the purpose of wringing every bit of his money's worth from her body, then why had he touched her? To prove he could rev up her libido? Or something entirely different? Everything about his behavior in the last twenty-four hours confused her. She'd assumed that he wanted a divorce and that he sought to make her pay with her body before he paid in cash. Now…she wasn't sure. If he'd brought her here merely to use her before he began legally shedding her, why would he insist he'd been faithful? Or speak her married name so emphatically, like he meant to underscore the fact that, at least on paper, she was still his wife.

Once, she'd believed that he loved her. He'd never said the words, but what he lacked in verbal affection he'd more than made up for in a hundred other ways, like his romantic, over-the-top proposal. Like remembering that she loved stargazer lilies and having huge bouquets stuffed with them at their last-minute wedding.

Like having chocolate mousse for her tonight?

Gia closed her eyes. Why couldn't everything be different? The night she and Jason had married, she'd been on top of the world. He'd been the most dashing groom. Somehow, in less than twenty-four hours, he'd seen to every detail of their elegant ceremony. He'd even had a selection of insanely beautiful wedding dresses delivered to her door so she could pick one and have it hemmed or tucked as needed.

That night, she'd been Cinderella at the ball, swept into his glittering world for an enchanted evening, fooling herself into imagining that she belonged beside him. Her phone ringing with the news of Tony's murder had been her clock striking midnight. Reality had ripped her from fantasy. Suddenly, she'd realized that her brother was gone forever, her parents didn't know she had a husband, and she had a mountain of responsibilities that weren't going to go away simply because she'd been foolish enough to marry a man she couldn't keep.

When she'd forced herself to let go of Jason mentally, Gia had been sure he would forget her within a month or two. Six at most. But nearly a year later, he seemed resistant to the idea of releasing her for good.

Was it possible he still cared?

Gia glanced at the clock. He'd only been gone ten minutes. Somehow, it felt like a week. But that wasn't new. For unending months after their marriage, being away from Jason hadn't been a mere ache, but a plague—a ceaseless yearning that had hounded her days and haunted her nights. After just a little taste of him tonight, the need thrumming inside her, demanding to be close to him was twenty times worse.

What was she going to do about their marriage? As much as she still had feelings for him, she didn't see how she could toss aside her common sense again. But even if the two of them living happily ever after was a fantasy, the thought of letting him go again made her heart constrict.

The door opened, abruptly ending her thoughts. Automatically, she curled her legs up to her chest to hide as much of her nudity as possible.

Jason quirked a brow. "Lower them."

He stood stock-still until she complied, flattening them on the bed once more and revealing her breasts.

"Spread them," he demanded.

She dug deep to tamp down anger—and the even more insidious arousal. No way could she let him know. Already, she'd begged him. Stupid move. Jason had so much command over her. Tipping her hand and revealing how much she wanted her husband would only give him more.

Still, she couldn't stop her trembling as she parted her thighs. His stare immediately dropped to her sex, and his eyes gleamed with satisfaction. She stung with both desire and shame.

"Excellent. More mousse?" he asked, sauntering to the nightstand and taking the crystal dish in hand.

The chocolate was scrumptious. Since Jason could usually take or leave anything sugary, she suspected he'd had someone whip up the dessert for her. The surprising gesture was sweet—a word few associated with him. But Gia had seen that side of him before and knew it existed. Yes, he'd been an ass tonight, but she had expected as much. He was angry and hurt, and she bore most of the guilt for their faltering marriage. Throwing his thoughtfulness in his face now would only be juvenile.

"Yes, please."

He relaxed, as if pleasantly surprised that she hadn't rebuffed him. Then again, after months of rejection, why should he have expected anything else from her? Guilt gnawed at Gia again.

"Open up." Jason sat on the edge of the bed and spooned up some of the mousse, then brought the heaping chocolate toward her mouth.

Willingly, she opened for him, cradling all the goodness on her tongue while he fed her. The independent woman in her probably shouldn't like this, but why lie? Sometimes, he could be so attentive, even tender, that she simply melted.

In silence, he lifted one bite after the other onto her tongue until she'd swallowed the last of it. Gia couldn't contain the happy little sigh that escaped her throat. "Thank you. That was incredible."

Jason brushed a piece of hair away from her face. "You're

welcome. How are your hands and wrists?"

Though she was still cuffed, everything was surprisingly comfortable. "I'm all right, except I don't know why you left the room with me restrained. I wasn't going anywhere."

"You weren't," he confirmed. "But that orgasm you pleaded for earlier is mine. I've waited nearly a year for it. I wasn't going to let you take it from me by your own hand."

"I wouldn't have."

He shrugged. "I wasn't taking chances. Are you still hungry?"

"Tonight's dinner was more than I usually eat in three days. I'm stuffed."

His lips tightened. "You've lost weight."

"I can't eat when I'm stressed."

Jason didn't comment directly, he just reached over to uncuff her wrist on the far side of the bed. His chest hovered near hers, their faces inches apart. Gia couldn't deny how much she craved his kiss again.

Instead, he stared, silent and inscrutable, as if trying to see down to her soul. His sharp blue eyes enthralled her. Stubble covered his strong jaw. His broad shoulders eclipsed so much of the room beyond. God knew he was good in bed. Maybe she could resist if she didn't love him.

Finally, he popped a latch, and her left cuff sprang free. Jason eased back and released the other, then began massaging her shoulders. "Do they ache?"

Gia wasn't dumb enough to lie. Besides, she deeply suspected that her wrists would be in those same cuffs again in the very near future.

"A bit."

"Come with me." He peeled off her shoes and helped her to her feet.

Swallowing down her questions, she trailed him to the massive bathroom as he began running the tub. As the water turned warm, he eased the stopper down and added a bit of some exotic bath oil with a hint of coconut and musk before turning to her.

At the gravity of his stare, she swallowed. With fingertips skimming her shoulders, he slid the baby-doll nightie down her arms and off her body. When she stood bare before him, raw lust seared his face. That expression said he wanted to lower her to the floor and fuck her right that second. Gia wanted to let him.

He held out his hand, looking her up and down. "Get in."

It didn't once occur to Gia not to comply. She closed her eyes in delight as the warm water enveloped her feet and lapped at her ankles.

Since she'd moved in with Mila and the kids, the little house's only bathtub was on the other side of the place, and Gia hated to intrude in the children's space. She'd missed the luxury of being immersed in warm, fragrant water.

"Sit back." Jason helped ease her down into the water.

Though she usually liked to wait until the tub filled to avoid the cold surface against her skin, she didn't argue. But when she lay back, Gia was shocked to realize the entire surface of the tub was comfortably warm.

"The back is heated?"

He smiled faintly. "Yes. It's also an air tub with colored LED lighting. The towels are heating now. So is the floor."

Wow. She never even stopped to consider such luxuries. Money had always been tight in her family. Now it was a downright issue. She'd better enjoy all this pampering while she could, but it was far more special because Jason shared the luxury with her. In her stupid heart, he did it because, despite his anger, he still wanted to take care of her.

"Thank you." She settled back again and closed her eyes.

"You're welcome," he murmured.

He ran his fingers through her hair. Another touch she'd always loved. And he remembered. Gia moaned as he gently rubbed at her scalp, brushed his hands over her temples, applied the perfect pressure to the back of her stiff neck. He touched her as if they didn't have a care between them. It would be so sinfully easy to slip again into the fantasy of being Jason's fairy-tale soul mate.

Once upon a time, she'd fallen hard for him. It had nothing to do with his money and everything to do with the very personal way he cared for her. Insistent, yes. Hands on, definitely. But she'd never felt more adored in her life than she did with Jason.

"Relax," he whispered.

Her eyes slid shut. "You're making it impossible to do anything else."

"Excellent." He gathered her hair in his hands and clipped it atop her head.

Then she smelled something new, a blend of lavender, rosemary, chamomile, and a few other scents she couldn't identify. Suddenly, his big hands covered her shoulders and began kneading, working the oil down her arms, then back up to her neck. She gave a low groan and melted against him.

"Jason," she whispered.

He bent and brushed his lips against her ear. "You like that."

"Hmm…" she breathed. "Yes."

When Gia had first arrived, she'd been sure that he would immediately force her into bed. Not physically. After all, she'd agreed to give him her body at any time in any way he wanted until their anniversary. But instead of ordering her surrender, he seemed intent on coaxing it from her. And he was doing a damn fine job.

"Still sore?" He massaged the tense muscles and tendons of her shoulders and arms, dissolving her accumulated stress with every gentle dig of his fingers.

"No."

"Good."

Jason dipped his hands in her bath water, rinsing them. Then he caressed his way up her hips, her waist. Gia's breath caught and held as his fingertips traced a path over her damp skin until he cradled her breasts in his hands.

"These are perfect," he murmured, thumbing his way toward her nipples.

They beaded in anticipation of his touch, tightening, lengthening. He captured them in his grip. She eased her head back against the rim of the tub and drew in a shaking breath before exhaling in an aroused rush. Why did he always turn her inside out?

He slid his cheek against hers, the stubble prickly soft. The slight abrasion of his skin added another layer of texture to his possession. His woodsy-musky scent surrounded her and reminded her of the hundreds of times he'd driven her to ecstasy with seeming ease. Now she was on his turf, playing by his terms…and heading for his bed again. For a blissful moment, she didn't regret it.

The last eleven and a half months had been so devastating, so stressful and terrible. Temporarily dropping all the crushing responsibilities for finding Tony's killer while juggling her small niece and nephew was such a wonderful, guilty relief. Giving Jason anything but her body wasn't smart, but Gia didn't think she could hide the fact that she still cared.

When Jason released her nipples then clamped down on them again, she arched into his hands, reveling in the way he cradled her in his grip. Pleasure clouded her thoughts, as if she'd consumed a whole bottle of wine. Tomorrow she would care that she'd given in too easily.

Tomorrow she might even resent him for being so able to unravel her restraint.

Tonight, she just didn't care.

He buried his nose in her neck and inhaled. "God, I've missed your smell. For a month after we left Vegas, I sniffed the nightgown you wore on our wedding night. It made me hard and hungry to fuck you every damn time. Just like I am right now."

"You're trying to seduce me." She couldn't seem to make her voice sound accusing.

"I don't have any plans to stop at trying. You're my wife, at least until the twenty-fourth. That's how I intend to treat you. I'm going to strip you, bind you, penetrate and possess you every chance I get."

She didn't doubt him. Jason might be motivated by revenge or a need to work through whatever residual emotions he had, and he might want to be indifferent to her in every way except sexually, but she sensed he wasn't.

"Stand." He grabbed a towel from the nearby rack.

As she complied with a shiver, he wrapped the warm terrycloth around her, tucking it between her breasts. Dizzy and off balance, Gia swayed closer. Her chest met his. As Jason wrapped his arms around her, she grasped his shoulders and eased her head back. She couldn't help but stare into his eyes. They didn't look crystal cold now, but a hot, dark blue. His jaw clenched. His nostrils flared. Desire tightened his face.

It might be the stupidest thing she'd ever done, but Gia lifted her face, stood on her tiptoes, and brought her mouth toward his. Jason met her halfway, his lips crashing over hers.

He held her tight and sank deep, as if he could inhale her all at once. The inexplicable need to be close to him, along with a sense of rightness, stunned her.

Gia opened herself to him and took the aggression of his kiss. It had been such a long time, and she wanted him, craved the sense of safety and care he inevitably gave her. She'd done far too much damage to their relationship to expect much more than lust in return, and she should probably use this time to work Jason from her system, in case he was doing the same. Problem was, she didn't want that at all.

The last year had proven that she didn't always get what she wanted.

Shoving the confusing tangle of her thoughts aside, Gia drowned in his scent, his taste. He made her body ache—and her heart yearn.

Lost in him, she gave herself over.

Suddenly, Jason tore away, drew in a breath, repositioned to get deeper, fisted her towel, and devoured her once again. Gia couldn't stop herself. Desperate for more, she stumbled over the rim of the tub and pressed her body to his.

Her husband lurched back against the bathroom counter, and she finally felt every inch of his hardness—chest, abs, thighs, as well as that cock she remembered filling her so perfectly. Gia whimpered as she curled her tongue around his, begging because she couldn't bother to part from him long enough to speak the words.

With a growl, Jason yanked back, panting. He scanned her expression for a long second with a curse before he lifted her and turned, plopping her on the counter. He ripped the corner of the towel from between her breasts. The terrycloth fell away, exposing her entirely. He remained fully clothed, and she felt so vulnerable under his hot stare. Determination stamped itself all over his face. He meant to have her now.

Gia's nipples peaked. Her stomach knotted with excitement as her blood fired hot and her pussy clenched. If he walked away from her again, she swore she'd shrivel up or go insane, so she did the one thing she knew would inflame him.

She lowered her gaze, noticing the big bulge beneath his fly, and spread her legs for him. "Take me."

* * * *

Jason clenched his teeth. It would be *so* easy to do that.

But instinct told him that he had to decide whether he merely wanted his pound of flesh…or to keep his wife by his side forever.

If he let Gia into his life again, he would have to remove feeling from their arrangement or risk her hurting him once more. But if he took her to bed now only to watch her slip through his fingers again later, then what?

At the thought, Jason was torn between leaving the room once more until he could be rational or fucking her absolutely senseless.

"Damn it," he muttered.

How had she crawled under his skin again so quickly? Or had he ever truly stopped caring? Jason knew the answer. It wasn't a comfort.

So he had to find some way to induce her to stay, figure out what she wanted and give it to her, no matter the cost.

His entire life, he had wondered why his father had been stupid enough to marry Samantha, knowing she cared about his money far more than him. Sadly, Jason understood now.

"Spell it out for me," he insisted, clasping her face in his hands and spearing her gaze with his own. "Who am I and what do you want from me? Exactly. I won't have any more miscommunication between us."

"I want you inside me, Mr. Denning." Gia's voice trembled.

She gave a shit about what happened here. If nothing but nerves caused her shaky tones, she wouldn't have sounded so damn steady when they'd argued earlier.

"We're not sceneing right now. Try again."

"J-Jason…"

He shook his head. "Who am I *to you*? Just some guy you want to fuck?"

She recoiled, shock raising her brows and dropping her jaw. "No. We might not have had an ideal first year or even a honeymoon, but legally we're still married."

"But I've never had the chance to truly be your husband, so where does that leave us?"

Gia tried to back away. "I thought you wanted sex."

Jason held firm. "I didn't ask what you thought I wanted. You're avoiding my question."

Her expression looked a bit guilty. "You're my husband."

"That's right. And…?"

The way Gia squirmed in his grasp told him that she wasn't ready to admit any feelings she might be having for him. Oh, she was willing to cede her body. Jason meant to use it to bind her to him. Once he'd managed that, he would work like hell to capture at least a corner of her heart. If that didn't work…well, he had more money.

"Spit it out. What do you want from me? Does tonight mean anything or do you just have a fire that needs putting out?"

"No," she insisted. "Why are you making everything between us sound so ugly?"

"I'm simply making sure I understand what you're begging for."

Her lips tightened. She leaned back against the mirror with a huff and grabbed for her towel to gather it around her body. He slammed his hands down on either side of her hips, pinning the terrycloth to the counter.

"Let me have it," she insisted.

"Answer me."

She gave him a little growl. "You're the one who demanded we spend this time together. What do *you* want?"

"For you to stop hiding from me and be honest."

Gia crossed her arms over her naked breasts. "What do you want me to say? I've never stopped wanting you. Fine. There's the truth, but I like you much better when you're nice."

"Nice?" Jason turned her words over in his head. "What the hell does that mean?"

"You know, like when you helped me into the bath and rubbed my shoulders, unlike when you accused me of being horny or desperate for just any man."

"Did you like it when I kissed you and shoved my fingers up your cunt?"

A little flush dashed up her cheeks. "You know I did."

Her admission wasn't loud, but he heard it. And he understood. Gia opened to him every time he treated her like a treasured lover. Was there any chance she actually still cared?

The thought revved him far more than it should.

"Put your arms around me."

It took her a long moment to release the grip on her biceps. Finally, she did and scooted closer, raising her arms to him slowly until she clasped them behind his neck.

"Good."

Her body heat rose and her scent swirled all around him. Hell, just having her here made him rabid with the need to claim her now. He should probably stop, get control of himself and the situation, regroup and plan. All he really wanted to do was consume her in a blistering conflagration so she never considered leaving him again.

Jason covered her lips with his own once more. He gave up anything that resembled careful consideration and seized her mouth with a scorching kiss, stroking deep, feeling her lips mold to his kiss. Gia's breath caught, and she grabbed at his hair. Desire pinged from her body to his and back, revving with enough charge to power Dallas on a sweltering day.

Gathering her thighs in his desperate grip, he pulled them wide and dragged her closer until his aching fly rested against her pussy. Jason cursed the zipper separating them. Why the hell hadn't he taken his clothes off, too?

Dragging in a determined huff, he broke away and pulled at his shirt, not really caring how he got the damn thing off. As he tugged, some of the buttons pinged onto the floor, but BFD. Claiming his wife again was far more important.

His jeans fell victim next to his blazing need to be inside Gia. He ripped at the snap and yanked down the zipper, then shoved them off until he, too, stood naked and needy.

Some part of him really hated wanting her so much. That voice screeching in his head sounded like his father—calculating and remote. But he wondered how he'd last another hour without her, much less the rest of his life. Jason had never been good at forming attachments, but with Gia it had just…happened.

Fuck, these feelings were so foreign. Even if they gave her too much power, he wanted to be inside her in the next sixty seconds or less.

Jason reached into the bathroom cabinet and grabbed a condom. "Tell me again you want this."

Gia nodded. "I do."

"Tell me you want *me*."

Her gaze clung to him as her face softened. "I haven't wanted anyone else since I met you."

At her trembling admission, his cock ached even more. If he hadn't had the same experience, he probably would have bowed to his inner cynic and assumed she was lying. But he knew firsthand how true those words could be.

"No regrets afterward," he warned.

Hesitation flitted across her expression. It bothered Jason. Worried him, even.

Finally, she shook her head. "No. I'm not going to feel whole until I'm with you again, at least this once."

Once, my ass. After he took her, there'd be no letting her go again. But no way was he going to argue when he could be immersing himself inside the slickest, hottest heaven he'd ever lost himself in.

"I won't hold back." He tore into the foil and rolled the condom down his aching cock.

"I wouldn't want you to."

And I won't let go. For better or worse…until death do us part.

The silent vow made, Jason swiped a pair of fingers through Gia's folds. She moaned, and her wet heat put all his worries to rest. His wife was every bit as ready as he felt, and later he would touch her at will, delight in seeing her flush and pant and whimper for the orgasms he vowed to give her. He'd also take her properly in the bed he intended to share with her for the rest of their lives. Right now, he needed to make her his again.

Jason clasped her thighs and dragged her ass to the very edge of the counter. He was damn thankful that he was tall and had long legs. And then he didn't think anything at all as he wrapped his hand around his cock and guided it to her swollen, weeping cunt.

As soon as he buried the head inside Gia's sweltering opening, he clutched her hips, fused his stare to hers, and began to tunnel inside. She gripped him like hot silk and made his eyes cross as pleasure instantly blazed through his body.

As he pushed deeper, she tensed and gasped. Jason gritted his teeth. It had been nearly a year for both of them. Of course she was tight. He fought the urge to shove his way balls deep and pound at her pussy. Damn it, he didn't want to be wearing this condom. Taking her bare and feeling her walls clench down on him in climax before he spilled his seed deep inside her, hoping she would swell with their child...

Hell, he had to stop thinking that before he lost all self-control. He'd waited way too long to be inside Gia again to rush this.

Slow strokes, easy pumps back and forth. She gripped his shoulders, her eyes widening with every inch he managed to work inside her.

"Gia." His voice sounded like he'd honed it with sandpaper. "Take all of me."

Fighting to get inside her, the friction of her tight flesh all over his... Fuck, it was unraveling him.

"I'm trying." She nearly cried the words.

"Deep breath. In...yes. Now let it out." Amazingly, she relaxed around him, and he sank a little farther, over halfway in.

"Jason," she keened.

He grabbed her hips tighter, his fingers biting. "I know," he panted. "Another deep breath. We're so good together. Once you let me in, I'm going to fuck you deep and make you feel so good. Just let me...yeah. Like that," he groaned as he slid completely inside her. "Oh, baby."

Gia grabbed his shoulders and mewled, moving in perfect rhythm underneath him.

"You feel so damn good. I couldn't think about anything all day but you." He caressed her lush ass and withdrew in a torturously slow stroke.

"I imagined this," she moaned. "I fantasized about us."

Her pleading expression fueled his urge to thrust deep once more. His need to spur her climax drove him to action. Once he finished, he intended to do it again and again until they were sated and spent and smiling.

Determined, he shoved deep inside her once more. This time, submerging was as easy as diving into a warm pool of water.

"Please." Her nails bit into him. "It feels so..."

"Perfect. Yeah." He thrust a fist in Gia's silky dark hair and fastened his mouth to hers, drinking her in and filling her every way he could.

Her whimper made him harder. His balls tightened and his heart twisted. He did his level best to undo her one relentless thrust at a time. Her spice filled his nostrils. She made love the way she lived life, with caring and honesty—throwing her whole self into it. Her pussy clung to him, as if she couldn't bear for him to leave her for even a moment. The sensations had him flirting with orgasm. And with every thrust, he only craved her more.

Gia tore her lips from his with a gasp. "Faster. Harder!"

Normally, he didn't take orders well from anyone, especially a submissive. But tonight, he couldn't disagree. "Hold on."

Jason slammed back inside her, deeper than he could ever remember being. His cock prodded her cervix. Her nails clawed his back. She cried out in pleasure. He set up a merciless rhythm, chasing their pleasure until his heart pounded in his ears and his legs trembled. Fuck, he wasn't going to last, and he had to make sure that she didn't either.

Jason slid his hand between them, fingertips circling her clit. Gia tightened and clawed at him, her cunt clamping down. She blinked up and held her breath, silently begging, every muscle braced in anticipation. Then she wailed out her climax. The sound bounced off the tile walls and floors, ringing in his ears. He wanted more of that.

"Come for me, baby. Yes..." he groaned as she sucked him deeper. "So. Fucking. Good."

As her peak stretched on, unrestrained and beautiful, his spine tingled, his balls tightened. Jason's self-control broke.

He wanted to be the man who gave her more pleasure than she'd ever known, the person she turned to when she needed someone to laugh with, someone's hand to hold, someone to share her tears. Whatever it took, whatever energy he had to expend or money he had to burn, he would be that man for her.

With a last long stroke, Jason centered his world entirely on Gia and let go. Her scent filled him. Her flesh surrounded him. His heart beat with hers as he shouted her name in a hoarse groan and gave her everything.

Chapter Five

Nine days later

Gia padded down the stairs, weak morning sunlight drizzling into the kitchen through the thick clouds. Mid-November had turned a bit cooler, and she curled her arms around herself, huddling in Jason's T-shirt, wishing she'd donned warmer clothes. Then again, he'd take them off in nothing flat. After all, she didn't need a stitch in bed.

As she landed in the big open space of the first floor, she found him pacing the great room wearing a pair of sweat shorts. He'd doffed his nylon tank and slung it over one thick shoulder as he pressed the phone to his ear. Even the sight of him made her tingle like a girl in the throes of her first crush.

"I need a report," he demanded as he stared out the window.

Residual sweat from his workout slicked his wavy hair from his face. The muscles of his back rippled and moved every time he shifted his weight, breathed—or made an angry gesture with his arm, as he did now.

"What do you mean there's no progress? That's not acceptable." Jason paused. "Time is the one thing I lack, so don't tell me to be patient. It's been a week. If we're not getting results, we need another tactic."

He walked to the other end of the room, toward the front door. Gia continued to gawk. His broad shoulders tapered into a lean waist, narrow hips, and muscled legs. The thin fabric of his shorts clung to his incredibly appealing backside. He had an athlete's body, one he pushed to its full potential nearly every morning in the gym downstairs. Today, he'd added extra cardio, making love to her before his workout until she'd screamed—repeatedly.

"You're asking me for suggestions? Isn't this your area of expertise?" Jason opened the front door, and his *Wall Street Journal* waited there. He bent to retrieve the paper and clenched it in his fist. "Do you need more money?"

The party on the other line said something, and Jason tensed even more.

"Then I don't want to hear excuses. Solve the problem." He turned just enough to reveal a chiseled profile and his flush of quiet rage. "You've got seventy-two hours before I cut you loose and find someone who can do what I've asked."

Her husband conducted business full throttle. She'd been privy to a few of his calls. It shocked her that he spoke fluent Japanese, at least when it came to money management. Whoever he talked to now didn't quite understand that Jason was used to getting what he wanted and would drive hard until he got it.

That described their relationship. She'd been trying to hold her heart separate from her body, but every night Jason rocketed her to the stars, urging her on and up until she was spent and dizzy. Then he held her close, their hearts beating together, until she wondered if she could separate from him again without crumbling.

For so long, Gia had coped by dealing with only the most pressing issues. The future and its associated problems, she'd shoved into a mental compartment marked "later" and locked away. Little by little, Jason pounded at her mental safety barriers like a battering ram. Gia felt perilously close to caving in. The possibility of parting ways with him for good on their anniversary filled Gia with dread.

"Try that. Spreading the word is critical, but do it carefully," he insisted, then turned back toward the kitchen. The moment he spotted her, his eyes darkened. "I'll have to call you back." Jason didn't wait for a reply. He simply hung up. "Good morning."

"Morning." The word came out breathy, and she kicked herself. She sounded almost as love struck as she felt. A man like Jason could use her feelings to wring all the sex and devotion from her he desired.

Would giving in be so bad? He no longer seemed to want revenge or simply to bang her out of his system. In fact, the way he talked to and touched her, studied her, and spooned her each night made her wonder if he had something else entirely in mind.

A shiver wracked her, part cold, part desire as she remembered how he'd bent her over the sofa last night to pump her with ferocious strokes of his thick cock as they looked out over the city's glittering lights. He'd growled in her ear that he craved her—and that she belonged here with him always.

It wasn't smart, but her body had flowed with his, her pleasure rolling up to him like the ocean at high tide. And damn it if her heart hadn't yearned to stop resisting and surrender.

"Sleep well?" he asked.

"Yes." She always did when she curled up beside him. "You?"

Jason smiled faintly. "A few hours. You know me."

She did. Mentally restless, he always worked on ways to make money grow or plot some business scheme to his advantage. Gia knew damn well his thoughts were hardly limited to commerce and interest rates. Every day he found some new way to engage her until she felt like the most interesting topic he wrapped his thoughts around. When Jason focused on something, he did it with single-minded fervor, and she couldn't deny how much she loved being the center of his attention.

If she could experience that every single day, it would be a dream come true. Then again, hadn't hoping for the fairy-tale ending and ignoring reality landed her in this mess?

Gia averted her gaze. "I can make breakfast this morning. What would you like?"

"No worries. I had a few things delivered. I've got fabulous breakfast burritos in the warming drawer and fresh fruit in the fridge. Give me a minute, and I'll have a surprise, too."

He never let her lift a finger. The pampering had been nice at first. Now, she felt without direction. Even if she wasn't staying forever, she had to contribute. "You know, I'm not useless."

He frowned. "Of course not. You're very capable."

"But you see to everything around here. Why won't you let me pitch in? I cook, Jason. I clean. I do laundry. I can even garden."

"But you don't have to. I employ people. Let them do their jobs. You're here to focus on us."

"I have. But what's the point of me having nothing to do? If it's to take a vacation, believe me, I haven't slept this much in a year. I haven't eaten this much ever. I'm ready to be productive again. You're still conducting business. Since you don't want me working on my brother's case, at least let me contribute in some way."

He sent her a sly grin with a flash of white teeth. "If you think you're not playing a vital role, let me assure you otherwise."

"By being available for sex?"

The smile fell off his face, replaced by a chilly warning. "By being my wife."

Suddenly, his ploy made sense. "You're trying to show me how you envision every day of our married lives."

On the one hand, she was more than a little touched. On the other, she couldn't live this way. Did Jason think that the "job" he paid her for in luxuries and physical pleasure was to be at his carnal beck and call?

He stiffened. "Would that be so terrible?"

"So if we stayed married, you'd insist I hang around and be available whenever you wanted me naked? I wouldn't do anything vital, like work?"

"I would take care of you in every way. Keep you safe, adored, and—"

"Bored out of my damn mind." She gaped at him. "I need purpose."

He stalked closer, eyes narrowed. "You came here exhausted and half starved. If that's what 'purpose' does to you, I won't tolerate it. I'm not expecting you to do nothing. I understand you're a determined woman with goals. I know your submissive nature drives you to help others. You've given a lot to your family. That's admirable. But you can't do it all at your own expense, Gia. Let me help you. Why should you give up food and sleep when I can provide them so easily and let you turn your attention to something else important?"

A half dozen relevant responses raced through her head. Her family wasn't his responsibility. But they'd already had that argument. She understood his point. They hadn't been married long, but did the length of time matter? Spouses were supposed to be partners in life. If her mother ever needed help and didn't tell her father, he'd be very hurt. Fine. Message received.

Naturally, Jason didn't want her important task to have anything to do with bringing Tony's killer to justice. Hunting Ricky Wayman down alone and cuffing him would bring her immense satisfaction...but the task was dangerous almost to the point of suicidal. And in the back of her head, Gia worried that even if she could manage to arrest the thug and a grand jury indicted him, the trial wouldn't see right served. Her brother's former partner, Patrick, had quickly recanted his statement that pinned the blame for Tony's murder on Wayman, so she couldn't rely on the lone eyewitness account to convict him. But last week she'd learned from another friend in the precinct that Patrick had bought a fancy new boat this past spring. She could guess where that money had come from, and it left a bitter taste in her mouth. She'd called Internal Affairs to report the incident, but hadn't yet heard a thing. Frustration was setting in.

If Jason didn't see her filling Tony's shoes again to care for Mila and the kids, and if she accepted that trying to bring Wayman to trial might be exasperating—not to mention risky—where did her husband think that left her? Just a guess, but she figured he would be much happier if she didn't strap on a badge and gun every day and patrol the streets of South Dallas. Gia had mixed feelings about that.

"I appreciate what you're saying," she began. "I just don't know where that leaves me."

Jason didn't answer immediately, and she tensed, watching him open the warming drawer under the oven with a couple of breakfast burritos inside. "Bacon or sausage?"

"Bacon," she answered automatically.

He grabbed the rolled foil item on the left, then retrieved a plate. As soon as he set her breakfast on the shiny black china, he reached into the refrigerator to pull out a cup of pineapple, bananas, and mandarin oranges. He continually surprised her with her favorite things, and she couldn't help but be moved, even when she was miffed.

"Take this to the table." He handed her the plate, then gestured to the breakfast nook.

"I need an answer."

"Eat. We'll talk."

Gia knew damn well that arguing with him when he expected her to fill her belly wouldn't get her anywhere. Shaking her head, she took her breakfast and plopped down at his table, looking out over the city. He lived in the clouds, her prince occupying his castle in the sky…and she could almost get used to sharing his kingdom every day.

Was she really thinking about staying? The thought was dangerous, but difficult to drown out. How could she do it with so many people relying on her? How did she admit to her family that she'd been married all this time? And how did Jason expect her to fill her days?

Despite all these obstacles, the sense of rightness when she was with him gripped her and never let go.

As she unwrapped the burrito, Gia heard the popping of a cork and turned. Sure enough, he was pouring champagne into a flute and adding a little orange juice.

Her jaw dropped. "A mimosa?"

"It's one of my mother's favorites." He shrugged. "I thought you might like it."

And he'd arranged this treat because he'd been thinking of her. The whole thing struck her as thoughtful and indulgent, if a little excessive. But he went above and beyond in taking care of her. How could she be angry about that?

Crap, he had her so confused.

As she took her first bite of heavenly warm egg-filled burrito and followed with a spoonful of the luscious fruit, Jason finished mixing the drink and brought it across the room, easing it directly in her hand. Beside her plate, he set a bottle of hot sauce. "Enjoy."

"I will as soon as you tell me what you see me doing with my next nine days." *Or the rest of my life?*

She gulped down half her mimosa, then had to hold in a moan. That tasted really good.

Jason pulled out the chair beside her and sat. Gia had the distinct impression that he collected his thoughts and organized his words.

"I hope you're willing to simply enjoy our time together, but if you genuinely need something to occupy you, come up with ideas and we'll discuss them. Do you want children someday?"

The change of subject made her head spin. "Of course."

He stood again and paced, paralleling the wall of windows along the north side of the kitchen with his long stride. Sharp and controlled, he pivoted to face her again when he reached the counter and ran out of floor.

"I do, too. And I want them with you. Let's cut to the chase. Tell me what you need to stay with me and make that a reality."

Gia blinked at him, unable to breathe for a long minute. "You want us to have children together?"

"Yes."

Nothing in his expression told her what he might be feeling. The only thing she sensed was edginess, a hint of anxiety. He wanted this, probably more than he wished her to know.

She tried not to soften too much. After all, who knew why he'd chosen her to procreate with. So he wanted her. And he'd given her every reason to suspect he cared. But neither of those truths added up to a reason they should create life together.

"I don't understand. What I need to stay? Um…" She tried to give him a coherent answer, but that proved hard with a nonsensical question.

"You know." He gestured impatiently. "Tell me what I'll need to provide in order for you to stay with me. A bigger house, a new car, diamonds, a trip to Paris… Whatever it is, consider it done."

Was he serious? "First, I'd need a life with fewer problems. I have to figure out what to do about my family. You and I would need to work out our differences and find some common ground. Another house with safe stairs is a must once kids start walking." She shrugged. "But buying me a car or jewelry or taking me overseas won't fix anything unless… Was that supposed to be some bribe to induce me to remain your wife and have your children?"

He bristled. "It's an honest exchange. I give you something you want so I can have something I want."

The idea was completely distasteful. "What makes you think I would even accept something monetary to enter into motherhood?"

His face turned colder. "You would hardly be the first woman. Several of my mother's friends had monetary provisions rewarding them for the birth of each planned pregnancy written into their prenuptials. Besides, once you accepted my offer to come here in exchange for a better divorce settlement, I saw no reason you wouldn't be amenable."

He'd thought wrong. Was that how marriage worked in his experience? "No! Children aren't a clause in a contract. People should have them because they're in love and want to grow their family so they can pass that love down to the next generation."

He raised a dark brow at her, a silent rebuke. "Love is…something movie producers and greeting card companies use to manipulate our emotions so we'll open our wallets. Usually, it's lust, loneliness, or the desire to display the 'right' wife on your arm. Over time, 'death do us part' is more about one being too fond of the dollar signs in their bank account to engage in a messy divorce. Gia…" He shook his head. "Unconditional love and eternal devotion are seductive thoughts, but they don't exist."

Every word horrified her. She stood to face him, shock bouncing inside her. "That's not true. I've seen them every day. I have no clue where you got your warped ideas but… If you really feel this way, why the hell did you marry me?"

"I wanted you."

"We were already having sex," she argued. "You didn't need to marry me for more of that."

"I wanted to call you mine. I still do. You fill some void I hadn't realized existed in my life. I enjoy spending time with you, pampering you, and fucking you. I'd like a family since I didn't have much of one as a kid. So I need to know what you require in order to make it happen. Give me your price."

"Your love," she choked.

His face closed up. "I could lie, but I'd rather not insult you. What else can I give you?"

Gia felt time stand still, the air stop. Pain crushed her, starting dead center in her chest and rapidly spreading like a disease.

"Without love, I can't stay."

"So that's it? You're going to divorce me on our anniversary and walk away because I won't give you syrupy words I don't believe in?"

"No." She approached him on bare feet. "I'm going to let you go so you can find someone you will fall in love with so you can see how real it is."

With a controlled sigh, he clenched a fist. "I don't want 'someone.' I want you. I'll treat you like a queen and give you the world. Can't that be enough?"

Gia's first instinct was to refuse. If she did, it would mean spending her life without Jason. Should she relinquish the man she loved over an ideal? Who was to say that he wouldn't eventually realize he more than wanted her? That maybe he even loved her deep down? Or was she rationalizing because he had her heart and always would?

Suddenly, her phone rang from a distant corner of the house. A quick listen told her the ring tone was Mila's. Had something happened to one of the kids?

Sending Jason a glance that pleaded with him to understand, she dashed for her purse upstairs.

He followed. "Who is it?"

"My sister-in-law," she tossed over her shoulder.

Cursing under his breath, he trailed her into the bedroom, watching with unwavering focus. Gia couldn't mistake his impatience to finish their earlier discussion. She felt the same.

Today had, perhaps, been their most honest conversation. Before they'd married, she and Jason had lived in the moment. She'd read enough about his upbringing online to know that hers had been vastly different. He must know that, too. Since she'd returned to Jason, they had shared space, but they hadn't really tried bridging the chasm between them.

This morning felt like a first step.

As the fourth ring pealed, Gia snatched her phone from her purse and hit the button, pressing the device to her ear. "Hello?"

"Hi, G," Mila greeted. "Sorry to bother you. Just a quick question. Where did you leave TJ's insurance card?"

Her sister-in-law had taken to calling Tony Jr. by his initials because Mila could no longer bear to speak her late husband's name.

"It's not in your purse or affixed to the fridge?" Gia asked.

"No. It's not in the junk drawer or with your mom, either. I've looked in the obvious places. Last I remember, you had it when you took him in for his cough."

Crap. Yes, she had—the day before she'd come to Jason's.

Gia plowed through her purse and found her wallet. The second she opened it, the little card spilled out. "I've got it."

"I need it."

Her heart stopped. "What happened?"

"Nothing. I totally forgot that TJ has a well appointment today. I wish they'd let me use my card, but I guess the insurance company is cracking down against members using the wrong one, so…" Mila paused. "Is there any way we can meet so I can get it? His appointment is at three."

A glance over her shoulder told Gia that Jason stood in the doorway, staring and conscious of every word she spoke to her sister-in-law. She barely managed not to wince. Introducing Jason to Mila might as well be introducing him to the whole family. No way would her brother's wife keep quiet about a man. But Gia already knew that crossing town to spend a few hours without him wasn't an option. She'd committed to spending twenty-four/seven with him until their anniversary.

"How about if I drop it off at the doctor's office and you can pick it up there? I have to get back downtown this afternoon, and I'd rather not fight rush hour traffic." Gia rubbed at a pain in her chest that couldn't be anything but a stab of guilt.

"Sure." Mila sounded a little surprised and hurt that she didn't want to meet for a cup of coffee or lunch, like they usually would, but her sister-in-law could be a one-woman inquisition. If Jason was anywhere in earshot, he would state the bald truth.

What a terrible way for her close-knit family to find out the two of them had been married for nearly a year.

"Great. I'll have it there by one or so." She sent Jason another glance for confirmation, and he nodded.

Then he slipped from the room and headed down the hall, toward the stairs. Gia breathed a guilty sigh of relief that he'd elected to let her finish her conversation in private.

"Perfect," Mila assured.

"How's the new nanny?" Gia almost held her breath, anxious for the answer.

"Incredible! I don't know how you managed to talk your new boss into paying for someone so amazing. The kids love Colleen, and she's made life so easy. I wish I could keep her forever."

A sad relief. Great that the woman was working out, but Gia's worry that she'd failed her family hurt. She'd given her all, but between work and hunting Wayman, there hadn't been enough of her to go around.

"Glad to hear it."

"They miss their Auntie G," Mila added.

"I miss them, too." She tried not to cry. In truth, she missed her whole family.

"Hopefully, you won't be busy much longer," Mila said gently. "Oh, the other reason I called… We've had to move your father's birthday dinner to tonight. I know it's short notice and you've got a tight job, but any chance you can make it? It would mean a lot to your parents."

"Tonight? Dad's birthday isn't for two weeks."

"Thanksgiving is late this year, so his big day falls on Black Friday. The Delvecchios are out of town that weekend for the holiday."

The family owned her dad's favorite little hole-in-the-wall for food. He wouldn't want to celebrate anywhere else.

"Your mom and I realized it this morning, so we rescheduled," Mila went on. "Please come."

How would that work? She doubted seriously that Jason would allow her to attend a family event without him. In fact, he'd told her just minutes ago that he wanted to be with her a lot longer than nine days. It stood to reason that he'd demand to meet the Angelotti clan.

When she and Jason had first eloped, she'd had a plan to invite her parents over for dinner, introduce Jason and let them get to know him over the meal, then announce that they were husband and wife. But once Tony had been killed, her plan had gone out the window. Gia didn't know how to broach the subject with them a belated year later. Or if she even should. She'd know what to do once she'd decided whether to stick it out with Jason or throw in the towel. But springing a surprise marriage on her father, especially when it might not last, wouldn't be much of a birthday gift.

"I want to come, but I'm really tied up here." Gia winced. "I'll see what I can do... If I get free, tell me again what time I should be at Delvecchio's."

"Five thirty. It was the only time they could take us last minute."

"I'm not sure I can be done with my downtown appointment this afternoon by five thirty. Don't be surprised if y'all have to go on without me." Gia made a mental note to ask Jason if they could shop for a gift today and drop it off at the restaurant before her family arrived.

"I was afraid you'd say that." Mila sounded disappointed. "If your schedule changes and you can make it, then come by. I know your dad would be thrilled."

"Sure. Yeah. Thanks for the heads up. If I end up having to leave the gift at the restaurant, I'll text you. Talk to you soon."

Gia shoved her phone in her purse again and turned suspiciously to the hall, wondering if she'd find Jason lurking there. But no. She crept downstairs and found him in the kitchen sipping coffee and browsing his newspaper.

"So we need to drop your nephew's insurance card by the pediatrician's office?"

His question rattled her. "I can take care of it and be back by two."

Jason's blue eyes turned dark, his entire expression disapproving. *Or not...*

"I'll be driving you, Gianna." He spoke her full name, telling her with just one word that she'd reached an unbendable boundary.

She tried to hold in a sigh. "I also need to drop off a little something for my dad. Would it be possible to stop by a mall first?"

"Of course."

"If you don't have time, I understand. You sounded like you were on an important call when I first came downstairs, so—"

"Nothing is more important than you."

His words made her stomach flutter. Honestly, she didn't understand her husband. He hadn't even pretended that he believed in love, yet he'd done everything to make her happy, comfortable, and sated since she'd walked through his door. If he'd told her that he loved her this morning, she would have believed him. Oh, his demeanor could be remote. But his *behavior* spoke volumes, every word saying so clearly that he cared.

Confused and yearning, Gia lowered her gaze. "Thank you."

"My pleasure. Why don't you shower? I'll set out something for you to wear. We'll leave when you're ready."

"I can find my own clothes. You don't have to…"

Gia stopped. No, Jason didn't have to choose her clothes, but his raised brow told her that he wanted to. In fact, he insisted. It should really bug the independent woman in her, but the idea that he sought to select every stitch on her body from the skin out excited her.

"All right," she murmured.

"Excellent. Off with you. I'll take care of everything else."

* * * *

Jason watched his wife walk up the stairs. She intended to keep him separate from the rest of her life. Not acceptable. He suspected Gia worried about her parents' reaction to their marriage. No, he wasn't Catholic, but Marco and Silvana Angelotti would surely find other redeeming qualities in him—namely that he would always take care of their daughter.

Later, he'd allow himself to feel disappointment in Gia's behavior. Now, he had other plans.

Before he'd asked Thorpe to reach out to his wife, Jason had examined his marriage from every angle and found three impediments to making their relationship last. He'd cured the first by bringing Gia here to actually spend time with him so she could see what their life together might be like. He hadn't completely fixed the second problem, but he'd started the process. It shouldn't take much longer. The last? Well, maybe today he could enact change…even if he had to force her to face her fear.

For now, he'd show her a pleasurable afternoon while he ironed out this new wrinkle between them: her insistence on love.

Frowning, he pulled out his phone and made a few arrangements, then headed upstairs to the bedroom he shared with his wife. That had a nice ring, and he had to admit that he'd been much happier since getting her under his roof. She looked better rested. He'd even managed to put a few pounds back on her. All in all, it had been a successful nine days.

Time to step up his game and close the deal.

Once in the master bedroom, he heard the shower running behind the closed bathroom door. Prowling to his adjoining walk-in closet, he opened his armoire and pulled out a few bags. He'd carefully chosen the contents of each over the past week. A bra here, a skirt there. Understated but sexy heels. A designer bag with a beautiful pop of bright pink. According to his assistant, these would thrill Gia, and he enjoyed buying her things she'd never buy for herself.

Next, Jason pulled open the jewelry drawer. Inside, he found the Tiffany blue velvet box with Gia's wedding ring tucked away and clutched it in his fist.

Nothing ventured, nothing gained...

With a decisive nod, he shut the armoire doors and laid all the items out on their bed, including the ring.

Quickly, he made use of one of the showers down the hall, then returned and dressed, just waiting for her reaction. It should be enlightening.

Chapter Six

About mid-morning, they pulled up in front of one of the swanky, old-money malls of Dallas. She'd heard of this place, but it was easily thirty minutes from her part of town, and she'd never had the bank account to shop here.

Gia pursed her lips. She couldn't blame Jason for bringing her to this mall when she hadn't been specific about which one she wanted. His condo wasn't far from here, and to a guy, one shopping center was probably as good as the next. Hopefully, at least one store would allow her to buy a present for her dad that didn't cost her an arm and a leg. But when they breezed in from the parking lot and the first merchant on her right was Tiffany, Gia didn't hold much hope.

And it reminded her of the little blue box Jason had put on the bed beside the ensemble—minus panties, of course—that he'd instructed her to wear. In every other way, the outfit was classy, well-made, and fit perfectly. She'd squealed over the raspberry-colored Kate Spade bag. Even the black Jimmy Choo kitten heels were surprisingly comfortable. Since the tags had still been on everything, she'd choked at the cost. Was Jason insane? Nine hundred dollars for a Roberto Cavalli skirt? She would never have even looked at something this pricy, much less bought it. But this was his show, so she'd worn everything he'd given her, hoping like hell she didn't spill anything and stain the garments.

Jason escorted her inside, then stopped her with a subtle grasp in front of the legendary jeweler. "Where's your ring, Gianna? I set it out for you to wear."

Damn. She'd known he would ask. "In my purse. I don't think wearing the ring is such a good idea."

"Because you don't think you'll be Mrs. Denning much longer?"

Gia hesitated. Everything between them was up in the air. Until she figured out whether she could stay with a man who might never say he loved her, she had to play it safe. "Because at this point we've only agreed to spend a few more days together. I'd hate to lose it while we're deciding about the future."

He didn't look happy with her answer. "Do you dislike it?"

It was far bigger than anything she'd ever imagined someone putting on her finger. She was almost afraid to find out how much he'd spent on it. Every minute she'd worn it last year, she'd checked to make sure the center stone hadn't somehow popped out or that the ring hadn't slipped off her finger.

"If you don't like it, I'll get you something else." He looked toward Tiffany & Co.

"That's not it. I just…" How did she put this into words? "The conversation we had this morning disturbed me. The point of marriage and family is love. Desire isn't enough."

"Do you really mean to give up on us because I won't say three silly words? Other than that one conversation, we're getting along perfectly. I've enjoyed this time with you more than I can express. Until this morning, I believed you felt the same. Am I wrong?"

Lying wouldn't solve anything. "No."

"Good. Having a realistic view of marriage in no way negates the fact that I care about you. You're not just a trophy or a body to me. I believe we can have a good life together. I've got nothing against roses and champagne. I'm happy to buy you all the lace you want. I'm too direct to ever compare your eyes to stars or whatever romantic drivel people spout. Beyond that, no two people should have their world revolve entirely around the other."

"None of that is love." Was he really that clueless? Where did he get these notions? She had a suspicion… "You know, we never talked about your parents. Tell me about them."

"Let me put your wedding ring on your finger and I will." When she opened her mouth to object, he shushed her. "If you lose it, it's insured. I'll replace it. Any other objections?"

At the moment? "No."

In truth, the ring was beautiful, but it was dangerous to entertain the fantasy they were a loving husband and wife out together for a relaxing afternoon before they returned home to cuddle on the couch to watch TV or make love.

"So what's the problem? Do you want to avoid wearing my ring more than you want to hear about my parents?"

With his tight jaw and down slashing brows, he turned away angrily. But when Gia curled a hand around his elbow and nudged him to face her, he looked more hurt than anything. Her resistance melted.

"I do want to hear." Gia dug into her purse and laid the cheerful blue box in her palm.

Jason's big fingers curled around hers, her ring sandwiched between them. When they touched, the electric contact gave her a jolt. He curled his other hand around her neck and cradled her head. God, she always got so lost in his eyes…

During their year apart, she'd often had dreams about him. No matter what happened during those episodes, when she woke, it was his eyes that haunted her. But she loved so much more about Jason.

His sophisticated precision and the relentless way he attacked life had always fascinated her, yes. He cut through the BS and simply said what others only dared to think. Once he'd zeroed in on her, he'd quickly snagged her attention and conquered her heart. Since then, he hadn't let go. Gia thought she had, but now she wasn't so sure.

"Baby…" he murmured as he bent to brush a kiss over her lips.

Gia closed her eyes, soaked Jason in, and opened to him. With something between a sigh and a groan, he took her mouth, plunging deep, his grip tightening on her. He took her breath as he stole her heart all over again.

She grabbed his shoulders, wriggling closer and fusing herself against him. How could she want him again so desperately? But like always, the moment their lips met, the passion sparked to a blaze that quickly became a conflagration.

Because she loved him. But according to him, he would never love her in return.

Damn it, what was she supposed to do about that?

As he let go of her hand and gripped her wrist to bring her closer, someone jostled them and cleared her throat. Gia looked up to find an elderly woman silently scolding them as she passed.

Jason smothered a laugh. "Guess she doesn't believe in PDA."

"Public displays of affection weren't big in her day. My parents don't mind indulging, but I remember my grandparents. OMG, the moment my mom and dad would kiss, my granddad would bluster and rail."

"That sounds nice, actually. I never knew my grandparents." With a sad smile, he plucked the box from her palm and opened it. "Give me your hand."

With her heart thumping, she did. When he removed the ring, he snapped the little case shut and pocketed it before sliding the gorgeous jewel on her finger. The moment hovered, breathless and profound as he settled the ring in place. It still fit perfectly, and the diamonds glittered in the light. Just like the first time she'd seen it, Gia fell speechless.

"I really will get you something else if you don't like it."

"Is that what you think?" She looked up at him, blinking in shock. "I love it. If I never told you that, I'm sorry. Wearing it terrifies me. Losing it would be crushing because it's the most beautiful thing I've ever seen."

Jason breathed what looked like a sigh of relief. If he didn't have deep feelings for her, if it—like her—was just a status symbol, would her opinion even matter?

"Tell me about your parents." She squeezed his hand.

His smile looked tight and cynical as he squeezed back and let go, strolling deeper into the mall. "Well, my father married my mother, his assistant, after he got her pregnant. He was fifty-five. She was twenty-three. He divorced his first wife, leaving her and their three college-aged children. My mother wanted wealth, and he wanted an upgrade on his piece of ass." He cocked his head and sent her a challenging glance. "Are you thinking, 'poor little rich boy with the scarred psyche?'"

Actually, yes. She might have grown up knowing her family watched every penny, but she'd never had any doubt they loved one another.

"Were they happy at all? Ever?"

He shrugged. "Mom was happy when she was shopping. I think my father was happy when he was showing off his pretty, young wife so everyone could see what great taste in women he had. They 'oohed' and 'aahed' that he could afford her. To this day, she's very expensive looking."

"None of that is happiness," she pointed out.

"I'm well aware of that." He took her hand in his.

"So they weren't affectionate?"

"The 'affection' my parents shared was outlined in their prenuptial agreement. If my father wanted more, it usually cost him at least a new Louis Vuitton bag."

"So basically, he bought her?"

Jason paused, then nodded. "I suppose, but she wanted it that way. He didn't object."

That explained why he spent ridiculous amounts of money on her and why he didn't believe in love. Why he'd been trying to buy his way into filling her womb with his children. He only understood what he'd seen.

"That's not the way marriage should be," she murmured.

"Forgive me if I don't believe you." He sent her a brittle smile. "Now, what do you need at the mall?"

Biting her lip, Gia vacillated. *Tell him? Don't tell him?* If she spilled, he'd insist they go to her father's party. The family would learn her secret…and there would be trouble. Besides, if she introduced Jason to everyone and they didn't stay married, she'd shock her parents and break their hearts. Her mom and dad were fairly hip about lots of things, but they were still Catholic. They didn't believe in divorce.

On the other hand, no one had ever shown Jason real love. Maybe he needed her far more than she knew. Or maybe she was inventing reasons to stay with him because she wanted to so badly.

She needed time to think.

"Just a little something for my dad," she hedged. "It won't take long."

He said nothing, just led her through the mall. Gia had the vague sense that he was disappointed. Or maybe that was just her guilt talking…

* * * *

It didn't take too long before Gia found a nice pair of wool-lined leather gloves and a striking plaid scarf for her father. She protested their expense and moved on. Since pinching pennies in Neiman's was counterintuitive, the second she sought the restroom, Jason went back and purchased the gift for her father. Marco Angelotti was his father-in-law, even if the man didn't know it. Besides, Jason had an ulterior motive.

Bag in hand, he waited for Gia at the end of the hallway outside the restrooms. She came out with fresh lipstick and a smile.

"I was thinking, if we start heading toward my parents' house, there's a sporting goods store Dad likes to browse that—" She peered at the bag in his hand. "What did you buy?"

"The items you think your father will enjoy. And don't say a word. He's important to you, so he's important to me. End of conversation."

She pursed her lips together. "It's not. There's no way I can afford those, so he'll know they didn't come from me."

"Take the price tags off and say you got a great deal." He shrugged. "Of course, you could always tell him the gift is from his daughter *and* son-in-law."

"I'm not sure that's a good idea. The first thing they'll want to know is if you love their little girl. If you can't say yes and mean it, they won't be welcoming."

If they had a drop of practical blood in their veins, they'd realize he could provide for her and any children they had in great style. They might not be thrilled that he'd joined the family, but he'd bet they'd be smart enough not to object.

"Leave that to me. I can be very convincing." He took her by the elbow.

Gia tensed, and Jason had no doubt she was flustered. Time to take his pretty wife in hand and start persuading her that love was just another four-letter word. She mattered to him. They could enjoy one another and build a solid foundation on which to raise children. And he'd spend every moment they had left together proving it.

"Come with me." Jason led her toward a section filled with clothing that looked well-made and stylish with a hint of sexy.

"Where are we going?"

"Indulge me for…" He glanced at his watch. "An hour or two. You don't have to be at the pediatrician's office for a while."

She frowned, still agitated about her dad's gift. "All right."

He grinned and led her to a rack of sexy black skirts that would hug her ass in the best possible way.

"Can I help you?" a very manicured fifty-something saleswoman asked them.

"No. We're just browsing," Gia answered.

"Yes," he contradicted. "My wife wants to try this skirt on." He spotted a shimmery blouse in a champagne shade that would look fabulous against her skin. "And that. I'd like to see some casual clothes, too. Classic, but not stuffy. Something age appropriate."

"Of course."

"She also needs lingerie and shoes." He rattled off her sizes.

Gia gaped at him. "Jason!"

He patted her hand. "Don't worry. We have time."

Because he wasn't going to hear a damn word about money. His subtle warning glare should tell her that.

"Will your wife need a purse or two? Any jewelry or cosmetics?" the woman asked.

"Yes. If you'll bring the purses with the outfits to the dressing room so she can see how everything looks together, I'd appreciate that. Also, we're going to need this block of dressing rooms to ourselves. My wife is very private, and I respect her modesty."

"Of course." The woman bowed her pale head deferentially. "I'll call some other associates and we'll be happy to bring you everything you requested."

"Excellent." He grabbed Gia's hand. "We'll wait for you inside."

The moment the woman hustled away, no doubt adding up her potential commission, Jason led his shocked bride to the fitting rooms against the far wall.

As soon as they walked into the partitioned area and saw that they were alone, she stopped and gaped at him. "Are you crazy? I don't need all that. I certainly can't affor—"

"Stop. Right. There." He glowered. "I asked you to indulge me and you agreed."

"I thought you wanted me to look at something interesting."

He shrugged. "Consider me spoiling you the most fascinating subject ever."

With a roll of her eyes, she sighed. "I appreciate what you're trying to do, but you don't need to buy me anything."

Jason studied her with a frown. She would spend every day and night until their anniversary with him for a healthy divorce settlement, but wouldn't accept his gifts during their marriage? "I didn't need a new Porsche last month, but it made me happy. Not everything is about necessity."

"Have you ever heard the words 'frugal' or 'economical?'"

"I have. They only apply when I wish them to. Don't worry about money, Gia. I have nine zeroes in my bank total. I can handle a day of shopping."

"I won't wear any of this when I go back to work."

Her argument was somewhere between tiring and insulting. "So I should not wish to buy things for my wife for the express purpose of seeing her look good or smiling?"

"That's not what I'm saying."

"Then explain. If I had to guess, you think that if I spend money on your clothing, I'll demand something from you in return."

"It feels a lot like you're trying to buy me, the way your father did your mother."

So she wanted his money without strings? That made sense to the cynic in him, but every other part of him protested that Gia wasn't mercenary.

Jason snorted. Either he was getting soft or his wife had played him well.

"Not at all. Let me put it to you this way: Would your mother ever object to your father if he wanted to do something nice for her?"

Gia paused, obviously trying to think of some way—any way—she could say yes to that and mean it. Finally, she gave a little huff. "No."

"Because if your father told your mother they could afford something, she would just accept that as fact."

Her long sigh told Jason he'd hit a bull's-eye. "Yes."

"Can you give me the same courtesy?"

"My father would never buy her all the things you're suggesting," she argued.

"He likes to make her happy, right?"

"Yes."

"Then if he had the means, I guarantee he would buy her everything in the store she wanted. Hell, you make it sound like he'd give her the world."

"He loves her."

"He values her above all others." And now they were playing a game of semantics. "Just like I value you. I fail to see the difference."

The sales associate saved him whatever argument Gia had on the tip of her tongue by coming in with an armful of bright but warm clothes for the coming winter. She set them in the first dressing room then disappeared and returned moments later with two fellow employees, who each carried in shoes and bags and a stack of lacy panties, sheer bras, and even a pair of stockings or two.

"I'll be back in a few minutes to check on you. If you need me sooner, there's a call button on the wall."

"Give us half an hour, please." He smiled politely, but it wasn't a request.

The woman didn't hesitate. "Of course."

As she left, Jason looked around in satisfaction. He'd been inside dressing rooms equipped with what his father used to refer to as the "man chair," but he'd never seen one outfitted with something between a chaise and a bed. It looked ready for sex. Draped in fuchsia, emerald, bright blue, and gold, he lounged back on the soft surface and watched his wife stomp toward the first dressing room.

"Problem?" he asked.

"You just take over everything. You bossed that woman around. You always tell me what to do. You even buy me things when I've asked you not to."

"The sales clerk is here to assist us. She doesn't seem unhappy with the tasks I've given her. And I fully expect that, by the time we've left, I'll have made any extra effort worth her while."

"Not everything is about money."

His pretty wife sounded naïve. "Most everything is. It's ugly but true. As for you..." He rose from the bed and prowled toward her. "It's a husband's right to provide for his wife, and maybe indulge her every now and then. If it will make you feel better, I won't ask you for a blow job in exchange for anything I buy. All I want is your company. Why are you angry?"

When he cupped her shoulder, she shrugged it off and turned away with a sigh. "I'm not angry. I just feel everything spinning out of control. No matter how I try to stop it—"

"That's the problem. You're trying to control not only this situation, but everything in your life. Baby, no one can." He turned her back to face him, something inside him hurting when he saw the tears gathering there. "When we met at Dominion, you agreed to my Dominance because you said you were ready to give me control. It took you months to truly let go, but every time you relinquished a bit of your tight grip and began to trust me, I was so thrilled and proud of you. During our separation this past year, you seem to have forgotten everything we once worked on."

"Because there was no one else to take on all this responsibility. I had to be strong."

That stung. "No one?"

She flushed and looked away. "After all these months, submitting still feels kind of foreign and irresponsible. Maybe I'm not wired for that any more."

Gia still believed she couldn't let loose and see to her own needs because she'd been so busy caring for everyone else's for months. She was mistaken. And he'd still love to paddle her for refusing to let him shoulder any of her burden. Arguing certainly wouldn't get him anywhere. He simply had to show her.

Jason pressed a kiss to her forehead, her lips, then stepped back. "Strip."

"What?" She looked at him as if he'd lost his mind.

"Did you have difficulty hearing my command?"

"No, I'm just—"

"Overthinking everything. I've given you a simple command." She wouldn't remember how much surrender fulfilled her until he gave her the experience again. Once she did, it would bring them closer. "I expect you to obey. Deep down, you want to."

Gia hesitated, her dark eyes searching his face as if looking for answers. "What if someone walks in?"

"Leave that to me." He smiled as he shut the door to the dressing room, enclosing them alone together.

After another hesitation, she nodded and dropped her hands to her blouse, her trembling fingers working the buttons.

Jason knew that Gia she was still a police officer who, if caught, would face censure for breaking the law. It had worried her in their past. After playing the role of parent to her niece and nephew, it would worry her even more. But she still trusted him enough to peel off the gauzy shirt covering her pretty breasts and slide it to the floor.

He began loosening his own shirt buttons, watching as she fiddled with the waistband of her skirt and hesitated. Gia had to work through this in her head. She'd always had an exhibitionist streak, but struggled with letting go away from the privacy of the bedroom.

"Off with the skirt. You didn't disobey me and wear panties, did you?"

"No." Gia sounded breathy and aroused, just the way he liked her.

"Good." He waited until she pushed the skirt down her hips and stepped out, holding it in front of her like a shield. "Hand it to me."

She swallowed nervously and paused, then finally held the skirt out to him. Perhaps he'd ease up and take pity on her if her nipples weren't peaking through her thin bra and she didn't already look wet.

Damn it, he couldn't wait to get his hands on her. It might sound trite, but every time he explored Gia's body, he found something new to appreciate, another way to savor her.

For now, he merely pushed her comfort zone by hanging the skirt over the top of the door behind him, far out of her reach. "Now your bra."

Her fingers curled up as she formed fists. She pressed her lips together. Jason could see the pulse beating furiously at her neck. His wife was going to give into him, and the thought drove him mad with anticipation. Fire seared his veins, engorged his cock. He fought the urge to grab her and tear the undergarment away, then shove her down on his stiff length until she took every inch. Instead, he snapped his fingers, letting her know that his thin patience had given way to expectation.

She let out a shuddering breath. "Jason..."

"Your safe word is still divorce. It's your only out. Unless you want to use it, give me your bra now. If you make me wait any longer, I'll spank you here and now. I won't care at all who hears."

Her eyes went round. Gia believed him. Good, because every word was the truth.

He held out his hand again. "You've got three seconds."

"You're pushing me."

And she was stalling.

"It's what a Dom does." He wriggled his fingers.

With a little wince, she reached behind her and pulled off her bra, then handed it to him. Jason barely looked. He was far too focused on her breasts, their natural weight plump and pretty as they rested gently on her chest. Her nipples stood straight and so beautifully engorged. He'd started this to remind her how satisfied she felt when she put her submission into his hands. But no way could he ignore how stunning she looked.

Without once taking his gaze from her, he slung her bra on top of her skirt. "Come closer. Cradle your breasts in your hands and present me your nipples."

At his words, she whimpered, but she did as he'd commanded, settling her palms underneath the weight of her orbs and lifting them up just enough to thrust their hard tips higher.

Jason watched her image reflected in the trifold mirror. They showed him her body from every angle, and he decided then to install one near his bathtub just so he could watch her emerge from the warm water, skin steaming and dripping, for his viewing pleasure.

Easing into the simple black and chrome chair behind him, he stared at Gia as she edged nearer. Hungry, ready, he itched to fasten his hands on her hips and drag her close enough to taste. Instead, he waited. She had to dredge up her courage and dig a little deeper into her submission with every step forward she took.

Finally, their knees bumped, and he cast his gaze from her nipples to her face. Nervously, she licked her lips. Smiling, he scanned the rest of her. Gia's flat belly twitched. She looked far wetter than the last time he'd peeked.

Excellent.

"Spread your legs."

She stepped out a few inches with her right foot, still supporting her breasts in her hands. God, what a gorgeous sight. Aroused, offering herself, so lush and wanton…

"Wider. Straddle my legs," he said, slouching in the chair and enjoying the view.

Gia frowned, her dark brows forming a frown. She glanced down toward his lap and stepped forward, the inside of her knee brushing his thigh. Awkwardly, she stumbled closer, spreading her legs wider until she straddled his own.

Every delectable part of her was on display for him. She might look hesitant, but he knew her desire and the need to submit had overcome her caution. Breathless, she stood, waiting, looking down at him with need glowing in her eyes.

"Tell me what you're thinking," he demanded softly.

"That you make me ache and want you when I shouldn't."

He petted her thigh, curled his fingers around to the back of her leg, and prowled up until he cupped her ass. "Why shouldn't you desire your husband? We won't get caught."

"You don't love me."

Jason pulled her into his lap, her thighs gripping his hips before he grabbed her chin. "I will place your needs above my own and take care of you until the end of time. I will never let you hunger or suffer or worry. I will bear your burdens, father your children, and hold your hand. No man will ever give you more."

And he refused to let this topic fester any more between them now. He'd rather drown out her thoughts with pleasure.

Cradling her head in his hands, he yanked her toward him. Her lips crashed into his. Gia gasped, conveniently opening to him. Jason took advantage, sliding inside to claim her with a ravaging kiss.

Intent on stealing her breath, he stroked ever deeper into the silky heaven of her mouth. He tasted the little butterscotch candy she'd sucked on just before they arrived. The musky dew of her cream wafted in the air between them. In his head, the two blended for a sensory buzz that had him reeling.

Jason urged her closer. Fuck, he had to get inside her soon.

But he had to fulfill her first. Gia needed to surrender, to pull that submissive part out of her and give everything over to him so he could make her feel safe. So she'd be whole. So they'd have a stronger bond.

As he broke away from the kiss, he nudged her back and helped her to her feet. He leaned to retrieve a skirt the sales associate had brought Gia to try on and ripped the belt from its delicate loops. "Turn around."

She closed her eyes as if she had to steel herself or find courage, but she did exactly as he asked.

"Keep your legs spread and give me your hands."

Gia looked at the two of them in the mirror, her gaze bouncing from her completely exposed body to his face, trying to read him. He remained purposely blank. When she'd submitted and pleased them both, he would make sure she felt his approval.

Finally, she stepped wide again and wound her hands around to the small of her back. He grabbed them with greedy glee and looped the wide cloth belt around her wrists, loose enough to allow blood to flow, but tight enough to keep her under his control.

Taking her hips in his hands again, he turned Gia to face him. "Pretty. I always like you bound and merciless. Now be a good girl and suck my cock."

Her breath caught, and she cut her gaze to the dressing room door. They had at least fifteen minutes before anyone interrupted them.

"Focus on me," he snapped as he unbuckled his belt and slid the button free. The zipper went down with a little hiss.

Gia's breathing picked up speed. She bit her lip as if nerves divebombed her, but her skin flushed and her nipples looked harder than ever. The fear of being caught was part of the game for her. It scared her, but not enough to stop playing.

"Yes, Master."

The words fell from her lips, an automatic response she'd given to him a thousand times when they'd played at Dominion. He'd always loved hearing her shaky little voice acquiescing to his every dirty demand. But now it meant so much more. Whether Gia intended it or not, she was letting him past her walls, allowing him back into her psyche, trusting him.

The thrill of that raced through him as she lowered herself to one knee, clearly intending to kneel to her task.

"No," he corrected. "Stand with your legs spread and bend at the waist. I want to see your pussy in the mirror."

She blinked at him. Somehow, he still managed to shock his little wife every now and then, and that gave him a supreme thrill.

As he wrapped his hand around his engorged staff, holding it up to her, she began to obey, bending to him slowly. About halfway down, he stopped her with a finger under her chin. "Open your mouth. Let me see how you intend to take me."

Her lips parted. Her brown eyes darkened. He released her face and filtered his fingers into her hair, bracing around her neck to urge her down.

As she wrapped her plump lips around his cock, he hissed in a breath at the shock of sensation. He focused straight ahead, staring down the line of her back and into the mirror. Every swollen fold of her drenched pussy reflected back at him, pink and scrumptious—and all his.

Gia curled her tongue around his length, worked the head with a series of slow licks and long pulls, then took him deep, right to the back of her throat. Heat. Thrill. Power. Jason felt drunk on them. But his wife intoxicated him most, her aching, almost desperate submission igniting his blood and torching him like gasoline on a bonfire.

"Good, baby. Yes…" He fisted her tresses and guided her to a faster rhythm. "Don't tease me or you know what will happen."

She bobbed her head, both nodding her agreement and razing him with a soft glide of lips back up his cock. Her teeth glided over the head. Biting back a moan, he urged her on even faster.

Fuck, she looked pretty and helpless. She sucked him like she wanted only his pleasure. She saturated him in a heady grip of desire. She was…his world. There was no way he was leaving this dressing room until she'd screamed her release.

He tugged gently on her hair. "Stop."

Gia licked her way to the head of his cock, then looked up. Their stares met. Her dark eyes looked doe-soft and yearning. He'd tapped into her submissive nature, and now she couldn't wait to give him more. She pleaded silently, as if she worried that she'd displeased him or that he'd spurn her. Immediately, he put her fears to rest.

Jason locked his lips with hers, breathing her in as he urged her mouth open and tasted her. Why did she reach into his chest and yank without mercy at the damnedest times? He wanted to consume her, shove her against the wall and fuck her madly. But he also wanted to slide his skin against hers, his heart beating in sync with hers. He wanted her beside him every damn night of their lives. Jason wasn't exactly sure why he'd fixated on her, but he couldn't deny the truth.

"Please..."

Gia's voice cracked. A glance told him that she neared the end of her rope. And if he didn't want to be interrupted, they were running out of time.

Jason fished a condom from his pocket and shoved it on in seconds before he snagged her arm and pulled her onto his lap, her legs dangling over the sides of the chair. He sought her opening and plunged deep, filling her cunt completely in seconds. Gia gasped sharply.

Because her hands were tied behind her, she had no choice but to rest all her weight on him. She also had no way to pull back. No leverage. No control, and he fucking loved it.

Fingers tightening around her hips, adrenaline and need charged through him as he lifted her up, then used his strength to control her slide down. Slow. Rough. Deep. Her moan shuddered as she tossed her head back. He gritted his teeth and hissed in pleasure. Yeah, he would give her every inch, every ounce of the heat scalding his cock—and she was going to take it.

"Is this what you wanted?" he growled.

"Yes." She barely managed the words between pants.

"Does this feel good?"

"God, yes."

Satisfaction soared. "You want your husband to fuck you?"

She nodded. "I'm aching..."

Beneath her, he rolled his hips as he lifted her, then lowered her back onto his erection. Tingles clawed up his spine. His body went electric as he watched her come apart for him. Her brown eyes darkened, softened as her cheeks flushed and her lips parted with a silent moan. Gia wriggled, trying to rush him. Her pussy clenched tight around his dick.

He impaled her on his length again and grabbed her nape, forcing her to look at him. "You don't determine the pace, do you?"

"No, Master," she whimpered.

He released her neck and again used his arms to lift her into his strokes. Faster. Rougher. Deeper. Jesus, she was like lightning in his veins.

Leaning in, he nipped at her shoulder, then bent and caught one nipple in his mouth. As he sucked, she let out a keening cry.

"That's it, baby. Make noise for me."

"I shouldn't." Worry wrenched the words from her.

"You will. I'll take care of everything." He pulled on her nipple again before switching to the other. "I just want to hear you."

His wife might be worried about being discovered, but this turned her on. Around him, she felt so slick and tight. So stunning and breath stealing.

"Yes..."

The flush broke out across her chest. Gia gushed all over his cock again. Her little whimpers picked up in volume. She was close.

"Come for me, my sweet wife, and scream."

Her hard breathing became outright pants, then she dragged in one long breath and held it. Jason pumped hard straight into her depths, praying he could fuse them together in a way that would last far longer than the orgasm and its afterglow.

Then he wasn't thinking any more as the ecstasy shot through him like he'd injected it straight into his heart. It zipped through his body, taking over. And as she let out a high-pitched squeal of pleasure in the sound of his name, he released everything he had to her, shuddering through every thrust, doing his best to claim her once and for all.

Chapter Seven

An hour later, Gia left the department store still blushing to the roots of her hair and dazed. Beside her, Jason held her hand and carried three huge bags of things he'd bought for her in the other. Behind them, two clerks carried the boxes of shoes her husband had insisted she needed. All eight pairs of them. When she'd pointed out that she only had two feet, he smiled and whispered that he only had one penis, but it really appreciated the view of her in sexy stilettos. Any other objection she'd raised, he'd waved away. His credit card had taken even more of a pounding than she had in the dressing room.

The thought made her blush again, especially when she recalled the way the sales associate had returned a few minutes later with a gentle clearing of her throat and a repressed smile. Gia herself hadn't been sure whether to smack Jason for inducing her to do something arrest-worthy or simply giggle. No denying that she felt happier, lighter than she had in over a year. Being with him fulfilled her, and it had nothing to do with what he bought her and everything to do with the way he coaxed her out of her comfort zone and made her feel special with just his touch.

She was head over heels in love with him again. Well, still. She sighed.

What could she possibly give him in return? A blue-collar outlook on life? Arrest procedures? He knew how to cuff someone without her pointers. Gia shook her head. She liked herself, but didn't at all see why a billionaire would pursue *her*. Was it because she'd left him for the better part of a year and he wanted what he saw as the unattainable?

The thought gnawed at her as they loaded the car and left the mall. It chewed some more at her as they glided down the highway, heading west toward her part of town. He drove his sleek black Porsche like he conducted business—aggressively and without paying much attention to the rules.

"You get a lot of speeding tickets?"

He grinned. "Maybe a few. What can I say? I like the adrenaline rush."

"You one of those idiots who jumps out of perfectly good airplanes with just a canvas backpack?"

"Yep." He laughed. "I love skydiving. I'll get you to try it someday soon."

"No thanks."

"Baby, we'll tandem jump. You'll enjoy it. I'll keep you safe," he promised.

For no logical reason she could think of, that actually made her reconsider. Jason would do exactly as he said. He would ensure that nothing happened except a crazy jump from five thousand feet and a smooth landing. She trusted him.

Of course, would she really be with him long enough to make that a reality?

Maybe…she should think about their future more. Yes, she was better rested and more relaxed since she'd come to Jason's condo. But if she stayed, it would only be because he made her genuinely happy. And because they were both in love.

Once in her neighborhood, she and Jason had a fabulous lunch at a nearby Japanese hibachi and sushi place she'd been wanting to try. Afterward, he drove her to the pediatrician's office, where she dropped off the insurance card.

When she hopped back in the car, it wasn't quite two in the afternoon. She assumed Jason would head back toward the city. Instead, he drove directly to her old house and parked in front of it.

Gia stared at the cozy little ranch-style abode. It hadn't been much. Small with an ancient kitchen and a crappy master bathroom. But she'd been proud of the little fixer. She'd bought it with her own money and spruced it up as finances allowed. Seeing it now gave her a terrible pang. She'd lost so much in the last year. Her brother. Her husband in so many ways. She'd also lost her independence and missed it deeply. The thought made her feel selfish, so she tried to squelch it. Truth was, she simply hadn't been prepared to shoulder the responsibility of her entire family while she'd been in shock and mourning.

"Why are we here?" Her voice shook.

"Why did you sell your house?"

Such a complicated question… "Long story short, after my brother's death, Mila couldn't cope without me. I was running myself ragged driving the nine miles between her place and mine, sometimes in the middle of the night when Bella was sick or Tony Jr. had nightmares, and grief was eating her alive. She really didn't function for a good three months." Gia paused. "My mom had just had a knee replacement. My dad was a great cop in his day, but he doesn't know much about being the primary caretaker for two kids under the age of three. It was just easier to move in with Mila."

"Why not rent your house out while you stayed with your sister-in-law so you'd have a place to come home to?"

She let out a huge sigh. After the way she'd avoided him for months following their wedding day, she owed him this explanation. He'd probably seen her disconnecting her phone and moving away as her means of avoiding him, rather than trying to deal with the tragedy and accept the obligations she'd suddenly inherited.

"When Mila learned she was pregnant again, my brother overextended himself to buy her and the kids the house they now live in. They needed a place with three bedrooms because if they put the baby in with Tony Jr., she'd keep him up half the night. Nothing worse than a cranky toddler."

Jason grimaced. "I'll take your word for it. So you…sold your house and gave her the money?"

"My brother would have done the same for me if our roles had been reversed."

"Your parents couldn't help out?"

"My mom raised kids and never worked outside the home, and my dad is retired. Their income is fixed and tight. Mila didn't want to burden them any more."

"You sacrificed a lot to help your brother's wife and kids."

Yes, including her marriage to Jason. "I'd help them all over again. Mila would never have been able to stand on her own this past year.

The kids are adorable, but a constant handful. But if I had to do it again, I'd try much harder to include you. In my head, leaning on you so much didn't seem fair."

"Giving me up was?"

Her only defense was that she hadn't believed he'd miss her that much. She still didn't know what it was about her he'd latched on to. "You're right. My sense of duty and my pride got in the way."

Jason sent her a pensive stare. "That can't happen again, Gia."

"I know."

He caressed the crown of her bowed head, a silent gesture of acceptance and forgiveness. "So you grew up around here?"

"Yes."

"Show me where you went to school."

It might be stupid, but his request made her feel giddy. Would he ask if he didn't care? No, nor would he fight for her to stay by his side. She hadn't bothered to truly open up to him before they said "I do." It wouldn't kill her to do so now. In fact, he was trying so hard to keep them together, putting...well, not his heart on the line, but his pride at least.

"Sure. I'd like that. You can tell me about your crazy high school days while I do."

It didn't take more than three minutes to reach her alma mater, but he was already regaling her with tales about playing football as a teenager. Even in the schools for the wealthy kids, they still pulled pranks on rivals and coaches alike.

He parked, and several of the male students stopped to gawk at his car. As Jason took her hand in his again, he patiently answered questions and even gave a few a peek at the interior. This relaxed version of her husband was giving, fun to be with. She more than respected the driven, take-no-prisoners man she'd married, but in this moment Gia really liked him, too.

Once the boys had gone, they walked the grounds of the school. The teenagers' day of learning had come to an end. Behind them, students peeled out of the parking lot as she and Jason walked together. On campus, they ran across the group of color guard girls taking advantage of the last of the nice weather before winter. They danced and tossed bright flags in the air to the beat of a dramatic tune.

After observing their routine and clapping at the conclusion, the girls giggled. Jason led her inside the halls and asked about her favorite classes, teachers, and memories. They watched part of a basketball game in progress and had a little footrace on the track. Since her husband was so athletic and he wasn't wearing heels, he won by a lot, but she laughed all the way back to the car, surprised to see that sunset was near.

Back at his sleek Porsche, he opened her door. Gia paused before climbing in, curling her hand around his shoulder and stepping on her tiptoes to kiss him. "That was fun. Thank you for a wonderful day."

His face softened. "You're welcome. I wanted to hear about this part of your life. Thank you for sharing it."

Gia blushed. They should be far past the innocent joys of "getting to know you," but here she was, feeling like an adolescent with her first love. A little backward since they were already married, but she liked feeling the butterflies in her tummy.

She smiled at Jason, wondering again what she could possibly give him to make him half as happy as he made her?

Jason slid into the driver's seat beside her and looked something up on his phone. Moments later, he revved the engine. It purred out of the parking lot, and she found herself lost in a haze of contentment.

Gia had married her husband once because she'd believed they would be happy together, but she'd never had the opportunity to test that theory. After today in particular, she knew she'd been right. Sex in a dressing room wasn't something she wanted often, but Jason somehow understood her craving for that edge of wild—within a net of safety. He always delivered. She was the one who had failed him, first that summer night long ago when he'd arranged a sensual tryst in the park. She had failed him again when she'd assumed he would want nothing to do with her family problems. She hadn't stood by their marriage.

"Thank you for refusing to give up on us."

He turned to her, stare sharp as he slid to a stop at a red light. "You're not angry any more?"

"More than anything, I was afraid. And I felt guilty. I knew so much of the blame for our separation could be laid at my feet. I didn't think I mattered to you any more and that you'd ordered me to your condo to punish me."

"And now?"

"I know you're trying to put us back together. Our last nine days have been better than anything I could have dreamed of."

Gia had a hard time admitting all that when Jason wouldn't tell her that he loved her. But he cared. Neither of them were perfect. Maybe they would grow together in time. Maybe…but it still bugged her. Could she live the rest of her life feeling his adoration but never hearing the three most powerful words a husband could give his wife? Were they a cliché or some vital glue that held a marriage together?

Jason reached for her hand and gave it a squeeze, then punched on the gas pedal when the light turned green again. "I'm relieved to hear you say that. We have another nine days together, and I'll enjoy every minute of them. But I would enjoy it more if you told me you would stay beyond our anniversary."

"It's crossed my mind. We have some issues to work through if we're going to try."

"We do. And I want to start now."

With those cryptic words, Jason took her hand from his and gripped the steering wheel. His stare on the road looked somewhere between focused and grim.

"What do you mean?"

He didn't answer right away, and she stared at the clock. Five forty. Her family would just be sitting down to her dad's birthday dinner. She hadn't had the chance to drop her father's birthday gift off at the restaurant, and it was too late now. Gia cursed under her breath. She would just have to hang onto it until her father's actual birthday.

She pictured her family chatting, singing, moaning over good food. They would miss having her there. The kids must be confused. She'd been a constant in their lives for the last year, and not seeing them felt like someone had punched a hole in her heart. They were so close to the restaurant… Gia thought of telling Jason about the gathering and suggesting they go. But as she glanced down at her three thousand dollar outfit and the gorgeous rock on her finger, she knew her parents would be shocked. If she remained Jason's wife, she would tell her family when they'd married and why she'd hidden the union from them, but not while they celebrated her father's birthday. Not in public. Not when she wasn't sure if she and Jason had a future.

As the familiar streets passed, she focused on Jason's strong profile and waited for an answer. Finally, he turned off one of the town's main drags and down an ancillary street, slowing down as they approached Delvecchio's. Her heart stopped as he pulled into the parking lot.

Crap! He'd overheard her on the phone with Mila earlier. "Jason…"

He shoved the car in park and turned to her. "You admitted that we have some issues to work through. The fact that I haven't met your family is a huge obstacle. I want to remove it now. Hell, do they even know we dated?"

No. She'd been worried when she'd met Jason that her folks wouldn't understand. He represented so many things her old-school, old-world parents didn't like—establishment and money. He'd never worked with his hands. He wasn't a part of the Church. No one in her family—not a single one of her sixteen cousins—had married anyone who wasn't both intensely Italian and devoutly Catholic. She didn't care about any of that, but her parents would. They would understand even less that she'd concealed her marriage from them.

Most of all, she didn't want to put her family through this upheaval unless she believed that she and Jason could truly make a life together.

"It's complicated."

"It's not," he contradicted. "I'm not who they would have chosen for you. I understand that, but it's your life and ultimately your choice. You say they 'love' you."

"They do, but—"

"No buts. If they value your happiness, then they will allow you to make the best decision for you and respect it. Am I wrong?"

"You're oversimplifying. They're parents; they always think they know best."

"You're an adult with your own life."

He was absolutely right. "But they've been the biggest part of it for years. I couldn't do without them."

"Well, I won't be your dirty little secret any longer." Jason gritted his teeth and sucked in a breath. "We are going to walk into that restaurant, and you're going to introduce me as your husband. Or you are going to say your safe word. Tell me again what it is."

"Divorce," she choked out.

"That's right. And we will never escape that possibility as long as you hide me from your family. All refusing to introduce us does is prove that you never intended to incorporate me into the important parts of your life."

"I need time." But as soon as the plea slipped from her lips, Gia knew she asked for too much.

"You've had nearly a year."

She had more objections, but they were all about her escaping her family's disappointment. About her not having to endure their shock and anger. Waiting did nothing but convince Jason that he wasn't important to her. And that wasn't true. If they could work it out, she wanted to stay with him. She loved him and wanted his happiness.

Her world tilted on its axis for a breath-stealing second. She steadied herself against his car as her thoughts raced. Could she even make him happy? Cold dread gripped her. Gia had no idea what Jason really saw in her. Maybe nothing.

Maybe that's why he cared but didn't love her.

God, she needed answers and she simply didn't have them.

"Gia?" he asked, concern deepening his voice as the setting sun slanted through the windshield and cast a golden glow over his inky hair and bronzed skin. He watched her with blue eyes, fixed and unwavering.

"I'm fine," she said automatically.

But she wasn't. She'd been that insecure girl who'd let self-doubt cloud her brain and screw her up. She'd let fear rule her—and still did. She wasn't a supermodel or a brainiac. She hadn't come from a gilded background or even finished college. All along, she'd been unclear what she could possibly give him, and the moment her family obligations had separated them, she'd allowed her doubts to creep in and craft a million excuses for why they should remain apart.

Self-flagellation and guilt blistered through her.

"Then it's time for you to decide. Do we meet your family or are you saying divorce?"

Instantly, Gia knew that if she uttered that word, he would take it literally and file tomorrow. On the other hand, if she stayed with him and he lost interest in a few months or years? It would hurt so much more.

No, she couldn't look at it that way. She refused to lose him again because of her fears or to save her feelings. It reeked of cowardice and self-doubt, and she would not be that woman. Even if she disappointed her parents, she had to believe they would never stop loving her. She owed it to them to come clean. And she owed it to Jason to try making him a part of her family.

"Let's go." She grabbed her purse from the floorboard and shoved open the car door, shaking from head to toe.

They walked through the shadowed parking lot. Jason took her hand, holding her father's professionally wrapped gift in the other, leading her to the door. He opened it for her, and the heavy wooden thing squeaked on its hinges. Delvecchio's wasn't big. The small bar area and takeout counter sat to the right, doing a steady business already. A dining area big enough for maybe fifty people lay beyond the hostess stand in front of a half wall just inside the foyer.

Gia swallowed, her palms turning sweaty as the familiar hostess turned to her. "Hi, Renee."

"Gia!" The Delvecchio's youngest daughter, only recently graduated from high school, called out to her with a little squeal. "I haven't seen you in forever." She eyed Jason not so discreetly. "Your parents said you weren't coming tonight. They'll be surprised to see you."

Completely. That filled her with an anxious dread, but she wasn't backing down.

"What corner did you sit them in? You know they're going to be loud, right?"

"Mila warned me." Renee winked. "They're in the big booth right outside the kitchen. Need a menu?" she asked Jason, looking a little star struck.

"I'll wing it." He gripped Gia's hand more tightly.

She flipped her gaze up to her husband. He'd pushed to make this meeting happen…but he was nervous. This mattered to him, and Gia found that endearing. Maybe she should still be mad at him. God knew she was so worried, she probably looked a charming shade of green.

"Can you have your brother bring a bottle of that Cabernet I like?" Gia asked the girl.

"Sure. Nick will take care of you. Holler if you need anything else."

She nodded at Renee and figured it was time to stop hiding behind the hostess stand.

Sucking in a deep breath, Gia led Jason around the partition concealing the restaurant from the front door. Instantly, she saw her family in the corner. Longing buckled her chest. Dad laughed. Mom held his hand. Mila rocked the baby while smiling at her folks. Tony Jr. played with a pair of plastic cars on the table, crashing them together and making explosive sounds. He looked so much like her brother sometimes that it hurt.

The boy looked their way, his dark eyes piercing, then they lit up with recognition. "An' Gia!"

As he clambered from his chair, nearly toppling it and his booster seat over, he darted across the restaurant toward her. Jason released her so she could crouch and welcome the happy child into her arms. The moment the little boy crashed into her, Gia reached back to right her balance and laughed. Automatically, Jason braced her with a hand on her back. She sent him a grateful glance before she turned back to Little Tony.

"How's our big boy? You been good for your mama?"

He nodded earnestly. "I helped."

"Of course you did."

"Colleen helped, too." The little boy grinned.

From his smile, Gia had no doubt that he liked the woman Jason had hired to help Mila and the kids during her absence. "That's great."

As she stood and ruffled his hair, Jason took her hand again and nudged her forward. She looked up to see her parents and sister-in-law all gaping and silent.

She held up her palm in greeting as she closed the short distance between her husband and her family. "Hi."

They all gave her the once-over before their collective gazes slid over to Jason. They studied him unabashedly. Her father frowned.

Her mother stood. "Hello, dear. Mila said you wouldn't be here. I'm glad you could make it. You brought a...friend." She smiled wanly. "Why don't you introduce us?"

Here went nothing.

"They're not just friends, Sil," Mila corrected her mother-in-law gently.

His frown morphing to a scowl, her father stood and looked Jason in the eye. "You dating my daughter?"

Gia sighed. "Daddy, be nice. If you'll give me a minute—"

"No, sir." Jason held out his hand and waited until her father shook it. "I married her."

What the hell? She turned a peeved glare at Jason, but he just sent her a cool glance.

Maybe it didn't matter if he'd blurted the truth. There was no good way to drop this bombshell.

Her mother gasped and blinked at her. "You're married to Jason Denning?"

He cleared his throat, and they looked around to see most of the restaurant staring at them. She recognized a girl she'd gone to high school with. Their neighbors down the street sat two booths away. She and Jason had managed to keep this marriage secret for nearly a year. Between crazy Twitter peeps and gossipy folks in the neighborhood, the truth would travel so fast, they might make the local ten o'clock news.

"Why don't we sit down, Mom?" She looked pointedly around her.

Mama pursed her lips. Her short dark hair didn't quite hide the flush of her cheeks. "All right."

Her father followed them. Mila just stared. This meeting wasn't going down as she'd hoped.

Awkward prevailed as they pulled up spare chairs. Gia lifted Little Tony and set him in her lap, glad to hold him again and have a buffer. "Mom, Dad, Mila, you've obviously heard of Jason Denning. He's my husband and he wanted to meet y'all."

"Why didn't you do the proper thing and ask me for my daughter's hand?" Daddy scowled.

Her mother looked uncertain. "Do you love her?"

Mila frowned. "How long have you been married and how did we not know about this?"

Gia slapped a hand over her face. "Can we skip the interrogation, please? Dad, we chose to elope. Mom..." She sighed. "Can you let me handle the whole love thing? I'm a big girl." Then she turned to her sister-in-law. "We married the night before Tony's death. When I got the phone call with the news, Jason and I were in Vegas. When we returned, everything was crazy, and I couldn't bring myself to lay more upheaval on any of you...so I made the choice to live separately from my husband while you needed me."

Her father's scowl deepened, then he leaned across the table to glare at Jason. "You supported this decision?"

"Not in the least. She slipped through my fingers for a while, but no more. I've been trying to convince her for nearly two weeks that we belong together. She's proving a little stubborn, but I intend to persevere."

Her father seemed to like that answer. A little smile lifted the corner of his mouth. "Good."

"Happy birthday." Jason set the present on the table between them.

Gia watched the exchange, stunned. Her father hadn't growled or thundered? She turned to her mother, keenly aware of the woman's confused stare. She also looked a bit hurt.

"I didn't marry him to upset you," Gia vowed.

With a tilt of her head, the older woman acknowledged that truth. "He's not Italian."

"Men of other nationalities can be equally wonderful," she pointed out.

Mom looked at her husband of thirty-two years. "Perhaps. I might be a little biased."

"I'm not Catholic, either, ma'am," Jason jumped in, sending her mother a reassuring expression and placing his hand over hers. "But I assure you that I'll always take care of your daughter and any children we have for as long as she'll let me." He smiled. "I'll probably do it even when she fights me kicking and screaming."

A reluctant grin tugged at her mother's lips—and broke the ice. "Which she will. My daughter is more than a little stubborn."

"And who does she get that from?" her father teased, pressing a kiss to Mama's forehead and dropping a hand to her thigh.

"You, of course," her mother quipped.

Her father laughed, then bent to murmur something in her mother's ear that made her blush.

Little Tony squirmed off her lap and ran around to his grandpa with his toys, looking for someone willing to join in the fantastic imaginary car crashes. Bella started fussing, and Gia's mother took the baby from Mila with a fond smile.

Jason's gaze bounced back and forth between her parents, seeming to look for any other objections he could stop before they began. Honestly, Gia couldn't believe they weren't more shocked or angry. In fact, they hadn't really protested much at all. Oh, they'd have words later, but she'd been sure the announcement would immediately cause World War III. So far...no.

Of course she was pleasantly surprised, but what the hell was that about?

A harried waitress came over a few minutes later, and Gia immediately recognized that the blonde was new. She smiled and asked for their order as Nick, the Delvecchio's son, brought the bottle of red wine she'd asked for.

"Thank goodness," Gia muttered as Nick poured the wine and gave Jason a speculative stare.

The second her glass was full, she took a long swallow and downed half. Gia still couldn't relax. She kept waiting for the other shoe to drop.

Dad opened his gifts with thanks and smiles aplenty. He loved what she'd picked for him. Wine flowed. Food came. Mila actually looked happy. Little Tony sidled up to Jason and wanted to play cars with him. Her husband was patient and attentive, and Gia watched, falling a little more in love with him every moment.

By the time they finished the food, her father was telling Jason jokes. Her mother patted his shoulder with a welcoming smile. Bella woke, and Mila stood, placing her in Jason's arms. He blinked and sputtered a bit, but her sister-in-law gave him instructions on holding her properly. The girl eyed Jason with an avid brown stare, then placed her little hand on his chin with a giggle. He grinned back.

Gia breathed through a sting of tears. He looked natural with children. He might have a ruthless bastard side, but he would also be a fierce protector who would move heaven and earth for his kids. When Jason caressed Bella's head, she also knew he'd be a giving but firm father—exactly like her own.

As the waiter took their food away, Jason engaged Mila in conversation about the kids and their habits.

Her mother rose from the table and kissed Dad, then turned to her with a pointed glance. "Why don't we go to the ladies' room?"

Mama wasn't asking exactly, and Gia knew the woman must have questions.

"I'm right behind you."

Jason watched as she rose, his expression bolstering her. Yes, she could handle whatever happened with her family. Gia had put off this introduction, building it up in her head to a terrible confrontation that simply hadn't materialized. He'd been right to give her a shove. She'd wanted to wait until she "knew" they would last to make him an official part of the family, but no couple had a guarantee of forever. It hadn't been fair to him.

She'd made more than one decision about her marriage that she regretted.

As Gia and her mother left the table and wended through the growing crowd to the restrooms, she felt Jason's eyes still on her. But when they disappeared into the ladies' room, her mother turned to her immediately.

"You've been married nearly a year and didn't tell us?"

Gia winced. Her mother rarely beat around the bush, but she was often gentle enough not to put someone on the spot. No mistaking her mom's determination for information now.

"I didn't know what to say."

Her mother frowned. "You thought the truth would upset us?"

She should have realized Mama would see right through her. "I know he's not Enzo."

"Honey…" Her mother's face softened with understanding. "You don't love Enzo the way you love Jason."

"Yeah. I wanted to for your sake, but…"

"Don't. I know your dad and I put a lot of pressure on you in the past, but Tony's death made us realize that no one is assured a tomorrow. We want every day you spend in this life to be a happy one. Enzo doesn't love you the way Jason does."

Well, since her husband didn't love her at all, according to him, she wasn't exactly sure how to reply to her mother. "It's been a really tough year, Mama. I cut Jason out of my life and it hurt so much. I don't know why he's forgiven me, why he wants me back, why he chose me in the first place. I'm scared."

"If loving someone doesn't scare you at least a little, then they don't really mean much to you." Her mother pulled her into a hug. "He chose you because you're beautiful and giving, because you're selfless and smart. What more could he want?"

"Someone like him. Someone raised in his circles with all the money and the advantages it buys. Hell, sometimes when he takes me out, I'm embarrassed that I don't know which fork to use."

"You didn't fall for someone raised in your circles. Do you love him less because he's not Italian or a cop or Catholic? Because he knows which utensil to use when?"

"No." When her mother said it, the whole idea sounded silly. "But I thought you might."

"Would you really have left him for good if your father and I didn't approve?" Mama cocked her head in a silent scold. "You're a grown woman, Gianna."

"I know. You're right." She loved Jason too much to leave him again. "It's what's in *my* heart that matters."

"Exactly. Does he make you happy?"

"Yes, but we have some unresolved issues between us."

"Then work them out. That's what people who stay married do. Talk. Be as honest as you can. Share your fears. Give him your worries."

Gia grimaced. "I haven't been really good at that. When I got the phone call about Tony, I just…broke away. I knew the family would need me."

"You gave up your happiness for Mila and the kids. Did you ever think that adding another member to the clan would make it stronger?

That maybe he could help you and lessen the burden for everyone?"

"No." And she saw it so clearly now that sorrow and guilt weren't clouding her. "I didn't really give him a chance. I just assumed he wouldn't want to be knee-deep in diapers and baby vomit and all the depressing reality of Tony's death and Mila's problems."

Her mother shot her a skeptical stare. "He hardly looks like the type who would crumble in the face of adversity."

Again, Mama was wise. "You're right. I feel like an idiot."

"You may have left originally because of our tragedy, but you didn't return to Jason for some reason I suspect is bigger than your obligation to Mila and the kids."

She hadn't trusted in what they had, in her appeal and ability to hold him. She had been sure that if she presented him with all her problems instead of her ass for a good spanking, that he'd get annoyed and leave. She'd lacked faith in herself, in him… "I have to fix it."

"There's my baby girl." Her mother smiled. "Show me your ring. It blinded me across the table so I didn't get a good look at it."

Gia laughed and held out her hand. Mama took it and peered down at the jewels.

"It's incredible." Her mother squeezed her hand.

"So is he."

"Then just be you and open up. Everything will work out."

They shared another hug before Mama disappeared into a stall. Gia did the same, then they washed their hands in silence before returning to the table. Jason was playing peekaboo with Bella and answering her father's questions about savvy investing while Mila watched with an indulgent smile.

"Are we ready to go?" Mama asked as she approached the table.

"Not quite." Mila grinned, then gestured toward Nick.

He came out with a big slice of Italian wedding cake all lit up with candles. Their waitress followed, juggling forks, a knife, and another bottle of wine.

As Gia took her seat beside her husband and gripped his hand, everyone at the table started singing, Little Tony screeching the words he knew at the top of his lungs. She laughed.

In this golden little moment, all was right with her world. Not perfect, but really close. She had to work on herself and cut Jason some slack. He didn't understand love…yet. But with time and patience, if she gave him her whole heart, he would.

As the song ended, her family clapped. Dad even looked a little misty-eyed—a first for her big, tough-guy father—as he thanked everyone. The group dug into the cake while her father lifted baby Bella above his head for an airplane ride, followed by a kiss. The day seemed more complete for having Jason beside her.

Once the dessert had been devoured, her husband rose and disappeared. Frowning, Gia watched. *What the devil was he up to?* He returned a moment later with a smug smile. Before she could puzzle that out, Nick nearly danced his way to the table with a beaming grin, then handed Jason his credit card.

With an absent scrawl, her husband signed the slip, and she looked down. She wasn't surprised that he'd paid tonight's bill, but the family could eat at Delvecchio's every week for a year and probably not spend that much.

Nick handed her father a gift certificate. "From your daughter and Mr. Denning. Happy birthday."

Daddy looked at the slip of paper and scanned it, then handed it back toward Jason. "A thousand dollars? You didn't have to do that. I can't accept…"

"Now I know where Gia gets it from." He sighed. "Please take it. If it makes you happy, it makes your daughter happy. And you know the saying… Happy wife, happy life."

"But it's too much," her father argued.

"If you enjoy this place, it's just right." Jason wrapped an arm around her.

She smiled up at him. He was trying so hard to fit into her family. Maybe he'd gone overboard, but she knew Jason meant the gesture to please, not bribe. No one had ever done something that nice for Daddy, and he deserved it. No doubt he would appreciate it.

"Thank you," she whispered.

"You can thank me later," he murmured hotly in her ear as a cell phone rang somewhere nearby.

"Not because you bought him something," she scolded.

"Then don't thank me. I just can't stay away from you."

Gia giggled. "You're so bad."

"Oh, just wait. I'll get much worse when we're alone. I might have a new paddle with your name on it. Or maybe we'll go for a swim in the pool on my deck and I'll fuck you there."

Out in the open, where anyone could see. Well…anyone with a helicopter or binoculars in a nearby building. But the idea made her more than wet. "I didn't bring a bathing suit."

"What a shame…" He grinned.

She fought down a shiver and a blush. Jason cradled her chin and lifted her face for a kiss as she heard a third ring, then her father answer the phone.

"Yes, this is Marco Angelotti." He pressed his finger to his other ear, trying to drown out the background noise in the restaurant.

Her mother grabbed her purse as Mila gathered Bella's little dish and spoon, then removed her bib. Little Tony retrieved his toys. And Gia glowed with happiness. Her family knew about Jason and they accepted him. They weren't angry or disappointed or throwing her out of the family.

All that time she'd wasted because she'd been worried about their reaction. If she'd taken Jason to meet her parents when they'd been dating, her father would have yelled and refused to let him in the house. Her mother would have cried, crossed herself, and asked why her only daughter was trying to kill her. Today…a whole different story. She'd never imagined that Tony's passing had caused them to change their outlook about the proper son-in-law.

"Can you repeat that?" Her father frowned.

Mama paused to send him a questioning look. He closed his eyes and clenched his fist. Gia's stomach dropped like a stone. Worry filled the void.

Beside her, Jason's phone dinged with a text. Nothing new since he constantly conducted business, but she wished all the noise and chaos around them would abate so her father could hear and they could all figure out what had him upset.

He pushed past Mama and Jason and marched toward the door. Everyone gathered their belongings and followed him out. Apprehension gripping her, she trailed after her family, then looked behind her to see Jason reading his phone before he darkened the screen with a satisfied nod.

"I need to see what's wrong with my dad."

"I'm with you," he promised, pocketing the phone. "Is he upset?"

"I can't tell for sure."

Jason grabbed his coat and escorted her out the door just as her father hung up the phone, his face pale and shocked. He stepped closer to his truck, shaking, then balanced himself against it, head bowed.

Mama curled up against him and lifted a palm to his cheek. "Marco?"

Gia ran to her dad, flanking his side and taking hold of his arm.

"What is it?"

He tensed, swallowed, then lifted his head to stare at them all for a long moment. His weighty gaze steadied on Mila before shifting back to his wife. "Ricky Wayman is dead."

Chapter Eight

Fifteen minutes later, they sat around the breakfast table in her parents' kitchen. Mama busied herself making coffee. Mila settled Little Tony in front of the TV in the next room, then put Bella in her playpen. Jason linked his fingers with her own. Daddy didn't say a word.

"Who gave you the news? What happened exactly?" Gia asked finally as Mila entered the kitchen again and Mama sat down with her steaming mug.

Her father sighed. "Sergeant Miller called. He still works at the precinct, right?"

She nodded. "He's retiring in March."

"He thought I'd want to know that Wayman had been killed. Apparently, he got into a fight with one of his homies and it ended with a gunshot."

Gia sat back in her chair, the shock still pinging inside her. A thousand emotions pelted her. Vindication warred with anger. Wayman had been an unrepentant thug, well known for selling drugs to kids. Whoever had shot him had probably done the human race a favor. But she'd wanted to arrest him and at least try to make him answer to a jury and the prison system for his crimes. His violent end shouldn't be surprising, not when he lived so violently himself. Still, the suddenness of it left her reeling.

"Do we know why?" she asked.

Mila breathed a sigh of relief. "Do we care why? He's dead, and I say good riddance. Wayman shot your brother in cold blood, and I hope he pays for what he's done in Hell."

"I can't disagree," her father said gruffly, sipping at his coffee. But he still looked shaken.

Mama reached out and tucked her hand in his. "I know I should look at it differently as a good Christian, but that criminal took something from me—from all of us—I can never replace. I couldn't bring myself to forgive him. Maybe now that he's reaped what he's sown, I can. I don't know. But I also know there's a mother out there tonight grieving the loss of her son. She will miss him at Thanksgiving and Christmas, every year his birthday passes, every time she sees something he would have enjoyed... Even if her son committed terrible deeds, my heart goes out to her."

Daddy nodded fiercely and wrapped his arms around her mother, breathing loudly into her hair as if trying to get a hold of his emotions. A long moment later, he kissed her head. "His death probably saved lives. And right or wrong, I feel a sense of closure now."

Gia didn't. She was relieved in a way, but even more, she felt cheated. The whole swirl of emotions barely made any sense to her. But right now had to be about her family.

Beside her, Mila sobbed quietly. "I know Wayman's death doesn't bring my husband back." Her breath hitched on his name. Still, she pressed on. "But I feel better knowing that man doesn't walk the streets any more and can't pull the trigger again. He can't rob any other woman of her husband or son. Maybe now, we can all move on with our lives."

Beside Gia, Jason squeezed her hand. She knew she should let go of her anger against Wayman and her driving need for revenge to focus on tomorrow, on building her own family with her husband. On the surface, that sounded great. But how did she just forget the fact that she'd *needed* to give her family—and herself—some finality before she moved on?

"We certainly weren't going to get closure from DPD," her father added cynically.

"What do you mean?" Gia frowned. Did her dad know something she didn't?

"Think about it. A good cop died and no one lifted a finger? The story of an officer murdered on the streets within days of Thanksgiving barely made it to the press. And Patrick recanted his eyewitness testimony after a few days."

"Yeah," she drawled. "And I have little doubt he bought a boat with the bribe that made him suddenly 'unsure' of what he'd seen. I even reported him to Internal Affairs. It's like…they're stalling or they just don't care."

"That's what I'm saying. Wayman was paying off most of the precinct, including the brass. I can't prove that, but I know he targeted your brother because Tony refused to be bought."

Gia sat back, feeling flattened all over again. It all made sense, and she should have seen it sooner. But no, she'd wanted to believe that the people she worked with weren't corrupt assholes more concerned with lining their pockets than justice. She felt damn naïve.

How was she going to return to work when her stay with Jason was up and look those people in the eye without wanting to rail and scream at them all?

Jason's phone rang. He pulled it from his pocket and glanced at the screen, then stood. "I should take this. You okay?"

She nodded. "Yeah."

Sort of, anyway. She might self-combust in the next ten seconds if her head didn't stop spinning. Hell, what else didn't she know?

"Excuse me for a minute." Jason nodded and ducked out of the room.

Gia watched him ease out the front door with his phone pressed to his ear, his posture telling her he was already in business mode.

"It's been a hell of a night," her father commented with a sigh.

She nodded, then reached for Daddy's hand. "It has, but I want you to know that I'm here for you all."

"No," Mila insisted, jumping out of her chair with her hands on her hips. "Hell, no."

Blinking, Gia stared at her usually reserved sister-in-law. "What the…"

"You listen to me." Mila wagged her finger. "Don't you dare give up one more minute with your husband! Tony and I had six wonderful years together. Even though they ended terribly, I wouldn't trade a second with him because I loved him. You gave me a year when your place was with Jason. Don't spend more time apart from him that you may someday regret. I should have been standing on my own two feet all this time. I will from now on."

"If we had known you were newly wedded, honey, we would have done so much more to pitch in and help." Mama's expression looked somewhere between miserable and guilty. "I let you handle everything because I felt lost myself. Taking care of the kids would have given me purpose and allowed me less time to wallow."

"You weren't up to it."

Her mother snorted. "I'm not ancient. I would have managed."

"I'd hoped dealing with the kids would give you less time to hunt Wayman," her father admitted. "I damn near did a jig when you were put behind a desk. You were too set on revenge to be looking for that killer."

"Daddy, I can take care of myself."

"I thought Tony could, too." He shook his head solemnly. "I kept fearing I'd get a phone call about your murder next."

"I wouldn't have risked myself."

Her father scoffed. "Don't lie to me."

Gia sighed as guilt ricocheted through her. "I was careful."

He shook his salt-and-pepper head. "Bullshit. You went into Wayman's 'hood with guns loaded and cocked. I made a couple of phone calls and tried to get you reassigned or put behind a desk, but I don't have any influence since I retired. Whoever finally realized that you were going to get yourself killed and did something about it, I want to shake his hand."

"I'm glad you approve." Jason closed the door behind him suddenly and crossed the front room into the kitchen with his hand outstretched.

Daddy took it, pumping vigorously. "You got Gia desk duty?"

"Yes, sir. I'm acquainted with the mayor. I might have suggested that if he wanted a healthy donation for his reelection campaign, he needed to make sure a certain beautiful female officer didn't get hurt in the line of duty."

"Well, hot damn!" A grin broke out across her father's face. "I like you even more."

"Thank you." Tears trembled in Mama's eyes.

Mila nodded, wearing a mirror expression.

She glared at them. They all approved of Jason's manipulation? What the hell?

Jason looked surprisingly grim. "Don't thank me yet." Then he turned to Gia and took her hands. "You know I'd do anything for you, that I would move mountains to keep you safe and happy."

"Yes," she said cautiously.

He'd proven it again and again these past nine days. Really, since they'd met. She might not always like the boundaries he gave her, but she couldn't deny that he had her best interests at heart.

"Always," he vowed, then faced her family. "That phone call I just took was from an associate of mine. A week ago, I hired him to spread the word in Wayman's neighborhood that I would pay anyone who brought information leading to the thug's capture a hundred thousand dollars."

Her father choked. Her mother gasped. Mila's jaw dropped.

"What are you saying?" Gia demanded.

"Once word got out, one of his fellow criminals didn't want to just give us information. Apparently, this one decided he could run the hood better, so he tried to turn in Wayman and collect a little money, too."

"Wayman would never go in quietly. He'd fight to the death… Oh my god." She pressed her hand to her mouth, shaking.

"Your reward put an end to him," Mila said.

Jason shrugged. "His fellow gangster's greed prompted him to turn on his 'buddy,' and Wayman chose to die rather than go to the station for questioning. Maybe I should cry or feel guilty, but I don't. I don't always get to use my money for something good, but I think in this situation, we got the best outcome possible."

"You *knew* I wanted to bring Wayman in myself," Gia said through her shock.

He nodded. "I knew it was going to kill you, too."

She couldn't argue that he hadn't done everything possible to keep her safe, but he'd completely missed the point. Later, when she was less stunned, she might not be so angry. But not now. "You didn't even discuss it with me."

"I saw no reason to mention it unless my plan actually worked. And I didn't know Wayman would rather die than be questioned."

"Did you think he'd just go quietly?" She tossed her hands in the air.

"Most people do, so yes. My intent was simply to get him into the station, which I hoped would lead to his arrest and eventual conviction. I did this for you."

She knew that logically, but somehow she had a hard time simply thanking him. "What gave you this crazy idea?"

"The night we met for Mexican food, I knew you needed closure.

The way you spoke suggested your family did, too. I knew you'd kill yourself trying to provide it. So I took care of it. It took me a few days to find the right person and another week for results but—"

"That phone call this morning, the one I overheard after I first woke up... That was him."

"Yes."

"You threatened to fire him."

"I wanted results. How does that make me the bad guy?"

It didn't, and in her head Gia knew that. But right in her gut where the anger and rage over Tony's death lived? Not so much. "You didn't talk to me about this."

"So you could tell me not to and go on risking your life?" he challenged.

She held up her hands, feeling seconds away from explosion. She didn't even know how to put everything she felt into words. Jason's heart had been in the right place, but that didn't excuse his interference.

"You had me put behind a desk, then you blackmailed me into spending a few weeks with you. You bought me clothes without consulting me, forced me to introduce you to my parents. And now you tell me that you had my brother's murderer turned to dust. When do I get to make some decisions about my own life?"

"Gia!" Mila screeched. "I couldn't be more grateful to him." She turned to Jason, then rounded the table to hug him. "Thank you. From the bottom of my heart, really. Thank you."

He put an awkward arm around her. "I'd do it again."

Meeting Jason's stare over the top of her sister-in-law's head, Gia dragged in a breath, trying to get ahold of herself. They'd been so happy an hour ago. She'd been almost convinced this could work.

Almost.

Her father grabbed Jason's hand again and shook it. "You did what I wish I'd had the means to do. My wife and I are grateful."

Mama nodded. "As far as I'm concerned, you're a permanent member of this family."

"That means a lot." Jason disentangled himself from Mila.

"Let's leave them alone," her mother suggested to the others.

Bella started crying, and Little Tony called for his mother. The women sent Jason one last grateful smile before they disappeared into the family room. Her father followed. As they retrieved the children, turned off the TV, and disappeared into the back of the house, the yawning silence suddenly enveloped she and Jason, threatening to swallow them whole.

"You're really angry with me?" he challenged.

"Yes." Fury growled at her, threatening to break free from its chain. "Apparently, I'm the only one. I know you did it for the right reasons, but…I can't believe you went around me like that."

Jason tilted his head. "You left me so few options. As long as Wayman was at large, you weren't going to stop obsessing. It takes two to have a marriage, and I can't be the only one fighting for us, Gia. I might make choices you hate, but damn it, at least I'm trying. What are you doing to keep us together?"

"You only offered that reward because you didn't think I was good enough at my job or strong enough to bring Wayman in."

"No. That's your insecurity talking. I did it because I knew you were brave and determined to keep going until the day one of you died."

His words knocked her back on her heels. For a long moment, Gia couldn't quite breathe.

"You've always made me feel so special and cared for—until this. Now you've just taken away my sense of purpose. Poof." She tossed her hands in the air. "All gone—without saying a word to me. Yes, I know you did it to protect me. But you tried to distract me with pretty baubles that don't mean a damn thing. I needed to make this world a safer place for my family by bringing Wayman down way more than I needed new designer clothes. And you just didn't get that love is more important than Prada. Or care. You might be able to buy another wife, but not this one. If you don't see that, I'm not sure we need to stay together."

He stiffened, then clenched his jaw as he stepped back from her deliberately and slowly. "You haven't discussed any of your plans with me for nearly a year, especially this obsessive, dangerous manhunt. Or your decision to move in with your sister-in-law and totally ignore your husband. But I digress… I'm sorry for not consulting you and for trying too hard. Neither will happen again. I've done everything I know to make you care about our marriage, but it's clear to me that we will never be a priority for you." He shoved his hands in his pockets. "Tell your family that it was nice to meet them. I have a reward to pay out tonight. Good-bye, Gia."

Jason raised his hand like he wanted to touch her. But he didn't. He simply clenched his fist and turned on his heel before he walked away. Her chest imploded as she watched him, the jagged and raw pieces of her heart a splintered heap. Gia wanted to call him back…but why? Loving Jason wasn't enough. She couldn't change him any more than he could fit her into the mold of women, like his mother, he understood.

As her husband shut the door quietly behind him for the final time, Gia knew that nothing would ever be the same again. A sob tore through her chest.

* * * *

Jason paced his condo. The November sun streamed through the floor to ceiling windows, blinding him. If he'd been able to drink himself into a stupor after last night's debacle, his hangover would be bitching at the light. As it was, he had nothing to blame his squinty, vampiric avoidance of the sun on except his bad mood. Why should the day be so fucking cheerful when he wasn't?

Stalking back into the kitchen, he grabbed a bottle of water and downed long swallows. He hadn't been able to run this anger out of his system, even after a punishing eight-mile jog on the treadmill. Business hadn't distracted him during his sleepless night. Neither had trying to logic his way out of this mess. No matter how he told himself that he'd failed at marriage and now he should move on, Jason couldn't make himself listen. He'd even tried to convince himself that Gia was just another woman who could be easily replaced. On paper, maybe. Something inside him wasn't buying it. He had no idea why.

She'd been a pain in his ass, with her quick Italian temper and headstrong ways. The woman wasn't logical. She'd taken a long time to give him her submission, railed every time he tried to set boundaries or keep her safe, insisted that she didn't need his money or his protection or…much of anything from him. Jason sighed.

In some ways, those traits were the very ones that had drawn him to her, which probably made him sound like an idiotic loon. But he'd enjoyed the challenge of coaxing her from her shell. Gia's independence coupled with her submissive nature had been so unlike anyone he'd met. The fact that she didn't seem to give a shit about his fortune was refreshing. Hell, he respected it. She'd wanted money from their divorce, yes. It disappointed him, but the businessman that lurked in his brain said that in her position, he'd want the sum they'd mutually agreed upon, too. His attraction to Gia was everything he'd thought and still more he couldn't quite put his finger on. Her loyalty, for sure. The way she so often put the people she cared about first.

Sadly, she'd never made him one of her priorities. So where did that leave him? Mooning over a woman who would never return half of his…what, sense of attachment? No. He'd mooned over some of his girlfriends in high school. What he felt was more than mere connection. Missing her now hurt like he'd lost something vital. A limb, maybe. But even more important.

Like his heart?

Jason downed another swallow of water, then huffed out a breath of air. Oh, shit. Was that even possible? He'd always believed that love was a fabrication, but what else explained why Gia would sacrifice so much of herself to help raise her niece and nephew? Risk her life to vindicate her brother? Worry so much about her parents' reaction to their marriage? She genuinely loved those people, would do anything for them.

Maybe she hadn't been able to love him because he didn't understand the meaning of love. His parents had been lousy examples. Samantha would never have lifted a finger to help raise the children of a relative grieving the loss of a spouse. She would have cheered Wayman's death and Jason's method for bringing it about because she wouldn't have had to get her hands dirty. She could simply spend another day at the spa, drink champagne, and think about how grand life was. Even his dad hadn't been a shining example of devotion. Jason had never said anything, but he had zero respect for a man who would leave his wife and three kids because he'd been stupid enough to bang his secretary and knock her up. All his life, Jason had seen "love" exchanged for a new pair of shoes or a trip to anywhere exotic.

Before she'd ever taken a dime from him, Gia had proven that wasn't love at all.

So what was it exactly?

Jason whipped out his phone and opened his browser to search. Dictionary results popped up. With a shrug, he figured that was as good a place to start as any.

1. *A deep, tender, indescribable feeling of affection and care toward a person, such as that arising from kinship, recognition of attractive qualities, or a sense of underlying oneness.*

That was a really convoluted way of saying he gave a shit about her way more than the average person and that he had a hard time explaining his feelings. Check.

2. A feeling of intense desire and attraction toward a person with whom one is disposed to make a pair; the emotion of sex and romance.

Check, though those were really clinical words to describe the feelings unsettling him. He'd never felt anything like this and he didn't have anything to compare it with. What her parents felt for one another? That had looked like love to him. When he'd seen Marco and Silvana, he'd been struck by an odd jealousy. Those two had been through hell together, would have done anything to make one another happy and whole. Jason couldn't deny he wanted what they shared.

3. Sexual passion.

Um…like mad. He wanted his wife all the time. Check, check, check.

Well, shit. He was in love. What a fine time to realize it now that Gia was gone.

If his mother could see him now, she'd laugh her head off—after she'd asked him for money, of course.

Jason gripped the phone tighter. What did he do about this mess? He'd been angry with his wife last night. He'd tried to help her and keep her safe, and he'd been hurt. So he had thrown in the towel. But really, he couldn't keep the relationship going for them. She had to want it, too.

Why didn't she? Was he that unlovable?

As he ping-ponged mentally whether he should let her go and call his attorney or find another way to lure his wife to his side, his phone rang. He stared at the display.

Gia.

His heart stopped. But he could only make one choice.

He stabbed the button with his finger and answered. "Yes?"

"Jason, I need to talk to you."

Her voice trembled, and he braced. Whether she felt guilty or angry or worried, she'd brought them to this place. Okay, he'd probably helped. Being decisive and in charge worked for him in business. It didn't translate quite as well in marriage. His mistake, and he'd already taken note for future reference. That, and the fact that he fucking missed her, were the only reasons he'd answered her call now. But without calm, productive conversation…their marriage could only be heading one place.

"I'm listening."

"Face to face. I can't do what I need to over the phone."

Do, not *say,* he noticed. Had she decided not to wait the eight days until their anniversary to file for divorce? Most women wouldn't pass up decent six figures just to be free a few days early. Gia? With her, anything was possible.

He could point out the pitfalls of bailing early on their agreement, but she was smart. She knew the score. And even if it made him foolish, he wanted to know what the hell was going on in her head. He wanted to see her, too. Might as well not kid himself. Besides, once she'd served him with papers and they started down the grand road to divorce, he wanted to look her in the eye and tell her that he loved her. In part because he knew he'd never feel like he'd given this his all until he did. And also because he wanted Gia to know exactly what she'd lost.

"When and where?"

"Four thirty. Lakeside Park, by the granite teddy bears."

The park he'd taken her to early in their relationship for their first scene together, a semi-public one meant to open her submission and fulfill a fantasy. The same one in which she'd called her safe word and nearly ended everything between them for good.

Symbolism. Fabulous. He loathed that shit.

"I'll be there."

"Thank you. See you then."

Before he could reply, she hung up. Jason cursed, then paced his empty condo. He had exactly eight hours to decide how to approach her.

Grabbing his gear, he left his place. Too many memories of Gia here pelting him now. He wished like hell he would have thought of that before he'd coerced her to stay in his home. He could have gotten a suite at the Crescent or something. But no. He'd wanted her in his personal space, in his bed, as if she shared his life. So she would experience what their marriage could be like.

Dumb ass.

Making his way out the door and to his Porsche, he drove the city aimlessly, past his boyhood neighborhood, past upscale shops and family neighborhoods. A pretty brunette pushed a stroller on the sidewalk, a napping toddler securely tucked in. The smiling woman looked visibly pregnant with another child.

Why couldn't that be his life? His family?

Damn it, he sounded maudlin.

His phone rang again. He couldn't see the screen while driving, but he pounced on it. "Gia?"

"Is that your wife or your latest girl toy?"

Samantha. He sighed. "Did you want something?"

"Well, I'm being a good mother this time and inviting you to my engagement party."

Jason recoiled. "That was fast. The guy you met at Neiman's?"

She sighed as if she didn't have a care in the world. "Geoffrey is a wonderful man. You'll like him. He takes such good care of me."

Whatever. "What do *you* like about him? I mean, besides his bank balance."

"Well, he's charming, of course."

"Do you love him?"

She gasped, affronted. "Would I marry anyone I didn't?"

Only four other times. "Would you take care of him through thick and thin?"

"Jason, Geoffrey is ten years younger than me and in perfect health. Neither of us are on our death beds."

And his mother was missing the point of the question completely, probably on purpose.

"Would you do anything to comfort him if he lost something priceless?" He couldn't compare Gia's unflagging support of her family after Tony's death against his mother helping her next fiancé through a missing cuff link or whatever. The questions were soaring right over his mother's head because she valued things far more than people.

She laughed off his questions. "I'm sure I'd find the appropriate words for such a moment and hand him a double Scotch. Where are you going with this?"

Jason winced and gave up explaining it to her. She had limitations, and he wouldn't change her. But one thought resonated in his head over and over: If he let Gia slip through his fingers, he'd probably wind up with a new wife every five or ten years, each one much like Samantha.

The thought sickened him.

But he couldn't control everything between them. He certainly couldn't make her love him.

Fuck.

"When is the party?"

"Tonight at eight o'clock." She rattled off an address, somewhere off of Mockingbird in Highland Park.

Old money. Naturally.

"I have a meeting at four thirty. If it wraps before then, I'll be there."

"Lovely. Don't disappoint me." Samantha hung up.

Jason ended the call and shook his head.

He felt sorry for his mother because she would never know anything deeper than the joy of pretty, shiny things for sale. She'd never really feel her heart. Moreover, he didn't want to be like her. He wanted what Gia's parents had.

He wanted Gia.

How could he impress that upon her when he saw her this afternoon? All his usual ideas—jewelry, handbags, shoes—took him in the wrong direction. She wouldn't care about any of that. She wouldn't take a trip to an alley with him, much less anywhere tropical and fabulous so that he could romance her unless she wanted to be with him.

Other than her divorce settlement, she didn't seem to care about money. In fact, now that he thought about it, her agreeing to spend eighteen days with him for the cash seemed out of character.

Unless the money wasn't for her at all.

He pounded on the steering wheel with a sigh. *Oh, hell.* He'd been so stupid.

But at least he knew what to do now.

A few errands and a lot of anxious waiting later, Jason pulled up at the park, locked his car, and headed toward their meeting point. The sun shined brightly, the thermometer edging toward the seventy degree mark as the last of autumn fought against a winter that would soon encroach. A few leaves still clung to the trees. Ducks swam in the nearby pond. Kids ran and laughed across the little stone bridge near the granite bears that served as monuments in the park. He'd grown up here and always thought of this place as a little slice of heaven, a refuge in the city.

Now being here just ate at his guts.

Jason glanced at his watch. Right on time. He looked around for Gia, leaning against a little railing, hoping like hell he'd made the right decision.

As he second-guessed himself, Gia approached in a pair of faded jeans, a simple coral-hued T-shirt paired with a beige sweater, and flip-flops. What she didn't wear was her wedding ring or a smile. Jason couldn't stop the anxious slide of his stomach to his toes.

He didn't want a goddamn divorce.

"Hi," she greeted. "Thanks for meeting me here."

He wanted to hold her. Fuck, he wanted to take her, possess her, convince her that she was his and always would be. But she put off a vibe that gave him pause. Not a fuck-off sort...but not precisely welcoming, either.

"Of course. What's on your mind?"

She drew in a not-quite-steady breath—a hint that she was nervous, too. "I've given everything that happened recently a lot of thought. I've made some decisions and taken some action."

Here it came, Gia telling him that she'd filed. He clenched his jaw, braced for the worst, and resolved to at least listen before he spoke. Then he intended to fight like hell. She might not see it yet, but they were right for one another.

"We made an agreement before I came back to you. I am determined to keep up my end of things, so I'll return for the next eight days if you want."

"Because you want the money from the divorce settlement?"

"Yes."

"So...you haven't filed yet?"

"No."

Thank God for that. "Then what? You plan to hire an attorney and just...go on with your life as if this never happened?"

"No," she said softly. Her expression broke, and he watched her fight tears.

It took everything inside Jason not to intervene and comfort her, to reach out and try to make everything okay.

"Then what?" He frowned at her, not understanding. "Explain."

"I won't be the one to file. I can't stop you if that's what you want, but..." She shook her head, tears gathering. "I'll never make the first move to end our marriage. I tried for a year to go on as if we never happened. I already know it's not possible."

His chest seized up. Breathing stopped. His heart thundered furiously. "Are you saying you don't want a divorce?"

"No." She emphasized her answer with a shake of her head. "I've given this a lot of thought. You've been trying to show me affection in the way you know how, with gifts. It's not an insult, and I have to stop being too proud to see that."

Gia *had* been thinking.

Relief poured through him. "I never once tried to hurt or offend you."

"And you've gone out of your way to help me. Trying to have Wayman arrested is a good example. I might not like your methods, but you meant to keep me safe and eradicate him from my life all at once."

"Two birds, one stone. I've been telling you my motives for a while."

"You have, and I…" She shook her head and curled her fingers together nervously. "I can't hate you for that."

"Protecting what's mine is in my nature. I know you don't like my methods—"

"But your intentions are in the right place, I know. Sometimes, I lose my temper and I get emotional. When I look back later, I see clearly that I overreacted. I've gotten pretty good at eating crow over the years. I wish you had told me that you intended to deal with Wayman, but I know you didn't mean to take away my opportunity for justice."

"I didn't."

"After I calmed down, I realized that I took my frustration out on you. I'm sorry."

"You always want to right the wrongs. I respect that about you. I'm sorry if I stepped on your toes. I might be a bit too accustomed to calling shots and making decisions."

"I've heard enough of your business conversations to figure that out. I just had to calm down enough to realize you didn't do this to hurt me."

"Never."

"And I wanted to be really mad at you for forcing me to introduce you to my parents." She gave him a wry, if reluctant smile. "As hard as it is to admit it, you were right. They really love you."

A bright spot in this mess. "I'm pretty fond of them, too. Your niece and nephew are adorable and clearly idolize you."

"They are a handful. I've loved every minute I've been with them." She sighed. "But we're not here to talk about the kids."

"No," he agreed. "You don't want a divorce. What do you want?"

"What do *you* want? When you left last night—"

"I was mad, too." A tight grin tugged at his lips. "I don't often lose control of my temper."

"Do you want these last eight days with me?" Gia looked like she held her breath. "You don't have to coerce me. I'm more than willing to give them to you."

Jason couldn't find her words anything other than endearing. "Why do you ask? Because you want to spend those days with me or because you need money?"

"Both," she admitted quietly.

He watched her closely, trying to puzzle her out, but her normally expressive face didn't give a lot away. "We can negotiate the time together. The money…" He reached into his pocket and pulled free a piece of paper he'd folded and placed there earlier after picking it up off the fax machine at his office, then he handed it to Gia.

She scanned it. "What's this?"

"Read it," he encouraged with a bob of his head.

With a frown, she did. Her expression changed from impatience to confusion. Finally surprise overtook her face, complete with a gasp. "You didn't!"

"What?" he asked innocently.

"You paid off my sister-in-law's house?"

She screeched the question, and he took a step back. "You're mad? I'm not trying to buy you, if that's what you think. I just thought that since you always worry about Mila and the kids—"

"Thank you!" Gia threw herself at him, arms encircling his neck, legs around his waist, squeezing tight.

Damn, the minute she touched him, he wanted to tear her clothes off, restrain her, and get as deep inside her as possible.

Not far away, he saw a few moms watching over their kids stop and stare at them. Public scenes were nothing new to him…but definitely not with kids nearby.

Jason cleared his throat and gently eased Gia to her feet. "Baby, as much as I'd love to do every fabulously dirty thing to you I can think of, now isn't the time."

She sent him a little scolding glance with a laugh, but she still blushed. "I know. I just… Wow, I know you paid off Mila's mortgage for me, and I can't think of anything that makes me happier."

Relief wended its way through his bloodstream. "Thank God. I finally figured out this morning that you wanted the divorce settlement to help your family, so I just took care of it. I know I didn't consult you first."

"It's the most thoughtful thing you've ever done for me." She grinned from ear to ear. "Mila is happiest being a stay-at-home mom, and even with my salary and the proceeds from the sale of my house, I could barely keep up financially. I didn't want her worrying about affording the house or wondering how they'd find the money to eat. Now, without a mortgage, she'll have enough left after Tony's death benefits to take care of their necessities and save a little for the future. She's going to be *so* incredibly happy."

"If you're happy, that's what matters to me."

"I'm thrilled. But..." She winced. "I still want the money from the settlement."

"On top of paying Mila's mortgage? All two hundred fifty thousand?"

"Yes. Today, if you can get it to me."

Jason's first reaction came from the cynic in him. She wanted money and she still intended to let the divorce happen? Why? Had she decided that she couldn't live without the swanky shopping? He stared down into those deep dark eyes of hers, the lush rosy lips and paused. Did her reasons really matter? If all he had to do in order to keep Gia was take her to the mall and buy her a few things to line her closet...

He frowned and put the brakes on that thought altogether. Gia wasn't Samantha. She'd been thrilled that he'd spent his money paying off a family member's house, rather than try to bribe her with baubles.

"Who needs the money?"

She bit her lip. "It's complicated. If you'll at least consider it, take me to your bank, and I'll show you what I'm thinking. Then...you can decide what you want to do about the money and about us."

Knowing his wife, the money would benefit someone else far more than her, at least directly. She would probably derive her satisfaction from knowing someone she loved no longer had to worry, but who? Her parents?

"Separate cars? You lead. I'll follow." They headed toward the lot.

Gia gave him a sheepish grin. She looked like such a sensual woman most of the time. Her beautiful femininity had caught his eye first. She was all curves and angles, graceful. At the moment, however, she looked a bit like a child with that smile.

"Can I ride with you?"

Jason palmed his keys. "You like the car."

She shook her head. "No, I'm fascinated by the way you drive. It's aggressive. And…sexy."

Jason laughed. "Hop in."

As he pressed the button on the fob, the car beeped and unlocked. He opened her door and helped her in, then shut her inside. Bracing against the car, he closed his eyes for a second, allowing himself a moment of triumph. She didn't want a divorce.

So what happened with them after this jaunt to the bank? Gia wouldn't tell him what she had in mind until she was good and ready. But any time he spent with her was a pleasure, so he played along.

Jason slid into the low, sleek vehicle, letting the black leather hug his body as he started the car and let it roar. He backed out of the lot, threw it in drive, then revved the engine. A smile crept up her face.

"You know, Officer Angelotti, I might break a traffic law or two today. Think you want to try to arrest me for that?"

Her smile disappeared, and she turned suddenly somber. "No."

Hell, what had he said? "Did I upset you? I was just teasing."

Face pensive, she licked her lips. He got hard at the sight and cursed himself. She was upset. As much as his cock wanted those lips around him, Jason had to focus on her.

"Sorry," he murmured.

"It's okay. It's not you. I'll explain after our stop."

Something still bothered her. Jason examined their conversation from every angle, trying to determine what. Their marriage? This errand? He came up blank.

A few minutes later, they pulled up in front of the bank. Jason emerged and opened her door, curiosity eating at him. Whatever she was about, he wanted this settled so they could deal with their marriage and their tomorrows…and start letting Gia know that she was his.

As they approached the door, she stopped and placed her fingers on his chest. "Before we go in, I want to say a few things."

He pulled her to the side to let another customer enter the branch and tried to rein his impatience. "Go ahead."

"Whether you want to give me the money or not, it doesn't change my decision. I won't file for divorce. Obviously, I can't stop you from doing it, and if you still choose to at the end of eight days, I won't expect more money."

His silly wife hadn't yet grasped the way he saw their relationship working, but as soon as he figured out what she was up to, he'd make a few things clear.

"All right. Anything else?"

She nodded, then took in a shaky breath. "Last night, I gave a lot of consideration to my future, all parts of it. I took a long, hard look at my job and decided that I can't keep working for a precinct where no one cares if justice is being served. When money becomes more important than right, I have no business being there. I talked it over with my dad. He understands. This morning, I quit."

The words stunned him. Happily, of course. He never thought he'd see the day that Gia gave up the pursuit of order and goodness. He loved the idea that she wouldn't be risking herself in the line of duty and possibly wind up a casualty like her brother, suddenly gone because some street punk had pulled the trigger. But Jason remembered their argument in his kitchen yesterday morning. She needed purpose in her life.

"If it's a decision you're happy with, then you made the right one. If you want my support, you've got it." And he would totally provide for her. If she never wanted to lift a finger again, he'd be happy to give her everything she needed.

"That's where the money comes in," she admitted, wrapping her arms around herself as a breeze whipped through her sweater.

"So it's a nest egg for the future?" Did she think she'd remain married to him but live separately?

"No, it's the beginning of my new purpose. If I'm not going to be a police officer, I've got to do something good with my life. So I'm going to start a fund to help the families of slain officers. It will provide assistance for everything from burial expenses to child care to financial planning for the future. And grief counseling, definitely. Whatever these survivors need, I want to make sure they get. The money from the settlement will allow me to get a good start on fundraising and assisting others."

Shock and pride both smacked him. God, Gia had the biggest heart. She made him feel alive for the first time in his life. Until her, he'd never known what it meant to think with goodness. Jason felt blessed to have her. If he had his way, he'd spend the next fifty years absorbing more of that love and giving it back to her.

"Did you already set up an account here?"

"No, but I did file the paperwork to create a nonprofit LLC so I could open one. Do you hate the idea?"

"No, baby. I love it. I think it's every bit as amazing as you are," he assured her. "Let's get this started."

An hour later, they emerged from the bank. Evening was just falling, leaving a bright orange-pink swath across the sky. Gia wore a smile of such serenity that she glowed. Jason had been attracted to her the moment he saw her, but he found her so much more beautiful because he knew how good she was inside as well.

"Congratulations," he murmured as he helped her into the car again.

"I'm really excited to get started. Thank you so much for doubling the contribution. I can do more for others much faster."

"My pleasure." He started the car and drove back to the park.

It didn't take long before they pulled into the lot again. Most of the minivans and SUVs had cleared out.

"So…that's everything I had to say." She looked at him expectantly. As Jason pondered the best way to tell her what was on his mind, she grabbed her purse and fished her keys out. "I'll…um, get out of your hair."

Jason reached out and grabbed her wrist. "No, you won't. I need to say a few things before anyone goes anywhere." And now that the moment had come for him to finally speak what was in his heart, he felt nervous as all hell.

She sank back into the seat but still didn't look relaxed. "All right."

Shit. He hadn't planned this speech exactly. Without knowing what Gia had on her mind, he hadn't been sure what to say. Usually, he went on with his thoughts and plans, then let everyone else adjust as necessary. Besides keeping him off guard, his wife deserved more consideration—especially since she always put everyone else first. No one did that for her, and he wanted to be the one she could count on.

"I'm listening," she assured softly.

He gulped down rare nerves and took her hands in his, clutching them. "Gia, baby, I don't want a divorce, either. I want you to stay with me and live as my wife. I want to take care of you and watch you grow this foundation in your brother's honor, be a part of your family…and start our own. W-will you do that with me?"

The beginnings of a smile broke across her face, and she pressed her lips together to squelch it. Even so, he saw the moisture gathering in her eyes and making them glisten. Damn it, if she wasn't the most beautiful woman he knew. "Really?"

"Yeah…" He squeezed her hands. "I've been thinking a lot, too. I love you."

Gia froze, completely silent. Then she shoved her purse to the floorboard and launched herself into his arms, pressing her lips to his with a need that floored him. The passion to become one with him flowed from her kiss, deep into his mouth where they joined...then straight to his heart. Over the gearshift, he held her tighter, wishing like hell he could pull her body completely against him and make her his all over again.

But first, he had to hear her say that she wanted what he yearned for, too.

He tore away. "Is that a yes?"

She panted, her slick, passion-stained lips parted and tempting and... Shit, he needed to keep his head together. This answer was too important.

"Yes." Gia brushed a solemn kiss on his mouth, then smiled softly at him. "Yes. I'd love that because I love you. So much."

When she gasped suddenly, then dove for her purse on the floorboard, he frowned. "Baby?"

After a wild dig through her purse, she came up with a triumphant grin on her face. "Put this on me?"

Gia handed him her ring, then kept something back in her other fist.

Jason wondered what little plot she cooked up now, but he smiled. "My pleasure, wife."

In the solemn silence, he slid the ring onto her finger. This time, he knew it would stay there. Joy lit up every nerve and jetted through his veins. He couldn't imagine being any happier than he was right now.

"There," she breathed, looking down at the symbol of their marriage all glittering in the falling light. "It's beautiful...but not perfect."

"It's not?"

Gia grabbed his left hand in hers, set it against her cheek, kissed his palm. Then she looked into his eyes and, with shaking fingers, she settled a perfect platinum band around his finger. "I bought it this morning when I figure out what I wanted. In our rush to Vegas, we never picked out a ring for you, and I wanted you to have something from me so you'd always remember that you're my husband."

Fuck if he didn't feel his throat close up as he choked on the moment. "It's incredible. I'll cherish it because you gave it to me."

"I love you, Mr. Denning."

"I love you, Mrs. Denning. Hell, I enjoy saying that." He laughed, filling with light and joy and more happy tomorrows. "I'll probably say it a lot."

"Good." She grinned, then gazed out the windshield. "I think all the moms and kids are gone."

He glanced around the empty parking lot. "I think you're right."

Gia opened the door, stepped out, and bent to toss him a come-hither look. "You know, I've been a very bad girl, Master."

Jason wondered what she was up to but figured he'd like it. "You have. I still owe you one hell of a spanking for deserting me for so long."

"You do," she agreed. "You'll always keep me safe, right?"

"Always, to my last breath."

Her smile filled with mischief. "Then spank me…and whatever else you have in mind. That is, if you can catch me."

Her words clicked through his brain and had registered with his libido by the time she slammed the car door and started jogging into the park. He'd finally have her here, where their relationship had almost ended once—and now she'd trusted him enough to surrender. She'd love him more than enough to make it sweet.

"It's on, baby," he muttered as he jumped out of the Porsche and clicked the fob to lock it as he ran after her. "When I catch you, I'm going to spank your ass red and take you right then, right there."

As she reached a towering tree, she curled her arm around the trunk, then peeked back at him with a grin that lit up her whole face. "I can't wait…"

Acknowledgments from the Author

This novella might never have been written if not for the clever, unflagging persistence of Liz Berry and M.J. Rose. I'm thrilled you two allowed me to be a part of this project and tell a story that hits so many notes near and dear to my heart. Huge appreciation for every author in the inaugural 1001 Dark Nights collection for seeing the potential in our collective power and going on this adventure with me. Special hugs to all the "Beach Babes" with whom I had a chance to share my enthusiasm for 1001 Dark Nights (along with many Jell-O shots): Lexi Blake, Cherise Sinclair, Lara Adrian, Larissa Ione, Lorelei James, and J. Kenner. I'm extremely grateful to Isabella LaPearl for her fabulous voice that helps me "see" everything I've written. And to Chloe Vale for her gently guiding editorial hand, along with her ability to see what I've somehow missed. I can never thank you all enough.

About Shayla Black

Shayla Black (aka Shelley Bradley) is the New York Times and USA Today bestselling author of over 40 sizzling contemporary, erotic, paranormal, and historical romances produced via traditional, small press, independent, and audio publishing. She lives in Texas with her husband, munchkin, and one very spoiled cat. In her "free" time, she enjoys reality TV, reading and listening to an eclectic blend of music.

Shayla's books have been translated in about a dozen languages. RT Bookclub has nominated her for a Career Achievement award in erotic romance, twice nominated her for Best Erotic Romance of the year, as well as awarded her several Top Picks, and a KISS Hero Award. She has also received or been nominated for The Passionate Plume, The Holt Medallion, Colorado Romance Writers Award of Excellence, and the National Reader's Choice Awards.

A writing risk-taker, Shayla enjoys tackling writing challenges with every new book.

Connect with her online:

Shayla Black:
Facebook: www.facebook.com/ShaylaBlackAuthor
Twitter: www.twitter.com/@shayla_black
Website: www.shaylablack.com

Pure Wicked
A Wicked Lovers Novella
By Shayla Black
Coming September 8, 2015

During his decade as an international pop star, Jesse McCall has lived every day in the fast lane. A committed hedonist reveling in amazing highs, globetrotting, and nameless encounters, he refuses to think about his loneliness or empty future. Then tragedy strikes.

Shocked and grieving, he sheds his identity and walks away, searching for peace. Instead, he finds Bristol Reese, a no-nonsense beauty scraping to keep her family's business afloat while struggling with her own demons. He's intent on seducing her, but other than a pleasure-filled night, she's not interested in a player, especially after her boyfriend recently proposed to her sister. In order to claim Bristol, Jesse has to prove he's not the kind of man he's always been. But when she learns his identity and his past comes back to haunt him, how will he convince her that he's a changed man who wants nothing more than to make her his forever?

Also from Shayla Black/Shelley Bradley

EROTIC ROMANCE
The Wicked Lovers
Wicked Ties
Decadent
Delicious
Surrender To Me
Belong To Me
"Wicked to Love" (e-novella)
Mine To Hold
"Wicked All The Way" (e-novella)
Ours To Love
"Wicked All Night" - Wicked And Dangerous Anthology
"Forever Wicked" (e-novella)
Coming Soon:
Theirs To Cherish
His To Take

Sexy Capers
Bound And Determined
Strip Search
"Arresting Desire" – Hot In Handcuffs Anthology

Masters Of Ménage (by Shayla Black and Lexi Blake)
Their Virgin Captive
Their Virgin's Secret
Their Virgin Concubine
Their Virgin Princess
Their Virgin Hostage
Coming Soon:
Their Virgin Secretary

Doms Of Her Life (by Shayla Black, Jenna Jacob, and Isabella LaPearl)
One Dom To Love
The Young And The Submissive
Coming Soon:
The Bold and The Dominant

Stand Alone Titles
Naughty Little Secret (as Shelley Bradley)
"Watch Me" – Sneak Peek Anthology (as Shelley Bradley)
Dangerous Boys And Their Toy
"Her Fantasy Men" – Four Play Anthology

PARANORMAL ROMANCE
The Doomsday Brethren
Tempt Me With Darkness
"Fated" (e-novella)
Seduce Me In Shadow
Possess Me At Midnight
"Mated" – Haunted By Your Touch Anthology
Entice Me At Twilight
Embrace Me At Dawn

HISTORICAL ROMANCE (as Shelley Bradley)
The Lady And The Dragon
One Wicked Night
Strictly Seduction
Strictly Forbidden
His Lady Bride, Brothers in Arms (Book 1)
His Stolen Bride, Brothers in Arms (Book 2)
His Rebel Bride, Brothers in Arms (Book 3)

CONTEMPORARY ROMANCE (as Shelley Bradley)
A Perfect Match

1001 DARK NIGHTS

CRIMSON TWILIGHT
A Krewe of Hunters Novella

NEW YORK TIMES BESTSELLING AUTHOR

HEATHER GRAHAM

On the Krewe of Hunters

By Heather Graham

I've always been fascinated by both history and stories that had elements that were eerie and made us wonder what truly goes on, what is the human soul—and is there life after death? When I was young, I devoured gothic novels and became a fan of Washington Irving, Edgar Allan Poe, Bram Stoker's *Dracula* and Mary Shelley's *Frankenstein*.

And with years passing—for some of us earlier in life and others later—we lose people. When we lose people, we have to believe that we'll see them again, that there is a Heaven or an afterlife. Sometimes, it's the only true comfort we have. I think it's a beautiful part of us—the love we can have for others. But it also allows for pain so deep it can't be endured unless we have that belief that we can and will meet again.

Having grown up with a Scottish father and an Irish mother, I naturally spent some time in church learning the Nicene Creed—in which we vow that we believe in the Holy Ghost.

I suppose people with very mathematical and scientific minds can easily explain away such things as "death" experiences shared by many who technically died on operating tables before being brought back. "Neurons snapping in the brain," is one explanation I've heard.

But I sadly lack a scientific brain and my math is pathetic, so I choose to believe that all things may be possible.

Have I ever sat down with a ghost myself? No.

But I have been many places where it's easy to imagine that the dead might linger. I've heard of many strange tales. And I love the chance that when a loved one needs to be soothed, when a right must be avenged, a ghost—or perhaps the strength and energy of the human soul—might remain.

Thus the Krewe.

Who better than an offshoot of a crime-fighting agency to help these wronged individuals—far too, well, *dead*, themselves—who wish to set the record straight?

I've had incredible chances myself to do wonderful things and while I haven't met a ghost, I have certainly been places where the very air around you feels different. Walking through the Tower of London, stepping into Westminster Cathedral—or standing at dusk on one of the hallowed fields of Gettysburg, you can easily feel seeped with history and the lives that went before us.

I've enjoyed working on the Krewe novels, setting them various places I've loved myself. Each year, a group of writers takes the Lizzie Borden house for a night. For promo, I've done a documented séance at the House of the Seven Gables. I've been on expeditions with ghost "hunters" on the Queen Mary, the Spanish Military Hospital, the Myrtles Plantation, and many more wonderful locations where history, time, and place took their toll on men and women.

Wonderfully fun things happen. The incredible owner of the Lizzie Borden Bed and Breakfast and Museum, has restored the house to as close to the way it looked the fateful day that Lizzie herself either did—or didn't—take an ax (or hatchet!) and give her mother forty whacks. (It was really somewhere between 18 and 20, but that doesn't work well in a rhyme!) One year, the Biography Channel was filming there and my newly graduated Cal-Arts actress daughter, Chynna Skye, played Lizzie Borden for the Biography Channel—and hacked me to pieces as Abby Borden. (What a charming mother/daughter shot, right?) I've stayed at the 17hundred90 Inn in Savannah in the room from which their resident ghost, Anne, pitched to her death. The management there has a wonderful sense of humor—they have a mannequin of Anne in one of the windows, waving to those on the tours that go by. We also happened to follow a then young recording and television star's stay in the room. She left the inn a letter, telling them that Anne had been in her luggage, messing up all her packing. Having spent time with ghost trackers who did seek the logical explanation first, all I could think was, "But did you look for the note from the TSA?"

A favorite occasion was at the Spanish Military Hospital in St. Augustine where, watching the cameras set up by my friends, the Peace River Ghost Trackers, I was certain I saw a ghost. But good ghost trackers are out to find the solid solution to a "haunting" first—it was pointed out to me that I was seeing Scott's shadow as he moved across the room.

While Adam Harrison first makes his appearance in *Haunted*, the Krewe of Hunters series actually begins with *Phantom Evil*, taking place in one of my favorite cities in the world, New Orleans, Louisiana. I have put on a writers' conference there every year since the awful summer of storms and flooding decimated the city. There are few places in the world with an aura of "faded elegance," of the past being an integral part of the present. There are tales of courage there, of tragedy, and of adventure. The cemeteries stir the imaginations of the most solid thinkers. There are many ghosts with the right to be truly furious at their earthly fates—not to mention some of the most delicious food in the world!

Jane Everett and Sloan Trent first meet during a wicked season of murder at an old theater in Arizona reminiscent of the Bird Cage. The Wild, Wild, West certainly had its share of violence and intrigue as well. Cultures came together and clashed, miners sought treasure, and the ever-present human panorama of life went on—including love gone wrong, hatred, jealousy, and greed.

And where ghosts might well linger. If they exist, of course.

For this story—while thankfully, nothing went wrong and it was an incredibly beautiful day!—I have chosen a castle in New England

and the seed of its imagining came from a real wedding—my son's.

Yes, in America, we have castles. That's because we've had men who lived with massive fortunes and could indulge their whims and have them brought over—brick by brick or stone by stone—from a European country. And there's just something about a castle...

So many things can go wrong at a wedding. What with dresses, a wedding party, nervous brides, nervous grooms, bad caterers, and so on.

But what could be worse than the minister—dead on the morning of the nuptials?

Dedication

For Franci Naulin and D.J. Davant

Yevgeniya Yeretskaya and Derek Pozzessere

and

Alicia Ibarra and Robert Rosello

And to all kinds of different, beautiful—wonderful weddings!

Chapter 1

"I say we fool around again," Sloan Trent said.

Jane Everett smiled.

They'd spent the night before fooling around—even though it had been their wedding eve— so she assumed they'd fool around again a great deal tonight.

Which was nothing new for them.

They'd finally made it out of the shower and into clothing and were ready to head downstairs. But Sloan was still in an amorous mood. He drew her to him, kissed her neck just below her ear, and whispered, "There's so much time in life that we can't fool around… so you have to fool around when the fooling around is good, right?" He had that way of whispering against her ear. His breath was hot and moist and somehow had a way of creating little fires that trickled down into her sex, generating an instant burst of desire.

"We've just showered," she reminded him.

"Showers can be fun, too."

"We're supposed to be meeting up with Kelsey and Logan and seeing a bit of the castle before we get ready for the ceremony."

"You never know. Maybe Logan and Kelsey are fooling around and showering, too?"

He pressed his lips to her throat and her collarbone, drawing her closer, making the spoon of their bodies into something erotic.

She wasn't sure what would have happened if it hadn't been for the scream.

More a shriek!

Long, loud, piercing, horrible.

They broke apart, both of them making mad leaps for the Glock firearms they were never without, racing out of their room to the upper landing of the castle's staircase. Of all the things Jane hadn't expected as her wedding approached, it was for the minister to be found dead—neck broken, eyes-wide-open—at the first floor landing of Castle Cadawil. Logan Raintree and Kelsey O'Brien, their co-workers and witnesses for the wedding, rushed up close behind them.

They all paused, assessing the situation, then raced down.

Reverend Marty MacDonald lay on his back, head twisted at that angle which clearly defined death, his legs still on the steps, arms extended as if he'd tried to fly. Sloan looked at her, shaking his head sadly. She felt as if all the air had been sucked from her lungs. Her blood began to run cold. Her first thought was for Marty MacDonald. She didn't know him that well. She'd met and hired him here, on the New England coast, just a month ago when she'd first seen the castle. She and Sloan had been talking about what to do and how and when to marry, and it had suddenly seemed right.

But now. The poor man!

Her next thought was—

Oh, God! What did this say for their lives together? What kind of an omen—

"Tripped?" Logan Raintree suggested, studying the dead man and the stairs.

Logan was the leader of the Texas Krewe of Hunters—the minidivision within their special unit of the FBI. Many of their fellow agents liked to attach the word "special" with a mocking innuendo, but for the most part the Bureau looked upon them with a fair amount of respect. They were known for coming up with results. Jane had known Logan a long time. They were both Texans and had worked with Texas law enforcement before they'd joined on with the Krewe.

Kelsey had come into it as a U.S. Marshal. She'd been working in Key West, her home stomping grounds, until she'd been called to Texas on a serial murder case. She and Logan had been a twosome ever since. One weekend they'd slipped away and quietly married. They told no one and it had become a pool in the home office, had they or hadn't they? If so, when?

Sloan had profited $120 with his guess. Sloan wasn't a Texan, though he, too, had worked there. Jane had met Sloan in Arizona during the curious case of the deaths at the Gilded Lily. He'd been acting-sheriff there at the time. Six-foot-four, broad-shouldered, wearing a badge and a Stetson, he'd been pretty appealing. That case put some distance and resentment between them, until solving it drew them together in a way that would never end.

"Tripped?" Logan said again, and she caught the question in his voice.

Logan and Sloan, and all of the members of the Krewe, worked well together. Logan and Sloan both had Native American mixes in their backgrounds, which brought a sense and respect for all beliefs and all possibilities.

Jane loved that about both men.

Of course, she loved Kelsey, too. She'd known Kelsey her whole life. Having grown up in the Florida Keys, Kelsey also had a keen interest in everyone and everything. She was bright, blonde, and beautiful, ready to tackle anything.

"So it appears," Kelsey murmured.

"Did you see anyone?" Sloan asked the maid, whose horrified scream had alerted them all.

The maid shook her head.

"I'm trying to picture," Sloan said, "how he tripped and ended up here, as he is."

"He had to have come down from far up," Kelsey noted.

Sloan rose and started up the winding stone stairway. "He'd have had to have tripped at the top of the stairs, rolled, and actually tumbled down to this position."

"Anyone can trip," Kelsey said, laying a hand on Jane's arm. "I'm so sorry."

Jane closed her eyes for a minute. She wanted to believe it. Tripped. A sad accident. Marty MacDonald had been a loner, a bachelor without any exes to mourn him and no children or grandchildren to miss their dad or grandpa. But did that mitigate a human life?

The housekeeper who'd screamed was still standing, staring down at the corpse through glazed eyes, her mouth locked into a circle of horror.

Jane felt frozen herself.

They were used to finding the dead. That was their job. Called in when unexplained deaths and circumstances came about. But this was her minister—the man who was to have married her and Sloan. She didn't move. The others still seemed to have their wits about them. She heard Sloan dialing 911 and speaking in low, even tones to the dispatch officer. Soon, there would be sirens. A medical examiner would arrive. The police would question them all. Naturally, it looked like an accidental death. But Jane always doubted accidental death.

But that was in her nature.

Would the police doubt so, too?

She felt a sense of hysteria rising inside her. She could wind up in an interrogation room on the other side of the table. *Did you do this? I think I know what happened,*" a hard-boiled detective right out of some dime novel would demand. He'd be wearing a Dick Tracey hat and trench coat. *"What was it? You were afraid of commitment. Afraid of marriage. You don't really love that poor bastard, Sloan, do you? You didn't think you'd get away with killing the rugged cowboy type of man he is. Tall, strong, always impossibly right. So you killed the minister. Pushed a poor innocent man of God right down the stairs!"*

Whoa.

Double whoa.

She didn't feel that way. She'd never felt for anyone like she did for Sloan. She was in love with his mind, his smile, his voice. The way he was with her, and the way he was with the world. They shared that weirdness of their special ability to speak with the dead. They also shared a need to use their gift in the best way. She definitely loved him physically. He was rugged and weathered, a cowboy, tall and broad-shouldered, everything a Texas girl might have dreamed about. He had dark hair, light eyes, sun-bronzed features, and a smile that could change the world.

Except that he wasn't smiling now.

"You just now found him?" Sloan asked the maid.

The woman didn't respond.

"Ms. Martin," Sloan pressed.

Jane had noticed the maid's nametag too, identifying her as Phoebe Martin. At last, the woman blinked, focused, and turned to Sloan, nodding sadly, like a child admitting an obvious but unhappy fact.

"Is anyone else here?" Sloan asked her. "I mean, besides you, me, Logan, Kelsey, and Jane?" He pointed around to all of them, using their first names. That was a way to make her feel comfortable, as if she were one with them. In situations like this, people spoke way more easily to authorities when they felt as if they were conversing with friends.

The maid, an attractive young blonde woman of about twenty-seven or so, shook her head. "Right here, no. I didn't see anybody. I was coming from the kitchen and saw him lying here. But, yes, yes, of course, others are around. They're always around. The castle is never left empty. The caretaker, Mr. Green, is somewhere about."

"Anyone else?" Jane prodded gently.

Ms. Martin nodded solemnly. "Mrs. Avery is in her office along with Scully Adair, her assistant. And the chef came in about an hour or so ago. So did two of the cooks. Lila and Sonia are here. They're with housekeeping."

Jane knew that Mrs. Denise Avery managed the castle. She'd dealt with the woman to rent the rooms they'd taken for the weekend, including the chapel and ballroom. The castle was actually owned by a descendant of Emil Roth, the eccentric millionaire who, in the late 1850s, had the building disassembled in Wales and brought to the coastline of New England. The owner, another Emil Roth, had been born with more money than he'd been able to waste. The Roth family had made their fortune in steel, then banking. The current Roth was gone, Jane had been told, to Africa on a big game photography hunt. Mrs. Avery was a distant relative herself. And while the current Emil Roth spent money, Mrs. Avery tried to make it.

"Miss Martin, perhaps you could gather them all here, in the foyer," Sloan suggested.

"Gather them," she repeated.

"Yes, please, would you?" Jane prodded.

"The police and the coroner will arrive any minute and everyone should be here when they do," Sloan said.

Phoebe Martin looked at them at last. "Police?"

"A man is dead," he said. "Yes, the police."

"But... he... fell," she said.

"Possibly," Logan said.

"Probably," Jane said firmly.

Phoebe's eyes widened still further. "Pushed!"

"No. All we know is that he's dead," Jane said. "The local police need to come and the death investigated. The medical examiner or the coroner must come, too."

"Pushed!" Phoebe said again.

"There is that possibility," Kelsey said. She glanced at Jane and grimaced sorrowfully. "But, he probably just fell. No one was there, right? We were all in our rooms, you just came to the landing and found him, and the others are in their offices or on the grounds working. Poor man! He fell, and no one was here. But we still have to have the police."

"The ghost did it!" Phoebe declared.

"Ghosts are seldom vicious," Kelsey said.

Phoebe's gaze latched onto Kelsey. "How would you know? Ghosts can be horribly malicious. Ripping off sheets. Throwing coffee pods all around. Oh, you don't know! It was *her*, I'm telling you. She did it!"

Phoebe was pointing. It seemed she was pointing straight at Jane.

"What?" Jane demanded, her voice a squeak rather than the dignified question she'd intended.

But then she saw that they were all looking behind her at the painting on the wall.

She'd noted it before, of course. Just about a month earlier while driving through the area after a situation in the Northeast, she'd seen the castle. It was open three days a week for tours, and she'd been there for the Saturday afternoon event. Mrs. Avery had led the tour and introduced them to Elizabeth Roth via the painting, a young woman who'd lost her fiancé on the eve of their wedding. Elizabeth, the daughter of the house, had been found dead of an overdose of laudanum on the day her wedding should have taken place. It was said that she was often seen in the halls of the castle, wringing her hands as she paced, praying for the return of her lover.

She was beautiful. Rich waves of auburn hair billowed around her face, with soft tendrils curling about her forehead. Her features were fine and delicate and even ethereal. The painting appeared to be that of a ghost, and yet, Mrs. Avery had assured, it had been done from life by the artist Robichaux who'd been a friend of the family. Perhaps he'd sensed the doom that was to be her future. John McCawley, her groom, had been killed the night before the intended nuptials, hunting in the nearby woods.

"Miss Martin, you're suggesting that Elizabeth Roth did this?" Sloan asked quietly.

Phoebe nodded solemnly. "There have been other deaths over the years. On this staircase. Why do you think we're not booked solidly for weddings?"

Sloan looked over at Jane. She stared back at him with her eyes widening. No, she had to admit, she hadn't done much research on the castle. It had just been beautiful and available, perfect for the two of them. Or so she had thought.

A wry half-smile played lightly on Sloan's lips. An assuring smile, she thought. One that conveyed what she already knew. Ghosts don't stay behind to kill. And something else. They both knew they would be together always, whether this turned out to be the wonderful event of a wedding or not.

"Someone else died here? On these steps?" Sloan asked.

Phoebe looked at Jane. "Last time, it was the bride."

Sloan stared at Jane again. She widened her eyes and gave her head a little shake. Another point she had not thought about either.

"What happened?" Logan asked.

"The bride fell. She tumbled down the stairs. The police said that she tripped on her dress and fell. She died in a pool of white. It was terrible!" Phoebe said.

"It doesn't seem to be a particularly dangerous staircase," Kelsey murmured.

Jane looked down again at Marty MacDonald, dead at the foot of the stairs, his eyes still open in horror. As if he'd seen something awful. His murderer? Or something else? Why the hell would anyone have murdered the man? She realized that Sloan was watching her, frowning, aware of how upset she was. Or maybe relieved? Last time, it had been the bride to die. Sloan gave her a warning look filled with empathy. One that said this was sad, but there was no reason to believe it was anything other than a tragic accident.

"It has to be the ghost. It has to be," Phoebe whispered.

He gave his attention back to Phoebe Martin.

"Must be a powerful ghost," he suggested, not arguing with Phoebe but trying to get her to converse, without really stating anything they knew about the ghost world. "The reverend was not a small man. Assuming that they exist, I'm sure that ghosts do have certain powers. But, personally, I do find it unlikely that the ghost of Elizabeth Roth pushed a man down the stairs."

"You don't know our ghosts," Phoebe said, sounding a little desperate. "Maybe it wasn't Elizabeth. Maybe it was John McCawley, her fiancé. Oh! Maybe his hunting accident wasn't so accidental. Maybe he's seeking revenge!"

There was no painting anywhere of John McCawley, but then, he hadn't lived to become a member of the family and only family members, Mrs. Avery had assured Jane, were pictured on the walls.

"Most likely the poor Reverend MacDonald tripped," Sloan said. "But that's still a sad, accidental death. I believe we should gather everyone on the property here. The police will be arriving soon," Sloan said.

"Of course. I'll gather the others," Phoebe said.

But before she could scamper off, a man in his late-twenties with sandy blond hair, a trifle long, dressed in a tailored shirt and jacket reminiscent of Lord Byron, appeared at the landing.

"What in the devil? What's going on down there?"

Miss Martin didn't scream in terror again. She gaped in astonishment, staring upward.

"Mr. Roth!" she strangled out.

Jane arched her neck to get a better look at the man. Mrs. Avery had informed her that the owner would be gone for the duration of time they were at the castle. He'd supposedly left several weeks ago.

"Hello, Miss Martin," he said gravely.

"Hello," he said to the others, coming down the stairs and carefully avoiding the fallen dead man. He seemed justly appalled by the corpse, sadness, confusion, and horror appearing in his expression as he looked at the dead man.

"Mr. Roth?" Jane asked.

He nodded. "How do you do? Yes, I know. I'm not supposed to be here. And I'm so sorry. Poor man. Do you have any idea... the banister is safe, the carpeting is... secure. I've had engineers in here to make sure that it's safe. But, poor, poor fellow! He must have fallen. Are the police coming?"

"On their way," Kelsey said.

"It's just a normal stairway," Emil Roth murmured, looking up the stairs again. "How does it happen?" The question seemed to be retrospective.

"Mr. Roth, we just heard that a woman died here in the same way. Is that true?" Sloan asked.

Roth nodded, disturbed as he looked down again, then away, as if he couldn't bear to look at the dead man. "Can we do something? Put a sheet on him, something?"

"What about others?" Logan asked. "Dying here."

Roth looked at Logan. "Sir, many died over the years, I believe. It was the Cadawil family home in Wales and the family died out. And here, my parents both died in the room I now keep. Of natural causes. A child in the 1880s died of consumption or tuberculosis. Only Elizabeth Roth died by her own hand. Yes, we had a tragic accident the last time we agreed to have a wedding here. The bride died. A terrible, incredibly sad accident. Oh, Lord. I just wish that we could cover him up!"

"Not until the police arrive," Sloan said. "Best to leave him for the authorities."

Phoebe was still just standing.

"Miss Martin, if you'll gather the others, please?" Logan said gently.

Phoebe moved at last, walking slowly away at first, staring at them all, then turning to run as if banshees were at her heels.

Jane heard the first siren.

She was surprised when Emil Roth looked straight into her eyes. He seemed to study her as if he saw something remarkable.

"How?" he repeated, and then he said, "Why?"

The sound of his voice seemed to echo a sickness within him.

The police arrived. Two officers in uniform preceded a pair of detectives, one grizzled and graying in a tweed coat, the other younger in a stylish jacket. Sloan, closest to the door where they were entering, stepped forward and introduced himself and the others with a minimum of words and explained the situation. A Detective Forester, the older man, asked them all to step away. A younger detective, Flick, began the process of having the uniform officers tape off the scene. Everyone was led through the foyer to the Great Hall. They sat and Jane explained that the minister had been there to officiate at her wedding to Sloan. Emil Roth began to explain that he'd been in Europe planning for an extended stay in Africa but that a stomach bug had soured that prospect, so he'd returned late last night, entering through his private entry at the rear of the castle, where once upon a time guests of the family had arrived via their carriages or on horseback.

The others at the castle were herded into the Grand Hall and introduced themselves. Mrs. Avery, the iron matron in perfect appearance and coiffure. Scully Adair, her young redheaded assistant. Chef Bo Gerard, fortyish and plump, like a man who enjoyed his own creations. Two young cooks, Harry Taubolt and Devon Richard—both lean young men in their twenties who'd not yet enjoyed too much of their own cooking. Sonia Anderson and Lila Adkins, the other maids, young and attractive, like Phoebe.

None of them had been near the foyer, they said.

They were all astounded and saddened by the death of the minister. A few mentioned Cally Thorpe, the young woman who'd died in her bridal gown, tripping down the stairs too. Everyone seemed convinced that it was an accident caused by the ghost of Elizabeth Roth. The medical examiner arrived and while he said he'd have to perform an autopsy, it did appear that the minister had simply missed a step near the second floor landing and tragically broken his neck.

"Sad," Detective Forester said. "Ladies and gentlemen, there will be an autopsy, of course, and I may need to speak to all of you again, but—"

His voice trailed as his younger partner entered from the foyer and whispered something to him. He suddenly studied the four agents.

"You're Feds?" he demanded.

Logan nodded.

"And you're here for a wedding?" Forester asked.

He seemed irritated. But, obviously, they hadn't come to solve any mysteries since they'd been here already when the death had occurred.

"We're here for our wedding," Jane said. "I love the castle. It's beautiful."

"So you're responsible for the minister being here?" Forester asked.

"Yes," she told him.

He stared at her as if it were entirely her fault.

Then Scully Adair, Mrs. Avery's pretty redheaded assistant, stood up, seemingly anguished. "It's not Miss Everett's fault that this happened. It's the castle's fault. It's true! People can't be married here. It was crazy to think that we could plan a wedding. Something bad was destined to happen."

"Oh, rubbish!" Mrs. Avery protested. "Sit down, Scully. That's rot and foolishness. The poor man had an accident. Miss Everett," she said, looking at Jane. "Not to worry. We can find you another minister."

Jane was appalled by the suggestion. Mrs. Avery made it sound as if a caterer had backed out of making a wedding cake. A man was dead!

"The ghosts did it," Phoebe said.

"Ghosts!" Forester let out a snort of derision and stood. "I believe the medical examiner has taken the body. I have a crime scene unit checking out the stairway, but then there will be hundreds of prints on the banister." He paused and looked around again at all of them. "None of you saw or heard a thing, right?"

"Not until I found him," Phoebe said.

"And then she screamed, and we came running," Sloan said.

Forester nodded. "All right, then, I'll be in touch. We'll be awaiting the M.E.'s report, but I believe we're looking at a tragic accident."

Jane knew what his next words would be.

"None of you leaves town, though. Yeah, I know it's cliché, but that's the way it is. I want to be able to contact each and every one of you easily over the next few days."

He stared at Sloan, Logan, Kelsey, and Jane.

"Especially you Feds."

Chapter 2

For a long moment, Sloan Trent had simply sat beside Jane when the meeting had ended and others, except for Kelsey and Logan, had moved on. Then Sloan had held Jane close in silence. The bond between them remained. Nothing, he thought, could ever break that. And then they sat together with Kelsey and Logan. Maybe they were all still a little numb. They'd come for such a joyous occasion.

"We *can* find a… a…" Kelsey began, but then she paused and Sloan wondered what she had been about to say. *Another minister?* Or, perhaps *a living minister?*

The body of Reverend MacDonald was gone—taken to the morgue. Mrs. Avery had retired to her office. Chef and the cooks had presumably headed to the kitchen. Mr. Green had gone back to the groundskeeper's lodge and the maids were cleaning the rooms above.

"I'm not sure that this is what we want for the memory anymore," Sloan said, slipping his arm around Jane's shoulder. She was handling it well, he thought.

Or maybe not.

She seemed stricken. But Jane was strong. She'd proven that so many times. Of course, this was different. She'd planned the perfect small wedding for them in a beautiful place with just a few close friends. The ceremony had never meant that much to him. If she'd wanted a big wedding, fine. If she'd wanted to walk into city hall and say a few words, that would have been fine, too.

He knew that he loved her. No, that was truly a mild concept for the way he felt about her. He'd known what people might refer to as "the good, the bad, and the ugly" in life. He'd experienced a few one-night stands, never knowing if they were good women or not. He'd had relationships with really fine people. But he'd never been with anyone like Jane. Smart, funny, beautiful. And she'd be just as beautiful to him in fifty years. She had the most unusual eyes, not brown or hazel, more a true amber. When she looked at him with those eyes, he saw the world and everything he wanted in life within them. The idea that someone else completed him as a whole seemed cliché, and yet he woke each day happy she was in his life. He worked well with her. They trusted one another with no question. Their commitment was complete. And it didn't matter to him a bit if it was legal. But since they did both believe in God, along with the basic tenets of goodness associated with most religions, it was nice to think that they'd have their union blessed.

Where or how meant nothing to him.

But women? They planned weddings. Big and small.

"We're not getting another minister," Jane said. "And we're not getting married here."

"But we're not leaving here, you know. Especially not us 'Feds,'" Logan reminded them.

Sloan was glad to see that Logan was amused rather than offended. Most of the time when they worked with locals, all went well. Sloan knew that because once upon a time he'd been the local the Krewe of Hunters—with Logan at the helm—had worked with. That had been the beginning for him. Now, he'd been with the Krewe for some time and he loved where he was, though he didn't particularly like murder and mayhem. But he'd known as a young man he'd been meant to fight for the rights of victims, whether living or dead. And working with the Krewe was the best way he knew how to accomplish that role.

Jane punched Logan in the arm.

The two had known each other for years. Logan had been a Texas Ranger. Sloan had spent time working in Texas, too, but Jane had been a civilian forensic artist who'd worked with Logan's group many times before any of them had ever heard of the Krewe of Hunters. They sometimes seemed like a brother and sister act.

"No matter what Detective Forester said, we all know damned well we're not leaving. Not until we know what happened to our minister," Jane said.

"It was an accident, don't you know?" Kelsey said. "That, or the ghost did it."

"We've yet to come across a malevolent ghost," Logan reminded Kelsey.

"And I don't believe for one minute that a ghost did anything," Kelsey said. She looked at Jane. "Have you seen any of the ghosts that haunt the place?"

Jane shook her head. "I didn't see any signs of anyone haunting the castle when I was here before, nor have I seen any yet. How about you?"

Kelsey shook her head. "But you and Sloan arrived much earlier. I thought that maybe while you were out in the garden, or over by the old graveyard, you might have seen someone."

"We're forgetting one thing," Logan said.

"What's that?" Jane asked.

"We're suspicious people by nature. We're called in to solve unexplained deaths, attacks, and other events. And this might have been accidental," Logan said. "Maybe Reverend MacDonald just wasn't paying attention. Don't forget, we never suspect anything but what is real and solid until we've given up on real and solid."

"Then again," Sloan pointed out, "if we're not suspicious, I don't think anyone else will be. Because it *appears* to be real and solid that our minister tripped and broke his neck tumbling down the stairs." He stroked Jane's dark hair and looked into her luminous eyes. "You met the Reverend MacDonald in the village, right?"

She nodded. "When I came here and saw the castle on the hill, I thought it was just perfect. I had gone into a coffee shop and the clerk there told me that it was open for tours. After I spoke to Mrs. Avery and discovered we could get this date, I went back down to the village and inquired about someone at the library. I met with Reverend MacDonald in the same coffee shop and he was delighted. He couldn't marry us on a Sunday because of his church services, but a Saturday would be marvelous. And I told him I'd have a room for him here, so that he'd be ready for the services."

"What else do you know about him?" Sloan asked her.

"Nothing, except that he's from the area. A bachelor. He loves when his youth groups have cookie sales. And the parents he works with are wonderful and love to work at creating carnivals to support the church."

"Doesn't sound like a man anyone would want to hurt," Logan said.

"No," Kelsey agreed.

"He looks great on the surface," Sloan murmured. He caught Logan's eye and he knew. What had happened might have been a tragic accident. But, they wouldn't just accept that as fact. They'd dig and see what might lie hidden beneath appearances.

"Okay, then," Kelsey said. "I'm up and off."

"Off where?" Jane asked her.

"To the local library. I'll see what I can dig up about this place," Kelsey said. "And then I'll head to the church and speak with people and find out what I can about our good Reverend MacDonald."

"Then I'm... not really off," Jane said. "I'm going to talk to Scully Adair. Bad things have happened here before. We need to find out more about the bride who died."

"I'll head into the village, too," Logan said. "And see what I can dig up by way of gossip there regarding both the reverend and the castle folk. I think I saw Mr. Emil Roth head out. It would be good to have a chat with him. The castle's hereditary owner should definitely know what there is to know about the castle."

"We'll meet back upstairs in a couple of hours?" Jane asked. "In the bridal suite? It's the biggest and gives us the most room to work."

"We might as well make use of the size," Sloan agreed dryly.

They wouldn't be laughing tonight, sipping champagne, eating strawberries and enjoying a totally carefree time as their first night of being husband and wife.

"You know, maybe you two are not going to become legally wed here," Kelsey pointed out, a smile in her eyes, "but there's no reason to make a perfectly good room go to waste."

"Don't worry," Sloan told her, smiling and meeting Jane's eyes. "We don't intend for you two to stay long."

"A man just died," Jane murmured.

"In our line of work, someone has frequently just died," Logan said softly. "And that really shows us just how important it is to *live*."

Jane smiled and nodded. "We have champagne and fruit and chocolate. And we're willing to share. We'll meet in the suite in about two hours. And we will know the truth."

Sloan looked at Jane as they all nodded. She was so beautiful.

Calmer where Kelsey could be animated, serene often in a way that seemed to make the world stand still and be all right for him. She could be passionate and filled with vehemence when she chose and courageous at all times—even when she was afraid.

God, he loved her.

* * * *

Scully Adair's place was the reception desk in front of the doors that led to Mrs. Avery's medieval and elegant office on the ground floor of the castle. Mrs. Avery, Jane thought, was going to be a tough nut to crack. She was all business and no nonsense. But, of course, if she heard Jane talking with Scully, she'd probably butt right in. So Jane waited, standing by the office door. Soon enough, Scully came out, her pretty features furrowed in a frown, her movements indicating that she was disturbed and restless. Her fingers fluttered as she closed the office door. There was a twitch in her cheek.

"Hey," Jane said softly.

She was glad that Scully didn't scream in surprise. Instead, her slender fingers flitted to her face. Her hand rested at her throat.

"Um, hey," she said. "I'm so, so sorry. I mean, what a wedding day, huh?"

"I'm not worried about my wedding," Jane said. "Sloan and I will marry somewhere soon enough. But were you going for lunch or a cup of coffee?"

Scully nodded with wide eyes. "Coffee, with a stiff shot."

"May I go with you?" Jane asked.

"Sure. I guess."

Jane fell into step with her as they walked along a corridor to the far end of the ground floor. There, an archway led into a cavernous kitchen. Pots and pans hung from rafters. A giant fireplace and hearth filled one end. Other than that, the place was state of the art with giant refrigerators and freezers, a range top surrounded by granite, a work table, and other modern appliances. There was also a large table in a breakfast nook. Old paned windows looked out over the cliff top where flowers and shrubs grew in beautiful profusion.

Chef Bo Gerard, a man who greatly resembled Chef Boyardee, and his two young assistants, Harry Taubolt—dark-haired and lean, a handsome young man in his mid-twenties—and Devon Richard, blond, a little heavier, a little older, and bearing the marks of teenage acne—were already there. They all looked morose. Each had a mug in front of him as if they were all imbibing in coffee, but a large bottle of Jameson's sat in the middle of the table between them. The three looked up from their cups and smiled grimly at seeing Scully, then leapt to their feet when they saw Jane.

"Miss, guests aren't really allowed back here," Chef Gerard said.

"Oh, leave her be. What, does she look stupid? They're going to look up everything about this place," Scully said. She walked past the table, heading toward the granite counter and a coffee pot. "Miss Everett, coffee? You can lace it or not as you choose. The guys already have the booze on the table. Me? My minister dead on my wedding day? I'd be drinking."

Jane smiled. "Coffee, yes, lovely, thank you."

She accepted a cup from Scully, who sat and poured herself a liberal amount of Jameson's from the bottle on the table.

Not about to let an uncomfortable silence begin, Jane dove right in. "Scully, you said that we shouldn't have been allowed to plan a wedding here. Why? What happened before."

"Scully!" Chef said.

Scully stared at him and then looked at Jane. "You know the legend, of course. I was so startled and so scared when I saw the poor Reverend MacDonald. I looked at *her* picture. I mean, seriously, who knows? Maybe she can push people down the stairs."

"Scully, you're an idiot," Harry Taubolt said, shaking his dark head. "You see ghosts everywhere."

"There are ghosts," Devon Richard said, staring into his cup. He looked at Jane then as if she had somehow willed him to do so. "There are ghosts. They can move things."

Chef let out an impatient sound. Harry snorted.

"You forget where you put things or what you've done, that's what happens," Chef said.

"No," Devon said, shaking his head firmly. "When I come out to the Great Hall and find a napkin on the floor, I know I didn't put it there. When I've preset a plate with garnish, then the garnish is on the counter top, I know I didn't put it there." He turned to stare at Harry. "And you know it happens. You just have to deny it, or you'd be scared."

"You think that Elizabeth Roth is the ghost?" Jane asked.

"No," Scully said.

"Yes!" Chef snapped firmly.

"An old ghost," Harry said softly. "Elizabeth was due to marry John McCawley just before the start of the Civil War. McCawley was from the South. He wasn't in the military, he hadn't made any declarations about secession, but the family wasn't happy about the marriage. I say one of them did McCawley in when he was out in the woods. Hunting accident? Hell, no one believes that. Nathaniel Roth, Elizabeth's brother, was out in the woods at the same time. He must have shot McCawley. And Elizabeth couldn't bear it or the fact that her family would be party to such a thing. She killed herself—that we know. And she hates the family. She couldn't be married here, so she won't let anyone else be married here. She pushed your minister down the stairs."

"She looked beautiful and gentle, not like a vengeful murderess," Jane said. She turned quickly to Scully. "Who do you think is haunting the place?"

"Scully," Chef said.

But Scully laughed. "Jane is an FBI agent. You think she can't find out?" Scully told Jane, "Mrs. Avery decided three years ago that she'd allow a man and woman from Georgia to be married here. Cally Thorpe was going to marry Fred Grigsby. Cally fell down the stairs, too. Detective Forester didn't mention that fact because he was working somewhere else when it happened. He'll know now, but, anyway, what the hell? That was ruled an accident, too."

"So," Jane said carefully, "you think that Cally was pushed?"

"How many people really just fall down the stairs?" Scully demanded and shivered. "I think I have to quit. I mean, I love this place, but we were alright before Mrs. Avery booked another wedding. What is the matter with that woman?"

"How many of the people working here today were working here when Cally Thorpe died?" Jane asked.

They looked around the table at one another.

"Let's see," Chef began. "Harry, you had just started. Devon, you'd been here a month or so. Mrs. Avery, of course, and Mr. Green has been here since he was a kid working with his dad on the property. Me, of course. I've been here eight years."

"What about the maids?" Jane asked.

"Just Phoebe. The other two girls started in the last few years," Scully said. "I've been here for five... oh, God! I was the one who found Cally. Her eyes were open, too. She was just staring toward the ceiling. No. It wasn't the ceiling. It was the painting." She leaned forward, focusing on Jane. "She was staring at the painting of Elizabeth Roth, right there, right where it hung on the wall."

"Maybe it's true," Devon said quietly. "Maybe we're all okay as long as no one gets married here. Maybe Elizabeth has remained all these years—and she'll kill someone before she allows a wedding to take place in this house!"

Chapter 3

Sloan had feared he might have some trouble with Emil Roth. After all, he was liable for what had happened, being the castle's owner. Even if lawyers could argue that the man wasn't responsible for another's accident on a safe stairway, he was liable in his own mind.

That had to hurt.

Sloan had seen him head out the front with the police when they'd left, and he hadn't seen him since, so he decided to take a walk outside first and see if he was down by the gates or perhaps just sitting on one of the benches in the gardens. While the castle was on a cliff and surrounded on three sides by bracken and flowers, beautifully wild, the front offered sculptures and rock gardens and trails through flowers and bushes and even a manicured hedge menagerie. Mr. Green apparently worked hard and certainly earned his keep. But Sloan couldn't find Emil Roth outside. He tapped on the caretaker's door and Mr. Green opened it to him, looking at him suspiciously.

"Yeah? You got a problem here? You gotta bring it up with management," Green said.

"No, sir. No problem. It's beautiful. I've never seen such a perfectly manicured lawn. Yet you keep the wild and windswept and exotic look around the place, too," Sloan said. "I was just looking for Mr. Roth."

"He ain't out here," Green said. He was an older, grizzled man, lean yet strong, his skin weathered and permanently tanned from years in the sun.

"Then, thank you. And, sincerely, my compliments. You keep this up all alone?"

"Two kids come to mow and hedge sometimes, but… yeah, I do most of it," Green said.

Sloan thought he might have seen a blush rise to the man's cheeks.

"I've been doing this since I was a kid, over fifty years now. The old Emil—this Emil's father—hell, everyone was named Emil in the darned family—just opened the place to the public about forty years ago. My dad was still in charge and he taught me. People like greenery. It's a concrete world, you know? Some people come just to see the grounds."

"I can imagine. Hey, so how has it been for you? What do you think? I mean, the castle goes way back, but even in the United States, it has a spooky history. The obligatory ghost," Sloan said.

Green narrowed his eyes. "Sure. All old places have ghosts."

"You've seen something," Sloan said.

"Naw."

"I can tell!"

"Sane people scoff at ghosts, you know."

"Only sane people who haven't seen them yet," Sloan said.

"Have you seen a ghost?"

"One or two, I'm pretty damned sure," Sloan said. "You gotta be careful—because people don't think you're sane once you mention the unusual."

Green nodded in complete, conspiratorial agreement. He lowered his voice, despite the fact that they were alone with no one remotely near them.

"There are ghosts around here. A couple of them. There's—" He hesitated, as if still not sure, but Sloan stayed silent, watching him, waiting. "—a man in boots and breeches and a black shirt who watches me sometimes. He tends to stay behind the trees, down toward what's left of the forest to the rear of the property. And as far as Elizabeth Roth goes, I've seen her. I've seen her often, from the upstairs window. Her room—Elizabeth's room—it's the bridal suite now. I guess you're staying in it."

Sloan nodded. "That's us. I'll watch out for Elizabeth," he said. "Tell me, has anything ever indicated to you that the ghosts could be—

mean? Vindictive?"

Green shook his head. "Naw, in fact... hell, one day I slipped on some wet grass and went tumbling down. It was summer and I blacked out. When I woke up, all dizzy and parched, a water bottle came rolling down to me. Now sure, bottles can roll. But I think John McCawley was there. He rolled that bottle to me. I took a drink, got myself up, and all was well. There's nothing mean about the ghosts in this place."

"You were here when another accident took place, right?"

Again, Green nodded. "Poor thing. That girl broke her neck on the stairs, same as the minister today. We checked the banister. The carpeting on the stairs is checked constantly to see that it's not ripped. The stairs aren't particularly steep or winding. Go figure. Bad things happen."

Sloan thanked Green and headed back toward the house. The foyer and Great Hall were empty. He heard voices coming from the kitchen but headed toward the stairs. At the top, he could see one of the maids.

Phoebe Martin.

She seemed to still be in shock and was stroking a polish rag over the same piece of banister over and over.

Sloan walked up the stairs. "You doing okay?" he asked.

"It's just so sad. How about you?"

"We're all right. Did you know Reverend MacDonald?"

"No, I'm bad, I guess. I haven't gone to church in years. And I was raised Catholic. I wouldn't have known Reverend MacDonald anyway. He was at the really small parish just outside town, and he was an Episcopalian, I believe."

"You never saw him around town?"

Phoebe shook her head. "No, I guess we didn't shop at the same places. And, I admit, I'm pretty into clubbing. Not many ministers go clubbing, I guess."

"Ah, well. I was hoping to talk to Mr. Roth."

Phoebe's eyes widened. "Can you believe it? He was here when this happened, and he wasn't supposed to be."

"Since he is here, I was hoping to talk with him."

"That's his suite, there, at the end of the hall." She lowered her voice. "That was always the room that was kept for the master of the house. And there has been a Roth here since the castle was brought to the United States." She hesitated. "You know, don't you, that the bridal suite was once Elizabeth Roth's room when she was alive?"

"I've been told."

Phoebe looked at him with wide, worried eyes. "You need to be careful. Especially careful now."

"I don't believe Elizabeth would want to hurt Jane or me."

"She hurt the Reverend MacDonald," Phoebe said. "I truly believe it."

"Phoebe, sadly, accidents do happen."

"They happen more often with ghosts," she insisted.

"What does Mr. Roth believe about the place, or do you know?" Sloan asked.

"He doesn't believe in ghosts. Which is good—I guess. But then, he's not here a lot. Too quiet for Mr. Roth. He likes Boston and New York and travel in general. I guess if I had his money, I'd travel, too."

"Everyone can travel some," Sloan told her.

"Sure," Phoebe said. "But, still... be careful, please."

"We'll do that. I promise," Sloan told her. "And perhaps, if you're worried, you might not want to work on the banister."

"Oh. *Oh!*" Phoebe said. "Right!" Gripping the banister tightly, she started down the stairs.

Sloan smiled, thanked her, and headed down the hall. He knocked at the double French doors that led to the suite. Emil Roth answered so quickly that he wondered if he'd been waiting for a summons.

"What can I do for you?" Roth asked.

Sloan studied the man. He was young to have such financial power, Sloan thought. Late-twenties, tops. And he seemed to enjoy the look of a Renaissance poet. His haircut would make him perfect for a Shakespearean play. But his gaze was steady as he looked at Sloan.

"Since you're here, I was hoping you'd give me a tour of the castle and a tour of your family history," Sloan said.

Roth stared at him. He was a man with a medium build and light eyes that added to what was almost a fragile-poet look.

"Sometimes, family history sucks, you know?" he said. "I'm sorry about your wedding. I mean, really sorry that a man is dead. By all accounts a good and jovial man. And I'm sorry that my family history is full of asses. But I don't think that it means anything. A man fell. That's it. He died. So tragic."

"I agree. But, we're not getting married today and we're still here. And history fascinates me," Sloan told him.

Roth grinned at that. "You're a Fed involved with a special unit that investigates when deaths that are rumored to be associated with something paranormal happen. I'm young, rich, and not particularly responsible, but I'm not stupid either."

Sloan laughed. "I wouldn't begin to suggest that you're stupid. I believe that, tragically, Reverend MacDonald fell. But I am fascinated with this place. Jane didn't really check out much of the history here. She fell in love with the castle. She wanted a small and intimate wedding more or less on the spur of the moment. And sure, under the circumstances, I'd love to know more about the 'ghosts' that supposedly reside here."

Roth grimaced. "The maids have been talking again."

"Everyone talks. Ghost stories are fun."

"So I hear. Mrs. Avery thinks that they create the mystique of the castle. I personally think that my ancestor's desire to bring a castle to the United States is interesting enough. But, we do keep up a lot of the maintenance with our bed and breakfast income, parties, and tours. So, I let her go on about the brilliance of a good ghost story. But, what the hell? I'll give you a tour."

"That's great. I really appreciate it," Sloan told him.

"What about your fiancée? Maybe she'd like to come, too?" Roth suggested.

"Maybe she would. I'm not sure where she is... I'll try her cell," Sloan said.

Jane was number one on his speed dial and, in a matter of seconds, she answered. He cheerfully explained where he was and asked what she was doing. She said that she'd be right there.

As they waited, Roth asked Sloan, "How do you like your room? No ghostly disturbances, right?"

"Not a one," Sloan told him.

"You should see people around here when they come for the ghost tours," Roth said. "They all have their cameras out like eager puppies. They catch dust specs that become 'orbs.' Sad. But, then again, we're featured in a lot of books and again, I guess my dear Mrs. Avery is right."

"I understand she's a distant relative," Sloan said. "Pardon me for overstepping, but it doesn't sound as if you like her much."

Roth grinned. "I'm that transparent? Sad. No, I don't like her. Her grandmother was my grandfather's sister. I guess we're second cousins or something like that. But, no, I don't like her. She's self-righteous and knows everything. I understand keeping the place up and keeping it maintained, but she's turned it into a theme attraction. I'm really proud of it as a family home. But… anyway, in my father's will he asked that I keep her employed through her lifetime—as long as she wishes. So, there you go. She's no spring chicken, but she's a pretty healthy sixty-plus. I have a few years to go."

Sloan heard footsteps in the hall and saw Jane coming.

They always managed a real balance when working, as did the others. Those in the Krewe of Hunters units tended to pair up—maybe there was just something special that they all shared and that created a special attraction. Jane had belonged to the Krewe before he had. He'd met her when she'd come to Lily, Arizona, his home, where he'd returned when his grandfather had suffered from cancer. She'd been both amazing and annoying to him from first sight. He'd been attracted to her from the start, falling in love with her smile, her eyes, her mind. In his life, he'd never been with anyone like her. She seemed aware of everything about him, faults and flaws and "talents," and she loved him. They hadn't been in a hurry to get married, but they'd both wanted it.

She met his eyes with the same open gaze she always did.

He walked to meet her, slipping his arm around her shoulder. "I'm really pleased. It's not a good day, certainly, but Emil Roth has offered us a real tour. History, and all else."

"That's kind of you, Mr. Roth," Jane said.

"But you saw the castle before, right? You took the ghost tour, didn't you?" Roth asked her.

"I took the tour. So I know about Elizabeth Roth and her beloved, John McCawley. He was killed in a hunting accident the day before the wedding, and then Elizabeth killed herself."

"Come on then. I do give the best tour," Roth said. "And call me Emil, please."

"Then we're Sloan and Jane," Sloan said.

Emil smiled and nodded. "Let's start in the Great Hall and go from there."

He seemed happy. Sloan looked at Jane. He took her hand and she smiled and shrugged and they followed Emil Roth. At the Great Hall, he extended his hands, as if displaying the massive room with its décor of swords and coats of arms and standing men in armor.

"Castle Cadawil was built in 1280 and the Duke of Cadawil held it all of two years, until the death of Llywelyn the Last in 1282 and the conquest of Edward I from the Principality of Wales. That's why, to this day, the heir apparent to the British crown is called the Prince of

Wales. Anyway, the castle wasn't a major holding. It was on a bluff with nothing around it that anyone really wanted to hold for any reason. So, through the centuries, it had been abandoned, half-restored, abandoned again. In the early 1800s, my self-made millionaire ancestor saw it there and determined that he could move a castle to New England. And he did so. Of course, when it came over, it was little but design and stone. Antiques were purchased and through the years, Tiffany windows added. My family apparently loved their castle. But then, as you know, tragedy struck before the wedding of Elizabeth Roth and John McCawley."

"What do you think about that?" Jane asked him. "Did the family love and welcome McCawley, or did someone hate him?"

"Enough to kill him?" Roth asked.

"He died in a hunting accident. Other men in the family were out there, too, right?" Jane asked.

"Yes, they were. And it's an interesting question. There are no letters or family records that reflect anyone's feelings on the matter and the two men involved would have been my great, great, great, grandfather, Emil Roth, and my great, great, grandfather, another Emil Roth. I don't like to think that my ancestors would have killed a man they didn't want marrying into the family."

"What happened?" Sloan asked. "McCawley was shot?"

"With an arrow, they were deer hunting," Roth said. "But, you see, they weren't the only ones out there. A number of wedding guests were there. You two wanted a small wedding. The wedding of Elizabeth Roth was the social event of the season."

"Of course," Jane said.

"No one saw anything? No one knew who missed a deer and killed a man?" Sloan asked.

"If so, no one admitted anything. He was found by Elizabeth's father who, of course, immediately rushed him back to the castle and called for a surgeon. But it was too late. Elizabeth came running down the stairs and—"

Roth paused in his speaking, looking troubled.

"And?"

"The story goes that John McCawley died at the foot of the stairs. The men carrying him paused there because Elizabeth was rushing down. When she reached him, he looked into her eyes, closed his own, and died."

"How sad," Jane murmured.

"And then, of course, that night, Elizabeth took an overdose of laudanum and died in the early hours of the following morning, when the wedding should have taken place."

He led them out of the hall.

"If you look at the arches, you can see that the foyer was originally a last defense before the actual castle. There would have been a keep, of course, in Wales, and a wall surrounding it. We have the lawn in front and the wild growth to the rear, except for where the grass is mown just out the back. Following along to the right of the castle, after the entry, you reach the offices and such and going all the way back, you get to the kitchen. Heading upstairs, are the rooms. Mine, of course, was always the master's suite. Where you're sleeping—and though they weren't actually married here, many a bride and groom have slept there—was Elizabeth's room. There are four more bedrooms. Your friends are in one. Reverend MacDonald was in another, and there are two more guest rooms. The attic holds five rooms. Phoebe lives in one and the other two maids come in just for the day or special occasions. Chef has an apartment over the old stables, and Mr. Green has an apartment on the property, too."

"Mrs. Avery doesn't live here?" Jane asked.

"Yes, she's on the property. You passed her place coming in. The old guard house at the foot of the cliff. But her assistant, Scully, lives in the village as do the other cooks."

He looked at Jane curiously.

She asked him, "Is there a big black spot on my face that no one is mentioning to me?"

Emil Roth laughed. "I beg your pardon. Forgive me. It's just that when I look at you and your face, tilted at a certain angle, you look so much like her."

"Her?" Jane asked.

"Elizabeth," Emil said. "Come look at the painting again."

Sloan wasn't sure why the idea disturbed him but he followed as they headed to look at the painting on the wall. Elizabeth Roth was depicted with her hair piled high atop her head, burnished auburn tendrils trailing around her face. Her eyes appeared hazel at first but when Sloan came closer, he realized they'd been painted a true amber.

Just like Jane's.

There was something in the angle of the features. It was true. Jane bore a resemblance to the woman who'd lived more than a century before her birth.

"Do you have roots up here? Maybe you're a long lost cousin," Emil teased.

Jane shook her head. "My family members were in Texas back when people were exclaiming 'Remember the Alamo!' I've no relatives in this region. It's just a fluke."

"But an interesting one," Roth said. "So, what would you like to see next?"

"Where is Elizabeth buried?" Sloan asked. "And, for that matter, her fiancé, John McCawley."

"I understand he never actually became family so he has no painting in the castle," Jane said. "But surely they buried the poor fellow."

"Absolutely. Out to the rear, at the rise to the highest cliff. They're both in the chapel."

"I think I'd like to pay them tribute," Jane said.

"If you wish," Roth said. Smiling, he turned to lead the way out of the castle. "Although, I will warn you."

"What's that?" Sloan asked.

"On a day like today, with a fog settling over the graves, people have been known to see ghosts wandering about."

Sloan looked at Jane. "That's okay. We'll take our chances."

Chapter 4

The old chapel had been brought over to the States from Wales, Roth explained as they left via the rear, out through the kitchen's delivery doors.

Jane was curious that he had chosen to leave by this route. If she remembered right, there were other exits, more elegantly designed, leading to the wilds of the rear and the cliffs that overlooked the sea.

Chef and his two cooks were no longer sitting at the table imbibing in coffee and Jameson's, she noted as they went through. They were all busy at some kind of prep work. She assumed that the employees ate dinner at the castle as well since they didn't need that much prep for four guests and the master of the house, who they hadn't expected to be there anyway.

Chef Bo looked up from his work at a saucepan and acknowledged Roth and stared broodingly at the others as they went through.

His two assistants just watched.

"There's another way out as well. The two arches at the end of the Great Hall lead to smaller halls that bypass this area," Roth explained. "And there's a servants stairway back there, too. I just thought it would be fun to see what was going on in the kitchen."

He was almost like a child who knew that he was in charge, and was yet surprised by it and curious as to his effect on others.

"Smells divine!" he called as they passed.

Three "thank yous" followed his words.

There was a large doorway under a sheltered porte-cochère when they stepped outside. Most likely, parking for large delivery trucks. They walked around one of the walls and were in the back. An open-air patio, set on stone, offered amazing views of the Atlantic Ocean. A light fog swirled in a breeze and seemed in magical motion, barely there. A fireplace, stocked with dry logs, remained ready for those who came out to enjoy the view when it was cool, and Jane imagined they might hold barbecues out there too. Bracken grew around the patio with wild flowers in beautiful colors. Other than the patio and the chairs, if one stood on the cliff and looked out or up at the rise of the castle walls, they might have been in a distant land and in a different time.

But Jane looked to her right.

At the base of a little cliff that rose to another wild and jagged height, was the chapel. It was surrounded by a low stone wall. Within the wall were numerous graves and plots. The chapel had been built in the Norman style with great rising A-line arches and a medieval design. Two giant gargoyles sat over the double wooden doors that led inside.

"Sometimes," Roth said, "I do feel just a bit like a medieval lord. Pity it's far too small and dangerous here for a joust."

"It's really lovely," Jane said.

"Yes, and I'm a lucky man," Roth said. "Primogeniture and all. The oldest son gets everything. Of course, in my case, I was the only child. If I do have children, I'll change things, that's for sure."

Somewhat surprised, Jane looked at Sloan.

Was that for real? If so, he seemed like a pretty decent guy.

She smiled.

There was that wonderful part of their relationship that seemed like an added boon. The ability to look at one another and know that they shared a thought.

"Shall we head toward the chapel?" Roth asked.

He stood a bit down on a slant from them. He wasn't really that small a man, probably about six feet even. But Sloan seemed to tower over him. Jane was five-nine and in flats, but with his Renaissance-poet look, Roth somehow seemed delicate and fragile.

"Thanks. We'd love to see it," Sloan said.

They followed him to the stone wall. There was a gate in the center and a path that led to the chapel. The gate wasn't locked. It swung in easily at Roth's touch and they followed him. He kept on the stone path and headed directly to the chapel where the door was also unlocked.

"You're not worried about break-ins of any kind?" Sloan asked him.

"Maybe I should be. I guess people do destroy things sometimes just for fun. But Mr. Green is always at his place. He hears anything that goes on. He only looks old. Trust me, he's deceptively spry. Caught me by the ears a few times when I was a kid. Guests here are welcome to use the chapel and the only way up here is by the road, so I guess it was just never kept locked. Progress, though. Maybe I'll have to in the future. It's really kind of a cool place. You'll see. Simple and nice."

It was indeed. Tiffany windows displayed the fourteen Stations of the Cross along the side walls, each with its own recessed altar. The high arches were clean and simple and there were five small pews set before the main altar. A large marble cross rose behind the altar.

"Actually, there's a time capsule in here," Roth told him. "Emil, who brought the castle over, is under the main altar with his wife. Their children are scattered along the sides. Sometimes, of course, the daughters moved away, but there are a good fifty people buried or entombed just in the chapel. But you want our own Roth family Romeo and Juliet. Over there—first altar. Come on."

His footsteps made a strange sound as he hurried along the stone floor. Sloan and Jane followed. There were six altar niches along each side of the structure. Someone had obviously been a stickler for symmetry. The first, closest to the main altar, had a window that depicted Judas's betrayal of Christ. The altar beneath it was adorned with a large silver cross. On exact angles from the prayer bench below the altar were two marble sarcophagi or tombs. One was etched simply with a name. John McCawley. The other bore just a first name. Elizabeth. Beneath her name was a tribute. *Daughter; the rose of our lives, plucked far too swift, and we left in life, adrift. In Spring she lived, in Spring she remains. There 'til our own sweet release, 'til this life on earth for all shall cease. Beloved child, we'll meet again, where sorrows end and souls remain.*

"It sounds as if she was deeply mourned," Jane said.

"They say that her father was never the same. He lived as if he'd welcome death every day."

"It's amazing he didn't fall apart completely and lose everything.

But, then, of course, she had a brother. Your great-great-great—however many greats—grandfather," Sloan said.

Emil laughed. "It was my great, great, great grandfather. And he apparently had a wonderful friend as an overseer who'd studied at Harvard. He kept the place going. So this is it. What else can I show you? I mean, you're guests. You're free to wander as you choose. And, of course, this was horribly tragic, but you were supposed to be married today. We'll do anything we can. If you want—"

"We're just fine," Jane said quickly. "Will you be joining us at dinner?"

Roth seemed pleased, as if she were giving him an invitation rather than asking a question.

"I'd be delighted. Much better than eating alone," he said.

"Chef seems busy. Don't others eat here as well?" Jane asked.

"They do. But when I'm here, I just wind up eating in my room," he told him. "And, actually, I have some e-mails to answer. Anything else, just knock on my door."

"We'll wander here for a minute, if it's all right," Sloan told him.

"My house is your house," Roth told them with a grin.

He left them.

When he was gone, Jane looked at Sloan and asked, "Anything?"

"Quiet as—a tomb. No pun intended, of course."

She grimaced at him and headed to the grave of Elizabeth Roth. She set her hand on the tomb, trying to feel something of the young woman who had lived such a short and tragic life. But all she felt was cold stone.

Sloan watched her.

She shrugged. "Nothing. But I can't help but feel that somehow, what's happened now, with Cally Thorpe and Reverend MacDonald, has something to do with the past."

"You really think it's possible that a ghost pushed them both down the stairs?" Sloan asked her, frowning.

"It's not something that we've ever seen. So, no, I don't. But I can't shake the feeling that it's all related."

"Why?" Sloan asked.

She smiled. "I guess that's what we have to figure out."

"Let's walk to the room," Sloan said. "Maybe Kelsey and Logan are back and have come up with something." He reached out and took her hand. "I love you."

She nodded. "I'm not worried about our lives. I'm just sorry that

Marty MacDonald is dead."

"If we can stop something from happening in the future, at least he won't have died in vain."

"Let's head up," she said.

* * * *

"There's no dirt to be found on the Reverend MacDonald," Kelsey announced. "His church is being draped in mourning, his deacon has sent for an emergency cover priest to take care of Sunday services. There are no allegations of his ever being flirtatious, too close to the children, or involved in any kind of scandal. But we have more reason to think it was just an accident."

"Oh?" Sloan said.

He was always amazed by the Krewe's ability to find whatever was needed to make their work go smoothly.

The bridal suite—Elizabeth Roth's room—actually consisted of a drawing room or outer area, the bedroom itself, two large dressing rooms, and these days, a small kitchenette area. Kelsey had managed to get hold of a work board. With erasable markers, she'd already started lists of what they knew and what they had learned. Staring at lists sometimes showed them what went with some other piece of information in another column. They were gathered in the drawing room, Sloan and Jane curled on the loveseat together, Kelsey at her board, and Logan thoughtful as he straddled a chair and looked at the board.

"Why should we be more prone to think that it was an accident?" Sloan asked.

"I spoke with the reverend's deacon. He's been battling a heart condition for a long time. It's possible he suffered a minor heart attack and fell," Kelsey said.

"Maybe the M.E. will be able to tell us more from the autopsy. Anything from your end, Logan?" Sloan asked.

"The reverend was well liked. No hint of improprieties or anything along that line," Logan said. "People were sad. But many of his friends did think he was a walking time bomb. Apparently, a lot of people knew about his condition. And he liked pastries. A woman in the bakery told me that she'd designed a whole line of sugar-free desserts to help him keep his weight down."

"Okay. No one out to get the reverend." Kelsey wrote on the board.

"Both Elizabeth and John McCawley are entombed in the chapel," Jane volunteered. "Along with the rest of the family."

"The caretaker, Mr. Green, sees the ghosts all the time," Sloan said.

"But I don't believe a ghost is doing this," Jane said flatly. "From what I've heard, both Elizabeth and John McCawley were good people—deeply in love. I do, however, have a suspicion that John's death wasn't accidental."

They were all silent.

Kelsey frowned and looked at Sloan.

Sloan spoke to Jane at last. "I don't know if we'll ever have an answer to that. Even if we were to meet their ghosts, they might not have known themselves. What we need to figure out is if someone is killing people here now, in the present, and stop them from killing anyone else."

"Of course," Jane said. She rose, stretched, and walked over to the board. "Personally, I find our young host to be interesting."

"You think that Emil Roth pushed the reverend down the stairs?" Kelsey asked.

"No, and I'm not sure why not. Except that he doesn't seem to be into a lot of family rot. He doesn't see himself as some kind of a lord of the castle. He's young and rich and spoiled, and I think he knows it. I'm not even sure that he likes the castle. He definitely doesn't like Mrs. Avery. He has to keep her here, though. It was part of his father's will. She's a distant relative."

"Ah, the plot thickens," Logan said dryly. "But why would she kill people?"

"To keep the ghost legend going? Maybe she wants some of the television ghost hunters to come in here. Great publicity for the place," Jane suggested.

"Logan," Sloan said, "let's call the home office and get someone there checking into financials for this place. As far as I can tell, the Roth family has more than Emil could spend in a lifetime, even if he tried wasting every cent of it."

"There's no reason for the man to have killed a minister," Kelsey said.

"Or anyone, really," Sloan noted. "But, we'll get a financial check done on the family and make sure. So, anyone get any dirt on the people living here?"

"Not yet. Observation may help," Sloan said. "We'll be dining with the master of the house, and I believe dinner is at six."

"Ah, yes, the wedding feast." Jane murmured.

"We can still—" Sloan began.

"No, we can't!" Jane said quickly. "The wedding feast will be fine, without the wedding."

"Okay, so, just take note here. We have a list of everyone in the house or on the grounds at the time of Reverend MacDonald's death. We've decided that the reverend had no outside enemies. We don't believe Emil Roth is involved, but we'll keep looking. According to what we learned about Reverend MacDonald, it really seems likely that it was a tragic accident," Kelsey said.

"And that would be better than the alternative," Logan said.

Jane rose and walked over to a table where a bottle of champagne sat in a silver bowl of ice with crystal flutes around it. She didn't make a move to open the champagne. She spun around. "I say we go down for a cocktail hour and keep talking with whoever comes near us."

"Okay," Sloan said, rising again.

"Sure," Kelsey agreed.

"Who knows? Too bad there isn't a butler here," Logan said.

"There should have been a butler," Jane said.

"Because the butler often did it?" Kelsey asked.

Jane smiled. "No, it's a castle. There should be a butler. But—" Her voice trailed as she looked at Kelsey's board. "I wish that I believed that Reverend MacDonald just fell. But I don't."

"A hunch?" Kelsey asked her seriously.

They tended to pay attention to gut feelings. But, of course, everyone was wondering if Jane wasn't influenced by the circumstances here at the castle.

"We'll get images of everyone in the house and send them to the main office," Sloan said. "They can find out things about the past by just running searches, and it will be much easier for them to do that than us."

She smiled. "Yes, please. And maybe we can take a walk right before dinner and see if we can chat with any of the locals."

"The locals?" Kelsey murmured.

"Local ghosts," Jane said. "Who knows just what they might know?"

Chapter 5

"How is everyone doing?" Emil Roth asked as they entered the Great Hall.

He was there before them and held a crystal decanter of something dark in his hand. He waved it about as they entered. Jane thought he might have been there imbibing for some time.

"Brandy," he said, "anyone want to join me?"

"Club soda with lime?" Sloan asked him.

"Wise man," Roth noted. "Since people seem to trip down stairs around here. It's best to keep a clean and sober mind. I, however, will just crawl up the stairs. It's hard to trip when you crawl."

He set down the decanter and poured a soda for Sloan, but as he handed the glass over he was looking at Jane. He shuddered, then smiled. "I'm sorry. So sorry! Really. It's just you do bear a strange resemblance to Elizabeth Roth."

"Resemblances can be strange, of course," Jane said. "But sometimes it just depends on what angle an artist gave to a rendering."

"You know a lot about art?" he asked her.

"Jane is a wonderful artist," Kelsey said.

"I'm a forensic artist," Jane said.

He shuddered again. "You draw or paint dead people?"

"Sometimes. But, sometimes, I paint the living. When they're missing, if they have amnesia, if we need to get their images out to the public for a reason."

He gave a slightly sloppy smile. "So you could sketch me?"

"Certainly," she told him.

"Ah, yes. You could, but would you?" he asked.

"If you wish," she said.

"How rude of me. A tragic day. It should have been your wedding. And here I am, asking you to sketch me."

"I don't mind at all," Jane said.

"I'll run up and get your sketch pad," Sloan offered.

Emil lifted his glass to Sloan. "Don't run, not on those stairs."

"I'll be careful," Sloan promised.

"Do you need an easel? Is there something else I can get you? Draw what you really see, too, okay? I don't need to be flattered and I'd like a true image."

Logan pulled out a chair at the table for Jane as he told Emil, "Jane has a unique talent for catching expressions and what makes a person an individual. I'm sure what you'll get is honest."

Jane laughed softly. "I won't try to be unflattering."

Emil drew out the chair across from her. "Am I good here? Do you need more light?"

"I'm fine. As soon as Sloan brings down the pad, we'll be set to go," she promised.

"Please," Emil told Logan and Kelsey, "help yourselves to drinks. I believe Chef will send someone in with hors d'oeuvres soon."

"Thank you," Kelsey told him. "Jane?"

"Diet cola, thanks," Jane said.

"Ah, nothing more exciting?" Emil asked her.

"We're just not feeling all that festive, I guess," Jane said.

Sloan arrived with her sketch pad and a box of pencils. She smiled and thanked him.

"Ready when you are," Emil told her.

"I've already begun," she said.

"You're not drawing."

"But I am studying your face," she said softly.

"Ah," he said. "Should I pose? Lean in? Rest my chin on a fist?"

"No," she told him, picking up a pencil.

She began to sketch. To her amazement, she thought that it was one of her best, and quickly so. She changed pencils frequently, finding light and shadows. She caught his youth, something of a lost empathy in his eyes, and a world weariness he might not have expected. She also caught a bit of the handsome young Renaissance man. Or, perhaps, a rich kid adrift because he could probably be more than what the world seemed to expect of him. When she finished, she hesitated, looking at him.

"May I?" he asked.

"Certainly," she told him.

He took the drawing and studied it for a long time. "Could I possibly have this?"

"Of course," Jane told him.

"May I snap a phone pic of it?" Logan asked him. "It's really excellent. I'd love to have it, too."

"Yes, definitely," Kelsey said.

Mrs. Avery came walking into the room, her lips pursed. She seemed unhappy that Emil appeared to be enjoying his guests. Perhaps she was just unhappy that he was there at all.

"Will you have hors d'oeuvres soon?" she asked politely.

"Yes, we will, Denise. But, first, come here. You must see this!"

"Really, Emil—" Mrs. Avery began.

"Oh, come, come, Denny! Come over here and see this. You must sit, too, if Miss Everett is willing. I'm quite astounded by the likeness she created of me." Emil said.

"I have business—" Mrs. Avery began.

"Yes, yes, you do. You work for me. Sit for a spell. Jane, will you?" Emil asked.

"If you wish."

"Will this take long?" Mrs. Avery asked.

"Five minutes," Sloan said.

Jane thought there was something firm in his voice. He used a tone she knew, though it wasn't often directed at her anymore. People complied with that tone.

Mrs. Avery sat.

She began to sketch and caught the woman's high cheekbones and thin lips. Because it seemed that the sketch was coming out a little too harsh, she set a tiny stray curl upon the forehead and down the face. The sketch caught the true dignity of the woman, but softened her as well. Jane was surprised to see Denise Avery's face as she studied the drawing.

She looked up at Jane with a smile. "That's really nice. Thank you."

"And she'll let you keep it, Denny," Emil said. "After Logan snaps a pic, that is."

"I would love to keep it. Thank you," she said.

Before she could rise, Chef stuck his nose and then his body into the Great Hall. "May I begin with the service?"

"Oh, not until Miss Everett does a sketch," Mrs. Avery said. "Come, sit!"

Jane looked at Sloan.

He grinned at her with pleasure. Logan, she knew, would get a snapshot on his camera of every shot. That night, he'd get every drawing, along with names, to their base. Then they'd know if everyone was who and what they claimed to be.

Before they were done, she'd sketched everyone working at the castle except for the two maids who only came in from nine to five—Sonia Anderson and Lila Adkins. Before she finished with everyone, she asked Chef to bring in the hors d'oeuvres. And as he and his assistants, Harry Taubolt and Devon Richard, served the food, Sloan began speaking with them. By the time she was done with her last sketch for the night—that of Scully Adair—it was agreed that they would all—guests, owner, and employees—eat together that night in the Great Hall.

"It's nice to be together," Scully told Jane, sitting beside her.

The food was all on the table and they passed things around.

It had all gone surprisingly well.

"Considering the fact that a man died here just hours ago," Devon Richard said.

"An accident," Harry said. "It's awkward, isn't it? I mean, none of us really new the reverend, so we can't mourn him as if we lost a friend. And yet, he died here, and we're having dinner."

"People still have to eat," Mrs. Avery said.

"Yes, I know. And work and breathe and go on. It's just that I feel we should be mourning," Avery said.

"And things shouldn't go on as if they were so normal," Phoebe Martin said. Then she laughed uneasily. "Of course, this isn't normal. I've never dined in the Great Hall before."

"This is our way of mourning," Emil Roth said, and they were all quiet for a minute.

"We should say something," Chef announced. "I mean, it doesn't feel right. It just doesn't."

Sloan stood. He'd wound up across the table from Jane. "Shall we join hands."

They rose and did as he suggested. Sloan said a little prayer for Reverend MacDonald ending with, "May he rest in peace, a good man. He'll reside with the angels, certainly."

"Thank you," Emil said when he sat.

"The hall is quite something. But, I can see why you like to eat in your room, Mr. Roth, when you're here alone," Mr. Green said. Even he had been called in for a sketch and dinner. "Of course, I do remember the days when the family was alive and cousins came from many different places, old aunts and uncles, too. Then, the place was alive with laughter, kids running here and there."

A silence followed his words.

"The castle is still a happy place," Mrs. Avery snapped. "You should hear the people when they come here. They love to laugh and to shiver! And our overnight guests are always delighted. Why, we have some of the best ratings to be found on the Internet."

"I wasn't implying that it wasn't happy," Mr. Green said. He looked quickly at Emil Roth. "I certainly meant no disrespect."

"None taken, my man," Roth said. "I say, pass the wine, will you, Phoebe? And do fill your glass first."

Phoebe looked at him, plucked up the wine, looked at him again, then poured herself a large glass.

Emil smiled at her and waited patiently.

Jane made a mental note that one of them would definitely make sure he got up the stairs okay that night. But as the wine flowed, the conversation became more casual. And when Chef and Harry headed to the kitchen to return with the dessert, Jane slipped away, determined to step outside for a few minutes. She headed out to the front. There were dangerous cliffs in the rear of the property, and she didn't intend to become a victim of the castle herself. She walked down toward the caretakers cottage where Mr. Green lived, then kept going, toward the guard house and Mrs. Avery's home.

She turned and looked back at the castle and saw the windows to her own room. They'd left the lights on. She stared upward for several seconds before her breath caught.

Someone in the room.

At one of the windows.

Watching her.

As she watched them.

* * * *

Jane was a special agent, the same as he was. She'd passed the academy and was in law enforcement. But she was still the woman he loved, the woman he was supposed to have married that day. So when Sloan realized Jane was out of the Great Hall, he followed. He didn't know why he felt such a sense of anxiety, but he did. He saw her, far down the path to the castle, as soon as he exited and came down the few stone steps at the entrance.

She was just standing on the path, looking back.

He hurried to her. She smiled as he came to her and pointed up at the castle.

"Someone is there," she said.

"Someone?" he asked.

"Were they all in the Great Hall?" she asked.

"When I left, yes."

"Then I believe Elizabeth does haunt our room," she said.

Sloan looked up. There was nothing there then.

She smiled. "No, I'm not losing it. Someone was there. Now, they're not."

"I believe you," he said.

"You know, I'm really not losing it in any way," she said, turning to him so that he slipped his arms around her. She smoothed back a lock of his hair. "I don't care where or when we marry one another. It doesn't matter. And it doesn't matter that we weren't married today. It does matter that a man died. A good man."

He smiled and nodded. "I know that."

Impulsively, he went down on a knee and took her hand. He kissed it both dramatically and tenderly and looked up to meet her eyes.

"I love you with the depth and breadth of my heart and soul. In my heart, you've already been my wife, my love, my soul mate, my life mate. Not to mention one hell of an agent. And artist, of course."

She laughed, drawing him to his feet and giving him a strong buff on the arm. "That started off so beautifully!"

"Hey, you are an amazing artist. And agent. You want to be an agent tonight, right?"

"I do," she told him. "It's just that speech, it could have stayed romantic."

"Want me to try again?"

"No!" She laughed. "I say we get back up there and make sure that Emil Roth makes it to his room."

"And then we'll make it to ours," he said.

"And then we'll make it to ours," she agreed.

Hand in hand, they made it back to the house. In the Great Hall, Mrs. Avery was saying that she needed to get some sleep. Chef told her that breakfast came early, and Phoebe Martin was headed upstairs, but when she saw Jane and Sloan come in, she stopped.

"Thank you so much, Jane, for the sketch. It's wonderful. And thank you both for somehow making a nice evening out of a horrible day. Good night. And don't forget, if you need anything—anything at all—we're happy to oblige."

"Thank you, Phoebe," Jane told her.

She scampered on toward the stairway. Jane followed her. As she did so, she heard Sloan and Logan talking to Emil Roth, convincing him that they'd see him to his room. It was time to sleep. The men and Kelsey were looking to see that Emil was safe. Jane followed Phoebe up the stairs, and then on up to the third floor.

Phoebe turned to look at her when she reached her door.

"Thank you," she said.

"You're welcome."

"You're worried about all of us."

"There was a lot of wine flowing down there at the dinner table."

But Phoebe looked at her with wide eyes.

"You don't believe that the reverend's death was an accident, do you?" she asked.

"Actually, we found out that he had a heart condition. That might have caused him to stumble. But we'll know more when the M.E. makes his report," Jane said.

But Phoebe still watched her. "That won't make any difference to you, will it? You think that he was killed."

Jane said, "The police seem to believe it was an accident."

"Do you think we're all in danger?"

"No," Jane said.

That wasn't a lie. Whoever the killer was, they were part of the castle crew. And the killer certainly wasn't in danger.

Phoebe shook her head. "Thank you for tonight."

"Of course," Jane said.

She left Phoebe to descend the stairs to the second level.

Careful as she did so.

* * * *

Within another ten minutes, everyone was where they should be or on their way to their own homes. Sloan watched as Jane came down from the attic level, her hand firmly on the handrail of the far less elegant steps that led from the second floor to the attic. She joined him, Logan, and Kelsey on the second floor landing by their rooms.

"One of us will be up through the night. I'm taking first shift and Kelsey will be second. You two deserve to get some sleep or whatever tonight."

"We're fine," Sloan assured him.

"We know that," Kelsey said, grinning. "We just want you to know that we're on the awake duty, or guard duty, or whatever you want to call it."

Sloan started to protest but Jane caught his arm. "Just tell them thank you, Sloan."

"Thank you," Sloan said.

Jane dragged him into the room.

"I'm, uh, up for whatever you're in the mood for," he said.

But she walked away from him, leaving him in the entry and heading into the bedroom. She stood there for a while and then walked back out.

"She's not here," she said.

"No?"

She shook her head with disappointment. "I thought that she would be. I thought that tonight we'd see her."

Sloan walked to her and took her gently into his arms. "Maybe she knows that we're here. Maybe she knows why we came. And maybe she's as good and sweet as history paints her. What she really wants is happiness for others."

She'd felt warm in his arms. Warm, soft and plaint, trusting, so much a part of him that their heartbeats seemed the same. But then she stiffened and pulled away from him. He realized that she was looking out one of the windows. The drapes hadn't been pulled closed. She walked to it and he followed closely behind her.

And he saw what she saw.

There was a man standing in the moonlight. He was by the caretaker's cottage, looking up. He seemed to be in breeches and a blousy poet's shirt. His hair was long, his thighs encased in boots.

"John McCawley," Jane whispered.

Sloan had to agree.

The figure in the moonlight faded.

Jane turned into Sloan's arms. "The past has something to do with this. I know it."

"We should get some sleep," he told her.

She nodded and headed into the bedroom. It was supposed to have been their wedding night. But he knew her. She was upset. The minister she'd brought to the castle had died here.

"I love you," she said.

"I know," he told her.

"I'll be in bed," she said. "Just give me a few minutes."

He let her go and walked over to the board Kelsey had set up that day, studying what she had written. *Who had something to gain from the death of a minister?*

He went over the names.

Mrs. Avery, he thought. The distant relative. The woman who had allowed Jane to book the castle for the wedding.

He walked into the bedroom. Jane hadn't even disrobed. She was lying on her side, her eyes closed, sound asleep. He laid down beside her and drew her into his arms. He held her as his mind whirled until he managed to sleep himself.

And then—

He woke.

He didn't know why. It was almost as if someone had shaken him awake.

But there was no one there.

Curious, he rose and walked back out to the foyer, then opened the door to the hall. Logan was opening the door to his room at the same time. Sloan looked down the other way. Someone was approaching Emil Roth's room in the darkness.

"Hey!" Sloan shouted.

The figure paused and turned to him. He could make out little of the person in the darkness. Whoever it was had bundled up in black pants, a black hoodie, and what even seemed to be a black cape of some kind. In the pale glow of the castle's night-lights, something gleamed.

A knife?

"Stop," Sloan demanded.

He stepped from his room, listening in the back of his mind for his door to close, for the lock to catch. He wasn't leaving Jane alone without a locked door. For a few seconds the figure stared at him and he stared back.

"Stop!" Sloan ordered again.

The figure began to run down the stairs at a breakneck speed.

Sloan raced after the person, Logan at his heels.

Chapter 6

Jane awoke to the sound of Sloan's voice, disturbed, aware she needed to be up. But she felt a soft touch on her cheek. Not the touch of a lover, rather the brush of gentle fingers that a mother, a sister, or a caring friend might give. For a moment she lay still, her Glock on the bedside table. If there was someone there, no matter how lightly they touched her—

She opened her eyes.

And saw Elizabeth Roth.

The ghost looked at her with sorrow and grave concern. And then, when she realized that Jane was awake, she vanished.

"No!" Jane said. "Please, help us. Don't go!"

But there were more shouts in the hallway and the apparition disappeared in a matter of seconds, fading from Jane's sight. Jane bolted up, grabbed her gun, and headed into the hall.

It was empty.

She cautiously moved out of the bridal suite. She backed her way to the door to Kelsey and Logan's suite and ducked her head in. Neither was there. Almost running, she made her way to Emil Roth's suite. The outer door was open. Taking every precaution, she pushed the door inward and made her way into the room. Like the bridal suite, it had an outer foyer area with a grouping of chairs and a wet bar. Roth family plaques adorned the walls along with prints of medieval paintings. She made her way through to the bedroom, pushed the door open, and quickly flicked on the light, hoping to first blind anyone who might have attacked Emil in the night, or who might be lingering in the room.

To her astonishment, Emil Roth was there.

And he wasn't alone.

She was awkwardly greeted by the sight of flesh. Way more of Emil Roth's pale body than she had ever wanted to see and a pair of massive, gleaming breasts. Way too much of a skinny derrière. Emil's flesh, a woman's flesh—sweaty, writhing flesh—writhing until she turned the light on and they both stopped moving like deer suddenly blinded by headlights.

The woman screamed.

Emil Roth roared. "What the hell?"

Jane instantly turned the light off. "Sorry—sorry! Your door to the hallway was open. I was afraid that someone was hurting you."

She heard the tinkle of the woman's laughter. And then, in the darkness, she realized she knew who the woman was.

Scully Adair.

"I wasn't hurting anyone, I swear!" Scully said. "But, please, don't say anything! Please, don't say anything to Mrs. Avery. I'll wind up fired—"

Scully started to rise.

Jane lifted a hand to her. "I won't say a word, I swear it. Please don't get up on my account. I won't tell Mrs. Avery a thing."

"Hey, now, I own the place," Emil said.

"Whatever!" Jane told them. "I will not say a word. It's between you all. Forgive me. Sorry, I'm out of here. Pretend I was never here. Just do what you were doing, I mean, um, you just might want to lock your door."

She flew back out of the room, shaking, slamming the door in her wake. The locks were automatic, she reminded herself. They'd been warned about that—step outside and it would catch behind you. For a moment, she leaned against the closed door. Visions stuck in her head that she prayed she could quickly clear.

She gave herself a mental shake.

If Emil Roth was fine, what was going on? Where the hell was Sloan? Where were Kelsey and Logan? She hurried to the stairway and gripped the banister tightly, looking behind and around her as she started down the stairs to the castle's foyer. Still, she saw no one. The giant double front doors to the castle were ajar. She walked outside. A moon rode high, the air was still, and a low fog lay gentle on the ground. There was a night-light coming from Mr. Green's cottage and a slightly lower light emitted from the guardhouse where Mrs. Avery was supposed to be sleeping. She wasn't sure why, but she walked the distance around the grounds, on alert, ever ready to be surprised by someone lurking in the night or watching and waiting. But no one accosted her. Instead, she felt as if she was being beckoned toward the chapel. She wasn't afraid of the dead. The dead had helped her many times. She made her way through the gate at the low stone wall that surrounded the chapel. She was afraid of the living. They were dangerous, in her mind.

But no one jumped up or slunk around from a gravestone or a tomb.

She reached the chapel door and pushed it inward. Someone was sitting in a pew, looking at the altar.

He rose.

She looked at John McCawley, tragically killed in a hunting accident the eve of his wedding.

He looked at her a long moment. "You see me? You see me clearly?"

"I do," she told him.

He seemed incredulous, then he smiled, and she saw that he had been a truly handsome young man with a grace about him. "Forgive me. I see people pointing into the woods and saying that they see me when I'm standing next to them. And the ghost hunters! Lord save us all. A twig snaps and they scream, 'What was that, oh my God!'"

"There are several of us here who see the—" She paused. She wasn't sure why, but saying "dead" seemed very rude. "Who see those who have gone before us."

"Really? Amazing and wonderful. I heard one of the maids whispering about it today. You do look like my love, like my Elizabeth. Are you a descendant?"

"I'm really not. I'm sorry," she told him.

"Ah, well, no matter." He studied her anxiously. "If you see Elizabeth—I know she's here. I see her at the window. But you—you with this gift of yours, if you see her, tell her that I love her. I wait for her. I'll never leave her. I love her in death as I loved her in life."

"Why don't you tell her yourself?" Jane asked.

He shook his head. "It's as if I can't breach the castle. I try to enter. I don't know why. The family arranged the wedding, but they didn't want us together. There were a number of us out that day—Emil Roth, father and son, among them. I watched the blood flow from me, but I never knew who'd done the deed. And yet, I prayed that my love would go on—that Elizabeth would rally and find happiness. She loved me, but she wasn't weak. She should have lived a long life and she should have found happiness. But she did not. I'll never leave her now. I will watch her at the window for eternity."

"I'll tell her," Jane said. "But there is a way—there is always a way. We'll figure it out, and you two may tell each other everything you wish to say."

As she spoke, she heard her name cried out loudly and with anguish.

Sloan!

"Here!" she cried. "I'm in the chapel."

A moment later, the door burst in and Sloan rushed to her, sweeping her into his arms. He was oblivious to the ghost, oblivious to everything but her.

He shook as he held her.

"Hey," she said. "I'm fine. Where have you been? Where are Kelsey and Logan?"

"Right behind me. There was someone about to break into Emil Roth's room. We all chased whoever it was down the stairs and out into the yard, but they disappeared as if into thin air," Sloan said with disgust. "I went back to the room and then I banged on Roth's door and—Roth is sleeping with his help."

"I know," Jane said.

Logan came striding in, followed by Kelsey. "There you are," Kelsey said, pushing Sloan aside to give Jane a hug. "We were worried sick."

Jane told them, "Hey! You guys left me."

"We were chasing a mysterious figure," Logan explained.

"The door locked, right, when I left?" Sloan asked, worried.

She nodded. "I just came out looking for you." She frowned. "Hey—now, we're all out here and Emil Roth is back in his room."

They turned as if they were one and went racing back to the castle.

They weren't careful then as they raced up the stairs.

At the door to Emil Roth's suite, they suddenly paused. "Whatever he's doing, we have to interrupt him. We're trying to keep him alive,"

Sloan said.

Logan nodded and banged on the door. Emil Roth, dressed in a silk robe, opened the door. Seeing them, he groaned. "You all again."

"Mr. Roth, someone was sneaking toward your door in the middle of the night. I believe they meant to cause you some harm," Sloan told them.

"It was me," said a squeaky, apologetic voice. Scully Adair, clad in an oversized shirt, her hair still in disarray, walked slowly out of the bedroom. She gave them a little wave. "Sorry. I'm so sorry."

Jane shook her head—trying to dispel unwanted images that rose before her mind's eye. "You don't need to apologize. You're both adults."

"But, Scully, it wasn't you," Sloan said. "It was someone wearing black, evidently sneaking around, who was headed toward Emil's door. We chased them, and whoever it was disappeared right outside the front door."

"Why would anyone want to hurt me? To most of the world, I'm worthless," Emil said dryly.

"You're not worthless!" Scully said passionately.

"You seem to be a fine enough young man, sincerely," Jane told him.

"But, beyond that, you are worth a fortune," Kelsey reminded him.

Emil Roth shook his head. "If I die, the only living heir—or heiress—is Denise Avery. But she doesn't just get everything. There are all kinds of trusts. The castle will be left to posterity. It will go to the village and be run by a trust and a group of directors."

"But she'd still make out all right," Logan said.

Emil waved a hand in the air. "She'd get a few million."

"Oh, Emil!" Jane said. "People have died for far less than a few million."

"But—Denise," Emil said.

Jane turned to Sloan. "Where was she when you all went running after the figure into the night?"

"We woke up Mr. Green and Mrs. Avery," Logan said.

"But both took their time answering their doors," Sloan said.

"Which, of course, is more than possible when you're sound asleep," Kelsey said.

"This can't be—real," Emil said.

"We didn't imagine the figure we chased away," Sloan said flatly.

"So what do I do?" Emil asked.

"You sit tight," Logan said firmly. "We're waiting on some answers from our home office, and the M.E.'s report. We'll have that info in the morning. For tonight, sit tight. One of us will stay in the hall through the next few hours. When the sun comes up, you'll be with one of us through the day until we get to the bottom of this."

"Really?" Scully asked. "I mean, the police said that it was an accident when the reverend fell. And someone was running around the halls? It could have been the ghost."

"It wasn't a ghost," Sloan said flatly. "It was flesh and blood that tried to get to you tonight, Emil. Dressed in black, sneaking around. And a man died here less than twenty-four hours ago. Let's be smart about this."

Emil nodded. "Yes. Thank you."

"Let's do what we can with the rest of the night," Logan said. "I'll take the hall first." He glanced at his watch. "Each of us takes an hour and a half. That gives everyone a few hours of sleep before morning. Kelsey, you relieve me. Sloan and Jane, you'll be up last."

"I meant to go home," Scully murmured.

"You can't now," Kelsey said flatly.

"But I'll be in the same clothing and Mrs. Avery—"

"I do own the place," Emil said again.

"You're a little shorter than Kelsey, but about the same size," Sloan said. "We'll get you some clothing. For tonight, sit tight."

They left Emil Roth and Scully Adair and adjourned to the hall.

"You know, we're forgetting people," Jane pointed out. "Chef lives over the old stables. I'm not sure where that is. And Phoebe Martin is up in the attic."

"The stables are down the hill and to the right of the gatehouse," Sloan said. "And the attic, you walked Phoebe up there tonight, right?"

"Doesn't mean she stayed there," Jane pointed out.

"But what would Phoebe or Chef have to gain from hurting Emil Roth?" Kelsey asked.

"The only one to benefit would be Denise Avery," Sloan said.

"But she was there, down at the gatehouse, when you banged on her door, right?" Jane asked.

"Oh, yes, spitting fire, warning us that she had the right to throw us out," Logan said.

"Let's get through the night," Sloan said. "And hope we get something to go on in the morning."

Logan turned to Kelsey. "Get some sleep. I'll wake you in a bit. And you two," he said to Jane and Sloan. "Go on in and—whatever. You have three hours."

Sloan slipped his hand to the base of Jane's spine and urged her toward their door. They entered and he waited for the click. He cupped her head between his hands and kissed her tenderly, the feel of his fingers feathering against the softness of her flesh an arousing touch. He had a talent for the right move at the right time. He could walk into a room and cast his head in one direction and she would just see that he was there and want him. He could be a joker. He could walk naked from a shower and tease and play and tell her that the offer was evident.

But, right now, he wasn't sure what was on her mind. He could always make her long for him.

"She's been here."

"What?" he asked her.

And she told him about waking up to the feel of something on her cheek, of Elizabeth being there and looking at her worriedly. She told him about John McCawley waiting in the church, forever watching the windows for his love.

"Why can't he come in the house?" Sloan asked her.

"Maybe he was never really invited inside—invited to be a part of the family," Jane suggested.

"Did you ask him about any of this?" Sloan asked.

"I didn't really have time. You screamed for me and he disappeared."

"We'll talk about this with the others tomorrow," he said. "And until then—" He paused, his fingers tracing a pattern down her cheek, his eyes focused on hers. "Until then, we'll get some sleep."

She smiled. "When this is over, let's go to an island. A resort. Maybe one of those all-inclusive ones. One where we have our own little hut on the beach."

"No ghosts," he said.

"No ghosts."

"Or Mrs. Avery."

"You think she's guilty?"

"She has the only motive," Sloan said. "Can you think of another?"

At the moment, she couldn't.

She kissed his lips with a promise for the future.

"Go to sleep," he told her. "I can't sleep anyway, right now. I'll take both our turns watching the hall. I'll be back in once it's full light. Logan will be up by then."

She headed into the bedroom, exhausted. She knew Sloan. He'd be pacing in the foyer area of their room for a while, thinking.

But she fell quickly asleep.

She awoke.

And felt Sloan's warmth beside her. She loved that she lay with him at night and woke with him in the morning. She even loved that they could disagree, even argue, that life with him was comfortable— and yet, she could see him, breathe his scent, watch him walk from the shower and want him as if they'd never made love before.

She rolled over to tell him that she loved him.

But never spoke the words.

A shrill scream pierced the castle's quiet.

Chapter 7

"I guess that Mrs. Avery wasn't responsible," Sloan said.

The scene was a repetition of the previous morning. Only now, it was Denise Avery who lay at the foot of the stairs, her neck broken.

Sloan looked at Logan, who'd been on guard duty. "What happened?"

"She was never on the second level to descend to the first," Logan said, looking at them.

This time, it had been Scully Adair—dressed in one of Kelsey's tailored work suits—who'd made the discovery when she walked down the stairs. Her scream had alerted the castle. Now, everyone was there, including Mr. Green.

Chef and Harry and Devon rushed in from the hall to the kitchen. Phoebe Martin had come running from the Great Hall and the two day maids, Sonia Anderson and Lila Adkins, hurried from the office. It was chaos, everyone asking each other if they'd seen Mrs. Avery.

"Whoa!" Sloan shouted. "Stop. All of you!"

They went silent.

Phoebe stared at Sloan with fear. Scully Adair seemed to be in shock. Harry and Devon just looked sick.

Chef shook his head. "I knew I should have taken that job out at the really haunted hotel in Colorado."

Mr. Green just stood there, hat in hand, shaking his head. "Sorrowful end. The reverend? He was a good man. Mrs. Avery? Not so much. Still, a sorrowful end."

"We're going to have to call the police," Jane said.

"Already dialing," Logan told them.

"Let's leave her as she lies for the M.E.," Sloan said. "We'll head into the Great Hall and wait for the police."

They obeyed like sheep. Chef, Harry, and Devon drifted to one side of the table—team kitchen. Phoebe Martin, Sonia, and Lila to the other side. Emil Roth—appearing to be in total shock—walked to his place at the end.

Scully looked at the room uncertainly. At last, she walked to the wall and sank down against it and seemed to curl into herself.

"Did anyone see her this morning?" Logan asked.

"I did," Mr. Green volunteered. "I saw her walking up to the castle from the guard house."

"Did you speak with her?"

"No," he said. Then, he added, "I only speak with her when I have to."

"We saw her—the three of us," Chef told them.

"Yeah," Harry said. "She came in telling us that if we were all going to get so chummy with the guests, Chef needed to plan cheaper meals."

"Nice," Scully muttered.

"Did you see her?" Jane asked the maids.

The three of them shook their heads.

"Not until she was there. At the foot of the stairs. But, I knew. The minute I heard Scully screaming, I knew," Phoebe said. She stared at Jane. "It's the ghost. She's angry. Elizabeth is angry. You tried to get married here when she couldn't. I think she's trying to kill you!"

Sloan cleared his throat. "I really don't think that Jane and the reverend and Mrs. Avery resemble one another in any way. Nor do I think that a ghost is killing people."

"So she just tripped?" Harry asked hopefully.

"Personally, I don't think so," Jane said matter-of-factly.

"But the reverend just fell yesterday!" Harry protested.

"And she fell today," Kelsey said.

"So, if she didn't just fall—" Harry began.

"Someone pushed her," Devon finished.

"And who would want to kill that old battle-ax?" Chef demanded sarcastically.

The police didn't knock, they burst right in. Detective Forester immediately looked at the FBI agents. "Four of you are still here—and another person is dead? What now?"

Everyone began to speak at once again.

Sloan assumed that Detective Forester was decent at his job. But he probably didn't deal with situations like this often. And Detective Flick, at his heels, merely followed the path that his boss took.

"Hey!" Sloan shouted. "Tone it down. Let the detective get his questions out in an orderly fashion."

They all went silent like errant school children.

"The ghost did it!" Phoebe said again. "The ghost did not want people getting married here. Maybe Elizabeth Roth didn't even want to hurt the reverend. He was just there and she had to stop the wedding. And so, to stop killing other people, she had to kill Mrs. Avery, who kept letting people try to get married here."

Forester stared at her as if she'd completely lost her mind.

"Who saw what happened?" Forester demanded.

"No one saw anything," Sloan said. "My co-workers and I were on the second floor. Scully Adair came down the stairs and found her."

"No one else was around?" Forester demanded of Scully.

Scully shook her head.

"Where were the rest of you?" Forester asked.

Mr. Green told him he'd never entered the house. Chef and cook said that they'd been in the kitchen, but that she had been in to see them just moments earlier.

"We had just gotten here," Lila said.

"We rode in together," Sonia said.

"I was still up in my room," Phoebe said.

"So she just fell?" Forester said, bewildered. "Someone has to know something." He spun on Mr. Green. "Who can vouch for you?"

Green just looked shocked. "I'm always outside."

"And you?" he demanded of Phoebe.

She stared back at him in horror. "Miss Everett walked me to my room last night. Damn you! Why will no one listen to me? The ghost did it."

"I want this place shut down to the public immediately," Forester told Emil Roth. "And no one leaves."

He made the announcement as if that were the answer to the dilemma.

"I don't really have anywhere else to go," Mr. Green muttered.

They heard activity at the door. The medical examiner had arrived. Forester told the group to stay in the Great Hall. Sloan ignored the order, getting a nod from Logan, and followed out on the heels of the detective.

The medical examiner shook his head as he stared at the corpse. "I'll get her temperature for time of death—"

"We know the damned time of death," Forester snapped. "Can't you tell if she was pushed or not?"

"When I have time for an autopsy," the man snapped back.

"Doctor," Sloan asked. "Did you discover anything yesterday that might have caused the reverend to fall? I heard he had a bad heart."

The medical examiner looked at him and nodded. "He was a walking time bomb. There was damage to his heart. Whether that caused his fall or not, I don't know. But he didn't suffer a heart attack before he came crashing down the stairs. And Mrs. Avery, I think she was in decent health. She certainly appeared to be."

Sloan said, "But she didn't fall from the top of the stairs. We were out in the hallway on that landing and we didn't see her." He actually hadn't been on the landing himself. Logan had been there. But, to Sloan's knowledge, Logan never missed anything.

"She fell from midway up?" Forester asked.

"She had to have. She was never on the second floor landing," Sloan said.

"It's a broken neck for sure," the medical examiner said. "If you want to know more, I'll be able to tell you in a few hours. She'll be an immediate priority at the morgue."

Forester thanked him. The medical examiner looked at Sloan and nodded. He had the feeling that he'd be getting any information just as quickly as Forester.

"What do you have to say?" Forester asked, looking at Sloan.

"I don't know what is happening any more than you do," Sloan said. "But three people breaking their necks on a stairway in a matter of years—two of them within two days? I don't see that as accidents, nor as coincidences. Something is going on here."

"You are saying that these people have been murdered?" Forester asked.

"I'd say it's likely."

"And what do you say we do to find out what is happening?"

Sloan was surprised. Forester's anger was all bluster. He was bewildered. There were no knives involved, no guns, no gang wars, and no obvious motive for killing. A husband hadn't gotten too angry with a wife. A mistress hadn't suddenly turned on a man who'd promised to leave his wife and marry her.

And yet, people were dead.

"Detective, we've been researching everyone here. We expect some reports this morning. But, questioning the people here could prove helpful."

Forester nodded. "I'll do it. Whatever you find out, you'll tell me, right?"

"Of course. This is your jurisdiction. We just happen to be here. We're happy to help. But I need to get together with my team."

Forester nodded and seemed better equipped to take control. "I'll see the employees one by one in the Great Hall. You and your team may return to your rooms. I'll send the cooks and the maids to the kitchen and start with Mrs. Avery's assistant."

Forester walked ahead of Sloan to return to the Great Hall. When they were there, he announced his intentions. "Chef, you and your helpers stay together. Miss Martin, Miss Anderson, Miss Adkins, you will stay together, too. You're welcome to wait your turn in the kitchen. Mr. Roth, we'll have to speak with you, but you're welcome to return to your room until Detective Flick comes to bring you down. Please understand, no one is being accused of anything but we must ascertain what happened here. Therefore, I need to speak with all of you, one by one. Mr. Green, you may return to your apartment. Just be ready to speak to us when we call you."

For a moment, everyone was dead still. Then, Chef rose. "Coffee sounds damned good. And breakfast. Detectives? Should I plan for you, too?"

Sloan was surprised when Forester looked at him—as if for approval.

"Chef, it's kind of you to look out for everyone," Sloan said.

He motioned to Logan, Kelsey, and Jane. As the others shuffled out, except for Scully Adair, who looked like a caged mouse, he and the Krewe members made their way to the stairs and up to the bridal suite.

"It wasn't Mrs. Avery after all," Logan said dryly, stating the obvious.

"Whatever motive could there be?" Kelsey asked.

"Motives for murder," Jane mused. "Greed? That seems to be out. Revenge? Who would have a motive for revenge against the reverend and Mrs. Avery?"

"Jealousy," Logan put in.

"Love," Jane said.

They all looked at her.

"Unrequited love?" she said.

"But who loved whom and wasn't loved in return?" Kelsey asked.

"Let's see what they've gotten us from the home office," Logan suggested.

He sat at Sloan's laptop, found his mail, and ran through everything that had been returned. "I sent them copies of Jane's sketches from last night along with names and everything else, and so far no one has a criminal record. Mr. Green has been here all his life. Our host, Emil, had some trouble with drinking and being rowdy in college, but that doesn't suggest he'd become homicidal. The maids? Lila Adkins is taking college courses by night. She hasn't even had a parking ticket. Sonia Anderson is halfway through a community college now. She wants to be a nurse. Phoebe Martin took the job here years ago when she was divorced. She took it because she could live at the castle, according to the records. Chef? He had offers all over the place but Emil Roth really liked him—they met at a restaurant in Boston— and offered him a husky salary. The two cooks? Devon Richard has applied to the police academy—with good scores. He'll probably be hired on when they have a position. And Harry Taubolt plans on staying to study with Chef. He wants a food career." He looked up at the others again. "Are we certain that Lila and Sonia left the castle last night?"

"Their cars were gone," Sloan said.

"I think we can rule them out. But how do we narrow down the others?" Kelsey asked.

"We're looking at Emil Roth, Scully Adair, Chef, Harry Taubolt, Devon Richard, Phoebe Martin, and Mr. Green," Logan said.

"Except that we know Emil Roth and Scully Adair were in Emil's room when whoever we saw on the stairs was sneaking around the house last night," Sloan said.

"So Chef, Harry, Devon, Phoebe, or Mr. Green," Jane said.

"And Mr. Green was in the caretaker's cottage when we went there. But he had time to slip in. The main thing is that whoever had been in the house just disappeared, as if into thin air. We need to find out where he or she got in and out of the house," Sloan said.

"We could start a search—" Kelsey said.

"Or just ask," Sloan suggested.

"Emil Roth," Jane said.

* * * *

Jane wasn't sure why but she felt the need to be in the room alone. Not that Logan, Sloan, and Kelsey weren't as good as she was when it came to communicating with the dead, but, in her experience, the dead sometimes chose who they would and wouldn't communicate with.

This time, she was certain, it was her.

Kelsey went down to the kitchen to talk to the cooks and maids. Sloan and Logan went down the hall to speak with Emil Roth about the architecture of the castle.

She sat quietly in the bedroom and said, "Elizabeth, I know that you're here. Please, speak with me. Tell me if you've seen anything, if you know anything that might help us."

The air didn't stir, and yet she felt that someone had heard her.

"I saw John McCawley last night," she said. "He wanted me to tell you that he loves you. That he'll never leave you. He watches you at the window. But you know that. That's why you go to the window. So that you can see him."

Slowly, Elizabeth appeared before her and walked to where Jane sat on the bed.

"I didn't kill myself," she said. "They said that I took the laudanum on purpose. My poor father believed that I did it myself. But, I did not."

That wasn't what Jane had expected to hear. "I'm so sorry. But who would have given you the overdose?"

"It was in the tea, I think," she said. "I believe it was my father's maid. She knew that father had no faith in John. Father was so mistaken. I hated his money. John hated his money. Everyone believes that if you have money, that's all that anyone wants. But I loved John. Maybe she believed that if John and I were both gone, and with mother gone, just my brother left… but she underestimated my father. He had loved my mother. There was no affair between them. And still, I'm certain that she tried her best. She had her brother kill John in the woods and make it look as if he'd been killed by my brother or my father! And then, of course, it was easy for her to make it look as if I were a suicide."

"What was the maid's name?" Jane asked her.

"Molly," Elizabeth said.

"What became of her?"

"My father fired her. She became uppity and thought she ruled the place. But he took care of her. He fired her and banned her from the property."

"And what did she do?" Jane asked.

"She left the house, cursing us all!"

"Did you know Molly's last name?" Jane asked.

Elizabeth shook her head.

Jane jumped up. "I have to get into your family's records."

"They're in the office. There's a display case there with the records from the 19th century."

"Thank you," Jane told her.

"How can that help?" Elizabeth asked her. "Our deaths were so long ago."

"I'm not sure, at the moment," Jane said.

She left Elizabeth and the room.

Greed was just one motive for murder.

But unrequited love and revenge were two others.

Chapter 8

"There are no secret entrances to the castle," Emil Roth told them. "But, of course, don't forget, there are two back entrances."

"But they can only be reached by the back, right?" Sloan asked.

Emil nodded.

Sloan looked at Logan. Their disappearing figure of the night before could have circled around the castle and come in through one of the back entrances. But what then?

"And there are servants' stairs that go up to the second landing and the attic," Emil said.

"Of course," Sloan said, irritated that he'd forgotten that in old places like this there was bound to be a second set of stairs.

Okay, one mystery solved.

"What are you thinking?" Emil asked Sloan.

"I'm thinking that someone has really been planning on attacking you and is getting rid of others in the hopes of ruining your life."

Emil looked at Logan. "Do you agree with that?"

"That's where we need your help," he said.

"I swear to you, I'm not the best human being in the world, but I'm not the worst. I haven't hurt anyone in a vicious business deal. I support equal rights. I'm decent," he said. "Not to mention, the only people here are my employees and you people."

"Is there any reason, say, Mr. Green, would harbor you any resentment?" Sloan asked.

"Not that I know of. He's happy, I'm happy. He tells me what he should do, and I tell him to go ahead and do it."

"What about the maids?"

"I overpay them. They have it easy."

"And Scully?" Sloan asked. She'd been with him—in bed—but that could have been part of a ploy. Perhaps two people working together.

"Scully," he said. "I love her."

Sloan and Logan looked at one another.

"Does she have an ex-boyfriend?" Logan asked.

True, they were both grasping at straws.

"Not that I know about. We started seeing each other about three months ago. Honestly, that's why I slipped back here and didn't go to Africa. We needed more time together. We wanted to be sure, really sure that we wanted to be together forever. And we are sure."

"Why was she so worried about what Mrs. Avery would think?" Sloan asked.

"Because, if we weren't really certain she wanted to keep her job. You know, everyone would have thought that she was after my money. She was so afraid of that. She has a degree in hospitality, so she could work anywhere. She's been offered good jobs by the major chains. But she wanted to stay here. Her mom and dad are here. Her dad isn't well. But to think she wanted my money? That was just stupid!"

There was a tap on the door and Sloan opened it.

Detective Flick was standing there. "Detective Forester would like to speak with Mr. Roth now."

"Of course," Emil said.

He followed Flick out. Sloan and Logan came too, but Flick motioned for them to hold back.

"Detective Forester asked that you head to the morgue. The medical examiner called. He has something. We want you to go so we can keep the questioning here going."

Sloan looked at Logan, who lowered his head to hide a grin. More probable, the medical examiner had specifically asked that the two of them come.

"We'll head right there," Sloan said.

"If you'll be good enough to tell us where it is," Logan said.

Flick gave them directions, then hurried ahead to make sure Emil

Roth made it down the stairs okay. Sloan strode quickly down the hall to tell Jane where they were going. But she wasn't in the bridal suite. He called her cell and she answered promptly.

"I'm in the office, looking at records."

"What are you thinking?"

"It's vague at the moment, but revenge is looking good."

"Who's taking revenge on whom?" he asked.

She laughed. "I don't know yet. But as soon as I do, I'll call you."

He hung up and he and Logan headed to the morgue. The village was quaint and small, but the morgue was state of the art. The reverend's body had already been claimed. Mrs. Avery remained. She looked small and thin lying on the morgue table.

"Here is what I want you to see," the medical examiner said.

They looked at the shaved head which revealed a dark bruising.

"I don't know about the reverend, but Mrs. Avery didn't take an accidental fall. She was struck on the head. And then she was pushed down the landing and the murderer was quite lucky. She broke her neck on the way down. Gentlemen, this is no accidental death. I'm classifying it a homicide!"

* * * *

Jane learned that Elizabeth's "Molly" was Margaret Clarendon. She'd been employed by Emil Roth from the time he'd moved into the castle until three months after the deaths of John McCawley and Elizabeth Roth. She'd died, unmarried, according to the records, sixth months after her dismissal, when she'd careened off a cliff. Whether she'd thrown herself off or fallen, there was no record. But her death had been labeled accidental. Had Margaret Clarendon thrown herself off the cliff? Remorseful for what she had done? Or bitter, because with all her machinations she'd failed to win the lord of the castle? No way to tell from the records. So Jane left the office and headed up the stairs again to the second level. As she climbed, she remembered to grip the handrail.

Halfway up, she ran into Scully Adair.

"Do you know anything?" Scully asked her anxiously.

"No, Scully, I'm so sorry. I wish I did."

"They questioned me forever. They think I'm a murderer!"

"Not necessarily, Scully. They have to question everyone like that," Jane assured her.

"They still have Emil in there," Scully said.

"He'll be fine," Jane said.

"I just wish he'd come out. They're talking to everyone so long."

"They're being thorough, listening for something someone might not even realize is a clue to what is going on."

"I'm going to get some coffee and something to eat. Do you want to come?" Scully asked her.

"I'll be there in a minute. I have something to check on," Jane said. "I promise, I'll be right along."

Scully nodded, then gripped the banister tightly as she went on down the stairs.

When Jane reached the bridal suite, she was alone. Elizabeth was nowhere to be seen and Jane didn't sense her presence. She went straight to her computer and video-phoned Angela at the home offices of the Krewe in Virginia.

Angela was with the first Krewe of Hunters. She'd earned her stripes in New Orleans. She was now married to Jackson Crow, the field director for all Krewe agents. While Jackson managed most of their commitments, there was still their overall head, Adam Harrison, who'd first recognized those out there with special intuition—that ability to talk to the dead. He was an incredibly kind man with a talent for finding and recruiting the right people for his Krewe.

Angela came online. She was a beautiful blonde who looked like she should have starred in a noir movie.

"Anything?" she asked Jane.

"So much!"

Jane told her about the morning's events, then said, "I need you to do a search on a woman named Margaret Clarendon, who lived here in the mid-1800s. Find out anything you can about her—before and after she worked for the Roth family."

"What are you thinking?"

"Elizabeth Roth believes that she was murdered, and that her fiancé was murdered, too. She thinks she was killed by this maid."

"And that will help you now?" Angela asked.

"I think so," Jane said. "There's no one to benefit from Emil Roth's death or from him being ruined. There has to be another motive."

"And you think Margaret Clarendon, despite the fact that she might have been a murderess, felt that ill was done to her?"

"We've seen it before. Sometimes there's a descendant out there who feels that they have to right a family wrong," Jane said.

"But remember that sometimes people just act on greed, jealousy, or revenge. Modern day psychos or self-centered asses," Angela reminded her.

"I'll watch from all sides," Jane promised her.

She said good-bye and they cut the connection. Jane drummed her fingers on the table for a minute, and then hopped up again. She was going to have to wait for results, but she couldn't sit idly by.

Time to try to pay a visit to John McCawley again.

* * * *

"Here's what I can't figure. If Mrs. Avery was hit on the head, she had to have been hit on the head with something. Where is that something she was hit with?" Sloan asked.

"Whoever hit her took it with them," Logan said.

Sloan was the one driving as they headed back to the castle. He saw a coffee shop and switched on his blinker, ready to pull into the lot.

"We're stopping for coffee," Logan said.

Sloan grinned. "I thought we'd try for a little more gossip."

"Sounds good to me. And coffee, too," Logan told him.

They went in and were noticed right away by the hostess, who stood at the cash register. A number of patrons were sitting around at the various faux-leather booths. They were definitely the outsiders, probably known as the people who were the guests at the castle. Where bad things happened.

"Sit anywhere?" Sloan said, smiling at the cashier.

"Wherever," she said.

He and Logan claimed a booth. A waitress came over, offered them menus, and took their orders for coffee. She scampered away, then returned quickly. She looked as if she was both anxious and afraid to talk to them.

She flushed as she poured the coffee and caught Sloan's eyes. "I'm sorry. I mean, it's a small village. You're guests at the castle, right?"

"Yes, we are. Sad business there, though," Sloan said.

"My God, yes! The poor reverend. Everyone loved him, you know. And now they say that Mrs. Avery has fallen down the stairs and broken her neck, too!"

Her nametag identified her as Genie.

"Yes, Mrs. Avery died," Sloan said.

"The poor woman," Logan agreed.

The cashier, apparently, couldn't stand being out of the know. She headed over to the table with a bowl of coffee creamers.

"Poor woman, my foot," she said. "Denise Avery thought she was better than anyone in town. She really thought Emil would run himself into the ground with drugs, or his stupid bungee jumping, or parachuting or whatever. He fooled her."

Sloan and Logan glanced at one another and up at the cashier. Her tag noted her name as Mary.

"Oh, I know!" she said. "I must sound horrible. But she came in here all the time and was rude."

"I applied to work at the castle," Genie said. "She looked at me as if I were flypaper. I didn't stand a chance. I wasn't pretty enough."

"You're quite pretty!" Sloan told her.

Which was true.

"Oh, no! Mrs. Avery wanted really pretty girls to work there. Even as maids. I mean, who cares what your maid looks like if she does a good job?"

"Hmmph!" Mary said. "That woman wanted to tease Emil. She wanted to get him going with whoever she brought in. And then remind him, of course, that he had a position in life, even if he wasn't fulfilling it. She just wanted to mess with that man."

"She's gone now," Genie reminded her.

Mary crossed herself. "It's not good to speak ill of the dead."

"But truth is truth," Genie said. "The reverend? He was a good man."

"Bad heart, though," Mary said.

"Oh, dear!" Genie said. "We are terrible. What would you like to eat?"

"What's fast?" Sloan asked.

"The special. Stew," Genie said.

"We'll take it," Logan told her.

"Sounds delicious," Sloan said.

It was actually terrible, or maybe it just seemed terrible because they'd been eating Chef's food. But it was fast and filling and they were out of there in no time. Sloan wasn't sure what they'd gained, but they'd gained something.

"Mrs. Avery was quite a manipulator," Sloan said.

"She was so determined to seduce Emil Roth with the maids, but he went and fell in love with Scully Adair," Logan mused.

Sloan looked at him. "Do we know what happened before he fell in love with Scully Adair?"

"It would be interesting to find out," Logan said.

* * * *

Jane was amazed at how quickly the day ended and darkness fell. It seemed that they'd just awoken with Mrs. Avery at the foot of the stairs. Then the police had come and begun their investigation. She had spoken with Angela, Kelsey had hob-knobbed with the kitchen staff and maids, and Logan and Sloan had headed to the autopsy. The hours had flown by, and as she came down the stairs, she could hear Detective Forester in the Great Hall. He'd certainly taken a long time with every single person who'd been in the house. She listened a second and realized from the slow answers he was receiving that Forester was now questioning Mr. Green. She thought about stopping by the kitchen, but decided to head on to the chapel.

She needed to talk with John McCawley.

She headed out again, just as she had the night before. There was no moonlight yet, the autumn sun fading, a brooding darkness hanging over the cliffs brought on by an overcast sky. She'd exited by the front to avoid running into anyone at the rear. She walked around the castle, from the manicured front to the wild and atmospheric rear, and hurried to the chapel.

John McCawley was waiting in front of the altar, staring up at it.

"Did you see her?" he asked, turning. "Did you see my Elizabeth?"

"I did," she told him. "And I told her and, of course, you know that she loves you. She thinks she was murdered. She didn't kill herself."

"What?" he asked.

"She believes that there was a maid at the house—Margaret or Molly—who wanted her father's attention. And that Molly believed that she could start by ridding the world of the two of you. And Molly had a brother—"

"David," John told her. "He was always coming to the stables, asking for any extra work."

"She believes that David shot you and that Molly poisoned her."

"Can you prove it?"

"Probably not after all these years," Jane said. "But you know. The two of you know. Maybe that's enough."

His face darkened and he began to frown. Jane thought that she had said something that disturbed him. But then she realized that he was looking behind her.

She spun around.

And saw a figure dressed in black.

She started to draw her Glock, but before she could something came hurtling at her. Ghosts didn't have much strength—thus the tales of rattling chains and squeaking floors and chairs that rocked themselves. But they did have something. And Jane was sure that John McCawley had used all of his strength to cast himself before her. She dove behind one of the pews, drew her gun, and fired. The solid *thunk* she heard confirmed that her bullet had found the wood of a pew.

She rolled and took aim again.

But there was no one there.

The wraith in black was gone, and so was John McCawley.

She rose. Her phone was ringing.

Angela.

She answered, watching the door to the chapel.

"I found out more about your Margaret Clarendon," Angela told her. "She does have a descendant working at the castle now."

Chapter 9

Detective Flick was waiting for Sloan and Logan when they entered the castle. He immediately directed them to Detective Forester, who had set up in the Great Hall. They sat and told him what they'd discovered at the M.E.'s office.

"We're going to need a search warrant," Forester said. "We need to find whatever object carries Denise Avery's blood."

"You don't need a warrant."

Emil Roth stood at the arched entry to the Great Hall.

"I own the property. I give you my permission to search every room. I believe there's a legality about guests in rooms, but I believe my guests will give you permission, too. Am I correct, gentlemen?"

"Of course," Logan said.

"Then I'll call in some backup," Forester said, "and we'll get to it tonight."

"I think that's an excellent idea," Logan said.

"Where are Kelsey and Jane?" Sloan asked.

"Kitchen, I believe," Forester told them.

Logan and Sloan headed out of the Great Hall to the kitchen. Kelsey was sitting there with Chef and Harry and Devon.

"Something to eat?" Chef asked.

"No, thanks. We had some horrible food in town," Logan told

him.

Chef grinned. "I do have the reputation for being the best around."

"I'd not argue it," Logan assured him.

"Why would you stop in town when you're staying here?" Chef asked. "And how were you out when the rest of us are prisoners here? Oh, yeah, I forgot. You're Feds."

Logan slid into a seat at the kitchen table. "We went to hear gossip."

Sloan remained standing. He still didn't know where Jane was. "We heard a lot of interesting gossip. Apparently, not many people liked Mrs. Avery. In fact, they seemed to think that she was trying to make everything in the world go wrong for Emil Roth."

Chef shrugged. "She treated him like he was a kid. When he hired me, not long after his dad died, they had a huge fight. I overheard them. She told him that he didn't have the know-how to run anything and that he shouldn't make decisions without her. I'm surprised he didn't kill her. He was the heir, but she acted like she owned everything."

"But he didn't kill her, did he?" Sloan asked.

"Emil?" Harry asked. "He's a decent guy. He's like a regular guy, but with money. He'd be normal as hell if people like Mrs. Avery didn't keep telling him that he had responsibilities as if he were Spiderman or something."

"Where's Jane?" Sloan asked them.

Kelsey, who'd been sitting at the table, frowned. "I'll go see."

"Wait. I'll just try her phone," Sloan said.

He dialed Jane's number and listened as they continued to talk.

"The people in town even seemed to think that Avery hired only attractive maids to try and get Emil involved with them," Logan said.

"Was that her plan?" Harry asked.

"I never had it figured as an actual plan," Devon said. "Go figure. That dried up old prune of a biddy setting Emil up for sex!"

"Did it work?" Logan asked

"At first, maybe. A few girls wound up being fired for various infractions. Oh, never for flirting with or co-habiting or whatever you want to call it," Chef said. "They'd be fired for failing in their duty, for disturbing a guest, things like that."

Logan heard an unspoken *but*. "What?"

"That all ended a few months ago," Devon said.

"Just spit it out, they know everything," Harry said. "They're Feds, remember? Emil is crazy about Scully Adair. And Scully is crazy about him. I don't know how they were managing to hide it from Mrs. Avery. All the rest of us knew."

"But, he did see people before that?"

"Yeah, sure. He's young, good-looking, rich. Who wouldn't have seen him?" Harry asked.

Jane's phone was ringing and ringing with no answer. Sloan ended the call and looked at Logan and Kelsey.

"Now we go and find Jane," he said. "She's not answering, and I'm pretty sure I know who we're looking for. Kelsey, go get the detectives. Logan, will you search the house? I'm heading out to the chapel."

"What can we do?" Chef asked.

"Stay put," Sloan told him.

* * * *

Jane cautiously stepped out of the church. The overcast sky seemed to have fallen closer to the ground, a dense fog rising to meet it. The graveyard, benign by day, now seemed to hold dozens of places to hide. Winged angels cast shadows over crooked stones. Trees grew at a slant and gargoyles loomed over tombs, warding off all evil. Standing in the doorway for the chapel, she was in clear view.

"You know I have a gun and I do know how to use it," she said, addressing the graveyard. "You might as well come out. I'm sure that you want me to think that Scully Adair is doing all this. After all, you know that Scully is a descendant of Margaret Clarendon. And you must have heard that there were a few references to the fact that Margaret was suspected of having helped Elizabeth along to her death. But, you know what? I don't think that Scully herself knows that she has any relationship to the castle. Margaret's child with Emil Roth went up for adoption. We only found out the truth because we have access to all kinds of records. Phoebe, you were good. I mean that scream you let out when you *found* Reverend MacDonald was really something. And the shock in your eyes? Amazing. So, you had an affair with Emil Roth. You thought you were the one. And I don't believe that you did kill Cally Thorpe. That was really just a tragic accident. But if people started dying at every wedding, that would give the castle a real reputation. But that wasn't enough. You figured you'd get rid of Mrs. Avery. Make it really ghostly. You hated her, because she sucked you in. She fed you the story about Scully and her being a descendant of Margaret. You thought you'd replay history, except this time you'd win!"

Jane barely ducked in time as a piece of broken plaster wing off a cherub came flying her way. By the time she was up again, her quarry had moved. Slinking low, she ran from one tomb to the next.

"Phoebe, my Krewe will have figured it out by now, too. Killing me will get you nowhere. Nor is there anywhere for you to go. You'll be arrested, and you'll face murder charges. If you give yourself up right now, I can try to help you."

Jane had moved away from the chapel a fair distance. Phoebe was leading her to the rear, a place where the graves began to ride down the slopes off the cliffs. She raised her head, trying to see in the near darkness. She thought she heard something—coming from behind her.

She was certain that Phoebe was before her!

Something thumped into the gravestone she'd ducked beneath.

An arrow.

She heard laughter from the fog-riddled graveyard before her, eerie in the strange dying light and the cool air.

"No one gets married here! They don't marry here. They *die* here!" Phoebe called to her.

Jane thought she heard a snapping sound on the ground, coming closer. She rolled quickly and slunk on the ground, staying low. She was armed and she could aim. But she couldn't make out a damned thing to shoot at.

"Brides die!" Phoebe cried, laughing.

The sound was both ahead and behind Jane.

In fact, it seemed to come from all around.

* * * *

Sloan was quickly on his feet, racing to the back of the house. At the rear exit from the kitchen, he thought that he felt someone behind him.

He turned.

And she was there. Elizabeth Roth.

She stared at him with a drawn face and worried eyes.

"I'll find her!" he promised.

"The fog has fallen," Elizabeth said.

"I'll find her!" he said. "Come with me?"

"I can't leave the house."

"Try."

She shook her head.

He couldn't wait.

He bolted out of the castle and was instantly astounded by the pea soup of New England fog he found himself within. He could still see the spire of the chapel, so he headed toward it. He made his way through the gate, down the path, and threw the chapel door open.

Jane wasn't there.

But he heard something.

Laughter.

Eerie in the strange fog. It seemed to come from the left, and then from the right.

"Jane!" he shouted. "Jane!"

He heard her reply.

And as he did, he realized that shouting had been a mistake. She was might be risking her life to shout out a warning to him.

"It's Phoebe and someone else, Sloan! Someone else with a bow and arrow, hunting us down," Jane shouted back to him.

He dropped to the ground just as something whizzed by his head. He tried to calculate the source of the arrow that had come his way. But whoever was shooting with a bow and arrow was now halfway around the church.

The laughter had come from the far rear.

On his hands and knees, he crawled around the graveyard.

* * * *

Jane tried to determine where she was, but with the distance they'd come she thought she might be in the back of the chapel, near the cliffs.

"I'm going to get you!" Phoebe said, her voice startlingly near.

She couldn't see anything. So how could Phoebe?

She didn't reply.

Then Phoebe began to chant. *"Good girls die, the bitches lie, the brides go straight to decay. This time round, the good girl dies and the bitch's lies will let her win the day!"*

"How do you see this as winning?" Jane cried out. "Emil is seriously in love with Scully. He'll marry her and you'll go to jail."

"Not true. Scully is right here with me. And if you don't show yourself now, she's going over the cliff!" Phoebe cried.

"I don't believe you. Scully was in the castle."

"She's here now. Wanna hear her scream?"

Jane heard a muffled cry.

Scully.

She winced, bracing against a gravestone.

"If you don't come out, she goes over the cliff right now!"

Sloan was out there, too, she thought. He had to be.

She'd be all right.

Or would she?

* * * *

Sloan kept silent and crept along the earth.

Another arrow flew past. That one, he was sure, had been sent blindly. He crept for what seemed like a lifetime but, looking at his watch, he saw that two minutes had passed. Another arrow flew by. This time he saw the arch and pattern.

He crept in the right direction.

Slow and silent.

At last he found himself behind the archer.

He waited and watched, forcing himself to be patient.

When the archer went to string another arrow, he pounced.

And together, they started rolling downhill.

* * * *

Jane realized there was nothing to do but stand. Her Glock was tucked into the back of her jeans.

"I'm here," she cried.

"Come out where I can see you!" Phoebe demanded.

"Where is that?"

"Come closer to my voice."

She did as told and tripped once over a broken stone, but then she saw images appear before her. Phoebe had somehow taken Scully hostage. She stood with Scully, close to the edge of the cliff, and held a knife to her throat.

"Drop the gun," Phoebe said.

"Let Scully go first," she said.

"Drop the gun, or she goes over."

"You're going to die or go to prison," Jane said.

Phoebe shook her head. "You'll be dead. And the whole thing will look like the crazy Krewe of Hunters unit—the *ghost unit*—went off the deep end and killed everybody. Then Emil will come back to me. He's young and sweet and pliable. He'll love me again."

"You were never anything but an affair to him, Phoebe. He loved Scully from the start."

"Put the gun down. She's already bleeding," Phoebe warned.

Should she pretend to do as instructed, then shoot? She could aim for Phoebe's head, but if either woman moved—

Someone lightly touched her.

And she heard a whisper that seemed part of the fog.

"Your love is behind you. Duck down. I'll do what I can."

Jane reached for her gun, dropped to the ground, and told Phoebe, "She's coming for you."

"Who?"

"The ghost of Elizabeth Roth. She's disgusted with what you're doing, trying to use the past to make a mockery of the present. She's there. At your side. Can't you feel her? She's touching you now."

"You're full of—" Phoebe began and broke off.

Elizabeth Roth was there, standing next to Phoebe, touching her hair.

Jane flew to her feet, sprinted forward, and caught Phoebe and Scully together, bringing them all down.

They landed hard, but Scully was free.

"Get up and run!" Jane ordered.

Thankfully, Scully had the sense to obey.

Phoebe still held her knife. She jumped to her feet in a fury, knife raised, ready to leap to where Jane had fallen.

But a shot rang out.

Phoebe paused midair. Then her body was propelled backward, disappearing into the fog. Jane heard her scream until a distant thud, flesh impacting rock, silenced everything.

An unearthly quiet returned.

Then shouts everywhere.

Logan and Kelsey. Forester and Flick. Chef and Harry and Devon and Lila and Sonia. All coming from the castle. Someone walked out of the fog toward her, gun in hand. Impossibly tall and broad and wonderful and always there for her. Her partner, in life, in work, and in breathing. Sloan didn't speak as he drew her to her feet and into his arms.

He just held her.

And their hearts beat together.

* * * *

"But, Mr. Green?"

It was Emil who seemed the most shocked. He'd trusted the man, thought he'd had a champion in him.

It was nearly morning again.

And, as the survivors gathered in the Great Hall while Forester's crew worked to find the bodies down the cliff, Sloan knew they were all grateful to know that there wouldn't be another one at the foot of the stairs that morning.

"Why Mr. Green?" Emil repeated.

"I think he just became involved with Phoebe. When you stopped seeing her, she started planning her revenge. I think she was trying to find a way to make her past part of yours. Instead, she discovered that Scully is a distant relative," Jane said.

"And," Sloan explained, "once she'd come up with her plan, she knew she needed help. And poor Mr. Green, alone and lonely. He was no match for Phoebe. He did what she told him. I believe she had him convinced that she had to do what was right for you and if so, she'd be with him forever and ever."

"But she wanted me," Emil said, confused.

"She didn't tell Green that part. She took care of the killing herself. But she needed him to help when it came to getting rid of you and Scully."

"As if she'd have ever gotten away with it," Logan muttered angrily. "The Krewe of Hunters doesn't lose. We come on harder and harder until a case is solved."

"We'll never really know what was on Green's mind, will we?" Kelsey asked.

Sloan lowered his head and shook it.

When he'd tackled Green, he'd subdued him and tied his hands. He'd never suspected, though, that the bound man would pitch himself over the cliff. But that's exactly what had happened once Green realized Phoebe was gone. He looked up. Logan was watching him, knowing what he was feeling.

"We try to save the victims first and always," he said.

"You saved Scully for me," Emil said.

Sloan decided not to tell him that Jane had saved Scully. He'd saved his own love and his own life with a well-placed shot.

"What will happen now?" Jane asked. "With this place?"

"I think I'll close it," Emil said. "Funny, I always dreamed I'd be married here one day. I'm not huge on tradition, but my parents were married here."

"I think you should be married here," Jane told him. "Prove to the world that the castle isn't evil. Only people can be evil. Make the castle a place of joy."

"She's right," Scully said.

"We get to be bridesmaids!" Lila said.

"Oh, yes! Except, of course, we get to be in on picking the dresses," Sonia added.

"You'll need a best man," Chef told Emil.

"And ushers," Harry said.

Detective Forester stood. "I'll at least expect an invitation. And one for Flick, too, of course."

"You got it," Emil promised. He looked at Jane. "But, you did plan to have your wedding here, you know?"

"But we're not the lord and lady of the castle," Jane said.

"I think we'll be headed for an island in the Caribbean," Sloan told him.

"You'll always be welcome here," Emil told them. "And anywhere I have holdings. And, I know that with Scully at my side, I'll make good. And we'll do good things. I swear it!"

"I believe you will," Sloan assured him.

"Flick and I will be leaving now," Forester said.

"I'll walk you out," Sloan offered.

Jane stood as he did. He smiled at her. They were both still muddy and grass-stained. They might not be married at the castle, but he did intend to make good use of the elaborate shower in the bridal suite as soon as he could.

They walked to the door and out onto the front lawn.

Emil was going to need a new caretaker, too.

But, as they waved good-bye to the detectives, Sloan was certain he'd never seen the place more beautiful.

Elizabeth Roth had realized that she could leave the castle. She stood with her beloved John down at the gates, oblivious to all else. She and John didn't notice the car that drove by them. They were engaged in a long kiss. And as the car passed, the sun rose high above them, crimson rays of extraordinary light raining down, more like twilight than dawn.

Sloan lifted a hand to shield his eyes, blinking against the glare.

When the light shifted, they were gone.

"Do you think—?" Jane asked.

"I don't know. But I do know they're together."

"Like we'll always be," she said.

"Shower," he said. "And then—"

"We'll fool around?"

"Isn't that how all of this started?"

That it was, she thought.

"Then, off to the Caribbean," he said. "Some place warm, with lots of blue water and sunshine. And we'll fool around for a lifetime."

She lifted her dirt-smudged face to his.

And he kissed the most beautiful lips he'd ever seen.

About Heather Graham

Heather Graham has been writing for many years and actually has published nearly 200 titles. So, for this page, we'll concentrate on the Krewe of Hunters.

They include:

Phantom Evil
Heart of Evil
Sacred Evil
The Evil Inside
The Unseen
The Unholy
The Unspoken
The Uninvited
The Night is Watching
The Night is Alive
The Night is Forever
(All available through Amazon and other fine retailers, in print and digital—and through Brilliance Audio as well.)

Actually, though, Adam Harrison—responsible for putting the Krewe together, first appeared in a book called Haunted. He also appeared in Nightwalker and has walk-ons in a few other books. For more ghostly novels, readers might enjoy the Flynn Brothers Trilogy—Deadly Night, Deadly Harvest, and Deadly Gift, or the Key West Trilogy—Ghost Moon, Ghost Shadow, and Ghost Night.

Out next for Heather the second book in the Cafferty and Quinn series, Waking the Dead—which follows Let the Dead Sleep. Go figure! (I guess they've slept long enough!)

The Vampire Series (now under Heather Graham/ previously Shannon Drake) Beneath a Blood Red Moon, When Darkness Falls, Deep Midnight, Realm of Shadows, The Awakening, Dead by Dusk, Blood Red, Kiss of Darkness, and From Dust to Dust.

For more info, please visit her web page, theoriginalheathergraham.com or stop by on Facebook.

When Irish Eyes Are Haunting
A Krewe of Hunters Novella
By Heather Graham
Coming February 24, 2015

Devin Lyle and Craig Rockwell are back, this time to a haunted castle in Ireland where a banshee may have gone wild ----- or maybe there's a much more rational explanation ----- one that involves a disgruntled heir, murder, and mayhem, all with that sexy light touch Heather Graham has turned into her trademark style.

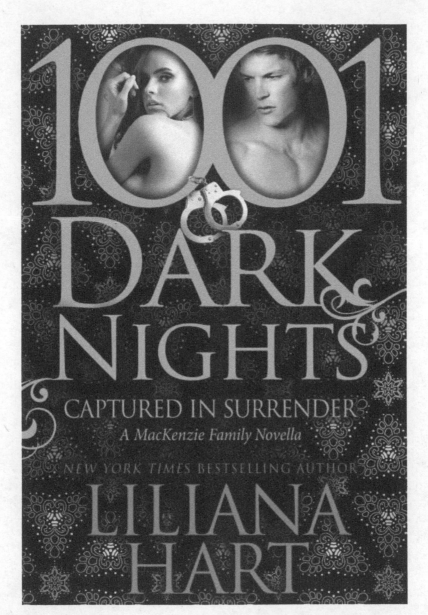

1001
DARK
NIGHTS

CAPTURED IN SURRENDER
A MacKenzie Family Novella

NEW YORK TIMES BESTSELLING AUTHOR

LILIANA
HART

Chapter One

She was taking a risk. A big one.

Naya Blade parked between two rusted pickup trucks and hit the kickstand of her bike with a booted heel. She turned off the engine and pulled the black helmet from her head, releasing long black hair that cascaded to the middle of her back.

The last dregs of an Indian summer lingered—the air like hot breath slapping against the face—the vegetation wilted and gasping for moisture. If the weatherman was right, there'd be storms rolling in sometime after nightfall, and the farmers whose livelihoods depended on their crops could breathe a little easier.

The rain would only make her job harder.

She dismounted the bike and hooked her sunglasses into the front of her black tank top, then ripped at the Velcro of the black leather fingerless gloves she wore and shoved them in her pack.

Her boots sent up plumes of dust as she made her way up the wooden steps to a row of identical shops, and her footsteps creaked across the clapboard sidewalk. She stopped in front of the glass doors of the diner, gave a quick wink to the two men playing checkers on the porch, and then opened the door to a jingle of bells.

The smell of grease and Pine-Sol rolled over and around her, and she felt like she'd walked back in time a few decades. The long Formica counter had pastries sitting under a glass dome, and a hand crank cash register sat at the other end. Red vinyl barstools with cracked seats lined in front of the counter, and booths with matching vinyl seats edged the perimeter. A television mounted in the corner crackled with static during a soap opera, and a single ceiling fan whirred lazily overhead.

"Good afternoon," the woman behind the counter said. "Just take a seat anywhere. It's only me working the counter today, so service might be a little slow."

"I'm not in a hurry." Naya headed to the far corner booth.

She moved with a sensual grace that had the two men at the counter following the sway of her hips and wishing they were forty years younger, and she tossed her pack into the seat before sliding in beside it, her back to the wall.

The trip into Surrender, Montana, hadn't been in her plans, but Jackson Coltraine had had other ideas. Some idiot judge in New York had released Coltraine on a million dollar bond after he'd gunned down his wife and her lover in cold blood. But Coltraine's family had money, and the judge didn't think he'd be a flight risk. *Moron.*

She'd been two steps behind him all the way across the country, until she'd caught a lucky break just on the border between South Dakota and Montana. Coltraine had come down with some kind of virus that had slowed him down. It was hard to run when you were bent over puking every five minutes. She'd been inching her way closer ever since.

When her skip crossed into Surrender, Naya could only shake her head at the irony. She'd sworn she'd never step foot in Surrender again. It didn't matter that it was a place that called to her—that she felt at peace here like she had nowhere else. What mattered was the man she'd left behind—the man who'd made her forget that she was nothing more than a woman—a woman who had the capability to love and deserved love in return.

Those kinds of thoughts were dangerous for someone with her independence, and she hadn't looked back since she'd walked away the year before. Though she'd wanted to. And Surrender never strayed far from her mind.

But fate had stepped in and kicked her right in the ass. Coltraine was in Surrender now. She could feel him. All she had to do was find him and then get as far away as possible.

"You're a little past the lunch rush," the waitress said, making her way to the table.

Faded red hair bushed from the top of her head and her rouge seeped into the deep creases of her skin. Her eyebrows were drawn on and her lipstick was fresh and cherry red, so it feathered out into the fine lines around her mouth. She wore jeans and a stained apron that wrapped around her bony body a couple of times.

She had a voice like a two pack a day smoker, and she looked like she didn't take shit from anyone. "We're about out of everything except for cold sandwiches and what's left of the vegetable stew. My name's Gladys."

Naya's lips twitched as the woman slapped down a plastic menu on the table. "A sandwich will be fine. And some coffee."

"Tourist season is over," she said, arching a brow. "Last of the vacationers headed out couple weeks back. It's still warm enough, but the weather's about to turn. You'll need a jacket by morning. You'd be smart to vacation somewhere else."

"I'm here on business."

"Never seen no businesswoman riding into town on a motorcycle. You a drug dealer?"

"No, ma'am."

Gladys harrumphed and fisted a hand on her hip. "It's a good thing too. Our sheriff helped the DEA shut down a drug ring not too long ago."

"Is that right?" Naya had briefly met Cooper MacKenzie on her last visit to Surrender. Her first impression of him was that he looked more like a criminal than a sheriff, but it hadn't taken her long to see he believed in justice—though she wondered if his brand of justice always lined up with the law. She'd liked him. He had a quick wit and a sarcastic sense of humor she could appreciate, but she was almost positive he wasn't going to be happy to see her again.

"Don't think because we're small that we let any trouble get past us. I got a sawed-off big as Leroy's arm over there behind the counter."

"I'm sure that makes your customers feel very safe," Naya said deadpan.

"And the deputies are just as qualified as the sheriff."

"Is it a big department then?" The last time Naya had been in Surrender, there'd been Sheriff MacKenzie, Deputy Lane Greyson, and the little busybody who worked in the office and knew everyone's business. They'd been woefully understaffed.

"We've got two deputies now, and he's got feelers out to hire more, though I don't think the city council is going to vote 'yes' on that. Cheap bastards. One of the deputies is ex-military. Doesn't say much. Looks like he'd be a good knife thrower—silent and deadly. But Lord, that man has a nice behind."

Yeah, that was a pretty accurate description of Greyson. "What about the other?"

"You sure do ask a lot of questions. I don't got time to stand around and blab all day. Let me get your sandwich and coffee."

Gladys went back to the kitchen with a swish of bony hips and a chip on her shoulder that probably weighed as much as she did. Naya had always found Surrender to be an interesting little town. Especially the mix of people who lived there. It was certainly different from her Brooklyn neighborhood and the one-bedroom apartment she rented. No one cared there what time she came or went, and no one sure as hell would stop to ask her personal questions. Small-town living and the slow pace was completely foreign to her.

Naya checked her e-mail and sent her boss an update on her progress, and a few minutes later, Gladys hustled back out with her food. The sandwich was thick as a brick and made her mouth water at the sight of it. Homemade potato chips were piled high beside it.

"Here you go," Gladys said. "And here's the check. The total is five, but I suggest you leave a ten."

"Seems reasonable enough to me." Naya slipped the photograph out of her bag along with a twenty-dollar bill. "Do you recognize this man? He would've gotten into town sometime this morning."

Gladys's penciled eyebrows raised almost to her hairline and she slipped the twenty into her apron pocket. "Don't recognize him. But if he's in town he won't be able to keep it secret long. I did see a dark-colored SUV driving past during the breakfast rush, but they didn't stop, and I didn't recognize the vehicle as belonging to anyone around here. We've only got the one main road in and out of town, and the bed and breakfast at the end of the strip is the only place for tourists to stay. Though if he's a good camper, there's plenty of places he could set up if he's got the supplies. Rawley Beamis owns the wilderness store and sells camping equipment and other gear. You might check there too. Is this guy your ex or something?"

"He's a fugitive. And he's dangerous. If you see him, give me a call." Naya passed her card over, and Gladys didn't even glance at it as she tucked it away with the twenty.

"I thought I recognized you." Gladys pinched her lips in a tight line. "You were here once before, and damned if old Duffey doesn't still talk about you every chance he gets. Your hair is longer now or I would've recognized you sooner. Girl, you are trouble with a capital *T*."

Naya winked and picked up her sandwich. "You bet. Being good is no fun at all."

Gladys cackled and headed back behind the counter. "Don't I know it. Take your time with your lunch."

As much as she wanted to, she couldn't linger if storms were coming, so Naya ate quickly and nodded to Gladys as she went back outside. The men who'd been playing checkers were still there, though it looked like neither of them had made a move since she'd gone inside.

Gladys had been right. There were a lot of places a lone man could hide in the area. Surrender sat nestled in a valley with only one road leading in and out of town. Businesses with matching black awnings and clapboard wooden sidewalks lined each side of the street in a neat row. The only anomaly was the large metal building that said *Charlie's Automotive* at the opposite end of the street.

The people of Surrender were ranchers and farmers for the most part. There were no subdivisions with tract-style housing. Neighbors were spread far and wide and there was no such thing as a quick trip into town. She had her work cut out for her. And if she could do it without running into the one person she was hoping to avoid, all the better.

She decided to take Gladys's advice and head over to the bed and breakfast and the wilderness store and show Coltraine's picture around. After that, her only choice would be to buy the supplies she needed and head out into the great unknown after him.

Naya looked up and down the street both ways and then moved back toward her bike. Her hands ran beneath the undercarriage out of habit to make sure no one had tampered with it while she was inside.

She felt him before she heard him—the energy spiking around her body increased the temperature by several degrees. The pull between them had always been electric—chemistry in its most basic form. But it was too late to run.

The handcuff snapped around her wrist and her helmet fell to the ground. Her arms were pulled behind her back as the other cuff snapped onto the other wrist. She gritted her teeth as the metal bit into her skin and she turned her head so she could look her captor in the eyes—green eyes with impossibly long lashes she'd always envied—and they were narrowed in suspicion.

"Hello, Naya."

"Well, well, well. If it isn't Deputy Greyson in the flesh."

Chapter Two

Lane knew the moment Naya had stepped back into his town. There was something about her that called to him, like she was a siren song and he couldn't help but answer.

It had been just over a year since he'd seen her last. Since she'd ridden into town on that wicked bike looking for her brother. Colton Blade had been in the military with Cooper MacKenzie, and he'd always told his sister that if he ever got into trouble, then Cooper was who he'd go to for help.

But Colt turned out to be a bad seed—alcohol, drugs, assault charges, bar fights…and attempted murder. Colt Blade was more trouble than he was worth in Lane's opinion—someone who'd been given too many second chances and pissed them all away. Naya knew it too. But she'd still come after him, hoping he'd listen to her when she asked him to go back and face trial.

Naya had found Cooper, hoping he'd seen or heard from her brother, but Cooper hadn't been in touch with Colt for more than a decade. Lane had just come in from lunch to see her standing there in the office, and despite her brave front, he'd seen the despair etched on her face.

The sight of her had been like a punch to the solar plexus. Her face was a study. It shouldn't have been beautiful—not if you looked at her features individually. Her face was angular and her cheekbones flat, attributing her Native American heritage. Her nose was long and straight and her chin slightly pointed. But her eyes were what made a man lose his mind—exotic in shape and the color of dark chocolate, fringed with full black lashes. Thick brows winged above them, giving her a perpetual look of challenge.

She was tall—close to six feet—and her jeans had hugged her curves in all the right places. The belly-baring top she'd worn had shown a pierced navel, and the muscles in her arms were sinewy and lean.

He'd been struck speechless at the sight of her, his cock going rock hard in an instant and the wild lust of need surging through his body like it never had before. He'd have done anything to keep her around longer, just to satisfy his curiosity and see if her lips were as soft as he imagined they were. To see if she felt the connection the same as he did. He'd seen the way her nipples had hardened when she turned her dark gaze on him.

It had been a no-brainer to volunteer to help her search for her brother. He'd done it as much for himself as for her.

He'd never believed in love at first sight, but the moment he'd met Naya, those beliefs had been reevaluated. Their chemistry had been palpable—a living, breathing thing. And the heat that sizzled between them was hot enough to singe anyone who got too close. He'd had no control over his body in that instant, and that's something that had never happened to him before.

It looked like things hadn't changed much. His dick was hard enough to hammer nails and the feel of her against him, the challenge in her eyes daring him to do something about it, made him want to bend her over the bike, strip off those skin-tight jeans, and slide right between the creamy folds of her pussy.

"You're under arrest," he said instead, taking a step back so she couldn't feel his arousal. He didn't recognize the sound of his voice, the low rasp of desire.

"Oh, come on now, Deputy." Her lips quirked as if they were sharing a private joke. "That fight wasn't my fault, and I am hardly to blame for all the damage that was done. If you remember, I believe I was otherwise—" she took a step closer to him so her breasts rubbed against his arm, and she whispered the words so he felt them blow across his lips, "—occupied when the fight started."

She'd definitely been occupied. They'd been in one of the back rooms at Duffey's Bar. They'd started out doing body shots of tequila, getting more daring with each one. A lick of salt across the top of her breast before the shot was thrown back, burning the whole way down. Another lick low on his belly, so her cheek pressed against his hardness as she swiped with her tongue.

It hadn't taken long until she'd borrowed his handcuffs and latched him to the gold bar that rimmed the pool table. And then she'd knelt in front of him and taken every inch of his cock like it was her last meal.

He remembered the bite of her nails on his thighs and the way she stared up at him with those dark bedroom eyes—dreamed about it for the past year until his body was so hot and his cock so hard that he'd had no choice but to stroke himself to completion just so he could get some damn sleep.

"I remember," he said. "And then your brother started breaking bottles and anything else that got in his way the moment he heard you were in town looking for him."

She nodded, the teasing glint gone from her eyes. "Colt would have killed you if he'd found us like we were. I had no choice but to head him off and get him out of town. Believe me, Surrender wasn't ready for Colt Blade."

"Sweetheart, I can take care of myself, even with one hand cuffed behind my back and my cock at full attention. I'm a cop. You seem to forget that on a pretty regular basis."

"You've certainly made sure I can't forget it now. The cuffs are a little tight, by the way. I'd prefer not to have bruises tomorrow."

"I'll take them off as soon as I can get you in a cell."

"You can't be serious," she said, freezing him with a glare.

"Dead serious. I wasn't even going to bring up the fact that you left me half naked and cuffed to a pool table, but you seem to have selective memory. And well, to be honest, I still find I'm a little pissed about the whole thing."

She smirked at that, her normal good humor restored and her eyes dancing with mischief. He wanted nothing more than to bite right into that lush bottom lip.

"A night behind bars might be worth it then. I hope you didn't get into too much trouble."

"I had an extra set of keys in the pocket of my pants. Which you kicked to the other side of the pool table before you ran out the door." He pushed her forward gently so she had no choice but to start walking. "You remember where the station is, don't you?"

"Come on, Lane. We both know you're not really going to arrest me. I've followed a skip into town."

"If he's smart, he's finding a place to hunker down for the night. Storms will be here soon. And yes, I am going to arrest you. The last time I checked, there was a warrant out for your arrest. Destruction of private property—"

"Bullshit. I was trying to get my brother out of there before he hurt anyone. The only reason that window broke was because I ducked when one of your upstanding citizens threw a chair."

"Uh-huh. Watch your step here," he said, leading her up the identical wooden steps on the other side of the street and down the long clapboard sidewalk. "Don't forget the broken bottles."

"Jesus, I'll pay the twenty dollars to replace the bottle of Jameson's I smashed over that idiot's head who threw the chair. He could've killed me. Maybe I should press charges."

"That's certainly your right to do so. Of course, we'd have to hold you in the cell a little longer while we got it all straightened out."

Lane nearly grinned as he heard her growl low in her throat. Naya Blade in a temper was a fine thing to see.

"Give me a break. This is about your ego, plain and simple. You got caught with your pants down—literally—" she snickered, "—and now you want good old-fashioned revenge. I had no choice in what I did that night and you know it. I had to get Colt out of there before he hurt anyone. He might be my brother, but that doesn't mean I don't know what kind of person he is. It was better all-around for us both to get out of town."

"And now you're back," he said, pulling her to a stop just in front of the Sheriff's Office.

He gripped her elbow and turned her so their faces were only inches apart. He felt the tension, thick with what had been left unsaid between them. "Tell me, Naya. What was I to you? A lark while you were searching for your brother? Or a distraction who fell right into the palm of your hand?" He took a step closer so her breasts rubbed against the front of his shirt, and she could feel the hardness of his cock against her jeans. "Did what we have ever matter?"

She lifted her eyes so the dark orbs were intent and focused solely on him. "You were the best thing that ever happened to me," she admitted. "But sometimes the best things come with a price. Sometimes a person's path is set before they ever take the first step. It was better that things didn't go further than they did."

The door to the Sheriff's Office opened and the spell was broken between them. Cooper MacKenzie leaned against the jamb with his arms crossed over his chest and his piercing blue gaze narrowed.

A year hadn't changed Cooper's appearance much. He still looked like an outlaw instead of a sheriff—his face scruffy with black stubble and tattoos covering his shoulder and most of one arm. He was a big son of a bitch—like all of the MacKenzies she'd met during her short visit—but there was something a little wicked, a little wilder, about Cooper that the other boys didn't quite have. He wore his badge and gun like they were an extension of his body, and the only difference she could see was the shiny gold band he wore on his ring finger.

"I've had forty-two phone calls since the two of you started walking this way," he said. "I'd suggest you get in here before the whole town is standing in the middle of the street to watch the show."

Lane inhaled slowly and then exhaled, counting as he did so. He and Naya were forever plagued by interruptions. But Cooper was right. Even now shop doors in town were opening and heads were popping out to see what was going on.

Naya turned to face Cooper and gave him a cheeky grin. "Sheriff MacKenzie. I bet you thought you'd never see me again. Miss me?"

Chapter Three

"Naya Blade," he said with a smirk. "I should've known the weathermen weren't talking about rain when they said a storm was coming." He stepped back out of the way so Lane could usher her inside. "As far as being happy to see you, I'm still up in the air on that. There aren't a lot of women I know who can beat me at pool and wreck a bar all in the same week. Looks like you're still making trouble."

"What can I say?" she winked. "I'm a woman of many talents."

"Well, I'm sure Lane would know that better than anyone," he smirked. "If I recall, you beat him at pool too."

"Don't make me kill you, Coop," Lane said, gritting his teeth so hard he thought they might turn to dust.

Cooper was one of his best friends and he'd made the mistake of telling him why it had taken him so long to get downstairs and get the fight under control. Cooper had laughed until tears had run down his cheeks, and he wasn't likely to let him ever forget it.

The station was a small square of a room with scarred wood floors and wood paneling on two sides. The third wall was dingy white and had maps of the area and persons of interest tacked to it. Two wooden desks faced each other. One belonged to the dispatcher and the other was shared between Lane and Joe Michaels, the other deputy. Since they were never in the office at the same time, crowding wasn't an issue.

The fourth side of the square room was made of iron bars that led to the cells. There were two of them, each no bigger than a walk-in closet, and neither of them saw much action except for the occasional drunk and disorderly. Surrender was, all in all, a mostly peaceful town.

Each cell held a cot, a toilet, and a small sink—and nothing else. A short hallway just behind Lane's desk led to Cooper's office, and farther down the hall was an exit door that led to the back of the building and the stairs to the apartment above the station.

Cooper had lived there before he'd gotten married a few months before, and now it was where Lane lived. It was a convenient location, but it didn't lend itself to a lot of privacy. He was always on call. But he didn't mind working. Work kept him busy. Kept him from thinking about things best left alone.

"You know what? You're okay, MacKenzie." Naya smirked and walked freely around the room, as if the cuffs restraining her wrists were no big deal. "Much more pleasant than *Deputy Holds a Grudge* here."

"If you think I'm getting in the middle of *that* particular fight then you are sadly mistaken," Cooper said. "And there's not much I can do about your current situation. You do have an outstanding warrant for your arrest, and you did leave town with a known fugitive in a suspicious manner."

Naya rolled her eyes. "Oh, for fuck's sake. You know that's all bullshit. I got my brother out of town and back where he belonged so he could stand trial."

"And how is your brother?"

"Serving twenty in Rikers."

Lane squeezed her arm gently and turned her so she could see his sincerity. "I'm sorry to hear that." He knew what it must have felt like for her to watch her only relative put away. She'd told him once she'd been close to Colt before he'd taken a wrong path in the road, and knowing Naya as he did, she probably wondered daily if there was something more she could've done to help him.

She shrugged and broke eye contact, and her voice held nothing but resignation. "It's what he deserved and probably what's best. Even though we're on different sides of the coin, you and I both stand for law and order. And we know it doesn't discriminate against blood. Colt made his choices. I'm only sorry he involved you guys in his mess."

"We've dealt with it before, and we'll deal with it again," Cooper said. "It's what we do. But just to be safe, I'd stay out of Duffey's way while you're here. He still bitches about the damage done to his bar."

"Good grief. I'll pay the damages just to not have to hear about it anymore. And if you don't let me go, you could possibly have a much bigger problem on your hands."

"She followed a skip into town," Lane explained when he saw Cooper's questioning look.

Cooper narrowed his eyes. "Damn, and I had sweet plans to spend the evening being stranded by the storm with my lovely wife."

"Go on home," Lane told him. "I'm on call anyway, and there's not much to be done about a skip tonight. Those storms are going to be bad. Hopefully, we won't lose power."

"I'm more concerned about having to rescue Tyler Claremont's cows from drowning like last time. I'd just as soon never have to go through that again." Cooper grabbed his keys and headed to the door. "In fact, I think I'll stop by there on my way home to make sure they're pinned up. I'll have Joe driving the roads tonight to check for areas of flooding. But make sure you tag me if things get bad. I can come in and hold down the fort, and I can deputize my brothers and cousins if need be for extra hands."

"It'll be fine. I was making my way around all the shops, reminding people to stay inside and hunker down for the evening, when I ran into our favorite bounty hunter here."

Cooper's laugh burst out and he shook his head. "Son, the fact that you've lived here two years now and still expect people to do as you ask them to constantly blows my mind. Surrender has a thousand of the most contrary people on the planet, and if you ask them to do something, you can be damned sure they'll do just the opposite."

"I might have let it slip that anyone caught purposely doing anything foolish would have to pay a two thousand dollar fine and do jail time for endangering the lives of rescue workers."

"I guess that's as good of a threat as any," he said. "I'm off for the night. You two stay out of trouble."

The door closed behind Cooper and the tension that had started to cool flared and simmered between them in hot waves.

"So tell me, Deputy." She watched him out of amused eyes and her chin was tilted in challenge. "Are you going to let me go so I can get a trail on my skip before the tracks are washed away? Or are we going to hunker down for the night and ride out the storm?"

A crack of thunder loud enough to shake the floor beneath them shattered the silence. Lane moved closer and watched her nipples tighten to small pebbles beneath the thin fabric of her tank top. Her hands were still cuffed behind her back and there was no way for her to hide the reaction of her body. Her lips opened on a soft sigh when he stepped in close enough to feel the heat between them, but he didn't touch. Not yet.

"It depends." His words feathered across her lips and her eyelids fluttered, heavy with arousal.

"On what?" She tilted her head slightly and leaned in, so he felt her words whisper against the corner of his mouth.

His cock was so hard he was surprised his jeans hadn't ripped at the seams. The pounding beat of lust drummed through his body so fast he had to grip the bars of the cell at her back to keep from tearing at her clothes and plunging balls deep inside of her.

"On the game we never finished. I think it's your turn to wear the cuffs and have your pants around your ankles while my face is buried between your thighs."

She brought her hands from behind her back, where the cuffs dangled from one wrist and a paperclip stuck out of the lock.

"You mean these cuffs?" she asked with a wicked glint in her eye.

Chapter Four

Instinct had him grabbing her wrists and jerking them above her head, and he quickly snapped the cuffs around the bars, holding her captive. He tossed the paperclip to the floor and it pinged loudly over the harsh sound of their breathing.

She rattled the cuffs against the bars and arched a brow at him. "I'd forgotten how fast you are when you want to be. I bet you were a hell of an Army Ranger. And now you're a big bad cop with too many skills and no place to use them. What are you going to do with me now?"

"I've always said your mouth was going to get you into more trouble than you could handle." He nipped at her bottom lip and watched her eyes go black with desire.

"Big bad bounty hunter," he whispered, mimicking her words. "I'm going to do exactly what I've thought about doing for the last year. No games this time. No interruptions. I'm going to fuck you until this need for you is out of my system. And then I'm going to do it again just for good measure."

She shivered and strained toward him, and he pushed her harder into the bars so she could feel the ferocity of his arousal. He felt the heat between her thighs and knew she was already wet for him.

Little mewls of pleasure escaped from her throat as the denim of his jeans pressed against her clit. It wouldn't take much to send her over the edge. But instead of giving into her demands, he took a step back and got himself under control, and then he smiled at the frustration that crossed over her face before she hid it. Turnabout was fair play. He'd been frustrated as hell for the past year.

The sight of her stretched out before him didn't do anything to cool the lust raging through his system. Naya didn't look like a woman held captive by her lover—like a woman about to submit. She looked defiant, the challenge in her eyes calling to every male instinct he had to dominate and take what was his.

Her arms were stretched over her head, cuffed to the bars, and her hair tumbled around her shoulders in a way that made him want to run his fingers through it while she took his cock into her mouth again. Her nipples pressed tight against her shirt and her breasts heaved with labored breaths.

Thunder rumbled again and it sounded closer this time, and then a few seconds later the pings of rain hit the awning over the sidewalk. It came down fast and furious, and flashes of lightning glanced off the windowpanes, filling the air with an electrical charge that only intensified the building need.

Lane went to the door and turned the lock for good measure and closed the blinds. And then he began the meticulous task of removing his clothes, enjoying the way Naya's eyes followed his every movement and the appreciation in her gaze.

"I always loved your body," she said, her voice husky. "But my, oh my, it's even better than I remember."

"I found the easiest way to get rid of the sexual frustration was to work out. You can only beat off so many times, and it's a poor substitution at that. Believe me, I've been working out a lot."

"Are the women in this town blind?"

"It wouldn't have mattered. Like I said, anything else would have been a poor substitution. I'm too old to fuck just to scratch an itch."

He unbuttoned the khaki shirt with the Sheriff's Office emblem over the breast pocket and tossed it over his desk.

* * * *

"Very, very nice," she purred, shifting against the bars.

He was built just how she liked a man—his shoulders broad and the muscles in his chest and abs well defined, but he'd packed on a lot of extra muscle in the year since she'd seen him, and her mouth watered in anticipation.

He unhooked his utility belt that held his gun and cuffs and laid it next to the shirt. Being restrained was exciting, but she wanted to touch, to run her hands over the muscles and taste and nip at every inch of flesh. Her panties were soaked and even the touch of her clothes against her sensitive skin was too much.

There was no way to hide the straining arousal behind the denim of his jeans. She remembered the feel of him—the thick rigid flesh she couldn't quite wrap her fingers around—the way it flexed beneath her touch. Not being able to have him inside of her, to finish what they'd started so long ago, had been one of her biggest regrets. He hadn't been the only one to have dreams the past year.

Lane unlaced his boots and set them neatly beside the desk, and then he stuffed his socks inside them. His fingers went to the button of his jeans. He flicked the button through the hole, unzipping them just enough to give himself relief from the constriction. The blue briefs he wore couldn't hold him, and she saw the head of his cock peeking above the elastic of his underwear. Lord have mercy, she was about to self-combust just looking at him.

"Don't stop now," she said when he seemed to change his mind about removing his pants.

"I think I'll leave them on, just to be safe." His grin was wicked as he teased her about their last time together. "I think I should even the score a bit first."

She rattled the handcuffs again. "It's not like I'm going anywhere."

He clicked his tongue and moved in closer, his hand glancing across the turgid bud of her nipple. Naya sucked in a breath as his fingers skimmed down her ribs and stomach until they reached the exposed strip of flesh between her shirt and her jeans. His fingers were calloused and rough in comparison to the smoothness of her skin.

He tugged lightly at the hoop in her belly button. "You have no idea what the sight of this little piece of metal does to me."

"Oh, I have an idea," she said wickedly. "But why don't you show me?"

He lifted the shirt—slowly—slowly—until it was raised over the black lace that barely covered her breasts. Her pulse pounded and blood rushed in her ears as he looked at her with such longing that she was afraid she might come without ever feeling his touch.

"Lane—" she panted.

"So fucking beautiful," he whispered reverently.

And then his mouth closed over the lace covered nipple and she swore she saw stars shooting behind her eyelids. His mouth was hot, damp, teasing, so every pull and tug echoed in her pussy. She moaned and arched against him, and finally—*finally*—he put his hands on her, grasping her ass and squeezing before picking her up so she could wrap her legs around his waist. But he never took his mouth from her breasts, switching from one to the other to give equal attention and driving her wild.

His hips anchored her to the bars and she barely noticed as they pressed unevenly against her back. She looked down in his eyes and saw the wickedness there. Lane wasn't flashy like Cooper MacKenzie. He stayed in the background, an observer, methodical in his thinking. And many would underestimate his strength and power because of those qualities. But the bad boy lurked behind those eyes and the mystery of it drove her crazy with lust.

She recognized the dominance in him—the Alpha he kept rigidly under control. And she knew she was in for the wildest ride of her life. If only he'd move a little fucking faster. Lane liked going at his own pace, but damned if she couldn't try to speed things up along the way.

"Dammit, Lane. More—"

She felt his laughter against her flesh and almost whimpered as his hand came up and undid the front clasp of her bra.

"I could spend hours right here, making you come just by sucking on your nipples."

Naya groaned at the threat. "For Christ sake. I'll be dead in a few hours if you don't hurry up and get inside me."

His teeth nipped once at the underside of her breast and his hands moved down to work at the button of her jeans. Desperation clawed at her and she shifted her hips to help him get the tight denim over her thighs. He peeled the black lace panties that matched her bra down with them and tossed them both to the floor.

"Oh, fuck!" he growled as he saw her for the first time. Her pussy was bare—smooth as silk—and her arousal creamed along the plump folds of flesh.

Naya was tired of waiting. She needed to come. Now.

His cock had never been so hard, so large and swollen. And the sight of Naya's pussy and the evidence of her desire made his balls draw up tight and his cum ready to explode. He worked the zipper the rest of the way carefully and pushed his briefs down so his cock sprang free. His hand went to the base and he squeezed tightly to hold himself off.

His breath labored in his lungs and his skin was covered in a fine sheen of sweat. The storm raged outside and the lights flickered with the intensity of the winds blowing against the power lines. He wouldn't have cared if they were in the middle of a hurricane. Nothing was going to stop him from this pleasure.

He only needed a second to get himself under control. But a second was all it took for Naya to take things into her own hands. She was every bit his match, in and out of bed. He watched in aroused awe as the muscles in her arms flexed, and then she slowly pulled the weight of her body up the side of the bars.

It took an incredible amount of strength and control. His cock jerked in his hand, and he squeezed tighter. She raised herself until the bare folds of her pussy were even with his face, close enough so he could breathe in the delicious scent of her. And then she lifted her legs and wrapped them around his neck, so her pussy was completely open to him, waiting for him. It was the sexiest fucking thing he'd ever seen in his life.

"Move faster," she panted.

With the opportunity right in front of him, he had no choice but to do as she asked. He cupped her ass to help take some of the weight off her arms. And then he devoured her like a starving man at a banquet table.

The taste of her hit his tongue like ambrosia, and they both groaned in unison as just the touch of his lips against her bare pussy had her coming in a liquid rush that he lapped up greedily.

She stared at him in complete shock. No one had ever made her come like that—not with just the first touch—as if he'd known exactly where to lick and taste so she'd melt into a puddle against him. He met her gaze steadily, the green of his eyes fevered in their intensity.

"Lane."

This time his name wasn't a demand on her lips. It was a plea. And she realized for the first time since they started their game of seduction the year before that she was in over her head. Because you didn't just get a man like Lane Greyson out of your system. A man like Lane would imprint himself on your body, mind, and soul. And there'd be no getting rid of him.

He noticed the panic in her eyes and the way she stiffened against him, but it was too late for both of them. She tried to unhook her legs from over his shoulders, but he kept her anchored. And then he licked her again, slower this time, never taking his gaze from hers. He licked and suckled and tasted until her head fell back against the bars and her hips began to move against his face.

"It's too much. God, Lane. I can't—"

He heard the desperation in the quaver of her voice. "You're mine, Naya. There's no running this time." He nipped at one of the swollen folds of her pussy, a teasing sting that had shivers racing up her spine.

Her breath caught when he soothed the sting of the bite with the flat of his tongue. And then he was licking inside of her over and over again, occasionally bringing his tongue up to curl around the sensitive bud of her clit.

"You're going to pay for this," she gritted out.

He nipped at her again. "I've already paid in full. A year ago. With a hard-on and a case of blue balls I haven't been able to ease. It's your turn to suffer, baby."

And then he thrust two fingers inside of her, filling her as his mouth went back to her clit. Naya arched against him and screamed, her fists squeezing the iron bars so hard she was surprised they didn't melt from the heat of her grasp.

He let her scream. The storm raging outside matched the one happening behind closed doors. She exploded around him, her pussy clamping around his fingers in an iron fist as cream covered his hand and the inside of her thighs.

"That's it, sweetheart." His voice was hoarse with his own desire and the need to bury inside of her.

Lane unwrapped her legs from around his neck, sure he'd have bruises there the next day, and brought them down so she was standing on her own two feet, though her legs quivered so badly he was afraid she wouldn't be able to support herself. Her head hung down, her hair covering her face, and her breathing was shallow and fast.

"It's my turn," he said, ripping at the thin tank top she wore so it fell to the ground in tatters. He wanted to see all of her, possess every inch of that sweet body. The lacy bra followed the tank top and then he cupped her full breasts in his hands, his thumbs rubbing across the nipples as she shuddered again beneath his touch.

The power she gave him went straight to his head. He pulled her arms down some, adjusting the cuffs, and then he turned her body so she faced the bars.

"Jesus, Naya." His finger trailed down her spine and she arched against him. "So fucking hot."

"Shut up and fuck me, Lane. I can't wa—"

He clasped his hands over hers around the bars and pushed into her from behind until he was balls deep. The muscles of her pussy quivered around him and he gritted his teeth to keep from exploding deep inside her. Her sharp cry was a mixture of pleasure and pain, and he paused to let her tight sheath adjust to the invasion.

She whimpered and arched, lifting herself more fully to him and widening her stance to make the adjustment easier. Sweat dripped from his brow and onto her back, and he looked down to see his cock buried between the round globes of her ass.

"Fucking beautiful," he breathed out, his head dropping back on his shoulders.

"Take me," she begged. "God, Lane. Take all of me."

So he did. His thrusts were short and hard, powerful enough that each one brought her up on her toes as she held the bars for dear life. The head of his cock rubbed against the sensitive spot deep inside of her over and over again, a fleeting feeling of pleasure and pain that grew in intensity as he kept up the frantic pace.

The sounds of flesh slapping against flesh and groans of pleasure were drowned out by booms of thunder, each one almost right on top of the other. Sweat slicked their bodies and their breaths labored.

And then his hands moved from the bars to cup her breasts before rolling her nipples between finger and thumb. He left one hand on her breast and brought the other down farther, until his fingers slid through the cream to find her clit.

"Oh, God—Lane!"

The touch was all she needed for another orgasm to rocket through her body. She threw her head back and pushed against him so the head of his cock hit the deepest part of her to intensify the orgasm.

This time her scream was silent, as if she didn't physically have any more to give. But he wrenched it all from her anyway. He kept the thrusts going, gritting his teeth to hold himself back, so every drop of pleasure was wrung from her body before he took his own.

His balls drew up tight and he felt the tingling at the base of his spine. And then he froze, holding himself completely still as realization struck.

"Fuck," he wheezed. "Condom." His body dropped forward and

his head rested on her shoulder as he tried to get himself under control. He bit her shoulder gently and her pussy contracted around his cock, making him groan with the torture.

He started to pull out of her, but she followed his movements so he stayed lodged inside of her.

"I'm on the pill. I'm safe." Her voice was as strained as his own. "Please don't stop."

He'd never taken a woman without that thin barrier of protection between them, even when she said she was on the pill. The risks were always too great. But the thought of risking it all with Naya had emotion bubbling inside of him that he couldn't explain.

"I've always used a condom," he said. Her muscles flexed around him again and he pushed a little deeper, teasing them both. "Always. But you make me forget."

"Finish it, Lane. Once and for all."

He didn't need a second urging. He plunged inside of her like a man possessed and he jerked against her as his orgasm hit with the force of a semi. Her muscles clamped around him tighter, sucking him deeper, as spurt after spurt of semen hit her inner walls. He stifled his groan against her neck as the spasms wracked his body violently.

He'd waited a year to get her out of his system. And he realized in that moment that a lifetime wouldn't be long enough. Naya Blade was his—for now and forever.

Chapter Five

The storm was as bad as the weathermen predicted, and it wasn't expected to stop for two more days.

Lane had managed to bundle Naya up in an extra rain slicker and hustle her up the back stairs to his apartment. He'd never seen her let down her guard before. She was always so tough, so in control. And now she was a puddle of satisfied woman. He had to admit the knowledge that he was the one responsible filled him with pleasure.

His apartment was no frills, just basic necessities and no clutter. His Army days had cured him of that. He got Naya tucked into his bed and watched her as she drifted into sleep. She looked right there, and there was a tug of longing inside of him for permanence. A longing he'd given up on long ago.

He'd seen too much before he'd settled in Surrender. His time as a Ranger had changed him. Watching friends die had a tendency to do that to a man. So in a sense, Surrender had saved him once he'd left the Army. All he'd wanted was peace and quiet. A simple life with simple needs. Cooper MacKenzie had offered that to him the day he'd walked into the Sheriff's Office looking for a job.

Lane was just about to strip out of his clothes and slip into bed beside Naya when the phone he'd brought up from downstairs rang. The electricity had gone off shortly after he'd gotten the cuffs on her wrists unlocked, and they'd fallen together in a heap on the floor in the darkness. He had no idea how long they'd stayed there, recovering from the cataclysmic event that had happened between them.

The generator at the station had kicked on about a minute after the electricity went off, but he knew there were a lot of people who didn't have generators and would be braving the storm and cooling temperatures without power. Summer was officially over if the icy slap of the rain that had pounded against him on the way upstairs was any indication.

He took the call and got dressed again in dry clothes, strapping on his utility belt and grabbing a couple of extra flashlights. He leaned over Naya in the bed and kissed her forehead, causing her to wrinkle her nose in protest. Her obvious disgruntlement made him grin. Naya was a prickly creature to be sure.

"Wake up, sweetheart. I've got to go out for a while."

Her eyes fluttered open and she turned so she could see him better. "I'm awake. I should probably get dressed and take off for the bed and breakfast. I've got to set out early to start looking for my skip."

"Stay," he said. "You're welcome to whatever you need here. There's food and a shower. And I doubt the roads will be good enough to do more than swim in the morning. We're all going to be stuck for a couple of days, including your skip."

She looked like she was going to protest. Staying the night in his bed promised something more than just fast and furious sex. He knew it. And she knew it too.

"Stay," he said again.

She finally nodded and pulled the covers back under her chin. "I'll stay. When will you be back?"

"God only knows. We've got power lines down and roads washed out. A couple of college kids coming home late are stranded out by Mill Pond. Joe's headed over there, and I'm going to go deal with the power lines. I hooked the boat to my truck earlier, so things should go fairly quickly."

"Have fun with that. And be careful." Her voice faded away as she drifted back into sleep.

Lane stared at her a second longer. He wanted to say more. To tell her what had been brewing inside of him this past year. He'd known she'd come back, because whether she realized it or not, this was where she belonged.

He loved her. He'd had plenty of time to think about it after she'd walked out of his life. They had a lot to learn about each other still, but he knew as sure as he was breathing that she was meant for him. He only had to make her come around to the same realization. And Naya was just perverse enough to run the other direction if he even hinted of such feelings. In the end, it would have to be her that made the first move.

* * * *

Naya sat up straight in bed, her heart pounding and her hands damp with sweat. The dream was always the same. She'd only been a cop for two years. But it had been two years too many. Long enough to watch her partner, Tony, gunned down for no good reason.

It had been a routine call for a domestic disturbance. They'd been to the same house more than a dozen times before. The woman never pressed charges, but the neighbors' complaints made a visit necessary. The woman would answer the door, her lip bleeding or her eye swelling shut, and she'd tell them she fell and that everything was all right.

It made Naya sick every time they took a call to that house because she knew one day the woman wouldn't be able to answer the door at all. And there was nothing they could do about it.

She'd known in her gut when they got that last call that things would be bad. Her instincts were never wrong. But she and Tony took the call and knocked on the door, just like they had so many times before.

The woman answered the door like she usually did, and Naya could see the red marks in the shape of fingers around her throat. Her pupils were dilated so they were big as black saucers, and a streak of blood was smeared under her nose. Her hands shook and she only cracked the door an inch or two. The terror on the woman's face was enough to send chills down Naya's spine. Something was different about this time, and Naya's hand automatically went to pull her weapon from her holster.

Tony tried to get the woman to come outside and talk to them for a bit without the husband interfering, but it was as if she were frozen in place. The shots that fired through the door took them all by surprise. And by some horrible stroke of bad luck, all three bullets hit Tony right in the middle of the chest.

If Naya had been the one to knock on the door that night—like she had almost every time before because she was a woman and the least threatening of the two—she'd be the one buried and gone instead of Tony. Naya had been given a second chance at life at the expense of her partner's, and it was something she'd never forget.

After the shots had fired, Tony's body had slammed back into her, falling on top of her, so she was trapped beneath his heavier frame. The breath was knocked out of her and for a few seconds, she was completely paralyzed. There was no amount of training or scenarios that could prepare you to catch your partner as he died.

Naya had still been on the ground, scrambling to her knees to call for backup, when two more shots sounded from inside the house—a shot for the wife and another the husband inflicted on himself.

She'd turned her badge and gun in that day, while Tony's blood had still been sticky on her hands. Nothing her captain could say would change her mind. She didn't have the guts to make it as a cop. But she had good instincts, and she had a nose for finding the bad guys. Becoming a bounty hunter was her only other option if she wanted to utilize her skills.

She shook herself out of the memories of the dream and looked around the room, trying to reorient herself to the present while repeating in her head that there was nothing she could do to change the past.

The rain still pounded down against the roof. It looked as if buckets of water were being poured onto the windowpanes, distorting the images in the street. Darkness still hovered in the sky, but she wasn't sure if that was because of the clouds or because it was still the middle of the night. No matter the time, she was wide awake and she might as well get up.

She stretched slowly, feeling the soreness in her muscles. Sex had been off her radar the last year—ever since she'd met Lane. No other man had measured up. She smiled smugly as a vision of his body and the thick stalk of flesh between his thighs drifted through her mind. She wasn't sure it was possible for anyone to ever measure up to that.

Her pack was on the chair in the corner of the room, and then she remembered her backpack of clothes was in the saddlebag on her bike. If her bike was still where she'd left it, that is, and not floating down the street with the cows and God knew what else.

The important thing was she had her paperwork to capture

Jackson Coltraine. She could pick up clothes and other supplies anywhere. She didn't care what Lane said about the roads. The itch at the back of her neck was telling her she needed to get out there and start looking. Coltraine was dangerous. And even sick, he wasn't someone to underestimate.

Before she could get back to work she needed coffee and a shower. In that order. So she rummaged through one of Lane's drawers until she found a spare T-shirt and she pulled it over her head, enjoying that the soft cotton smelled of him. Then she headed to the kitchen to see what more she could learn about the man who'd become her lover.

The way someone lived spoke a lot about a person. Lane's apartment was sparse—only a couch and a flat screen TV on the wall in the living room. There were no pictures or other collectible type things sitting around. Her own apartment looked much the same way, but mostly because she was never there and hadn't even unpacked all of the boxes that were still in storage. She wondered what Lane's excuse was because he obviously spent time here. Cooper had said Lane had been in Surrender two years.

The appliances in the kitchen were clean and well used. There was food in the refrigerator—not TV dinners and other various dips that most bachelors would have—but real food that made up ingredients for recipes. It was obvious the man cooked. It bothered her that she wanted to dig deeper—to learn more about the man he was. But she wouldn't lower herself to snooping past what was right in front of her eyes.

That kind of personal information was reserved for long-term relationships, not lust-filled flings.

She'd bitten off more than she could chew with Lane, she thought, searching through cabinets in the kitchen until she found what she needed for the coffee. The chemistry between them had been undeniable when they'd met a year before. It had been a game. A way to pass the time before she left town again. But now it was something more, and there was no way to go back to what they'd had before.

Lane had been a constant worry in the back of her mind the past year because despite her intentions when they'd started out, he'd gotten under her skin and stayed there. She couldn't let him get too close—close enough to know her secrets and her shame. What if she let herself fall in love with him and then he ended up not liking the person she was? A person who could stand by helplessly as three people died around her. A coward who couldn't pick up her badge and gun again to protect and serve.

Naya waited impatiently for the coffee, glancing at the clock above the microwave to see it wasn't quite dawn yet, and still Lane wasn't back from wherever he'd gone. She looked outside again, hoping the rain had magically stopped while the coffee had been brewing, but no such luck.

It mattered not. She'd wait a couple hours, gather a few supplies, and then set out to find Jackson Coltraine. He was still recovering from whatever illness he'd picked up, so he'd be weak, unable to move as quickly or adapt in harder conditions. He'd be looking for a place he could lay low for a while until the rain passed and he could recoup some of his strength. She only hoped he decided not to endanger any of the citizens of Surrender. Coltraine was dangerous and desperate—two things that made for a deadly combination.

The coffee trickled into the pot, and she finally lost patience and stuck her cup beneath the drip. She took the first scalding sip, feeling the blood start to move through her veins, and then she took it with her to the shower.

The bathroom was as clean and sparse as the rest of the place—white towels and washrags stacked in the cabinet above the toilet and a white shower curtain. She turned on the water, glad to see it was more than a trickle, and then stripped out of Lane's shirt and got in, taking her coffee with her and enjoying the dual stimulation to get her brain back in working order.

She knew the moment he stepped into the bathroom. Her senses were too honed for her to not recognize the change in the air. But she also recognized that it was *him*. Her head dipped back under the spray, rinsing the remaining shampoo away, and then she pulled the curtain back.

"Holy shit. What happened to you?" she asked, her eyes widening at the sight of him. This was not the sexy encounter she'd been envisioning in her head.

He'd stripped out of his shirt and had dropped it in a sopping heap on the floor. Despite the protection of the shirt, his chest and arms were covered in streaks of mud. So was his face. Blond stubble whiskered his cheeks, but splatters of brown covered the left side of his face all the way to his hairline.

"I had to track down the truck from the electric company. They'd taken a wrong turn and had to abandon their truck because the water was rising too fast. So I had to unhook the boat and go get them. I gave them a ride so they could take care of the power lines before anyone got hurt. It's as bad as I've ever seen out there. The people without generators are going to be without electricity for a few days."

He worked at the buckle of his belt, but the leather had gone stiff and was crusted with mud, so it wasn't easy to get off. Naya leaned down and turned the water a little hotter because his lips were blue and his teeth chattered. He finally got the belt loosened and his pants shoved down. The fact that he'd left the dirty clothes on the floor was a telling sign for how exhausted he must be.

"Hand me a towel and I'll get out and toss your clothes in the washer," she told him.

"Leave them. I'll have to throw them away anyway. And I'd rather have you for company in the shower. I'll let you scrub my back," he said with a leer. It would've been more effective if he hadn't been asleep on his feet.

"You've got another thing coming if you think the sight of you covered in mud and God knows what else is going to turn me on."

"I'm not sure I'd have the strength to do anything but drop you, so I think you're probably safe."

"And the romance is dead," she grinned. "That didn't take long."

"I'll romance the hell out of you once I get some sleep." He stepped into the tub with her and hissed as the hot water hit his skin.

"Why, Deputy Greyson. I believe you've become a smartass over the past year. I must've been a bad influence. You're always so serious."

"You make that sound like a bad thing. I like to think of myself as responsible and the voice of reason."

He ducked his head under the spray of water and started scrubbing away the mud. "I moved your bike over to Charlie's Automotive, by the way. And I grabbed your backpack while I was at it. I figured you'd probably need a change of clothes. Though you might want to toss them in the dryer first as they're a little damp."

Naya's heart did a small flip in her chest that he'd thought of her. It was the little things, her mother had always told her, that made a relationship last. She found herself in a hurry to get out of the shower and back on solid ground as those thoughts entered her mind. What she and Lane had was *not* a relationship.

"Why does it smell like coffee in the shower?" he asked quizzically.

Naya blanked her face from the panic she was sure had probably been showing there.

"Here." She handed him the mug and waited while he took a long, lukewarm sip.

"This is a little weird, as I've always been under the impression that coffee should be drank while not naked and soaking wet."

"I guess it's my job to get you out of your rut and bring some excitement to your small-town life." Her hand smoothed back his hair before she could help herself. "And being serious isn't a bad thing," she said in response to his earlier statement. "I think you want people to underestimate you. You sit back and watch, and you read people fast and accurately. It makes you good at your job and complements the way Cooper works as well. He's the flash. The one who intimidates. The one they focus on while you get in and work the job from behind the scenes. The two of you make a good team."

"It's pretty early in the morning to be psychoanalyzed." The annoyance in his voice was obvious, and she hid a grin while she passed him the bar of soap and another clean washrag. There'd been parts of being a cop she'd been good at too. Just not the most important ones.

"Surrender isn't as bad as you make it out to be," he said, breaking her out of her thoughts. "It's a good place to live. A good community that cares about each other. The people here just do things differently. But mostly it's entertaining, unless you're waist deep in raging waters, listening to people who should be tucked away safe in their homes while they yell out instructions."

Naya snorted out a laugh. "I can only imagine the excitement."

"After I got the power lines taken care of, I drove out to help Joe with the stranded kids. The road is completely washed out. There's no way through from either side or around unless you go by boat, and the water is moving fast enough that it's better you don't try it unless it's an emergency. People are going to be stuck in their houses for days until it goes down, or until they get restless enough to unhitch their boats and go joyriding. So probably by noon."

Naya smiled at the obvious affection he had for the people of Surrender, even as the affection equaled the exasperation.

"Those kids were stuck on top of their car and it took all of us to get them down and to safe ground. Their car washed away about five minutes after we got them to safety." He wiped a hand over the scruff on his face. "I'm too tired to shave. Cooper's downstairs in the office this morning so I can get a few hours of sleep. We're going to be spread thin the next week or so."

Naya looked him over from head to toe, the water running over the tight muscles of his abdomen and thighs, and the very rigid length of arousal.

"I thought you were too tired to do anything but drop me?" she asked, quirking a brow at the impressive sight below his waist.

"You shouldn't have brought coffee into the shower. I find I'm feeling very much awake at the moment. Rejuvenated even."

"Yes, I can see that. Still, I'm not sure I want to take a chance on being dropped." She pressed her palms against his chest and then slid them down slowly. "I should probably take matters into my own hands."

She wrapped her hand around him and squeezed, and then watched with delight as his head dropped back and a hiss of pure pleasure escaped his lips.

"Excellent idea," he said, bracing his hand on the shower wall as she dropped to her knees before him.

She stroked him from root to tip, watching him out of those dark eyes, and the sight of her kneeling in front of him—the water raining down and droplets catching on her hair and eyelashes like tiny diamonds—had his cock jerking against her hand. Her breasts were full, her nipples puckered and pink, just waiting for his mouth.

Wanting her was like breathing.

Her tongue flicked out and licked up the sensitive underside of his cock. His balls drew tight and he gritted his teeth as the pleasure gathered at the base of his spine. When she reached the swollen crest, her tongue curled around it and lapped at the pre-cum he hadn't been able to hold back.

"God, Naya," he rasped. "You're killing me." But his hand fisted in the back of her wet hair and brought her closer. She was a drug—addictive and sweet.

She stopped teasing him with gentle licks and strokes and enveloped the crest of his cock in her mouth, surrounding him with wet heat. She made swallowing motions and he swore he felt his eyes roll back in his head as she suckled him long and slow, while stroking the base of his shaft.

"Fuck," he groaned. "Take more. Suck me down, sweetheart."

She purred around him as he tightened his hold in her hair and he felt the vibrations all the way through his body. Her hand came up and cupped his balls and he widened his stance for balance and pressed harder into the tile wall.

He looked down into her slumberous gaze and watched as his cock disappeared into her lush pink mouth. It was heaven. It was torture. And though he was only moments from coming, he wanted to be inside her when the moment came.

"Stand up," he said, tugging on her hair.

Her nails bit into his thighs in protest and she opened her mouth wider, relaxing her throat as she pushed forward and took him down as far as she could go. It was impossible to take all of him, but the feel of his head hitting the back of her throat was pure ecstasy.

"Enough or I'll come," he growled.

Her eyelids fluttered closed and she ignored his pleas, completely lost in his pleasure. He finally gave up the battle and felt the orgasm rip through his body and down his cock before shooting into the back of her throat.

His shout echoed off the tiles and mixed with her hums of pleasure as she drank him down. The intensity of it flattened him, but he'd be damned if he was going to take without giving in return.

He pulled her head back and he felt the beast inside of him rage with lust as she licked a pearly drop of cum from her swollen lips. And then he lifted her up by the arms and pushed her back against the tile, his cock rooting between the slick folds of her pussy before sliding home.

Her legs wrapped around his waist and his arms went beneath her ass, supporting her. He couldn't be gentle. Couldn't be smooth or show her finesse. He had to fuck her in the most basic sense of the word.

His thighs bunched and muscles quivered as he pistoned between her thighs. He felt the bite of her teeth against his neck and heard her muffled scream, but the pain barely registered.

Her pussy clenched and pulsed around him and her legs squeezed him tighter as her body burned like a furnace from the inside out, her orgasm so powerful her muscles clamped around his dick so the pleasure melded with pain.

"Lane," she cried, her nails digging into his shoulders as she thrashed against him.

He felt his balls constrict and knew it should have been impossible for him to come again so soon. But even as he had the thought, his cock jerked inside her and his cum spurted against her inner walls.

He was wrecked. Probably for life. Their hearts pounded against each other in perfect time and muscles quivered while flesh cooled. His legs were shaky, and he let her down slowly, hoping she could support her weight because he wasn't sure he'd be able to hold both of them up for much longer.

Her eyes were closed and he soaped the washrag, wiping the evidence of their lovemaking from between her thighs, and then he turned the water off. Chills pebbled her flesh and he found his movements lethargic as he reached for towels. He could sleep for a week.

"Come on, love. We'll help each other to the bed."

"I'm not sleepy," she murmured, her head dropping to his shoulder as he dried them haphazardly.

"I can tell." Amusement made his lips twitch. Naya was definitely grumpy when she was tired. "You can hold me while I catch a couple of hours then."

She grunted what he assumed was her assent and they stumbled toward the bedroom, drops of water still dripping from their hair. They fell into bed in a tangle of limbs, and Lane pulled the covers over them so they were cocooned in the warmth.

"I need to get back to work at noon," she said. "I've got to catch Coltraine while he's weak and not expecting me."

"It's too dangerous with the water levels the way they are."

"That's why I've got to go. Gotta catch the bad guys and put them away."

She went limp in his arms and he kissed her forehead while she slept. "You'd have made a hell of a cop, love."

Her breathing was even with sleep but she answered. "I wasn't a good cop. Good cops don't let people die."

And then she didn't say anything else as sleep claimed her fully, but the words she'd spoken echoed over and over in his mind. Had she really been a cop? And if so, who had she let die? His mind wasn't going to be at ease until he knew the answers.

Chapter Six

Lane dozed off and on for an hour before finally giving up and rolling out of bed.

Naya was dead to the world, but he still moved quietly as he pulled a work shirt out of his closet along with a pair of clean jeans. He laced his boots and strapped on his weapon and then went into the other room to get his heavier raincoat.

He saw the file lying on the table next to her bag and he didn't worry about overstepping the boundaries of privacy one bit as he flipped it open to the papers inside. He studied the picture of Jackson Coltraine and read through the particulars of his crimes and arrest. He was considered armed and dangerous, and the thought of Naya going up against someone like that didn't sit well with him. It wouldn't hurt to start his own search and see what he came up with.

He left her a note so she'd know he was downstairs at the station, and then flicked the lock as he closed his front door behind him. The awning that covered his doorway wasn't built to keep off the driving horizontal rain, and he pulled his hood up as it immediately battered against him.

The rain sliced at his face as he hurried down the stairs and slipped in the back door. He heard Cooper's irritated voice on the phone as he walked toward the front room. He hung his jacket on the peg and waited until Coop got off the phone.

"Damn, boy. You look like you've been rode hard and put away wet," Cooper said with a grin. "I thought I told you to take some time to sleep."

Lane felt the flush of embarrassment in his cheeks. He'd never been one to share the details of his private life with his friends.

"I got enough sleep to last me a while," he said. "Who was that on the phone?"

"That was Wally Wilkins telling me he was going to take his boat and round up some extra deputies." Cooper rolled his eyes and leaned back in his chair, propping a booted foot on the corner of the desk. "Damned fool is going to end up swamping the boat and then we'll have to stop what we're doing and go rescue the whole lot of them. He says we need more help and wants to know what to do if people start looting."

"Jesus," Lane said, imagining the worst outcome.

"That was pretty much my thought too. I assured him there was no reason for him to leave his house. He has a generator and plenty of food and water. But he told me if Rory Jenkins from down the road tried to come steal some of his provisions—"

Cooper glared at him when Lane couldn't quite hold back a snicker. "I shit you not the man said provisions, as if we're in the middle of the Dust Bowl and the Great Depression. He said if Rory tried to steal from him, then he was going to shoot him dead as a doornail."

"He just wants an excuse to shoot Rory because Rory Jr. got Wally's daughter, Jo Beth, in trouble and didn't offer to marry her. Rory Jr. ran off to join the Army instead, and I've heard it's because his father told him to take the first train out of town and take it fast."

Cooper winced and Lane nodded in agreement. If Rory Jr. ever came back to Surrender, they could have a real problem on their hands.

"I can't tell you how comforting it is to know that of the thousand people in this town, that over half of them are registered firearms users," Lane said, shaking his head at the horror.

"I wouldn't feel too comfortable with those statistics, because you know the other half are unregistered users. This is the middle of nowhere. Everyone and their dog has a gun. Hell, even my wife keeps a gun in her desk at the library."

"That's city property. Is that allowed?"

"I gave her a special permit. Considering the drug trade that was happening only a few months ago around this area, I felt it was better to be safe than sorry."

"Speaking of better safe than sorry, I got a look at the paperwork on the skip Naya is tracing. Jackson Coltraine. He's Caucasian. Brown and blue. About six foot. He comes from money, so he's not going to be used to roughing it, and he caught the flu a few days back in South Dakota. He held a small-town doctor hostage and then bashed him over the head after he gave him some samples to treat the symptoms. It's slowed him down quite a bit. And with the rain and flooding—"

"You think he's going to hide somewhere he can get easy access to food and stay dry," Cooper said, finishing his thought.

"Yeah. And with no way in and out around Mill Pond, I was thinking he might try to hit either the Coleman or Newton barns, or maybe those empty hunting cabins. It might be worth checking out."

"Agreed. But for God's sake, don't let it slip to anyone we've got a fugitive on the loose."

"Too late." Lane scrubbed his hands over his face and wished he'd been able to get more sleep. "Naya showed his picture to Gladys when she stopped in the diner for lunch yesterday. Every person I ran into last night while trying to clear the roads and area mentioned it to me."

"Great. Now Wally will want to get his boat and gather a posse to hunt down Coltraine. Damned fool man makes me wonder how he keeps getting elected to the city council."

"His mother is one of the vote counters."

"Huh," Cooper grunted. "I reminded Wally that he voted down hiring the extra deputies we need. We're all running thin around here and they're going to throw a fit at the overtime we'll be putting in because of it. I'm going to force the issue and hire more deputies whether the city council approves or not. I don't care if I have to get my whole damned family to apply the pressure. Being a MacKenzie still means something in these parts. So keep your eyes and ears open if you know of anyone who'd like a job in law and order where they're grossly underpaid."

"You paint a hell of a picture," Lane said, mouth quirking in a grin. "I can see now how you persuaded me to join the ranks." The thought of hiring new deputies made him think of Naya and what she'd said in her sleep.

"I need to ask you something," he finally said to Cooper. If you couldn't trust your closest friend, who else could you trust?

"Is this about the bounty hunter?" Cooper asked, waggling his eyebrows. "You seem a little old to need pointers, but I'll give it my best shot."

"I'm amazed every day that you managed to find the one woman on this earth who can put up with your juvenile sense of humor."

"Pretty great, isn't it?" Cooper said with the smile of a man who was newly and happily married. "I'm just messing around. Don't be so serious."

"That's the second time I've been told that this morning. I find it an annoying assessment of my character."

"Greyson, you're the best man I know next to my own brothers. You're solid all the way through, and I know I can trust you no matter what the circumstances because you see through the bullshit and you'll always do what's right. You're the person I'd call to watch my back if I needed it. And after everything you've been through, I'm surprised you're not more serious than you are. Now tell me what's bothering you about your bounty hunter."

Lane blew out a breath, feeling a little uncomfortable at Cooper's praise—and it was high praise indeed. Cooper wouldn't let just anyone cover his back.

"Last year when Naya came into town looking for her brother, did you run a make on her?"

Cooper's eyebrows rose. "You're asking me that *after* you come down here with that bite mark on your neck?"

Lane stared at his friend without squirming under his scrutiny, and Cooper finally let out a sigh and dropped his feet from the desk to the floor.

"Give me a second," he said and went back into his office for a minute. When he came back out, he had a thick file in his hand and he passed it over. "I ran a make on her because that's the kind of trusting guy I am. And you can bet she knows I ran her because she's just that good. But I'm going to give you a little advice because I'm newly married and I clearly understand women."

Laughter burst from Lane's chest before he could control it. "I'm sorry. Wasn't it you who spent three days sleeping on the cot in the back room a couple of months ago because of how well you understand women?"

"That was a slight—setback," Cooper said with a wry smile. "I've also learned all about compromise, and I'm going to tell you straight out not to look in that file if you care for her as much as I think you do."

Lane let out a breath he hadn't known he'd been holding. "I think I have to look. She mentioned something earlier. That she was a cop. That she'd let people die."

"Ask her about it," Coop repeated.

"You told me that I cut through the bullshit and that you always know I'm going to do what's right. I do care about her. But I need to know if my instincts are off on this one and she's not the woman I think and hope she is."

Cooper sighed and handed him the file, and Lane weighed it in his hands, knowing what he found inside could change everything. Or nothing. He flipped it open without regrets and was greeted by the sight of her picture taken at the academy. She looked much the same as she did now, only there was a naivety in her eyes in the photograph that had long since been lost.

He read the overview of her short career and how it had ended, and his heart broke for her because obviously she was still suffering from the loss of her partner and the victim. She'd had no family left to lean on, and he couldn't imagine that her line of work let her have time for close friends or lovers.

"You should have listened to MacKenzie's advice," Naya said in a voice cold enough to give him frostbite. "If I'd wanted you to poke through my personal life, I would've given you the file myself."

Chapter Seven

Lane and Cooper both looked up sharply because Naya had managed to get past both of their guards. She hadn't made a sound coming through the back door, and there was no telling how much of their conversation she'd overheard.

Cooper felt bad for his friend. If looks could've killed, Lane would be six feet under. One of the things he'd always appreciated most about Lane was his ability to never let others see what he was feeling or thinking. If the death rays Naya was shooting from her eyes bothered Lane in any way, he wasn't showing it.

"I saw a couple of boats hitched up to pickup trucks out back," she said, turning her attention to Cooper. "Any chance I could borrow one so I can start tracking my skip? I'm thinking he's probably hiding in a barn or an empty house. And he would've tried to get as far outside of town as possible before the storm hit to reduce his chances of being seen."

Cooper looked between Lane and Naya, both of them working so hard at trying to hide what they were feeling that they were missing what was staring them in the face. He let out a breath and decided he was too old for this. He'd found his woman. Everyone else was on their own.

"Yeah, that's the same conclusion we came up with." Cooper

moved to the maps tacked onto the wall and pointed to a spot with his finger. "These are your two most likely areas. He would've had a lot of miles to cover before the storm hit. Surrender is bigger in square miles than it looks, and the ranches cover hundreds of acres. The next town over is Myrna Springs, but it's another two-hour drive with nothing in between, so I doubt he'd have kept going before the storm hit."

"Any empty buildings in that area?" she asked.

"A few. Mostly old hunting cabins and a couple of abandoned barns. The people around here know flooding is a possibility during the rainy season so houses are built up on higher ground. The barns too. It's just the overflow from the lakes that make the roads flood like this."

"What was he driving?" Lane asked, moving to stand beside them so he could see the maps.

Naya kept her gaze on the map, trying to run scenarios in her head while not letting how close Lane was standing to her make her uncomfortable. "He stole a dark blue Tahoe in South Dakota. I found a gas station attendant who remembered seeing it once we crossed the border into Montana, and Gladys from the diner remembered seeing a dark SUV driving through town yesterday morning. There aren't a lot of places to stop out here for him to boost another, so I have to assume he's still driving the Tahoe."

"Any word of an abandoned vehicle sighting?" he asked Cooper, since he'd been on call all morning.

"Nothing yet. But sometimes those back roads don't have a car on them for days. There are hunting cabins here and here," Cooper said, circling the spots on the map. "One of them is in the flood zone, so unless he's an idiot, he's probably not camped out there. But the other one has possibilities. You'll definitely need a boat to get there though."

"I'll take her," Lane said. 'You've got Wally and his posse to deal with."

"Thanks for reminding me," Cooper said dryly. "Maybe I'll just get them all to meet me at Duffey's and get them drunk so I can arrest them."

"You always have the best ideas. I guess that's why you make the big bucks."

Cooper grinned and slapped Lane on the shoulder.

"I don't mean to interrupt your male-bonding time, but I don't need a guide. I can take the boat and be back before it gets dark."

"Sorry, sweetheart. Those vehicles are police property. So that means you're stuck with me."

Her smile was sharp as a blade, and Lane felt the cut from where he stood. "Let's get moving then. If we're lucky, I can be back in New York by this time tomorrow." The words were meant to slice, as if what they'd shared between them had been nothing.

"Let's get moving then. I'd hate to get in your way." Lane grabbed his rain jacket and tossed a spare to Naya, and then he dug around in the closet for rain boots that came up to the knee. "You'll need these or you'll be looking for your shoes in the muck."

"You guys don't mind me," Cooper said, taking a seat in Lane's desk chair. "I'm just going to sit back and enjoy the show."

"I'm certainly glad it's not illegal for me to do this," Naya said, flipping up her middle finger at Cooper. He cracked out a laugh as she tossed the door open and stepped out onto the sidewalk.

"I couldn't have said it better myself," Lane said, following her out into the storm.

* * * *

Water and mud slushed up from the tires of his Bronco and the wipers swished frantically in the thankless task of clearing the windshield.

The trek from downtown Surrender to the country roads was a slow and painstaking process. Limbs had fallen across the roads, and debris, like trashcans and other items found in yards, had been carried some distance from their homes.

"Why did you say you hadn't been a good cop?" Lane asked, breaking the silence since it looked like they were going to be stuck together for a while. "I know you're pissed that Cooper ran a background check on you and that I read it, but I didn't see anything in that paperwork that said you'd been anything other than good at your job."

"You had no right looking into my private life. And I know what kind of cop I was better than anything written in those papers. But it's done, Lane. And I don't want to talk about it or rehash the past."

She turned her head and looked out the side window, and Lane gripped the steering wheel a little tighter in frustration. Also in trepidation, because what he was about to say hadn't been spoken before. Not even to Cooper.

"I was career military," he said softly, his voice barely audible over the rain. "I'm thirty-six, by the way. I enlisted just after 9/11 and hit the ground running. I was a Ranger, so my unit was put in some pretty sticky situations. Over and over again we'd be deployed and come back as a whole unit. When my commanding officer took retirement, his job was offered to me."

Naya had turned some in her seat so her attention was focused on him. Lane kept his eyes on the road, sticking toward the high ground and looking for a good place to unhitch the boat. They wouldn't be dry and warm for much longer.

"It's harder when you're in command," he said. "The sense of responsibility weighs on you. Your only thought going in and out is to make sure your men survive and to leave no one behind. Three years ago my unit was deployed to Kandahar, Afghanistan. There were eight of us doing a routine sweep when we heard yells—terrified screams of women and children and shouting from men. Militant leaders had set a trap for us, using children as bait, though we didn't know at the time that the children were their own—ones they were already training to join their ranks."

He felt the sympathy—the pity—in her stare, but she remained silent.

"The terrorists had gathered the children in the middle of the street, holding guns to their heads while they yelled for us to come out and see what we had caused. My men followed procedure and surrounded them. My sharpshooters were in place, and I'd called for an extra unit to come back us up. But one of my rookies didn't cover himself as he should have—a simple mistake he'd never get the chance to correct. They'd placed shooters at the top of the buildings to pick us off, and they took the shot as soon as they saw him."

Lane would've given anything for a drink—something to wet his throat so the words came out easier, and something to burn on the way down so it reminded him he was still alive. But there was nothing, so he forged ahead.

"All hell broke loose. Bullets flying from every direction. There was nothing to do but cover and wait for help to arrive. By the time it was over, I'd lost all but two of my men."

"I'm sorry," she whispered.

"I could've made different choices," he said, pulling the truck to a stop and backing up to position the boat. "It's torture to hold command, to make choices and demand that your men continue to follow orders even when they're dropping like flies around you. The two who survived—"

He paused and turned off the engine, the silence deafening as he gathered his thoughts. "We managed to regroup and stick together until the backup units came to lay down cover so we could get out. But we watched as the ones firing at us began to seek out the fallen soldiers and gather their bodies in a pile. They doused them with gasoline and set them on fire while we stayed hidden—helpless to do anything about it." His breath was controlled as he let it out softly. "Make sure your men survive and leave no one behind. I failed on both accounts."

She reached out hesitantly and took his hand, squeezing it gently. "I understand what you're saying, and I know this wasn't easy for you to tell me. Why did you?"

"Because I understand what it's like to feel like you didn't do enough. And I understand what it feels like to have no one around to bring you out of the abyss and the nightmares when things get bad. I didn't have a family to come home to. I was an only child and my parents died in a car wreck when I was seventeen. And after the mission in Kandahar was finished and I'd turned in my retirement papers, I pretty much roamed aimlessly for an entire year, living off my pension and traveling from place to place. And then one day I found myself in Surrender and I met Cooper MacKenzie. Before I knew what was happening, the people here became a kind of family, and I found the guilt of surviving didn't weigh quite as heavily as it once had. I'm saying it doesn't hurt to lean on someone every once in a while."

Chapter Eight

Lane's words ate at her while they worked to unhitch the boat and get it into the water. The rain jacket and boots hadn't helped much. They were both soaked to the skin by the time they got into the boat and Lane started the engine.

She didn't have the luxury of falling into a town and job that could become her family. Her brother was in prison, her mother was dead, and her dad had left for parts unknown when she'd barely been walking. Her neighbors didn't know her and there were so many people in New York, no one glanced her way as she walked down crowded sidewalks. She was utterly alone. And maybe what Lane said was right. Maybe the dreams wouldn't be so hard to bear if there was someone to hold her when she woke from them.

Lane steered the boat with expertise, and she had to admit she was glad he'd come along with her. She wouldn't have gotten very far in unfamiliar territory in these kinds of conditions. Limbs swirled in the fast-moving brown water where the roads had once been.

"Look there," she said, pointing through the trees some distance away. It was hard to be sure of the color, but a vehicle had been overturned by the water and only the tail end was visible.

"Let me see if I can get closer. There are too many trees to maneuver through." Limbs scraped along the bottom of the boat, and

Naya pulled her hood around her face to keep the rain out so her vision was clear.

"Could be it. I think it's dark blue, but it could be black."

"Close enough for us to check it out. The first hunting cabin is just up the way."

He put the boat in reverse and headed back to the main road, and Naya dug in her bag for her extra cuffs and the homemade weapon she used to stop the skips who wanted to run.

"Whoa! What the hell is that?" Lane asked, looking very nervous all of a sudden.

Naya grinned and held up the modified sawed-off shotgun. "It shoots sandbags," she explained. "It doesn't hurt the skips too bad, but it doesn't feel real good either when one hits them in the chest with that much force."

"I can imagine. I'll pretend I didn't see that. I'm almost positive it's not legal."

"Sure it is. And pretty damned effective too. I only have to shoot once and it knocks them on their ass. Then all I have to do is slap on the cuffs."

"We're going to have to talk about this fascination you have with handcuffing people," Lane said, arching a brow at her.

She felt her lips twitch and looked the other way so he wouldn't see. She wanted to be mad about him invading her privacy. If she was mad, it'd be easier to walk away. To go back to being alone with a justified reason.

They almost missed the hunting cabin because of a tree that had been knocked over, blocking it from sight.

"Well, I don't think he's staying there." Lane idled the boat a few feet away. "This is residual from the lake runoff. The cabin is in the flood zone, which is why no one uses it anymore. It's just a one-room shack like most of the hunting cabins around here, so what you see is what you get."

Water rushed through broken-out windows and the door hung on one hinge, banging back and forth against the cabin as the water pushed past it.

"Let's head to the other one," she said, starting to feel the prickle of unease at the base of her neck. She gripped her weapon tightly as Lane nodded and drove the boat farther up the road.

"We'll have to get out here and walk to land level," he said, docking by a tree. "The other cabin is on higher ground."

Naya was glad Lane had loaned her the boots when she rolled out of the boat and into water that hit just below her knees. The temperature had dropped steadily and it didn't help that her jeans were soaking wet and her hair plastered to her head, snaking beads of frigid water down the collar of her shirt.

Lane took her arm and they waded to higher ground. Their boots sucked at the mud and the slight incline was slippery enough that she lost her balance a couple of times and had to grab Lane's shoulder to keep from falling.

"Stay low here," he whispered. "The cabin is just over this rise and there isn't a lot of cover if you come at it direct. We'll split off in either direction and come at it from the sides."

It was easy for her to picture him as a commander. His orders were precise and direct, and he had no doubt that they'd be followed to the letter. She nodded and watched his fingers as they counted to three and then gave the "go" sign. Naya crouched low and moved from tree to tree, using them as cover, though she wasn't sure anyone would be able to see that far from the cabin because of the heaviness of the rain.

Her heart thudded in her chest as the little cabin came into view. He was in there. She knew it. Could feel it. No lights showed from the inside, but Coltraine would keep it dark if he suspected someone was outside trying to look in.

She'd be the most exposed on her run from where she was hidden to the side of the cabin. The rain made everything more difficult—more dangerous. She caught movement on the opposite side of the cabin and saw Lane move into position similar to how she was. And then he gave the signal to go and they both ran up to the sides of the cabin, staying low and against the wall once they got there.

There was no back door in a one-room hunting cabin, so they had no choice but to go through the front. She crept around the side of the house and met Lane at the front door, his weapon down at his side. Visions of the last time she'd stood in front of an unknown threat with someone she cared about flashed through her mind and she grabbed Lane's arm, squeezing so he would know to let her go in first.

He looked down at where her hand rested and then back at her face and shook his head. She could see the compassion, but also the steel behind it. Lane would never let someone walk through the door in front of him. It wasn't in his nature.

"On three," he mouthed. "You go low. It'll be fine, love."

He started the count and on three his foot slammed into the door, knocking it back on its hinges. She went in low, her makeshift weapon ready to fire if need be. The first thing she noticed was the smell. Bitter sickness filled the air and she brought her arm over her nose and mouth to block it.

A low moan sounded from the corner of the room, and she and Lane both turned in unison and pointed their weapons at Jackson Coltraine. He was at least twenty pounds lighter then he'd been when he'd left New York a month ago. His face was gaunt and dirty and his clothes ragged. He lay huddled in the corner, and his eyes burned bright with fever.

"Just take me," he said, holding out shaking hands in surrender. "I'm fucking sick. Get me a doctor. Take me in."

"Jesus," Lane said, his mouth tightening in a thin line. "That's just pathetic. Let's get him back to the boat and into town. He can spend the night in jail while we get Doctor MacKenzie to come out and take a look at him. It'd be a shame for him to die before he was able to go to trial."

"It'd at least save some taxpayer money."

"Are you two going to shut up and arrest me or not? I think I might need to throw up again."

"I'll let you take point here," Naya said, elbowing Lane in the side. "You've got the badge."

"You'll owe me one."

"That never turns out to be a bad thing," she winked.

"I said arrest me already! This is police brutality, having to listen to you yammer on."

"Shut up, Coltraine," Lane said, pulling him to his feet and slapping cuffs on. "And if you throw up in my boat, you're going to be sorry."

Chapter Nine

Cooper handed her a cup of hot coffee. They'd brought Coltraine back into town and gotten him behind bars. Coltraine wasn't someone to be trusted, and she didn't want to see anyone hurt because they'd let their guard down. Coltrain might be sick and weak, but he was still dangerous.

She warmed her hands on the cup and didn't care that her chattering teeth knocked against the cup every time she tried to take a drink. Thomas MacKenzie had already been in town helping his brothers make things more organized and assisting those who were without electricity, so they hadn't had to wait long for him to make his way to the jail.

"You should get a shower and get warm," Lane said, coming up beside her. He held his own cup of coffee and his clothes were as soaked as hers. "He's not going anywhere for a while."

"Do me a favor and go into the cell with Doctor MacKenzie. I don't trust Coltraine."

"I can do that. If you'll go up and stop being so stubborn." He handed her his keys so she could get inside. "Your lips are blue."

Naya rolled her eyes and headed down the hall toward the back door and then up the stairs to the apartment. Her time in Surrender was running out. She shouldn't feel such panic at the thought of leaving. This wasn't her home. But Lane was here. And the thought of going home to her own empty apartment wasn't at all appealing.

She'd spent her life on her own, never needing anyone. Her partner had been the closest thing she'd had to a mentor and friend, and he'd died right in front of her eyes. She always thought of his death as a kind of payback for letting herself care for him. Everyone close to her in her life had abandoned her. But the thought of Lane doing the same made her heart hurt. It was why it was best she suck it up and leave before she had to face the disappointment.

She showered quickly and changed into a pair of Lane's sweats she'd found in his drawer. They were much too big for her, but they were warm, which was all she cared about. She brushed the tangles from her hair and left it to dry around her shoulders, and then went into the living room where her belongings were stashed.

She didn't have much to pack, hardly anything at all, but she went through the process anyway to make her leaving more permanent in her mind. She'd set the bags on the table and gone to the kitchen to make more coffee when she heard the knob turn and Lane come in.

His eyes automatically went to her bags and then his heated gaze found her. He stared at her a few seconds, and she wondered what was going through his mind.

"I'm going to grab a quick shower. There's sandwich stuff in the fridge if you're hungry."

She assumed that meant he wanted a sandwich too, so once he went into the bedroom, she started assembling ingredients on the counter. When he came back ten minutes later, Naya's mouth went dry and her throat closed at the sight of him. He wore only a towel tied precariously at his hips.

The knife she'd picked up to cut the sandwiches clattered to the counter, and she forgot what she was doing—that she was trying to keep her distance.

"I—your sandwich. It's ready."

He smiled but didn't say anything as he came toward her. Her nipples hardened against the soft texture of the sweatshirt she wore and her breasts felt heavy. Liquid desire gathered between her thighs and the pulse in her throat jumped as his hand reached out to touch the side of her face.

"Lane—"

"Ssh, sweetheart. Just kiss me." His lips touched the corner of her mouth and then trailed lightly over her jawline.

"This is a mistake," she managed to get out as his teeth tugged at the lobe of her ear. "Don't make this harder than it has to be."

"Why would I make it easy?"

She didn't have an answer to that question. She only knew he'd ruin her if he touched her again. Her hands came up and rested against his chest, the silky hairs tickling her palms, and she meant to push him away. But he moved in, trapping her against the counter so she felt his hard cock pressing against her stomach through the towel.

"Just a kiss, Naya."

It seemed unreasonable to deny him such a simple request. His thumb brushed across her bottom lip once, making her tremble. She'd never trembled for any man. And then his lips touched hers and she was lost in the sensation. This man belonged to her—he was the part of her that had been missing all these years.

He pulled the sweatshirt over her head and jerked the sweatpants down her hips. The towel he wore fell to the floor, rasping over her skin as it went down, but his mouth continued to work its magic, slanting over her lips while his tongue danced erotically against hers.

His hands were gentle, the complete opposite of the need she felt building inside of him and the way his cock pressed against her stomach and branded her with its heat.

He surprised her by picking her up in his arms and carrying her to the bedroom, closing the door behind him with his foot. He laid her on the bed gently, following her down and settling between her thighs while he continued to kiss her. His hands were broad and rough as they made their way over her body, touching every inch of her skin, heating her from the inside out and driving her wild.

The change between them was palpable—panic inducing—and for a moment she wasn't able to breathe as emotions swept through her. It would be easier if he took her as he had before, if it was hands and mouths and a fast coupling that could camouflage the feelings wreaking havoc on her heart and mind.

She needed to touch him. Her hands came up to his shoulders, testing the strength of them before skimming her nails lightly down to the center of his back. Her neck arched as his lips suckled at the sensitive flesh there and she opened her legs, wrapping them around his hips while he slid the rigid stalk of his cock between her bare folds, probing at her entrance.

He didn't enter her—not yet. But he teased them both, heightening the pleasure and prolonging it while they memorized every inch of one another.

"Lane—" she moaned.

"Look what we have, Naya. Would you deny it? Would you run from it?"

She shook her head against the pillow. It was too late for her to deny anything. And she was no longer sure she had the strength to walk away, even as she resigned herself to getting her heart broken once more by someone she loved. *Love.* God, how had that happened?

"Please, Lane. Just love me."

"I am," he whispered. "I do."

And then she felt him probing at her vagina just before he slid inside, his movements slow and easy—tender. She arched against him, accepting all of him, and she wrapped her arms around him in an embrace as he began to move. A slow rocking of flesh against flesh that prolonged the tension building inside of her, so it kept her hovering just on the edge of fulfillment.

"Look at me, Naya," he said, grasping her hands and holding them on either side of her head.

Her eyelids grew heavy, and her whole body arched in anticipation, as if it were on the precipice ready to fall into oblivion. She looked into his eyes and fell deep into his gaze, and then her body clenched and her pussy convulsed as the orgasm rolled through her like a wave. His eyes went opaque and he jerked against her just before he followed her over the edge.

He rolled to his side and brought her with him so she was snuggled close. His heart pounded against her hand and their bodies were damp with sweat.

"I love you," he said, kissing her forehead. "I loved you a year ago when I first met you."

A joy so profound she wasn't sure she could contain it all filled her, and all she could do was hold him tighter. She couldn't speak. And she didn't see the sadness in his eyes when she didn't return the words.

Chapter Ten

The next morning came sooner than Lane wanted. During the night, he and Naya had made love multiple times, turning to each other over and over again. He'd thought she'd eventually say the words he needed to hear, but she never did. But it had *felt* like she loved him every time she touched him, loving him with her mouth and hands and body.

But as soon as the first hint of sunlight peeked through the bedroom window, it was as if the night had never happened. She'd rolled out of bed and dressed, stopping only long enough to make the coffee she seemed to need to survive.

He pulled on a pair of sweats and followed her to the kitchen, wondering how to say what he wanted without scaring her more than he already had.

"Stay," he said. "Don't go back to New York."

She looked up at him in surprise. "I've got to take Coltraine back and get him booked."

"I told you I loved you."

"I know. I love you too. You've made me realize I've kept myself closed off, not letting people in because I've been too afraid of getting hurt."

"So is that it? You've realized what you've been missing and now you're just going to go back to New York and leave Surrender behind? Can you really do that? Just walk away without giving it a chance? Surrender healed me when nothing else would. But I'd leave in a heartbeat if it meant I got to spend another day—another lifetime— with you."

His breathing was harsh and something that felt an awful lot like fear clutched at his belly when he saw the look of surprise on her face. He could feel her slipping out of his grasp like grains of sand.

"And I know I don't have the right to ask, but I'm going to anyway because I've got nothing left to lose. Could you stay? Could you be happy here? Leave the city and your job and your friends for a small town with a bunch of people who will want to know every inch of your past, present, and future?"

She clasped her hands in front of her and took a step closer, her gaze never straying from his. "No," she finally said. "I couldn't stay here for that reason."

Lane felt as if someone had just knifed him in the gut and he was bleeding to death. His body was numb. He'd laid himself bare and she'd rejected him. And dammit, he wouldn't do it again. He had his pride. He nodded stiffly and then turned away to head back to the bedroom. If he didn't escape now he'd end up on his knees begging.

"I couldn't stay here for them," she said before he could get away. "But I could stay here for you. I *will* stay here for you. I told you I loved you too. I meant it. I've been without a family for too long. Be mine."

He felt the smile spread across his face. "Is that a proposal?"

"No, but I'll say yes when you decide to ask me."

He opened his arms, waiting, and then he let out the breath that had been trapped in his lungs as she walked into his embrace.

"It turns out Surrender is in need of another good cop. What do you say to that?"

"I say one step at a time, Deputy Greyson. One step at a time. But feel free to love me in the meantime."

"Always," he said, leaning down to seal the deal with a kiss.

Acknowledgements from the Author

Thanks to my readers who keep asking for more MacKenzies. This is for you. And thanks to Liz and MJ for inviting me to be a part of this amazing project.

About Liliana Hart

Liliana Hart is the *New York Times* and *USA Today* Bestselling Author of more than twenty-five novels. She lives in Texas in a big, rambling house, and she's almost always on deadline. She loves to hear from readers.

The Promise of Surrender
A MacKenzie Family Novella
By Liliana Hart
Coming December 15, 2015

Gretchen Hunt is the newest agent at MacKenzie Security, but she has a lifetime of experience since she spent most of her career in the military police. When she's paired with Justin Livingston for an assignment, she finds that right and wrong isn't as black and white as she once thought it was. Especially since her new partner is one of the greatest jewel thieves in history.

Also from Liliana Hart

THE MACKENZIE FAMILY SERIES
Dane
A Christmas Wish: Dane
Thomas
To Catch A Cupid: Thomas
Riley
Fireworks: Riley
Cooper
1001 Dark Nights: Captured in Surrender
A MacKenzie Christmas
MacKenzie Box Set
Cade
Shadows and Silk
Secrets and Satin
Sins and Scarlet Lace
The MacKenzie Security Series (Includes the 3 books listed above)
Sizzle
Crave

THE COLLECTIVE SERIES
Kill Shot

THE RENA DRAKE SERIES
Breath of Fire

ADDISON HOLMES MYSTERIES
Whiskey Rebellion
Whiskey Sour
Whiskey For Breakfast
Whiskey, You're The Devil

JJ GRAVES MYSTERIES
Dirty Little Secrets
A Dirty Shame
Dirty Rotten Scoundrel
Down and Dirty

STANDALONE NOVELS/NOVELLAS
All About Eve
Paradise Disguised
Catch Me If You Can
Who's Riding Red?
Goldilocks and the Three Behrs
Strangers in the Night
Naughty or Nice

1001 DARK NIGHTS

SILENT BITE
A SCANGUARDS WEDDING

A Scanguards Vampires Novella

NEW YORK TIMES BESTSELLING AUTHOR

TINA FOLSOM

1

At the sight of Ursula's pale neck, Oliver felt a shiver race down his spine and shoot into his balls like a lance. It was a pleasurable kind of pain that he experienced: intense, yet at the same time he didn't want it to stop.

His fingers elongated, and his fingernails turned into sharp barbs. They were the claws of a beast because that's what he still was inside, what he would always be, despite his refined exterior and the gentle shell he wore for everybody.

Ursula was the only one who knew better because she saw it every day and every night: the hunger that still simmered so closely under the surface. The insatiable hunger for blood. But it was different now.

Right after his turning, he'd sunk his fangs into any neck that was unfortunate enough to cross his path. Now, over half a year later, his taste had become much more sophisticated. Still, there was nothing refined about it. Nothing gentle or sweet. Nor civilized.

Only one thing had changed. He cared about the woman who offered her neck night after night more than he'd ever cared about anybody. He'd fallen in love with her before ever tasting her blood, before he even truly knew her, and he wouldn't hesitate to sacrifice his own life in order to save hers.

They hadn't been apart since the night he'd first bitten her, when she'd freely offered him her vein, despite the ordeal she'd been through for three long years. Despite the disgust she'd associated with the act until then. But Ursula had pushed her fears aside and given herself to him, trusted him and put the nightmare she'd experienced at the blood brothel aside.

For him.

Because she trusted him not to hurt her.

"What's wrong?" Ursula's voice came from the closet from which she removed her clothes and packed them into several large boxes.

"This!" He pointed to the moving boxes.

She tilted her head to the side and sighed heavily, her almond-shaped eyes begging for understanding. When she pushed a strand of her straight, raven-black hair behind her shoulder, the gesture reminded him of what it felt like when he buried his face in her hair and smelled her unique scent, a scent that came from her special blood. Blood that had the power to drug a vampire. Blood so addictive that his friends and colleagues at Scanguards had tried to keep him from her when they'd first found out.

"But we agreed," she said softly.

Oliver took a step toward her, the beast inside him howling and demanding to be let out of its cage. "I know we agreed, but that doesn't mean I have to like it."

"It's not easy for me either," she replied, dropping a stack of T-shirts into a box and moving toward him with cat-like grace.

He'd always found her beautiful, ever since the first night she'd literally fallen into his arms in one of the dingiest parts of San Francisco. He realized that he'd never had a chance at resisting her, not even if her blood had been ordinary. Not even then would he have been able to disentangle himself from the Asian beauty who made his heart race whenever he looked at her.

Though his heart wasn't the only organ that coveted her.

How he was supposed to survive without her, he couldn't fathom.

"Please," she whispered when she reached him, placing her palm on his cheek. "Don't make this any harder than it is."

At her choice of words, he took her hand and slipped it to the front of his jeans, pressing it against the bulge that had formed there. The bulge that was ever present when he was near her.

"Harder?" he echoed. "I don't think it can get any harder."

Ursula chuckled. "Is that all you think of?"

Oliver slid his hand on her nape, pulling her to him. "No. I also think of not being able to do this."

He brought his lips to hers, gently pressing against her mouth. When he licked against the seam of her lips, she parted them lightly, and her breath rushed toward him.

"Hmm," she hummed.

"Won't you reconsider?" he coaxed her.

"I can't."

But he didn't want to accept her answer. "Imagine what you'll be missing." He captured her mouth fully and slid his tongue between her parted lips, exploring her warmth, dancing with her tongue.

Ursula severed her lips from his. "Oliver, we don't have time."

"Just one last time," he insisted and busied himself with tugging on her T-shirt, sliding it up her torso.

"But—"

He silenced her protest with a kiss and slid his hands underneath her shirt, caressing her soft skin. When his hands moved high up and encountered her bra, he stopped for a brief moment. Why she bothered to wear one, he wasn't sure. Her young breasts were perfectly firm and round and needed no support. Besides, she never wore it for long, because he always found a way of stripping her of it so he could caress her boobs whenever he wanted to—which was frequently.

It took Oliver all of two seconds to find the clasp of her bra and open it. Immediately, he slid his hands under her bra and cupped her breasts, squeezing them lightly.

She moaned into his mouth, and at the same time he heard her heartbeat accelerate. Touching her breasts and fondling her nipples never failed to arouse her. Even though they didn't have the time for this now, she responded to him as if her body couldn't help itself.

"There you go, baby," he murmured, releasing her lips for a brief moment. "You want this too." He inhaled her heady scent. "You can't wait to feel me inside you."

"Oliver, this is crazy. We have to get to the airport." Despite her protest, she didn't push him away but pressed her pelvis against his rigid cock.

"We have a few minutes."

And he was going to take advantage of the time they had left. Without allowing her any further protest, he pulled her T-shirt over her head and slipped the bra off her shoulders, dropping it carelessly to the floor.

"Undress me," he ordered while he gazed at her beautiful breasts that were topped with dark nipples. Hard nipples. Yes, there was no denying that she was as aroused as he.

Ursula let out a sigh.

"You know I'll make it worth your while. I always do," he whispered, pressing a kiss to her neck and grazing her skin with the sharp fangs that had already descended.

She shivered under the contact. "Oh God."

No more protests came over her lips. Instead, her hands went to work, freeing him of his shirt, then opening the button and zipper of his pants. When she pushed them over his hips, he helped her and stepped out of them. Before she could free him of his boxer briefs, he helped her take off her own pants.

She wore only a tiny G-string that barely covered any of her enticing flesh. On top of it, the material was practically see-through and hid nothing from his vampire vision.

Oliver licked his lips in anticipation of what would happen now. He loved satisfying two of his greatest cravings at once. Two birds with one stone. Not only was it utterly thrilling to take her blood while he was inside her, in his and Ursula's case it was also necessary. Only after she achieved an orgasm would the drugging effect of her blood be muted for a short while so that imbibing on it wouldn't turn him into a crazed addict. Less than an hour after her orgasm, her blood would be just as dangerous as before and therefore off-limits to him.

Oliver slipped his hand into her panties, combing through the neatly trimmed triangle of curls that guarded her sex, and headed farther south. Warmth and wetness greeted his foraging fingers. Instantly, his cock began to jerk, wanting to feel what his fingers felt.

"Take my cock out," he ground out, impatient for her touch because no matter how often he'd made love to her in the last few months, every time was different and new. And more thrilling than the last time.

Moments later, he felt her hands push down his boxer briefs, sliding them down his legs. Then one hand wrapped around him.

"Like that?" Ursula asked with a provocative tone in her voice.

"Yes, just like that, as if you didn't know it."

She squeezed his cock in her hand, making his heart pound into his throat.

"Fuck, baby!"

He groaned loudly and threw his head back, for a moment reveling in her tender touch. Then his fingers moved, bathing themselves in her wetness before sliding higher again to where her center of pleasure resided. When he slid one finger over it, pressing lightly, her eyelids fluttered and her throat released an audible gasp. He knew her body so well, knew exactly how to make her purr like a kitten, how to make her writhe underneath him in ecstasy, and how to make her shudder in his arms. And he couldn't get enough of it, of seeing her lips curl into a sensual smile, her eyes darken with passion, and her body tremble with desire.

Because in turn it caused a reaction in him: his entire body began to burn with need, the need to possess her, to make her his forever. Desire scorched him from the inside. The smoldering embers of his love for her ignited anew every time he looked at her sinful body, every time he kissed her sensual lips and touched her silken skin. It was as if she'd bewitched him by looking at him with her almond-shaped eyes as if he were the only man who mattered to her.

Just as she looked at him now.

"Take me," she murmured, her lips barely moving. "I need to feel you."

"I thought you'd never ask."

Within seconds he'd placed her on the bed, stripped her of her panties, and spread her legs. He'd taken her every way possible in the last few months, but what he still liked best was Ursula underneath him and looking into her eyes when he drove into her. He loved seeing her reaction when he plunged into her tight pussy and stretched her. Loved the way her breath rushed out of her lungs when he drove deeper than she thought he could. Loved the way her breasts bounced from side to side and up and down with each thrust.

"Don't make me wait," Ursula begged now.

A smile built on Oliver's lips. He hadn't even noticed that he'd been simply staring at her, feasting his eyes on her beauty. "No, my love, I'll never make you wait."

Then he brought his cock to her nether lips and plunged forward, seating himself balls-deep. A shudder ran down his spine and shot into his balls, threatening to unman him. It was always like that with her. The first thrust into her tight, silken sheath always did that to him because it was the moment he remembered what he missed most when she wasn't lying in his arms, panting. He missed the way she imprisoned him within her. The way she chained him to her body and her soul with only the tiniest squeeze of her interior muscles that she was probably not even aware of.

Whenever he felt her squeeze him like that, it felt as if his heart were being squeezed in the same way. As if she held his heart in her hand. Because she did. Because his heart belonged to her.

When he felt Ursula's hands on his hips, urging him to move, he complied with her wishes, falling into a rhythm that she dictated. Slowly, he drove in and out of her, shifting his angle so that with each descent his pelvis rocked against her clit. At the beginning of their relationship, she'd had problems letting herself go, but they'd overcome that obstacle and Ursula now responded to him freely and without inhibitions, her body pushing against him to increase the pressure on her clit. He reacted to her sign and started moving faster while he tried to stave off his own need to climax, a task which became more and more difficult by the second.

He tried to distract himself, but as he looked down at her, he saw how small rivulets of sweat ran from her neck through the valley of her breasts. It made her skin glow even more intensely and her scent more powerful, drawing him to her even more.

"Oh, God, baby!" he ground out, all too aware that his fangs were at full length and itching for a bite. "I need you to come!" Only then could he plunge his fangs into her lovely neck and find his own release.

"So close," she whispered between pants.

"What do you need, baby? Tell me!"

"Please."

Her back arched off the bed, her breasts thrusting toward him. Oliver dipped his head and captured one nipple, sucked on it greedily, his fangs grazing the sensitive peak. Underneath him, Ursula shivered, her body trembling now.

He moved to the other breast, repeating the same action, while he continued driving his cock deeper into her tight pussy. His hips worked at a rapid tempo, thrusting and withdrawing in quick succession. Another few thrusts and he would be unable to hold back his need to plunge his fangs into her flesh; another few thrusts and he would take her blood and allow it to drug him despite the disaster this would spell for both of them. Despite the fact it would destroy him.

His entire body began to tremble, and he knew he'd lost. This was his doom. Ursula was his doom, just like they'd all predicted. He wasn't strong enough to resist the temptation her blood represented.

His lips widened as he set his fangs to either side of her nipple and took a last breath. He pierced her skin and closed his eyes, knowing he'd failed, when a shudder went through Ursula's body as her orgasm washed over her.

Relief flooded him at the same time as warm blood rushed into his mouth and down his throat. Had he been able to speak, he would have thanked her for having saved him once more, but he couldn't let go of the breast he was sucking on. Her blood tasted rich and sweet. Perfect. And to take it from her breast had become one of his favorite places to drink. Right along with her inner thigh, where he could soak in her arousal at the same time as he fed from her.

"Oh, yes." She encouraged him now, her hand sliding to his nape to press him closer to her breast.

Oliver knew how much she loved feeding him like this because it was something only he did. None of the leeches at the blood brothel she'd been imprisoned at for three long years had ever been allowed to take her blood from anywhere else than her neck or wrist.

With one last thrust, he came and flooded her tight channel with his seed. His entire body shook from the intensity of his climax. It took long moments before he could think clearly again and was able to retract his fangs from her breast. Gently he licked over the two small incisions, sealing them instantly. There would be no scars. His saliva guaranteed it.

Oliver dropped his head next to hers, breathing heavily.

"Wow. I love it when you do it like that."

He lifted his head to look at her. "How?"

"All out of control."

He shook his head. "It was close. I almost bit you before you climaxed. But I—"

She put a finger to his lips, stopping him from continuing. "Almost. I'll make sure it won't happen."

Oliver dropped his forehead to hers. "I thought it had gotten easier, but it hasn't. What if one day you won't come in time?"

"Then we'll deal with it. Together." She gave him a soft slap on his backside. "Besides, you can always make me come."

He chuckled. "That's what a guy likes to hear." He pressed a gentle kiss on her lips.

"It's time to go," she murmured back.

"I know."

2

Ursula fidgeted as she nervously watched the escalator that descended from the arrival level to the baggage claim area at San Francisco International Airport where she and Oliver were waiting. She turned to him.

"You know what to tell them, right?" she asked.

Oliver clasped her hand then led it to his lips, pressing a soft kiss on her knuckles. "Don't look so anxious! Your parents will wonder whether something is wrong."

She sighed. "Well, that's because something *is* wrong. I've been living in sin with you, and if they ever find out—"

"What are they gonna do? Force me to marry you?" He chuckled. "Guess what? That's what we're gonna do anyway."

"Still, there's no need to upset them."

"Upset them? I thought they liked me."

"They do," she hastened to assure him. "Though I'm sure they would have preferred if I married a nice Chinese boy instead."

Oliver grimaced. "Hey, two out of three ain't bad."

"Two out of what three?" she asked.

He lifted his fingers and started counting. "Good looking and great in bed." He shrugged.

Ursula shook her head and rolled her eyes. "Yeah, about the latter.

I'm sure my parents wouldn't appreciate the fact that I shacked up with you for all these months while they thought I was living at the dorms at UC Berkeley."

"Shacking up with me? I'd hardly call it that." He gave her a soft smile, his eyes dropping to her lips and his head inching closer. "Actually, I preferred it when you called it 'living in sin.' It's got a much nicer ring to it."

Ursula nudged him in the ribs. "You're terrible. I wish you'd take this seriously."

"You mean the 'living in sin' part? I take it very seriously. And I thought you liked it. I did. Immensely."

She felt her entire body flush with heat. He could do that to her with the way he gazed into her eyes, his mouth parting, and his fangs starting to elongate as a sign of his desire for her.

"Oliver, your fangs," she whispered under her breath.

He closed his mouth instantly and swallowed. "See what you do to me. You start talking about sin, and I turn all primal."

She couldn't help but smile. "Maybe then it's a good thing we're getting married. At least then it won't be considered a sin anymore."

Oliver bent to her, placing a soft kiss near her ear. "I don't care what it's called. It won't change the way I feel about you. Nor the fact that the next week will be pure torture for me."

She lifted her eyes to meet his look. "It's the only way we can hide from my parents what's been going on the last few months."

He let out a resigned sigh.

"Let's go over the story again, just so we don't trip ourselves up," she suggested and cast another look up the escalator as more people started to descend.

"Okay," Oliver agreed. "You've been living at the dorms, but in order to prepare for the wedding, you moved into the guestroom in my parents' house today, and your parents will be staying in my room, while I move in with Samson until the wedding." He shoved a hand through his unruly dark hair. "I hope I can remember to call Quinn Dad. At least Rose I can still call Rose."

"Why?"

"Well, she's not my mother. I'm only related to Quinn as my sire. So, we should tell your parents that Rose is my stepmother. That way, I won't trip myself up when I address her as Rose."

Panic gripped Ursula. Last-minute changes to an established plan always spelled disaster. "Did you talk to Quinn and Rose about that already?"

Oliver squeezed her hand. "Don't worry about it. I discussed it with them and also with Blake."

Relieved, Ursula let out a breath. "Okay. And Blake knows what to say and do?"

Blake, who was human and Rose and Quinn's fourth great-grandson, could be a goofball, but she hoped that he would stick to the plan they'd put together and help them fool her parents that the Ralston-Haverford-Bond family—Quinn Ralston, Rose Haverford, Blake Bond, and Oliver, who had taken Quinn's last name after his turning—was a typical American family and didn't consist of three vampires and a human.

"Blake will be on his best behavior. I promise you that."

Ursula rolled her eyes. "Right."

"I'll keep him in line. He's still scared shitless that I'll bite him again. So, don't worry about him."

She smiled at him softly. "But that's a bluff. I know you won't bite him. You don't even like his blood."

Oliver pulled her closer, turning her into his body. "That's because you spoiled me with yours. Everything else tastes like battery acid to me." He inhaled deeply. "Oh God, I can smell your blood now."

Ursula shivered as he placed his lips on her neck and kissed her gently. "You've gotta stop. People are looking at us."

"You're killing me, baby. I hope you know what you're asking of me to stay out of your bed for an entire week." He lifted his head, and their gazes locked. The rim of his irises shimmered golden, a sign that his vampire side was emerging.

She caressed his cheek. "I know, my love. I'll make it up to you later."

"How?" he asked, his voice a husky murmur.

She chuckled quietly. "Since when don't you have any imagination?" She let her hand slide to his neck and scratched her fingernails against it, feeling how his skin turned to gooseflesh underneath her touch.

Oliver groaned. "I can't wait. After this evening, I've gotten the taste for a lot more." His eyes seemed to penetrate her. "To suckle from your breast was—"

"Oh, no!" she interrupted him in panic. She'd just remembered something. "My bra!"

He looked at her, startled. "What's with your bra?"

She grabbed his arm. "It's still in your bedroom! I didn't pick it up. Where did it go? Did you pick it up when we moved the boxes with my stuff to the guestroom?"

He shook his head. "I don't think so. I didn't notice it anywhere."

Ursula's pulse raced. "Oh God, my mother is gonna find it and then she'll know."

"Is it really gonna be such a problem?" he asked softly.

"Yes!"

Oliver sighed and pulled his cell from his pocket. "Fine. I'll take care of it."

"How?"

He unlocked his cell and started typing. "I'll text Blake to look for it."

"Blake?" Embarrassment swept through her. "You can't have Blake look for my bra!"

Oliver tilted his head to the side. "Rose went out shopping, so she can't do it. So if you don't want your mother to find it in my room, then it's going to have to be Blake."

Ursula ground her teeth. "Oh, crap!" Her gaze drifted to a crowd of people coming down the escalator.

He chuckled. "I'm assuming that's a 'yes'?"

She nodded reluctantly and glanced at him as he pressed "send" on his cell phone before slipping it back into his pocket. She'd had no choice, because she'd just spotted her parents at the top of the escalator. There was no time to come up with another solution.

"They're here!"

From the top of the escalator, her parents descended, their eyes scanning the waiting area below. Her mother, a petite woman with impeccable taste and style, wore a costume that looked like it was designed by Chanel, though Ursula knew that her mother would never spend that kind of money on clothes. She was a veritable bargain hunter, and Ursula was sure that she hadn't spent more than a hundred dollars for her entire outfit including her shoes and her fancy handbag.

Involuntarily, Ursula had to smile. Her mother would be shocked if she found out how much money Oliver's family was spending on this wedding. Her parents were well off, with her father earning an exceptionally large salary as a high-level diplomat for the Chinese embassy in Washington D.C., so there was no need for her mother to be frugal, but it was so ingrained in her that she just couldn't help herself. It seemed almost like a sport to her.

Ursula waved as she caught her father's eye. He beamed at her, then touched his wife's arm to point to where Ursula and Oliver stood waiting. Excitedly, her mother waved back, but Ursula's gaze wandered back to her father. It seemed as if he'd lost weight. His face looked paler than usual too. She shook her head. The neon lights weren't flattering for anybody's skin tone. It had to be an optical illusion or the fact that he was tired from the flight.

When her parents reached the bottom steps of the escalator and stepped off it, Ursula flung herself into their arms, reaching around them both and hugging them tightly.

"I missed you!" she said, pushing back the tears.

"We missed you too, Wei Ling," her father said, calling her by her Chinese name as he did so often.

"You're going to squash your mother if you hold on any tighter," Oliver said from behind her and put a hand on her shoulder.

Ursula stepped out of their embrace, wiping away a tear that had escaped her eye.

Oliver moved to her side and stretched out his hand toward her mother first. "It's very nice to see you again, Mrs. Tseng."

Her mother took his hand and shook it, then put her other hand over it to clasp it. "Young man, maybe it's time to stop calling me Mrs. Tseng. My name is Hui Lian," she said with the Chinese accent that even after two decades in the US had not diminished.

Oliver grinned. "I'd like that very much, Hui Lian." Then he turned to her father and shook his outstretched hand. "It's good to see you, sir."

"Call me Yao Bang. And considering you're stealing my only daughter from me, I'm rather happy to see you too. It's good to know she'll be in good hands."

Her parents exchanged a look.

All of a sudden, a strange sense of unease slithered down Ursula's back like a snake. A cold shiver followed.

"Well, let's get your luggage so we can get you home," Oliver announced and motioned toward the carousels.

* * * *

He shouldn't even be on the arrival level at San Francisco International Airport, but he'd followed a particularly tasty smelling woman who'd made her way down there from the departure level where he'd been about to check in for the red-eye to New York. When he'd smelled her enticing blood, he'd decided to get one last *snack* before his flight and had followed her.

He was done with San Francisco. After he'd been captured by people from Scanguards, the self-appointed police force and self-righteous group of vampires who thought themselves above everybody else, they'd incarcerated him and others like him for several months and forced them to undergo a detox program. Rehab they'd called it!

He and the other vampires had been addicted to special blood from Chinese blood whores that a blood brothel in Hunter's Point had provided. But one day the blood brothel had disappeared and shortly afterwards, Scanguards had killed its owner and the guards, taken the girls away, and rounded up the clients. To make them undergo treatment!

What a crock of shit that was! He knew that now. And the reason he knew it was because there at one of the luggage carousels, one of Scanguards so-called bodyguards stood, his arm around one of the blood whores he recognized. And from the fragments of conversation he picked up, he realized that this vampire, who he'd met before and whose name was Oliver, if he wasn't mistaken, was getting married to this blood whore.

Hadn't the people from Scanguards said that all the blood whores had been sent home? Clearly, they'd dished up a bunch of lies, trying to pacify him and the other addicts, while behind their backs they were keeping the blood whores for themselves.

His mouth salivated as the girl's smell drifted to him. He pulled the scent deep into his lungs. Instantly, his sense memory projected vivid images into his mind. He'd never experienced anything as exhilarating as the blood of these women. It was special, and it acted like a drug to a vampire. He'd experienced that drug and had never felt a high as powerful as when he'd been suckling on the neck of one of the blood whores.

His gut clenched as the same hunger resurfaced now. He'd thought he was clean, but it appeared rehab hadn't worked. He wanted the drugged blood of this woman. And it wasn't fair that the people from Scanguards kept this treat for themselves. What hypocrites! They'd made him and the others suffer through the symptoms of withdrawal while they gorged themselves on the delicious blood.

The woman he'd followed earlier was forgotten, as was his flight to New York. He wasn't leaving. No, he would stay and get his fair share. The Chinese girl on Oliver's arm would become his meal. He would show those arrogant men from Scanguards that he had just as much a right to this blood as they.

He would show Oliver that he had no right to monopolize her.

3

Oliver set the two suitcases down inside his room and turned around, motioning his soon-to-be in-laws to enter.

"I hope you'll be comfortable here."

Ursula's parents stepped into the room and let their eyes roam, while Ursula walked in behind them, her eyes equally examining the bedroom, though he was sure she was searching for her bra. Blake had not texted him back, therefore it was possible that he'd either not received the text instructing him to search for the bra or was out.

"We could have easily stayed at a hotel," Ursula's mother said. "There was no need to go through all this trouble."

"No trouble at all," he replied quickly. "My parents thought it would be best if you two took my room. And Ursula will be in the guestroom. That way, you're all together, which makes it much easier for all the wedding preparations."

Ursula's father looked at his daughter. "You're staying in this house, Wei Ling?"

"Uh, yes, Dad, but only because of the preparations for the wedding. I just moved my stuff from the dorms this morning. It would be such a trek each day to get over the bridge from Berkeley and back. I would waste too much time, and there's so much to do," Ursula replied hastily.

"I don't think it's appropriate for you to stay in the same house as Oliver. It's bad luck," her mother cut in and turned toward Oliver. "I'm sorry, Oliver, but we can't do that. We can move to a hotel with Ursula. Somewhere central."

Oliver took a steadying breath. Ursula had warned him that her parents were old-fashioned as well as superstitious. "It's really not an issue. I won't be staying here this week. I'm going to stay at my boss's house until the wedding."

Mrs. Tseng raised an eyebrow. "Your boss's house? That's very generous of him to let you stay. Well, then, of course . . . " She exchanged a look with her husband.

Ursula's father nodded. "Thank you, Oliver. That's very thoughtful of you. This looks very comfortable and spacious."

Relieved, Oliver pointed to a door. "You have your own bathroom and sitting area so you can relax. But feel free to use any part of the house. I'll show you around once you've had a chance to freshen up."

His sensitive hearing picked up the sound of footsteps on the stairs. Then a human smell drifted to him. He recognized the smell immediately. A moment later, Blake popped his head through the door.

"Hey!" he said.

"Hui Lian, Yao Bang, meet my half-brother, Blake. Blake, these are Ursula's parents, Mr. and Mrs. Tseng."

Blake let a big smile spread over his face as he walked toward them and shook their hands. "So nice to finally meet you. Ursula talks about you day and night."

"Day and *night?*" her father repeated, aiming a stern look in Ursula's direction.

Crap! Oliver thought. Leave it to Blake to say something that could get them in trouble. "What Blake means is Ursula speaks of you whenever she visits. You know, during the day."

Oliver felt sweat build on his nape. He tossed a displeased glance at Blake who shrugged, while Ursula's parents looked at their daughter.

"Yes, I told you, Dad. Oliver's family invites me over for dinner quite often," Ursula added and smiled.

Well, it wasn't entirely a lie, only that Ursula had become *Oliver's* favorite dinner and that after being invited to stay for the first time, she'd never left. But then, those were only minor details, albeit details they had to keep from her parents. Together with the other minor detail they had to hide: the fact that they were guests in a vampire household, and that their daughter was marrying a vampire.

What the hell had he been thinking? This would never work! Not his union with Ursula. No, they would be perfect together, but keeping the secret about what he was from her parents.

"When will we meet your parents, Oliver?" Ursula's father suddenly asked.

"They should be back any minute. I believe Rose had some shopping to do," Oliver replied, glad that the subject had turned to something less precarious than sleeping arrangements and how much time Ursula spent at his house.

"Rose? You call your mother by her first name?" Yao Bang asked in surprise.

"Well, she's my stepmother, so I've always called her Rose instead of Mom."

"Ah," Ursula's mother interrupted. "So, Rose is your mother then, Blake?"

"Yes, but, uh, well, since Oliver always called her Rose when we grew up, I call her Rose too."

Oliver turned so Ursula's parents couldn't see his face and rolled his eyes at Blake. Did he have to change the rules of the game? They'd expressly discussed who would call whom what. And now Blake threw a wrench into the whole machinery. Soon, this would blow up in their faces.

"Uh, I see," Mr. Tseng commented. "Well, as long as you all get on." Then he turned to peruse the room once more, his wife doing the same.

She walked closer to the bed and placed her handbag onto it.

"Oh, dear!" Mrs. Tseng suddenly said with a start and looked in the direction of his nightstand. Oliver followed her gaze, but Ursula's father was blocking his view.

Oliver turned to Ursula next to him, catching her panicked look, while he heard how her heartbeat accelerated. Clearly, she was thinking the same as he was: his mother had spotted Ursula's bra on the floor.

He had no choice now. He had to wipe her parents' memories to make sure that they never remembered seeing Ursula's incriminating underwear in his bedroom. He took a deep breath when he felt Blake's hand on his shoulder. Instantly he turned to him. His half-brother gave a slight shake with his head and dropped his gaze. Oliver followed it to Blake's jeans pocket. A little bit of black lace peeked from it. He grinned and shoved it down with his hand, making it disappear from Oliver's view.

Oliver mouthed a silent "thank you" to him and turned back to his future in-laws. If Mrs. Tseng hadn't found the bra, then what was she looking at?

With trepidation, Oliver took a few steps to walk around Mr. Tseng and saw what Mrs. Tseng was finding so offensive.

He had to stifle a laugh when he finally set eyes on the offending item. There, between his nightstand and the bed frame, one of his boxer briefs had gotten caught and hung suspended between the two pieces of furniture.

"I'm so sorry," he said hastily, grabbed the item and balled it up in his fist, then attempted to shove it in his jacket pocket.

"Maybe it was too inconvenient to get you to give up your room after all. We really shouldn't have imposed," her mother said.

"No, no. You're not imposing at all. I'm sorry. I guess I was in a hurry today."

Yeah, he sure had been in a hurry—in a hurry to make love to Ursula one more time before he was forced to move out of the house until the wedding. When he'd gotten dressed after they'd made love, he'd been in such a daze that he hadn't found his boxer briefs instantly and simply grabbed a new pair from his chest of drawers.

When he heard sounds behind him, he sighed in relief. The cavalry had arrived.

"Well, it looks like our guests are here," Quinn said from the door as he walked in, his wife Rose on his heels.

"I'm so sorry we weren't here to greet you," Rose instantly apologized and stretched her hand out to Ursula's mother.

"This is Rose, my stepmother, and this is Quinn, my father," Oliver introduced them. "Dad, Rose, these are Hui Lian and Yao Bang Tseng."

He watched as the faces of Ursula's parents turned to surprise while they shook hands and exchanged greetings with Rose and Quinn.

"You both seem so young," Ursula's mother said finally. Mr. Tseng nodded in agreement.

"Good genes," Quinn replied with a broad smile on his face.

"We get that all the time!" Rose chirped with a soft laugh and exchanged a loving look with her blood-bonded mate. "We were practically kids when we met. We got married when we were very young."

Oliver swept a quick gaze over Quinn and Rose. Both didn't only look like they were in their mid-twenties, they also looked nothing like him or Blake. While both he and Blake were dark haired, their supposed parents were both blond and had fair skin. There was no family resemblance among the four of them and rightly so. Quinn had sired Oliver with his blood and turned him into a vampire when he lay dying after a horrific car accident, and Blake, though he was their blood relative, hadn't retained any of Rose's and Quinn's fair looks. Blake was six generations removed from them, and they were in fact his fourth great-grandparents.

"I hope you'll both be comfortable here," Quinn continued.

"We didn't really want to put Oliver out by taking over his room," Ursula's father replied, motioning to his surroundings. "But thank you very much. I'm sure we'll be very comfortable here."

"Excellent!" Quinn agreed.

"Once you've unpacked and freshened up, why don't you come downstairs, and I'll show you around?" Rose offered. "It'll be chaotic in the next few days with preparing for the wedding, so I've had the kitchen stocked with everything you might need, and rather than have regular sit-down lunches and dinners, I figured everybody should just help themselves to anything they want. Don't you think so too?" She smiled at Mrs. Tseng.

Ursula's mother looked at her somewhat stunned, but then nodded.

Rose smiled. They'd agreed on this arrangement when discussing how to hide the fact from the Tsengs that neither Rose, Quinn, nor Oliver consumed any food. "It'll be so much easier considering we'll all have different schedules. What with the tent being built, the last-minute fittings for the dress, and whatever else comes up."

"A tent?" Ursula's father suddenly asked. "What for?"

Quinn stepped forward and put his arm around Mr. Tseng's shoulder. "I'll show you." He led him to the window and pointed to the garden below. "We'll have a large tent erected that will cover the entire backyard. The ceremony and reception will take place there."

Oliver watched as Mrs. Tseng stepped next to her husband. "Oh, that sounds nice."

Ursula nudged closer to Oliver, and he instantly pulled her against him, stealing a kiss while her parents looked out the window.

"It'll be perfect," he whispered into her ear, gently nibbling on her earlobe. "And afterwards, I'll make you mine forever."

4

He'd been watching the house half the night until Oliver emerged and left on foot shortly past two o'clock. He was alone. The blood whore wasn't with him. She was still inside the house, together with her parents and two other vampires, as well as a human male.

He waited until Oliver had completely disappeared from his view before leaving his hiding place across the street and approaching the house.

It would take some planning to get to the girl, since she was still surrounded by too many people, two of which were vampires. Had they all been human, he would simply walk into the house now and snatch her. The humans would turn into collateral damage. However, the two vampires could be trouble.

But he wasn't giving up easily. He'd continue to observe and find a weak spot. Like a tiger, he would lie in wait and watch his prey until an opportunity presented itself. Then he'd make his move and steal the blood whore right from under their noses. If the vampires who ran Scanguards thought they could put up rules for others but not live by them themselves, then he'd show them what he thought of that.

His gaze wandered to the windows on the upper floors. Some of them were still illuminated. He stood still and watched. Waited. He knew how to do that, how to stand silently without moving for hours.

How to barely breathe so as not to make a sound. How to remain almost invisible. How to blend in.

Inside him, his hunger grew. Though it was impossible, he thought he could smell the blood whore's blood from where he stood in the shadows of a lush tree. Yes, he'd missed that smell, that taste. He'd missed it while he'd been in rehab. While this crazy psychiatrist Dr. Drake had blathered about restraint and willpower as they'd sat around in groups to talk about how they *felt* about their addiction. Oh, he'd hated those sessions! But he'd played along because he knew if he didn't, they'd never release him. It had taken a long time. Longer than for many of the other vampires. He'd been among the last group to be released from the underground cells at Scanguards, which had turned into a clandestine treatment center complete with daily visits by Dr. Drake and his hot little assistant with the enormous rack.

Shame that she was a vampire. Had she been human, he would have dug his fangs into her tits first chance he got. Instead, the prisoners had been fed bottled blood. Cold, lifeless blood. He'd hated that too. But again, he'd played along. All so they would release him.

And while he'd been suffering in his cell, fighting against his hunger for that special blood, fighting his urge to lash out at his captors, Oliver had been gorging himself on one of the blood whores. Well, not for much longer. Soon, she would be his.

I'm coming for you, *Ursula*.

* * * *

Oliver greeted Delilah, Samson's wife, who opened the door for him.

"So we've got you back for a week," she said smilingly and kissed him on the cheek.

Behind her, Isabelle staggered into the hallway before falling onto her butt, chuckling.

"Wow!" Oliver exclaimed and walked toward the toddler. "She's walking!"

"Yes, she started last week, and every day she gets more secure on her two feet. I think she might be able to walk at your wedding."

He stretched his arms toward Isabelle and lifted her up. "You mean she could be our little flower girl?"

"Just in case, I bought her a cute pink dress so she's got something appropriate to wear. But don't tell Ursula yet, because I don't know whether she'll be walking well enough by then." She stroked her hand over Isabelle's dark hair. "I had no idea that hybrids grew up so fast."

Isabelle beamed at her, flashing her tiny fangs.

"Oh, no, Isabelle! What did we talk about? No showing of fangs! Just like we practiced. There'll be a lot of humans around this week, and we don't want you to expose us, do we?"

Isabelle dropped her lids and closed her mouth, clearly understanding her mother's words.

"Now try again," Delilah encouraged her.

The toddler parted her lips and flashed her mother another grin. This time no fangs showed.

"Perfect." Delilah kissed her on the cheek and Isabelle reached her arms out to her.

Oliver released her and handed her over to her mother. "I'm sure she'll do perfectly fine." Then he changed the subject. "So, is Samson home or is he at headquarters?"

Delilah motioned to the back of the house. "He's in his private office. Drake is here. And so are Gabriel and Zane. Samson said to join them when you arrive."

"Thanks." He turned toward the long wood-paneled corridor leading to the back of the house.

"Oh, and Oliver," Delilah called after him, "I prepared the newly renovated guestroom in the attic for you. That way you won't get woken by Isabelle."

He looked over his shoulder. "Thanks, Delilah. Hope it wasn't too much trouble."

She made a dismissive gesture with her hand. "No trouble. We love having you here. Samson misses you."

In many ways, he missed Samson too. For over three years, when he'd still been human, he'd worked for the owner of Scanguards as his personal assistant. He'd been his eyes and ears during the day, watching out for him while he slept, trading shifts with Carl, his vampire butler. Oliver sighed heavily. He missed Carl. They'd been friends despite the fact that they couldn't have been more different. But Carl was gone.

Oliver pushed away the sad thoughts and knocked at the door to Samson's study.

"Come!" Samson's voice came from the inside.

He turned the knob and opened the door, then closed it behind him. Samson sat at his massive desk, while Dr. Drake, Gabriel, and

Zane lounged on the sofa and the comfortable armchair.

"Hey, Oliver, you're just in time. Dr. Drake just arrived to give us an update," Samson greeted him and motioned him to sit.

With his short black hair, his hazel eyes, and an imposing over-six-foot frame, Samson was every inch the boss. He was the founder of Scanguards, the national security company that provided bodyguards to celebrities, politicians, and other wealthy individuals and organizations who could afford their services.

Opposite him, Dr. Drake, the only vampire psychiatrist—and one of the only two vampires trained as medical professionals in San Francisco—looked scrawny and lanky. Oliver had always found him an odd sort, though Samson and several others at Scanguards had used his services at one time or another.

"Great!" Oliver took a seat on the couch next to Zane. "Hey, guys!"

"Hey!" Zane ground out, clearly not happy to be in the same room as Drake.

He'd once been forced to attend a session with the psychiatrist and apparently not enjoyed it. Not that Oliver could blame the bald vampire. Zane wasn't one for *soft* things, emotions and the like. He was a lean, mean fighting machine, even though Oliver had seen glimpses of a softer side inside him when he'd first met his mate, Portia, a young hybrid. But at the moment, none of that softness was apparent. Zane looked as if he wanted to kill somebody.

"I think it was too early to let them go," Zane now bit out, looking at Gabriel for reinforcement.

Gabriel stroked his chin with his hand, contemplating his answer, then pushed a strand of dark hair, which had come loose from his ponytail, behind his ear. Oliver couldn't help but stare at the large scar that ran from his ear to his chin, a souvenir from the time when he'd been human. While the scar was ugly, there was something intriguing about Gabriel that made him an imposing figure who could drive fear into anybody.

"Dr. Drake gave everybody the all clear," Gabriel replied.

"What's going on?" Oliver asked, tossing a questioning look at his colleagues.

Dr. Drake sat up straighter. "As I was starting to elaborate, we terminated the rehab program. Scanguards did a fabulous job at rounding up all former clients of the blood brothel and bringing them in."

Zane snorted, his boots scratching loudly against the wooden floor. "I don't need you to tell me that we've done a good job."

Samson gave Zane a reprimanding look. "Let him talk."

The bald vampire leaned back and folded his arms over his chest. Oh yeah, Oliver could tell Zane was pissed. And he wasn't one to sugarcoat his opinions. If he didn't like something, he'd let you know. He and Zane had butted heads more than once. Nevertheless, he liked the guy. Zane's gut feeling was better than anybody else's. And in a fight, he was lethal.

Drake cleared his throat. "Well. Some of the patients were doing better than others. I believe it was a matter of willpower and motivation. Some responded to positive reinforcement better, and those were the ones we released a few weeks ago. I understand that Scanguards is still keeping an eye on them?"

Samson nodded and motioned to Gabriel.

"That's right," Gabriel answered. "But there has been no erratic behavior. All of them seemed to have integrated well again."

Drake nodded. "Good, good. And with the drug, so to speak, out of their reach, it's certainly made things easier."

The drug. Yes, the blood of all the Chinese women who'd been held at the blood brothel was indeed a drug to vampires. Highly addictive, utterly delicious, and producing a high. Oliver could only imagine it. He'd never gotten high from Ursula's blood, because they were taking precautions. He only bit her after she'd climaxed, because an orgasm diluted the potency of the blood for a short time.

"Yes, they're all back at home. All but Ursula," Oliver said almost to himself.

"Oh, I almost forgot," the doctor said. "Congratulations on your upcoming wedding!"

"Thank you!"

"Can we get on with business?" Zane interrupted.

Drake looked as if he wanted to roll his eyes but refrained from doing so. "Last night we released the remaining vampires in our care. They've proven to us that they are strong enough to fight the temptation and have conquered their addiction. They're all clean now. I don't believe we'll have any more problems with regards to this issue."

"Proven how?" Zane shot back. "By sitting in some stupid group sessions, babbling about how they felt?"

Drake narrowed his eyes. "Yes, by talking about their feelings, which is a proven psychological tool."

"I'll give you a tool. A stake is a tool," Zane muttered under his breath.

Samson rose. "You know as well as I do that we couldn't simply kill those men because of their addiction. We had to help them." His gaze drifted to Oliver, and Oliver instinctively knew what his boss was thinking of. Samson had helped him when he'd been in the gutter, when he'd been an addict and running with a bad crowd. He'd given him a chance to lead a productive life instead.

"I have to agree with Samson. We had to help them," Oliver added. "They are our fellow vampires. If we don't help them, who will?"

If Samson hadn't helped him and given him a job, he wouldn't be here now. And if Quinn hadn't saved his life by turning him into a vampire when he lay dying after a car crash, he would have never known what love was.

Zane clenched his jaw. "I just hope it won't come and bite us in the ass one day."

Oliver caught Zane's gaze and for a moment, their eyes locked. Was Zane's concern valid?

5

"You have *four* bridesmaids?" Her mother nearly gasped at the revelation.

"Yes," Ursula replied, using her fingers to elaborate. "There's Portia, who's married to Zane. She's a little younger than I. Then Nina who's married to Amaury. And Maya, Gabriel's wife. Plus Lauren. She's a good friend of Portia's and I like her a lot."

Still, her mother kept shaking her head. "No, no. That won't work."

"But, Mom, those are my friends. Besides, they've already got their dresses." Ursula looked across the table to her father, who had his head buried in his newspaper. He dropped it slightly and shrugged. "Dad," she pleaded.

"That's your mother's domain. You know I don't get involved in women's business."

The frown on her mother's forehead deepened as she rose from the breakfast table. "Don't you have any other friends? Anybody from college?"

"What's wrong with those friends? You haven't even met them yet. How can you be against them?" Ursula felt herself get defensive. Her mother often had that effect on her.

"I'm not against your friends," she insisted and sighed heavily.

"But you need more of them."

Ursula's forehead creased. "More?" She was perfectly fine with the friends she had. Besides, the only person she really wanted to spend time with was Oliver. But of course, he wasn't here. He had to stay at Samson's house during daytime.

Her mother stepped closer and gripped her chin, making her look up. "Have I taught you nothing about our culture when you grew up? You can't have four bridesmaids. Four means death. And you don't invite death to a wedding."

"Hui Lian, don't you think you're being a little overly dramatic?" her father suddenly interrupted.

Then it clicked for Ursula. Why she had forgotten that fundamental fact she didn't know. Maybe it was simply the stress of the wedding preparations that was getting to her.

"But you can't ask me to tell one of them that she can't be my bridesmaid. That wouldn't be fair. Dad, please help me here." All four of her friends were looking forward to being bridesmaids.

Her mother softly stroked over Ursula's hair. "Of course not, Wei Ling. That's why you'll have to find four more. We'll need eight bridesmaids. Eight will bring you luck."

Relieved, Ursula exhaled. "I guess I could ask Delilah and Yvette."

"Who are they?"

"Delilah is married to Samson. You'll meet him soon. He's Oliver's boss. And Yvette works for Scanguards too."

"So Yvette is one of the secretaries?"

Ursula shook her head, suppressing a laugh. If Yvette heard that, she'd have a fit. "No, Mom, she's a bodyguard like Oliver."

"A woman?"

She could firmly see the wheels in her mother's head turn.

"Well, maybe she's not the best choice then. We'll probably never find a dress for her."

Ursula pulled back. "What? Why not?"

"Well, if she's a bodyguard, you know . . . " Her mother hesitated and lowered her voice. "She's probably very butch. Isn't that what it's called? I mean, if she's a bodyguard."

Ursula shook her head in disbelief. "Oh my god! Just because she's a bodyguard doesn't mean she looks masculine. There's nothing butch about Yvette. She's one of the most feminine women I know."

Her father dropped his newspaper and folded it, a smirk on his face. Ursula met his gaze and had to grin when her father rolled his eyes, a gesture that luckily Ursula's mother didn't notice.

"Oh!" At least her mother had the decency to blush. "Well, in that case . . . But we still need two more to make it eight."

Sometimes Ursula really wondered how her mother could still hold on to all the prejudices she'd grown up with, while she'd lived in Washington D.C. for the past twenty years and had been exposed to a diverse population.

"Do you have any other friends you can ask?"

Ursula searched her mind. "I guess we could ask Rose. I'm sure she'll do it."

"Well, it's unusual to have one's future mother-in-law as a bridesmaid, but I guess we don't have much choice."

"Don't let Rose hear that. I don't want her to think we only asked her because we were in a jam." Luckily both Rose and Quinn were still asleep and would remain so for another few hours.

Her mother let out an outraged breath. "Wei Ling, you make me sound like I have no tact. Did you hear that, Yao Bang?" She glanced at her husband, who simply acknowledged her words with a smile, knowing that she didn't really expect an answer. "Of course, I won't say anything to Rose."

Ursula refrained from rolling her eyes. Instead, she contemplated who could become her eighth bridesmaid. She didn't know many women in San Francisco. She'd only attended a few classes since her escape from the blood brothel and had not really connected to anybody. Her life was with Oliver. Besides, the need to keep his secret had made her cautious about whom she invited into their home. She had to choose somebody who knew about vampires.

. . . or was a vampire herself. Vera.

"I know a very nice Chinese lady. I can ask her."

"A Chinese woman? That's wonderful. Who is she? Do we know her family?"

Ursula chuckled. "Mom, just because she's Chinese doesn't mean you know her or her family." It was highly unlikely considering Vera had been a vampire for some time. And she didn't exactly move in the same circles as her parents. Ursula was certain of that. Vera ran a high class brothel in Nob Hill, whereas her parents rubbed shoulders with other diplomats and government officials in Washington D.C. "There are hundreds of thousands of Chinese people living in San Francisco."

The sound of the doorbell startled her. She looked to the wall clock. Rarely anybody ever visited a vampire household this early. It was barely past ten in the morning.

She was about to get up to see who was visiting when she heard heavy footsteps coming down the stairs.

"Coming!" Blake called out to whoever had rung the bell.

A moment later, she heard the door open and another familiar voice greet him: Wesley, Haven's brother.

"Hey, hope I'm not too early, but you said the tent guys were starting early."

Their voices came closer and within a few seconds, both humans entered the kitchen. Well, technically Wesley was a witch, though his powers left much to be desired. According to what both Blake and Oliver had told her, Wesley had still not been able to gain all his witch powers back that he'd been robbed of shortly after his birth.

"Hey, morning, guys!" Blake greeted them, then pointed to Wesley. "This is Wesley Montgomery. Wes, these are Ursula's parents: Bang Tseng and Liliana Tseng. Did I get that right?"

Ursula cringed and shook her head, indicating to Blake that he'd just butchered her parents' names. "It's actually Yao Bang and Hui Lian."

Blake scratched his head, grinning unashamedly. "Oops! Well I knew it was something like *Bang Bang*." He made his hand into a gun, pretending to shoot. "That's kind of how I remember things. You know, associate the words with something familiar. Sorry. And *Liane*— so is that a diminutive of Lillian?"

Ursula rolled her eyes. Wordlessly, she mouthed, *stop it*, while swiping her index finger horizontally across her throat. She could always count on Blake to screw things up.

Meanwhile Wesley politely shook her parents' hands. "Nice to meet you, Mrs. Tseng, Mr. Tseng. I hope you had a good flight."

Her parents smiled at Wesley, clearly relieved not to have to listen to any further butchering of their names.

"Did I hear that the tent will be built this morning?" her father asked.

"Yes, that's why I figured I'd come and help out. To supervise the workers. Make sure they don't mess things up and break stuff," Wesley offered.

Her father turned to her. "Is Oliver not coming to help with that?"

"He can't. He's protecting a client today," Ursula answered quickly, pasting a regretful expression onto her face. "Last-minute booking. They couldn't find anybody else on such short notice. It's their busy season, Dad."

He raised an eyebrow. "Oh, I had no idea there were seasons for bodyguards."

"Oh yeah, totally!" Blake chimed in. "Whenever there are any political or big society events, we get a lot more bookings."

Her father gave Blake a scrutinizing look. "So you're a bodyguard too."

Blake nodded proudly. "Yes. I work for Scanguards too."

"Me too!" Wesley piped up, as if this were a competition. And between those two guys it generally was.

"Hmm, so if you two are bodyguards at Scanguards, why is it that Oliver had to take a booking when he should be taking care of these things, rather than one of you helping with the wedding arrangements?"

"Uh," Blake mumbled.

"Neither Blake nor Wesley are fully trained yet," Ursula said quickly. "They don't have all their certifications yet, so they're not allowed to protect a client on their own."

The explanation seemed to satisfy her father. "Well, good, then."

Another ring of the doorbell interrupted them.

"That'll be the tent guys. I'll let them in," Blake announced.

As he walked back into the hallway, Wesley on his heels, Ursula felt her mother's hand on her arm. She turned to her.

"We'll need to somehow get dresses for the extra four bridesmaids," her mother announced, looking at the list in her hands.

"I'll first have to talk to them."

"Good. Call them and while you're talking to them, ask them for their dress size, and then we'll need to go shopping. Do you have a local seamstress who can help us make alterations if we need to?"

Her mother was a veritable waterfall of questions.

"And when we've found the right dresses, they can meet us for the fitting."

"But can't we just get the dresses, bring them here, and then have everybody try them on and then get a seamstress to make the alterations here?" Ursula suggested. Having Yvette, Rose, and Vera meet them for a fitting during the day would be impossible. As vampires, they had to avoid daylight. Only the humans and the hybrids would be able to do a daytime fitting.

"That's too complicated. We'll have to do it right at the shop."

"But that won't work."

"Why not?"

Ursula scrambled for an excuse. "Well, they work during the day. They can't take time off."

"Rose works?" Her mother's head motioned to the ceiling. "But she's still asleep."

"Uh." Panic raced through Ursula. "Well, she starts a little later. I'm sure we can do something one evening."

Her mother gave her a displeased look. "You're making this all very difficult, Wei Ling! I'm just trying to help you."

"I know, Mom," she said quickly in order not to upset her. "I really appreciate it."

"Well, then, let's not waste any more time."

Ursula already sensed how this week would turn out: stressful, exhausting, and chaotic. And she dreaded every single minute of it, knowing that Oliver wouldn't be around much. Maybe pretending to her parents that she and Oliver didn't have an intimate relationship hadn't been such a good idea after all. Maybe she should have just come out with it at the beginning. Her parents would have been upset at first, but at least Oliver would have been able to stay at the house. And she would have a shoulder to lean on and arms around her to wipe away the stress of planning a wedding.

6

The door to the tradesmen entrance which opened to a narrow path leading along Quinn's house stood open, and two men were carrying heavy metal rods through the walkway.

The moment the sun had set, Oliver had walked the short distance from Samson's Nob Hill house to Quinn's mansion in Russian Hill. He'd not taken the car to Samson's, because there was no extra parking in the garage, and parking on the streets of Nob Hill was virtually impossible.

Oliver followed the workers through the narrow walkway that led into the garden, curious to see how far they'd gotten.

When he reached the garden, he looked around. Several men were busy, connecting metal rods to build a scaffold that would eventually be draped with huge canvas panels to create a tent that covered the entire backyard and connected seamlessly to the back of the house and its back entrance. A sliver of it would also drape around the other side of the house to lead to the French doors in the living room so that the guests wouldn't have to trek through the kitchen or the dirty tradesmen entrance to get to the tent.

Things seemed to be moving at a swift pace, but Oliver knew it would take a good two days until the tent was operable. Only then could other things be brought in, like tables, chairs and decorations.

Oliver turned away from the workers and walked through the open door into the kitchen.

Wesley stood over the kitchen counter, munching on a sandwich.

"Hey!" Oliver greeted him.

The wannabe witch lifted his hand in greeting, his mouth too full to speak.

"Where is everybody?"

Wesley swallowed before he answered. "I suppose with 'everybody' you mean Ursula?"

Was he indeed that transparent? At any other time he would have denied it, but he missed the woman who would soon be his wife and his mate, and he couldn't care less whether Wesley wanted to tease him about it.

"So? Where is she?"

"Out shopping with her mother."

"Do you know when they'll be back?"

Wesley shrugged. "I heard something about bridesmaid's dresses. That's when I tuned out."

"And Ursula's father?"

"Probably still upstairs. He wanted to lie down and rest. I think the whole racket down here seems to have tired him out." Wes set down his half-eaten sandwich and walked to the door that led into the hallway, peered outside for a moment, then closed it again and turned back. "So while we're alone, I wanted to ask you for a favor."

Oliver lifted an eyebrow, always suspicious when Wesley wanted something because whatever it was, it generally led to a minor disaster. "What kind of favor?"

Wesley rubbed his neck. "Well, you heard about the puppies, right?"

"Haven's Labrador puppies that you once turned into piglets with your magic?"

A sheepish grin spread over Wesley's face. "Yeah, it's just, I've been trying to turn them back into dogs, but it hasn't worked."

Surprised, Oliver couldn't suppress the chuckle that built in his chest. "Are you telling me that they are still pigs?"

"Haven is none too happy about it either. So, I hit the books and came across this spell that should work. Only thing is, I need a few drops of vampire blood to—"

"No way!" Oliver interrupted. "Go hit up your brother!"

Wesley made a grimace. "He's already turned me down. So I

figured maybe you'd wanna help out."

Oliver narrowed his eyes. "Is that why you volunteered to help out with the wedding preparations, so you can get me to give you some of my blood?"

Wesley huffed, outraged. "As if I would do that! I'm helping out because I want to. I thought we were friends."

"You're totally transparent, Wes!"

He shrugged. "So? Come on. It's just a few drops. I brought a little vial. You won't even feel it. It's just a pinprick. And it's all for the greater good. If I can't turn those pigs back into dogs, they'll eventually turn into bacon and sausage."

Oliver rolled his eyes. "Which I believe are the nicknames Blake gave them."

He knew Wes all too well. He would nag and be a total pest until he'd gotten what he wanted. It was better to get it over with. Besides, Wes was right. Giving him a few drops of vampire blood wouldn't hurt, nor would it be harmful to anybody. After all, vampire blood had great healing properties.

"Fine. But you owe me one and don't think I won't collect! Only a few drops. And it'll be the only time," he conceded.

Wesley beamed. "I swear!" He pulled a small glass vial just big enough for one fluid ounce from his pocket. "Here, just half-full is fine."

Still shaking his head, Oliver elongated his fangs, bringing them to full length. Instantly, he felt power surge through him, a result of his vampire side emerging. The lingering scent of Ursula drifted to his nostrils and cocooned him. If she were in the kitchen now, while his fangs were extended, he didn't think he could resist biting her. The bottled blood he'd consumed at Samson's had nourished him yet not truly satisfied him. The only thing that could truly satisfy his hunger was Ursula's blood and her body writhing beneath his.

"Uh, Oliver," Wesley prompted him, pulling him from his thoughts.

Swiftly he brought his thumb to his lips and pricked it with one of his fangs. He held the vial under his bleeding digit and let it drip into it, watching as the level quickly rose to midway.

"Oh, Oliver, you're here."

Oliver's head snapped to the door leading into the hallway. Ursula's father stood there, looking somewhat pale.

When their gazes met, Yao Bang's eyes widened in shock and

disbelief. "Oh, no!" he pressed out. "That can't be!"

Oliver's forehead furrowed, while Wesley ground out low under his breath, "Your fangs!"

"Shit!" Oliver cursed, but it was too late.

He hadn't retracted his fangs, and his future father-in-law had seen them. He made a move toward him and noticed him shrink back toward the door. At the same time, Wesley snatched the open vial that Oliver still held in his hand.

Oliver tossed Wes an angry glare. Because of him, he'd exposed himself.

Wesley shrugged. "Wipe his memory then."

Yao Bang's mouth opened for a scream, but Oliver was on him before it could leave his throat, clamping his hand over his mouth and preventing him from escaping by clutching him to his body. At the same time, he reached out his mind to the older man and sent his thoughts to him.

You saw nothing. You came into the kitchen for a snack and saw me and Wesley making sandwiches. That's all you saw. You never saw my fangs. You never saw any blood.

Yao Bang's eyes went blank, the fear in them wiped away. Relieved, Oliver released him and stepped back.

"Oliver," Yao Bang murmured, before he staggered a few steps forward, reaching out his arms to grasp for support.

Oliver grabbed hold of him before he could fall, then felt him go slack in his arms. He was unconscious.

"Crap!"

"What did you do now?" Wesley asked.

"I didn't do anything!" Wiping somebody's memory didn't have that kind of effect on humans. Nobody had ever fainted after he'd wiped his memory. This was not right. Something had gone wrong. "Shit, shit, shit!" Ursula could never find out about this. "Call Maya! Now! Get her here as fast as she can. Tell her to take the side entrance so Ursula won't see her when she comes back."

Wesley pulled out his cell phone and dialed.

Oliver gently lowered his future father-in-law onto the ground and checked his vital signs, when his sensitive hearing picked up the opening of the front door. He inhaled sharply. Shit! Ursula and her mother were coming back. Panicked, he looked around the kitchen, wondering what to do.

"Why don't you bring all the dresses upstairs into my room, Wei

Ling? I'll make some tea," Ursula's mother said from the hallway, her voice coming closer as she walked in the direction of the kitchen.

"Okay, Mom." He heard Ursula's reply, accompanied by footsteps on the stairs.

The kitchen door opened before Oliver could make a decision as to what to do with Yao Bang and how to explain his unconsciousness.

"Oh my god! Yao Bang!" Hui Lian said, running to where he lay on the floor. She stroked her hand over his head. Then her eyes shot to Oliver.

An inadequate excuse already sat on his lips, but he didn't get to utter it.

"We can't tell Ursula about this. Promise me." Her eyes pleaded with Oliver.

Surprised, Oliver pulled back. What did she know? Did she have an inkling that he was an immortal creature and knew what he'd done to her husband? But how?

"He has these fainting spells. The doctors think it's maybe anemia. But we didn't have time for more tests before the trip. Oh God, I hoped this wouldn't happen."

"Maya is on her way," Wesley interrupted.

"Maya?" Hui Lian asked, her eyebrows pulling together in confusion.

Oliver put a reassuring hand on her forearm. "She's a doctor. She'll check him out. He'll be fine." Relief washed through Oliver. Wiping Yao Bang's memory hadn't done this to him. He'd looked pale the moment he'd stepped into the kitchen. He'd probably been about to faint even if he hadn't seen Oliver's fangs. Still, Oliver felt responsible for what had happened.

"But we can't have Ursula see the doctor arrive. She'll be worried. She doesn't need this in the week she's getting married," her mother claimed.

"I'll distract her and keep her upstairs until Maya is gone again."

Hui Lian gave him a grateful smile. "Thank you so much. You're a good man."

For a moment their eyes locked, and for the first time, Oliver felt affection for Ursula's mother. She wanted only the best for her daughter and didn't want to destroy Ursula's happiness even if that meant keeping things from her. That's what they had in common. They would both keep secrets from Ursula if that meant she would be happy.

7

Ursula dropped the shopping bags on the floor of Oliver's room where her parents were staying and plopped onto the bed, kicking her shoes off in the process. All she wanted was to curl up into a ball and hide. She was exhausted and her nerves were strung so tightly, they would at this point snap at the slightest confrontation with anybody. Spending time shopping with her mother had been pure torture.

She stared up at the ceiling, sighing heavily, when the door opened. Immediately, she sat up. A smile formed on her lips when she set eyes on her visitor: Oliver.

"Hey, baby!" he greeted her and pulled her into his arms as he sat down on the bed.

Before she could even utter his name, his lips slid over hers and kissed her hungrily. While he'd always been a passionate kisser, Ursula felt that this kiss was more intense, more urgent than normal.

Oliver released her after several heart-pounding seconds.

"Looks like you missed me," she murmured against his lips. "Maybe we should be apart more often."

He growled low and deep. "Don't tease me. You know how I get when you play with me."

Ursula couldn't help but chuckle. She loved it when Oliver went all primal and possessive, when she should despise exactly that character trait in any man. Having been imprisoned for three years by crazy vampires should have scarred her forever so that she never wanted another man to act all possessive about her. But somehow when Oliver did it, it felt right. She wanted to be his. Forever.

Ursula ran her fingers along his neck and saw him visibly swallow when she brushed the artery that throbbed under his skin. "I wish we could start our new life together without all this fuss."

Oliver pulled back a few inches, looking at her quizzically. "What fuss?"

She made an all encompassing motion with her arm. "This. The wedding, the bridesmaids, the shopping, the flowers, everything."

"What? But we're doing this for you. I couldn't care less about a big wedding. Hell, if I had a say, I'd drag you to a secluded place with a big bed and blood-bond with you right now."

"I never wanted a big wedding either. But look at it now." She pointed to the window, indicating the large tent that was being built out there. "I'm not sure I'm prepared for all this."

"Then why are we doing it?" Oliver pushed a strand of her hair behind her ear, and she leaned into his palm, loving the way his touch comforted her.

"My parents. They want this. They think that if the wedding is perfect, the marriage will be perfect too." Particularly her mother believed that. Her father could have maybe been talked into something smaller and simpler, but even he had no chance once her mother had made up her mind.

"Our marriage will be perfect. I promise you that."

Ursula sighed. "But this wedding will be a disaster." She pointed to the shopping bags. "Do you know how many stores my mother dragged me to so we could find matching bridesmaid's dresses for the extra bridesmaids?"

"Extra bridesmaids? Are four not enough?"

"Four is a bad number in Chinese. It means death. So when Mom found out, she almost had a stroke! She insists that we have eight bridesmaids because eight is a lucky number."

Oliver shook his head. "She can't possibly believe that!"

Ursula rolled her eyes. "You don't know my mother! She's superstitious, controlling, a perfectionist and she drives me—"

"Don't, Ursula," he said softly, placing a finger on her lips. "Your mother only wants your best. She wants you to be happy and would do anything for you."

Ursula felt her eyebrows snap together. "How would you know that? You barely know her."

He smiled. "I just have a feeling. Trust me. She's doing this for you. Don't spoil it. I know you're stressed."

"Stressed is an understatement. I still have to get all the bridesmaids together for a fitting, and since half of them are vampires, we can't do it during the day. I'm running out of excuses why it will have to be at night. And then there's the cake, and Mom wants me to make wedding favors, and we still need to shop for some special table decorations. And then there are the flowers—"

"Stop, baby. I'll take care of some of those things for you."

"You would? Really?"

He pulled her against his chest. "Of course I will. It's my wedding too. How about I'll take care of the flowers and the cake? You won't have to worry about that at all."

Ursula threw her arms around his neck. "You're the best!"

Oliver grinned unashamedly and winked at her. "I'm the best at a lot of things. Do you want me to remind you?"

She gasped, pulled out of his arms, and shot a panicked look toward the door. "We can't! If my mother walks in here and sees us, she's going to give me a lecture on premarital sex, and I'm really not in the mood for that."

Oliver chuckled. "Your mother is busy in the kitchen. She won't disturb us for a while."

"You don't know her. Besides, it doesn't take forever to make tea. She'll be up here any moment." Ursula hopped off the bed and walked to the window. Below it, the tent was being built even though so far, it looked more like a scaffold used to paint a house rather than a tent. Several men still worked and floodlights had been installed to help them see in the dark. "When will the tent be up?"

She heard Oliver rise and walk to her. Then he pressed his body against her back und put his arm around her waist. "Maybe another day or two."

"Oliver?"

"Yes?"

"Do you sometimes think back to when we met?"

"All the time."

She turned her head halfway to look at him. "I'm glad it was you whose arms I collapsed in. You saved me."

Oliver smiled and shook his head. "No, *you* saved *me*. I was on a downward spiral. If I hadn't met you that night, I would have slid deeper, until one day I would have fallen prey to bloodlust. I was lucky to have found you."

She lifted herself on her tiptoes and turned in his arms. "I hope we'll always be as happy as now."

"We'll be even happier once we're blood-bonded. Then I'll be able to protect you better."

His words surprised her. "What do you mean?"

"I'll be able to sense when you're in danger because of the bond. And we'll be able to communicate telepathically."

She knew all about that aspect of the blood-bond. But some of his words made her ask, "Why would I be in danger?"

He shrugged. "Just saying. If anything ever happens, I'll know."

Ursula slapped his shoulder. "Don't spook me! Nothing will happen. I'm safe here."

He pressed a kiss to her forehead. "Yes, you're safe with me."

"It's too tight," Delilah complained.

She was one of eleven women assembled in the living room of Quinn and Rose's mansion, eight of whom were trying on their bridesmaid's dresses. Ursula tossed a glance in her mother's direction, who was assisting the seamstress in making some adjustments to Yvette's dress—or rather bossing the poor woman around.

Her mother hadn't heard Delilah over the din of voices in the room, which was currently off-limits to the men. In fact, Blake had been posted outside the door to make sure none of the workers carrying chairs and tables into the tent would accidentally step inside the room of scantily clad women.

"Let me help you," Ursula offered and approached Delilah.

Delilah, the pretty dark-haired woman with the green eyes, had a great figure, though she was a little rounder around her hips than some of the other women assembled. No wonder, she was the one who had borne a child a year earlier and seemingly had trouble getting rid of the last few pounds of pregnancy weight.

"Thank you, Ursula. I don't mean to be complicated, but if I zip it all the way up, I won't be able to breathe. I can't squeeze my boobs into this dress." Delilah glanced at her apologetically. "And I swear I didn't have any cookies in the last two weeks!"

Ursula chuckled and caught Maya's eye, who stood close and now approached. Maya let a long look wander over Delilah, then leaned in closer.

"I doubt it's the cookies, Delilah." Maya's eyes twinkled. "If you don't mind my saying so as your physician, it's generally not cookies that make your boobs swell."

Ursula noticed how Delilah sucked in a breath. "You don't think—" She stopped herself and ran her hand along her torso before resting it on her belly. "But, we've tried to be careful." Her cheeks colored prettily.

Ursula didn't have to be a brain surgeon to figure out what Maya was alluding to. "Are you saying Delilah is pregnant?" she whispered so nobody else in the room could hear them. Except maybe the other vampire females in the room, whose hearing was superior to that of humans: Rose, Yvette, Vera, as well as Portia and Lauren, who both were hybrids, half vampire, half human.

Maya smiled at Delilah. "I think you should come in for a test in the next few days. So we can be sure. I would love to study your pregnancy from beginning to end this time. Last time I only got the tail end of it."

"That is, if I'm really pregnant. I could well be just getting fat!" Delilah joked.

"With a man like Samson?" Maya looked at Ursula, and Ursula couldn't help herself but laugh.

"Maya is right. I mean I don't know Samson that well, but if he's anything like Oliver, then I'm surprised you only have one child so far." Shocked at her own words, Ursula slapped her hand over her mouth, then quickly scanned the room to see if her mother was close by. To her relief, she was still harassing the poor seamstress and giving her tips on how to do her job.

When she turned back to Maya and Delilah, both women were chuckling.

"Guess our Oliver has become quite a man," Delilah said, the affection for him shining through her words and eyes.

Ursula dropped her lids, suddenly embarrassed. "My parents don't know."

Ursula felt a hand on her forearm and looked up. Maya squeezed her arm briefly. "And they won't hear it from us."

"Thank you!"

"So, about the dress," Delilah started.

"Don't worry," Ursula said. "There should be enough inside seam so the seamstress can let it out to make it wide enough so you can breathe comfortably. Let me get her."

She walked to the seamstress, who knelt in front of Yvette to adjust the seam of her dress, and tapped her on the shoulder. "Ms. Petrochelli? Could you please help out my friend Delilah? Her dress is too tight. You'll need to let a little bit of the seam out."

"Too tight?" her mother interrupted, a panicked look on her face. "But you said she wore a size six. We bought her a size six."

"Yes, but it's just a little too tight." Ursula tried to calm her down, but it appeared it was already too late. Her mother had switched to panic mode and was already moving toward Delilah.

With a sigh, Ursula looked over her shoulder and watched how she stepped behind Delilah to try to zip her up. Then she gesticulated wildly and Ursula had to turn away. She couldn't watch. It would only make her stress about things even more.

"Your mother takes things too seriously," Yvette suddenly said, making Ursula look at her and smile.

"Don't all mothers?" She simply shrugged then let her eyes wander over Yvette's red dress. "You look great in this. It's totally your color."

Yvette smiled broadly. "I love it. I was just a little surprised that you chose red for the bridesmaid's dresses. Normally the bridesmaids get to wear some ghastly color like pink or orange, just so that they can't upstage the bride."

"Red means good luck at a Chinese wedding. The more red the better. Besides, with all of you except for Rose and Nina having dark hair, I figured it's a color that would look good on all of you." She chuckled. "And Rose and Nina can wear any color they want anyway."

Yvette laughed and winked at her. "Yes, blondes have all the fun."

Ursula had never seen her so lighthearted. As she joined in Yvette's laughter, she heard her mother's shocked gasp and turned, wondering what had gone wrong now.

Her mother stalked toward her, eyes wide, a dismayed look on her face. "Why didn't you tell me?"

Instinctively, Ursula backed away. Had somebody let it slip that she'd been living with Oliver? "Tell you what?" she managed to ask, trying to buy herself some time.

"About Oliver's date of birth!" Her mother's cheeks were flushed as her voice rose.

The other women fell silent and were suddenly all staring at them.

"Why didn't you tell me that he was born on the fourth of April?"

Ursula stared blankly at her mother. "What?" And who had even told her? She looked at the faces of her bridesmaids and saw Rose shrug and make a helpless gesture.

"Your mother asked so she could get a horoscope done as a surprise gift," Rose said apologetically.

"The fourth day of the fourth month, Ursula! How could you keep this from me?" her mother asked again.

That's when it finally clicked. It was a bad omen. With four meaning death in Chinese culture, for the groom to have two fours in his birth date spelled disaster. Ursula didn't believe in these superstitions, having grown up mostly in Western culture, but her mother was still too engrained in the old beliefs.

"It doesn't matter, Mom!" she answered.

"It matters! Have you no respect for your heritage? No belief in our culture?"

Ursula vaguely heard the chiming of the doorbell.

"I don't care when he was born. I love him!"

Her mother shook her head. "We have to change things. I'll have to get a horoscope done and see whether there's a day you can marry him that will counteract his date of birth. A day that'll be luckier than others."

"That's ridiculous! I'm not doing this! I'm getting married in two days, and that's that!" Ursula ran toward the door.

"Ursula!" her mother shouted.

"Mrs. Tseng," she heard Vera's voice. "Maybe I can help. I'm an expert in Chinese numerology."

Ursula pushed back the tears as she opened the door and stepped into the corridor. She doubted that Vera could sway her mother. After all, Vera was the owner of a brothel. Yes, she was Chinese, but did that really mean she knew anything about the superstitious beliefs her mother held or how to dispel them?

* * * *

He'd snatched a couple of folding chairs off the truck that was parked outside the house and simply marched into the garden without being stopped by anybody. In the tent, he placed the chairs around a table while his eyes took in his surroundings.

Various different workers were busy erecting a podium with a canopy on which undoubtedly the ceremony would take place, while others carried in tables and chairs and set them on the wooden boards that had been placed over the grass in order to form an even floor.

From what he could see, none of the workers were vampires. And if one of the humans realized that he didn't belong there, he could use mind control on him and make sure there would be no trouble.

Looking over his shoulder, he made sure nobody was taking any notice of him, and stalked to the door that led into the back of the house. He entered quickly, finding nobody in the large eat-in kitchen. He pushed the door to the hallway open and spied a human standing watch in front of a door. A tall young man who couldn't be older than twenty-five. He could overpower the human within seconds if he had to.

He'd nudged the door open a little wider when the doorbell chimed.

The human sighed and walked to the entrance door, turning his back to him. It was all the time he needed to exit the kitchen and advance silently into the corridor. Quickly, he dove into another room, which he identified as a laundry room by its smell even before he opened the door, and closed the door but for a sliver, so he could spy into the hallway from his hiding place. He was only a few steps away from the stairs that led to the upper floor. That's where he wanted to go to find Ursula's room and wait for her there. Eventually she would go there. All he had to do was wait.

"Hey Samson, Amaury!" the human greeted the two vampires who now entered the foyer.

He felt like growling but suppressed the urge. The boss of Scanguards and one of his high-level partners showing up here was inconvenient. He didn't need any more vampires on the premises than there already were. It was hard enough to avoid the ones already in the house. He had to be careful not to get too close to any of them or they might be able to smell him and realize he didn't belong here, even if he was hidden somewhere. He hoped that the fact that he was hiding in a laundry room that smelled of bleach and laundry soap helped disguise his scent.

"Hey, Blake!" Samson replied.

"What are you guys doing here? I thought you were babysitting Isabelle."

"I left her with Zane."

"Well, in that case, wanna help out?"

Amaury laughed. "Not likely. We're just here to pick up Nina and Delilah."

Blake motioned his head to the door he'd been watching earlier. "They're still in there for the fitting. I'm afraid you can't go in there right now."

Just at that moment, the door opened. The scent drifted to him even before he saw her emerge. Ursula came running out of the room and nearly collided with Amaury's massive frame.

"I'm sorry. I didn't see you, Amaury," she apologized hastily, her voice thick with tears.

"Something wrong?" Amaury wrapped his palm around her forearm when she tried to push past him and head for the stairs.

She shook her head and pulled herself free of his grip. "Nothing!" She sniffed.

Blake made a few steps toward her. "Is it your mother again?"

Ursula nodded.

"What's going on?" Samson asked, his eyes darting back and forth between the two humans.

Ursula turned back to them. "She doesn't like Oliver's date of birth!" A sob dislodged from her chest and she whirled around and ran up the stairs.

"Ah, crap!" Blake cursed.

"Shouldn't one of us go after her and calm her down?" Amaury wondered.

In his hiding place, he narrowed his eyes. No, he didn't want anybody to go after her, because she was just where he wanted her. She'd be in her room, alone, crying her eyes out for whatever reason. She wouldn't even hear him open the door and enter. She would be face-down on her bed. He hadn't thought it would be so easy.

Blake shook his head. "Just give her some time alone. Ursula and her mother have had a few blowouts like that. It'll pass."

When both vampires nodded in agreement, relief washed over him.

Perfect!

Now he only had to wait for those three to leave the hallway and he would be able to walk upstairs and grab her. Only a few more minutes.

"So, where's Oliver?" Samson asked.

"He's out with Wes. Something about the flowers," Blake replied.

Samson and Amaury exchanged a look. "Excellent. Then he won't be able to overhear us."

"About what?" the human asked curiously.

"About the wedding present. We need your assistance." Amaury motioned to another door, the first one next to the entrance. "Let's go into the study."

Blake tossed a look back at the door he'd been guarding. "But I'm supposed to watch that none of the workers goes in there while the girls are still trying on the bridesmaid's dresses."

"It'll only take a couple of minutes," Samson assured him.

Moments later the three disappeared into the study and closed the door behind them.

He grinned. Finally, things were going his way. He looked up and down the corridor, then pushed the door open wide and approached the staircase, walking on tiptoes. Once he set his foot on the first step, he knew he was safe. The plush carpet on the stairs swallowed the sound of his footsteps as he ascended.

On the landing, he turned and inhaled. He could smell the faint scent of the blood whore's special blood. It made his gums itch. His fangs descended in anticipation of the special treat he was about to enjoy.

He walked along the corridor, each step bringing him closer to his goal. He reached the door and put his hand on the doorknob.

"Ursula!" A female voice came from below. At the same time somebody came running up the stairs.

Cursing silently, his head snapped toward the sound as his feet automatically readied themselves for a quick escape. He caught a glimpse of the back of a head and a red dress as a woman came into view. She hadn't seen him yet, but she would in a second or two when she turned on the landing.

One of the bridesmaids.

But not one of the human ones. She was a vampire, as her aura indicated.

Fuming inside, he dove into the nearest room and closed the door silently behind him.

He could still hear her as she approached Ursula's room and knocked. "Ursula, honey, it's Vera. I calmed her down."

Then the door was opened.

His hands balled into fists while he tried to calm himself. There would be other opportunities like this one.

He just had to be patient.

But for tonight, there were entirely too many vampires in the house. He'd have to get out before anybody recognized him and realized what he was up to.

"Red?" Oliver stared at Wes in disbelief as the human brought the car to a stop in front of Quinn's house. "You turned the piglets red?"

Wes shrugged. "Well, it was my first try. I just have to work on the spell. I'm sure the second time it'll work like a charm."

Oliver already started shaking his head before Wesley's last sentence was even out. "No!"

"Oh, come on! I just need a few drops. That's all!" Wes begged, casting him a puppy dog look meant to soften him up.

But Oliver didn't cave. "I said no! Clearly, whatever spell you're trying out isn't working. There's no need wasting any more of my precious blood on it." The only person who'd get his blood would be Ursula. It was part of the blood-bonding ritual, and it would make her immortal while she remained human—and fertile. Once they were bonded, she would be able to conceive his child.

"But I really think it's going to work the second time. I just have to get the dosage right."

Oliver sighed. "Wes, I hate to say this, but don't you think that maybe witchcraft isn't exactly your calling?"

Wesley slammed his flat palm against the steering wheel. "I was born a witch! And I'll be damned if I can't get that back!"

"What do you have to prove? Just find something else that you're good at."

"Easy for you to say! Haven is a vampire, and Kimberly is a great actress. And what am I? Am I the only sibling who can't make anything out of himself? Don't you understand? I want to be somebody. I want to do something useful."

Oliver shook his head, though in a way, he understood Wes all too well. "But you are somebody. You're training as a bodyguard with Scanguards. Isn't that something?"

Wes turned his head away and looked out the side window, staring into the dark. "And you know as well as I how I got that position. Because I offered my blood the night you were turned, Samson felt obligated. Do you think he would really have offered me to train as a bodyguard if I hadn't practically blackmailed him?"

"Are you telling me you're having scruples about that?"

Wes shrugged. "I just wonder sometimes about what would become of me if Hav and Scanguards didn't exist. You know." He glanced at Oliver. "I need to have something that's independent of it. Something that's just mine."

Slowly, Oliver nodded. "I get that. I do. But you can't force it." He reached for the door handle and pushed the car door open. "It'll happen. Just be patient."

Then he exited and walked up to the entrance door. When he reached it, he felt a strange tingling sensation creep up his nape and stopped. He inhaled deeply, picking up many unfamiliar as well as familiar scents. Shaking his head to rid himself of the odd sensation, he pulled his key from his pocket and inserted it into the lock. The motion pushed the door inward. It hadn't been locked.

Cautiously, he stepped into the well-lit interior. Voices drifted to him from the open living room door and the kitchen in the back. Maybe one of the workers had left the door open when he'd left. He would have to speak to Quinn about security at the house during the wedding. It was bad enough that so many contractors marched in and out at all hours of the day, but to know that they were careless and left doors open so that anybody could just walk in off the street was inexcusable.

Just because the latest threats of the operators of the blood brothel and their customers, as well as the vampires who had special mind-control skills and had nearly crushed Scanguards a short while ago, were dealt with, didn't mean they had no enemies.

"Hey, Oliver. Glad I'm catching you alone."

He looked up and saw Maya walk through the living room door and approach him.

"Hey, Maya." He pointed to the bag in her hand, a red dress peeking out of it. "I see you guys tried on your bridesmaid's dresses. Nice color. I had no idea they were red."

She smiled. "A Chinese good luck thing, I guess." She tossed a quick glance over her shoulder. "I just thought I'd let you know. I looked in on your future father-in-law. He's doing fine. I did a blood test, and his doctors are correct. It's just a bit of anemia. Nothing to worry about. I've given him some meds to tide him over until he's back home."

"That's a relief. At least that means we don't have to worry Ursula with it. She's stressed out enough." The last couple of days she'd seemed frazzled most of the time. And he didn't like that look on her, the look that said that she wanted all this to be over.

"Uh, about that."

"What?" he asked, instantly worried.

"Ursula and her mother had another blowout tonight."

He shoved a hand through his hair. "About what?"

"Your date of birth."

"What's my birthday got to do with the wedding?"

"Apparently everything. You have two fours in your date of birth."

"So?"

"In Chinese that's bad luck."

"Damn it! Superstitious crap!"

"Well, of course it's superstition, but it's not any different than Westerners finding Friday the thirteenth unlucky. Unfortunately, it's really upset Ursula." Her eyes turned toward the ceiling.

"I'll take care of it. Thanks, Maya." He ran up the stairs, taking two steps at a time. Nobody had the right to upset the woman he loved, not even his soon-to-be mother-in-law. Particularly not over a stupid thing like a birthday.

Without knocking, he entered the guestroom. "Ursula!"

She wasn't alone. Vera had her arms wrapped around her and stroked her hand over her hair. Both looked up when the door fell shut behind him.

"Just in time," Vera said calmly and rose from the bed.

Immediately, Oliver pulled Ursula into his arms and rubbed his hands over her back. "I'm so sorry, baby. I just heard. Tell me, what can I do?" He looked at her tear-stained eyes, and his heart bled for her.

Before Ursula could answer, Vera replied, "I have an idea of how to fix this."

Oliver looked at her. "How? Last time I checked, nobody could change their birthday at will."

"Well, technically your birthday is the day you were turned into a vampire, which I believe was August 8. And that means you have two 8's in your date of birth, and that's very good luck."

"Yes, but you can't exactly tell Ursula's mother that without telling her I'm a vampire."

"Of course not! But I can use mind control to make her think she heard August 8 instead of April 4 when Rose told her your birthday."

Ursula eased out of his embrace and sat back on her heels. "That's not a solution! We can't keep wiping my parents' memories when something happens that they don't like."

"But we did it after you escaped those vampires. We had to."

"Exactly. We had to!" Ursula said firmly. "But this time we don't. Just because my mother has some crazy-ass idea about numerology doesn't mean that we have to wipe her memory. We have to reason with her."

Oliver rolled his eyes. "Reason with your mother? Aren't you asking a little too much?"

Ursula braced her hands at her hips. "What are you saying?"

"I'm just saying that she's not likely to listen."

"You don't know her like I do!"

Oliver jumped up from the bed. "Well, I'm not the one who's crying and all upset, am I?"

"I can't believe you said that!"

Shell-shocked, Oliver backed away. Were they just having their first fight? They'd never argued before. For several long moments, he simply stared at Ursula, who held his gaze without flinching.

"Well, no wonder I always dreaded family visits," Vera said calmly. "Brings the worst out in people."

Oliver shot Vera a look, then dropped his head. "I'm sorry." He raised his lids to look at Ursula, slowly placing one foot in front of the other to approach her again. "It's just, I hate seeing you unhappy. It hurts me. Here." He placed his fist over his heart. "I can't stand it when I can't help you."

Ursula reached her arms out to him, and he eased into her

embrace, pressing his head against her chest and encircling her with his arms.

"I'm sorry too. It's just all so overwhelming. Every day there's something else that goes wrong."

He lifted his head. "Nothing else will go wrong, I promise you. Our wedding day will be the happiest day in our lives."

A smile formed around her lips. "Are you saying that after our wedding day we won't be as happy again?"

He chuckled. "That's not what I meant."

"What did you mean?"

"Want me to show you?"

"Uhm," Vera's voice interrupted.

Darn, he'd forgotten that Vera was still in the room. He grinned at her sheepishly. "Thank you, Vera, for being there when Ursula needed you."

"No problem."

"What shall we do about your mother now?" Oliver asked.

"Nothing," Ursula said. "My mother is getting what she wants with everything else: the wedding dress, the bridesmaids, the wedding date, and the decorations! But I'm not going to compromise on the groom."

Oliver grinned. "That's my girl!"

10

After much crying, Ursula had reached a truce with her mother. As long as everything else at the wedding was arranged so that it compensated for Oliver's *unfortunate* date of birth, as she called it, she would look past it and not mention it again. This meant that her mother would include every good luck charm she knew in the wedding decorations, almost as if she thought she could ward off the bad luck Oliver's date of birth brought.

Ursula had agreed, not wanting to alienate her mother any further. After all, she was her parents' only child, and this would be the only wedding her mother ever got to arrange.

Finally, the day had arrived. In a few hours, she would be married to Oliver. The house was already swarming with catering staff.

Her mother was still not back from the hairdresser, and her father had decided to take a short nap, claiming he hadn't yet adjusted to the time difference between Washington D.C. and San Francisco.

When she heard a soft rap on the door to her room, she instinctively knew who it was. Was she already feeling the special connection that only blood-bonded couples had? She swore she could sense his presence in the house from the moment he'd entered shortly after sunset.

"Come in."

Oliver slid inside, quickly closing the door behind him. "Hey!" He was still wearing jeans and a T-shirt.

"You'd better not get caught in here or my mother will have a fit!"

He chuckled and pulled her into his arms. "You're not wearing your dress yet, so I think it doesn't count."

Smiling, she wrapped her arms around him and pulled his head to her. "Does the bride get a kiss?"

"Since you're asking so nicely," he murmured, sliding his lips over hers and capturing them.

When his tongue slipped between her lips and started to explore her with long and sensual strokes, she sighed contentedly. She'd missed him during this week, even though she'd seen him every day. But there'd never been a moment for them to be alone. Somebody had always been there.

Oliver's hands roamed her body, his fingers caressing her just like his tongue did. Warmth and desire filled her, rushing through her body like a flashflood. Her entire body tingled pleasantly, and the place between her legs hummed, yearning for a touch. His touch. His kiss. She'd never believed that love could be like this: all consuming, passionate, while at the same time comforting and safe. Yet she felt safe, safe with a vampire, the very creature she had once feared. Oliver had made her forget all her fears and shown her that even a vampire could love.

She felt his love now. It burned brightly and steadily. With every touch and every kiss, she felt it. And tonight, after the ceremony, she would feel it in his bite. His loving bite, how lovingly and silently, he would make her his forever. How he would bestow immortality on her without robbing her of her humanity. How he would make himself vulnerable because once they blood-bonded, Oliver could only feed off her. His body would reject all other blood. In fact, it would make him violently ill if he ever drank blood other than hers.

For a vampire to bond himself to a human required ultimate trust. She felt that trust between them.

When he finally severed the kiss, she breathed heavily.

"We've gotta stop, baby, or there won't be a wedding, because I'll tie you to my bed and won't let you go."

She chuckled. "Would that be so bad?"

He shook his head and wagged his finger playfully. "And deprive myself of seeing you walk down the aisle in your beautiful white dress while—"

"White dress?" she interrupted him.

He pulled back a little, his eyebrows snapping together. "Yes, of course."

"Oliver, I won't be wearing a white dress. My dress is red. White is bad luck at a Chinese wedding. Red is good luck."

She watched as Oliver's facial expression changed to one of dismay. "Uh-oh!"

Trepidation rose in her. "What?"

"You said white is bad? How about white flowers? We can have white flowers, right?" he asked, grimacing.

Her stomach plummeted. "White flowers? Oh, please don't tell me you got white flowers for the wedding." She searched his face.

"I didn't know! I swear I had no idea," he insisted.

Ursula covered her face with her hands. "Oh no! This is not happening!" She sniffed, trying to push back the rising tears. "I should never have told you to take care of the flowers! I should have done it myself. Oh my god, my mother is going to be livid!"

"Baby, I'll fix it!"

She lowered her hands. "You can't fix that! You'll never get that many red flowers now! It's only a few hours till the ceremony. If there'll even be a ceremony! Once my mother sees the flowers, she'll insist we call the whole thing off!"

Oliver cupped her shoulders, forcing her to look at him. "I'll fix it. Whatever it takes! But this wedding will happen tonight, one way or another! I'll get rid of the white flowers. I promise you. When you walk into that tent in a few hours, the flowers will be red. Please trust me!"

The look which he gave her was penetrating. For long seconds, she simply stared back at him. What choice did she have? She had to trust him to make this right. Silently she nodded.

He pressed a quick kiss to her lips and left the room.

Oliver raced down the stairs. Shit! He'd screwed up. He couldn't remember if Ursula had ever told him about not getting white flowers, or whether she'd simply assumed he knew. It didn't matter now. There was no need wasting time by blaming somebody. What was done was done. And now he had to undo it. Swiftly, and without her parents, particularly her mother, noticing.

At the foot of the stairs, he nearly collided with Cain, one of his colleagues. The vampire with the permanent stubble looked as if he'd been born in a tuxedo. Before tonight, he'd only ever seen his fellow bodyguard in street clothes and had no idea how well he wore formalwear.

"Cain, hey!" he greeted him.

Cain glanced at him then the stairs and smirked. "Snuck in a visit to the bride?"

Oliver sighed. "Just as well that I did. Has her mother come back from the hairdresser yet?"

"Haven't seen her." He motioned to the guard who stood at the entrance door. "Bob's been here for the last hour, just like you requested. I've got another one of my men at the side entrance. The catering staff will use the side entrance and the guests the main entrance."

Oliver nodded approvingly. "Thanks for taking care of that. It makes me feel better." A glance at the bodyguard whom Cain had called Bob told him that the man was a vampire. He leaned closer to Cain and dropped his voice to a low whisper. "And the guy at the tradesmen entrance. Is he a vampire too?"

His colleague nodded.

"Good. I need somebody to watch that Ursula's parents don't enter the tent."

"Something wrong?"

"You could say that."

Cain tilted his head toward the door to the living room. "Thomas and Eddie just arrived. Maybe they can watch the entrance to the tent. I would do it myself, but I still have to do a sweep of the perimeter."

"I'll ask them."

Not losing a second, Oliver marched into the living room. Thomas and Eddie stood near the fireplace, talking in low voices, though he could hear what they were saying thanks to his superior vampire hearing. His vampire colleagues were both blond, but they looked very different tonight. They had exchanged their usual leather biker uniform for elegant black tuxedos and looked like eligible bachelors from a TV show. Only, the two weren't single. In fact, they were married—to each other.

"Thomas, Eddie!" Oliver called out to them, interrupting their— very intimate—conversation. The two lovebirds had only gotten together a short while earlier and by the looks of it were still in their honeymoon phase.

"Oliver, the man of the hour," Thomas replied with a smile.

"Is this how you're getting married?" Eddie asked, shaking his head.

"'Course not. But I need your help right now. Can you guard the tent for me?"

Thomas raised his eyebrows. "You think somebody's gonna walk off with it?"

Ignoring his joke, Oliver said, "Just guard the entrance and make sure that neither Ursula's parents nor any of the other humans enter the tent."

"Sure, we can do that. But why don't you want them to enter the tent?"

"Because the flowers are white, and they need to be red. Or it's bad luck."

Eddie shrugged. "Okay, that makes no sense, but if you want us there, we'll do it, right?" He looked at his partner, who nodded.

"Thanks guys!" Relieved, Oliver rushed out of the room and into the kitchen. Several members of the catering staff were feverishly working on preparing food. But the person he was looking for wasn't in the room. Leaving the kitchen, he pulled out his cell and dialed a number.

"Yeah?" Wesley replied.

"I need you to do me a favor. Can you come to the house right now?" Oliver walked along the corridor when the door to the basement and garage opened.

"I'm already here." Wes stepped through the door. Behind him, Haven appeared, and a moment later, Blake.

"You're not dressed yet?" Blake asked. "The guests will start arriving soon."

"What were you guys doing down there?" Oliver asked, ignoring Blake's question. It would take him all of five minutes to get dressed.

Wes gave a noncommittal grunt and brushed some dust from the sleeve of his tuxedo. "Nothing. What's up?"

"There's a problem with the flowers."

"What problem?" Wes asked. "They looked perfect when they came this morning. I made sure of it. Hey, if they screwed something up after that, it's not my fault! Besides, I was doing you a favor!"

Oliver grabbed his friend by the shoulder. "Hey! I'm not blaming you. It's not your fault. It's mine. They're the wrong color. We can't have white flowers at the wedding. It's bad luck. I need them to be red."

Wes tossed him a not-my-problem-look. "There's no way you can get a florist to supply that many red flower arrangements in the short time we've got left. Even if you went to several florists, they wouldn't have enough to replace all the current ones."

"For once, Wes is right," Haven added.

Wes glared at his brother. "I said I'm sorry! Okay? I'll deal with the dogs after the wedding."

"You mean the pigs?" Blake threw in, chuckling.

Wes whirled around to Blake. "You're not helping!"

"Stop it!" Oliver ground out. "That's not important now. What's important is that Wesley turned the pigs red." And that unfortunate incident would now provide the solution to his problem.

Haven loosened his bow tie. "Well, at least somebody agrees that my little brother has no business practicing witchcraft." He tossed a sideways glance at Wes.

"One of these days you're going to change your opinion on that," Wes warned.

"Quiet!" Oliver shouted, and at last all three fell silent and stared at him as if he'd finally lost it. Maybe he had. "Wes, I need your help. You have to turn the flowers in the tent red. Now. Before Ursula's parents see them."

"How?"

"You turned the pigs red. Use the same spell!"

A wide grin spread over Wesley's face. "Does that mean you're going to donate a little more of your blood?"

"Just for this one spell," Oliver conceded.

Wesley dug into his inside pocket and pulled out a glass vial.

"You always carry a vial around with you?" Blake asked.

Wesley winked at him. "First rule of a bodyguard: you've always gotta be prepared."

Haven rolled his eyes. "More like first rule of an opportunist."

Wes shrugged. "I need a few things from your pantry too. And a few minutes to mix the potion. Preferably where nobody can walk in on us."

"The gym downstairs," Oliver suggested.

Instantly, all three shook their heads.

"How about in the laundry room?" Haven suggested instead.

"That'll work."

It took fifteen minutes after Oliver had *donated* some blood before Wesley's potion was ready for use. Making sure Thomas and Eddie were at their places to watch that nobody entered the tent, Haven stood inside the tent, blocking the walkway to the tradesmen entrance so none of the catering staff would disturb them during the spell, while Blake blocked the kitchen door so none of the waiters or kitchen staff could look into the tent from there.

"Do your thing," Oliver said, waving his arms at the white flower arrangements that stood on the tables and decorated the podium as well as the rods that held the tent up.

There were tables and chairs for over a hundred guests in the tent. While the tablecloths were white, the white covers for the chairs sported red bows. And the napkins were equally red. He had to admit he liked the rich color. It reminded him of Ursula's blood.

"Step back," Wesley warned and walked into the middle of the tent.

Oliver heard him mumble something incoherent—presumably the spell—before he tossed the vial with the potion on the ground.

Instinctively Oliver took another step back when red smoke rose from the broken glass vial. As it swirled around, one by one the flowers turned red. But the flowers weren't the only things that took on the magical color: the tablecloths and chair covers also turned red.

Oliver shrugged. It couldn't hurt.

Wesley turned around to him, smiling broadly.

Next to Oliver, Haven hissed in a breath. Then he took a few steps toward his brother, hugged him roughly, and slapped him on the shoulder. "You did well, Wes! I'm proud of you."

If Oliver didn't have enhanced vampire vision, he would have missed the wet sheen that built in Wesley's eyes as a reaction to his big brother's compliment.

Finally Wesley had achieved something to win the approval of his brother. Maybe screwing up on the flowers hadn't been so bad after all.

Oliver smiled. Nothing else could go wrong now.

11

For almost two hours he'd watched all the guests arrive. Nobody noticed him standing in the shadow of a hedge on the other side of the street. They were too busy parading in their fancy clothes. More humans than vampires arrived for the event, many of the humans Chinese. Clearly, the bride had a large extended family, though none of her relatives seemed to carry the special blood. Even from across the street he would have been able to smell it, so attuned was he to it.

Human valets were parking the guests' cars, and a vampire guard at the entrance door checked the invitations. Another vampire guard stood at the tradesmen entrance through which the service personnel, the waiters and kitchen staff, entered.

He'd dressed appropriately. In his black tuxedo he would blend in with the guests as if he belonged there. Only the vampires on the premises would know he didn't. But soon they would all be in the tent at the back of the house, and the only one he'd have to deal with was the one guarding the entrance door.

The house was lit like a Christmas tree. It made it easy for him to watch the goings-on. When the living room started to empty out, he knew that the guests were taking their places in the tent. It couldn't be much longer now.

He lifted his eyes to the upper floor. In one of the rooms, Ursula would be waiting, alone, while everybody else would be in the tent.

It was time.

Calmly, he crossed the street and walked up to the entrance door, out of sight of the vampire guarding the side entrance. The door to the house was open, but blocking it was a vampire guard. The guy didn't know him, and that was his advantage.

He flashed a charming smile at the guard. "I hope I'm not late."

The vampire motioned to the interior. "It's going to start in a few minutes." Then he nodded to him. "Your name? And your invitation please."

"Michael Valentine," he answered and reached into his jacket pocket. "Uh, and here's my invitation."

With a single swift move, he pulled a stake from his inside pocket and plunged it into the guard's heart, before the man could even react.

The vampire disintegrated into dust. Michael turned to assure himself that the vampire guarding the side door hadn't heard anything suspicious. There was no sound coming from the tradesmen entrance. Quickly he swept the set of keys, cell phone, and loose change that remained from the vampire into the bushes.

Unimpeded, he entered the house. Without hesitation, he walked up the stairs, when he heard the music in the tent starting. But there would be no ceremony. No wedding. No blood-bond.

I'm coming for you, Ursula.

* * * *

"I think that's our cue," her father said when music came drifting up from the tent.

Ursula turned away from the full-length mirror in the guestroom and faced him.

He smiled back at her. "You look beautiful, Wei Ling. You're a woman now. You make us very proud, me and your mother."

"Even though I'm not marrying a Chinese man?"

"That was never very important to me." He chuckled. "Now, your mother, that's another story. But she'll get used to it. Don't worry about it."

"Thank you, Dad." She leaned toward him and kissed him on the cheek.

For a moment, she hesitated. There was so much she wanted to tell him, to confess who Oliver was and what he'd done for her. How he'd rescued her from a life in shackles. Her parents knew nothing of it. After her release from the blood brothel, Oliver and Scanguards had gone through great lengths to wipe her parents' memories and done the same with everybody who knew about her three-year disappearance. But there were moments like these when she wanted to tell the truth, though she knew it would only lead to pain.

"I love you, Dad," she whispered instead. "For everything you and Mom have done for me."

Somewhat embarrassed, her father smiled. "Time to go and meet your husband."

"I don't think so!" A menacing male voice came from the door as it shut behind him.

Ursula whirled her head around to the intruder and almost tripped over her long red dress. Her breath caught in her throat when she recognized the man. Though she didn't remember his name, she knew he was one of the former clients of the blood brothel. Leeches, she and the other girls had called them.

"What is this?" her father asked, outraged. "Get out!"

"Only once I have what I want!" the vampire snarled, his eyes now glaring red, and his fangs descending.

Her father gasped, but Ursula knew the vampire's look all too well. He'd come for her blood.

"What are you?!" her father choked out as he moved in front of Ursula as if to protect her.

But Ursula knew her father was no match for the vampire. No human was. She squeezed past him, glaring at the leech.

"Oliver will kill you if you harm me!" she warned.

"He won't catch us. We'll be long gone by the time he realizes."

At his words, Ursula shook her head in disbelief. No! He hadn't simply come to attack her here and drink her blood, he was planning to kidnap her!

"No!" she screamed, but she knew that the music in the tent would prevent her scream from reaching Oliver's ears. He would stand there at the podium, waiting for her in vain. Waiting, while she was being kidnapped.

"Now come to me, and I won't hurt you," the vampire promised, then added, " . . . much."

"Leave my daughter alone, you monster!" her father yelled and jumped toward him before she could stop him.

"No! Dad! No!"

But it was too late. With one punch, the vampire knocked her father clear across the room and into the wall, where he collapsed with a groan.

"Oh no! Dad! No!" She ran her eyes over his body. She couldn't see any blood, but the impact could have left internal injuries. Inside her, anger and worry collided. "You'll pay for this!"

The vampire chuckled, and the sound made her shiver in disgust. Like a tiger, he approached, setting one foot in front of the other. Slowly, as if he enjoyed this and didn't want it to end too soon. Like a cat playing with a mouse.

Frantically she looked around the room for anything she could use as a weapon, but came up empty.

She was at his mercy now.

"I've waited for this for so long," her attacker confessed. "All those days in my cold cell I was dreaming of this, of finding another blood whore. I'd almost given up."

"Get away from me!" she warned again. "Oliver will kill you."

A moan from where her father had collapsed told her he was alive. She cast a quick glance in his direction and realized he was trying to move, but struggled.

"Maybe," the vampire hedged. "But only after I've gotten what I wanted." He fletched his fangs and took another step toward her.

Like a cold fist, fear clamped around her heart. She could see it in his eyes now: the madness. He wouldn't be able to stop drinking from her once he started. He would drain her.

Tonight, on her wedding night, she would die. And her father would have to watch helplessly.

12

Oliver watched as Blake tied the wedding rings onto the tiny pink pillow and handed it to Isabelle. The toddler grinned up at them, looking adorable in her pink dress. Together with Delilah, they all stood at the French doors of the living room that led to the tented walkway leading into the tent. The music from the tent where a string quartet played came through the loudspeakers into the living room.

"You sure she's gonna be able to do that?" Oliver asked and grinned.

Delilah exchanged a look with her daughter. "Of course she is. Aren't you, Isabelle?"

The toddler beamed.

"Now go into the tent just like we practiced."

Isabelle turned around and staggered along the path, still a little wobbly on her feet. Delilah followed her closely, ready to catch her if she fell.

"Well, it's almost time," Blake said, grinning. "You can still change your mind, you know. I'll take her off your hands in a heartbeat."

Oliver boxed him in the side. "Not a chance."

His half-brother chuckled. "Just thought I'd give it one last shot."

"Hey, thanks for being my best man."

"Glad you asked me."

Suddenly the door to the corridor opened. "Are we too late?" a familiar voice asked.

Oliver swiveled on his heels and saw Dr. Drake rushing in, his Barbie-doll receptionist on his arm.

"Sorry, I hope this is the right entrance, but there was nobody telling us which way to go. Luckily the door was open." He shrugged apologetically.

"The guard outside should have directed you," Oliver said.

"What guard?"

Oliver's heart stopped. Without answering, he charged past Drake and rushed into the foyer. He ripped the entrance door open, but the vampire guard Cain had stationed there was gone. He turned back toward the foyer when he stepped on something. He bent down and inspected the item. A dime was wedged between the grout of two travertine tiles.

Though finding a lost coin wasn't something unusual, the hairs on Oliver's nape rose and a cold shiver ran down his spine.

Something wasn't right. Cain would have never pulled the guard off his post.

Blake came running from the living room. "What's going on?"

Oliver was already charging toward the stairs leading to the upper floors. "Alert Cain and have him sweep the premises for any intruders. Discreetly. I don't want anybody to alarm the guests."

"Got it."

But Oliver barely heard Blake's reply. He'd been a bodyguard long enough to know when to listen to his gut feeling. And his gut feeling told him to make sure Ursula was safe. That it was presumably bad luck to see the bride in her wedding dress before the wedding didn't matter.

When he entered the upper floor, his suspicion was confirmed. Ursula was in danger. A muffled cry drifted to his sensitive ears. A human wouldn't have heard it, but he had.

He flung the door to the guestroom open and barreled into the room, assessing the situation within a split second without slowing his movements.

A vampire pressed Ursula against the wall, his hands preventing her from fighting against him, though she kicked her legs against his shins, while the vampire's head neared her neck. Panic and desperation shone from Ursula's eyes. A few yards away, Yao Bang struggled to rise from the floor but appeared weak and dazed.

The vampire's head whirled around, noticing Oliver instantly. He snarled, his eyes glaring red, his fangs protruding from his lips. Oliver recognized him now. He was one of the addicts that Scanguards had treated.

"Michael Valentine!" Oliver ground out.

Valentine narrowed his eyes and moved so fast a human would only see a blur, bringing Ursula in front of his body like a shield, his arm wrapping around her upper arms so she couldn't move them, and the claws of his other hand pressing against the soft flesh of her throat.

"One move and I'll slice her open!" he warned.

Oliver arrested in his movement. He couldn't risk Ursula's life, and he knew that one slice of Valentine's sharp claws across her neck would kill her almost instantly. Oliver wouldn't even have enough time to turn her into a vampire to save her life. She would die.

He had to buy himself some time. "You won't kill her," Oliver hedged. "You want her special blood."

A flicker in Valentine's eyes confirmed that he'd guessed right. The vampire was still an addict. Zane had been right. Rehab hadn't worked on everybody.

"Get away from the door!" Valentine ordered.

"No!"

Oliver flicked his gaze to Ursula, who had been the one to voice the protest.

"Don't do it. Don't let him take me. I'd rather die than be imprisoned again." Her eyes pleaded with him.

He knew what was going through her mind. If Valentine took her, she would face the same ordeal as she had for three years while imprisoned in the blood brothel.

"I won't let him take you," he promised her.

"I don't see how you can prevent it," Valentine said and started walking sideways, pulling Ursula with him.

"The house is crawling with vampires. You'll never get out!"

From where Ursula's father lay on the floor, a gasp came. But Oliver couldn't turn his face to look at Yao Bang, though he knew his eyes were open and he was watching them in horror.

Valentine let out a mocking laugh. "They're all in the tent in the back of the house." He motioned to the window. "We're going out the front."

Oliver was poised, readying himself to attack. His eyes searched the room for any weapon because he carried none in his elegant tuxedo. There had been no place to conceal a stake.

A few more steps and Valentine would be at the window. Oliver's breathing accelerated. He had to do something now.

As Valentine dragged Ursula with him, her dress caught in the legs of a chair and she stumbled sideways. Valentine held on to her, but the claws on her throat slipped momentarily.

Seeing his chance, Oliver pounced. His claws lengthened in mid-flight, and his arm pulled back for leverage then swung forward to punch Valentine's shoulder to knock him back and make him lose his grip on Ursula.

Ursula fell, her balance uprooted by the power of the impact. Her legs, already tangled in her long dress and the petticoats beneath, lost their footing, and she fell forward. From the corner of his eye, Oliver saw her reach for the chair to brace her fall, but he couldn't help her, because Valentine's claws were coming toward him in a one-two punch that knocked Oliver's head sideways.

Without as much as a breath in between, Oliver aimed a fist at Valentine and hit the side of his neck, whipping him sideways. As Valentine fell against the window frame, Oliver's eyes darted around. But there was no time to find anything to fashion a stake from.

Valentine pushed himself off the window frame with such speed and agility that Oliver was taken by surprise when his attacker body-slammed him, tackling him to the ground. Oliver landed hard with his back on the wooden floor, making the floorboards moan in protest.

A claw came toward him, but Oliver blocked it with his forearm, pushing back while he twisted underneath his attacker. The rage flowing through his veins gave him added strength, and he managed to toss Valentine off him. However, his opponent was agile and found his feet at the same time as Oliver rose to his own.

This time, Oliver didn't let Valentine's next punch find its intended target. Instead, Oliver twisted on his heels and evaded him gracefully.

Their combined grunts and groans filled the room and mingled with the heavy breathing of Yao Bang and Ursula, who'd both managed to get to their feet.

Ursula had run to her father, and from the corner of his eye, Oliver caught a glimpse of the two as Ursula tried to calm her father, while her eyes darted around the room, seemingly looking for something. But he couldn't concentrate on her, because fending off Valentine's kicks and punches took all his concentration. And in the uncomfortable tuxedo, he felt less mobile than usual, though his opponent had the same handicap, wearing a tuxedo as well.

With every blow, Oliver realized more and more that he and his opponent were of equal strength. They were equally tall and well built. What he needed was an advantage. Because it could be minutes until one of his colleagues came up to this floor to find them.

Oliver gritted his teeth and punched harder. Valentine swayed on his feet, giving Oliver hope that he was tiring, but it wasn't the case, as he found out an instant later. As fast as a bullet train, the other vampire jumped to the side, gripped the chair, and slammed it against the wall, breaking it.

"Shit!" Oliver cursed, as he saw Valentine clamp his hand around one of the wooden legs that had broken off.

Now his opponent had a stake.

The evil grin on Valentine's face confirmed that the bastard couldn't wait to use it.

"Guess that's it," Valentine said with a self-congratulatory smirk, then jumped toward Oliver.

The power of the impact slammed Oliver backward and the back of his knees hit the bed frame, making him tumble onto the bed, landing in a supine position. Valentine jumped onto him, pinning him and trapping one of his arms under his knee.

With his free arm, Oliver fought his attacker as best he could, but Valentine had both arms available to fight. On his left Oliver perceived a movement, something red clouding his vision, but he didn't dare turn his eyes away from Valentine.

Triumphantly, the other vampire lifted the stake while Oliver tried to push him back with his free arm. To no avail: the hand holding the stake lowered.

"Fuck!" he pressed out from between clenched teeth.

Oliver heard a cracking sound. Had a bone in his forearm broken? He couldn't tell for sure, but he only knew that he couldn't hold Valentine off much longer. And once Valentine had killed him, there was nobody stopping him from getting Ursula.

"No!" he screamed. "Noooooo!"

With his last ounce of strength, he pushed Valentine back, managing to catapult him off him. Valentine staggered backward a few paces, when he suddenly stopped dead in his tracks, his eyes widening in surprise and shock.

A groan came from his throat. Then he disintegrated into dust. Behind him, Ursula stood, her arm stretched out, holding a makeshift stake. He recognized it as a piece of the chair. It hadn't been his forearm breaking. Ursula had broken a leg off the chair and used it as a stake.

She had saved him.

Oliver jumped from the bed and ran toward her, wordlessly pulling her into his arms. He pressed her trembling body to him. For a few moments, he couldn't speak.

"It's over," she murmured.

"I'm so sorry." He kissed her.

From the hallway, several people came running. Cain burst into the room first, followed by Blake and Zane.

"Where is he?" Cain yelled.

Oliver pointed to the floor where dust had settled. "He's dead."

Cain sighed in relief. "He killed Bob, who was stationed at the front door. I found some of his belongings. Who was he?"

"Michael Valentine."

"Fuck!" Zane cursed. He'd been the one who'd first interrogated Michael Valentine when he'd come to Scanguards' attention. And Zane had also been the one who had guessed that rehab wouldn't work on all the addicted vampires.

"You were right. Rehab didn't work for all of them," Oliver said to Zane. Then his gaze fell on Yao Bang who still stood where Ursula had left him only moments earlier, looking at them cautiously. He appeared uninjured.

"Buy us some time downstairs," Oliver ordered, looking at Blake.

"And say what?"

"Wardrobe malfunction. Whatever," Oliver said. Then he looked at Zane and Cain. "Are we sure he was the only one?"

Both nodded. "Positive."

"Good. Then give us some privacy." He motioned to Yao Bang and his colleagues nodded knowingly. They realized what he had to do now.

When the door closed behind the two vampires, Oliver looked at Ursula. She ran to her father and wrapped her arms around him. "Are you hurt?"

He shook his head. "Just a few bruises."

"We have to wipe his memory," Oliver said to her, avoiding her father's eyes.

Ursula nodded with a grim expression on her face. "I'm sorry, Dad, but it's for the better. You should have never seen this."

Oliver took a step toward him, but Yao Bang stretched out his hand as if to stop him. "Please don't!"

"It won't hurt. I promise you. You won't even know."

Yao Bang shook his head. "Please. Whatever you're gonna do, don't do it. Leave me my memories." He pointed to the floor where the vampire had died. "I don't *want* to forget what dangers are out there."

Ursula shook her head vehemently. "Dad! Please! You'll only worry if you know."

Yao Bang's eyes softened when he looked at his daughter. "Wei Ling, my little one, but I've worried until now. I've always worried about your safety. When you moved to New York to go to university, I worried about you. Because there is so much evil in the world. Now I won't have to worry any longer. Don't you see?" He pointed to Oliver. "Now I know you'll be protected."

Oliver watched as Ursula's forehead wrinkled in surprise. "But aren't you shocked that I'm going to marry a vampire?"

A kind smile curved her father's lips upward. "He loves you. When he attacked the other vampire to save you, he didn't hesitate even a split second." Then he shrugged. "Though I guess a vampire wouldn't have been my first choice, particularly since I didn't think they existed. But at least that means he can protect you from other vampires."

Ursula sighed.

"Please, by leaving me my memories, you're granting me peace of mind," Yao Bang pleaded.

Oliver exchanged a look with Ursula, then he took a step toward her father and stretched out his hand. "I have your word that you'll never divulge our secret?"

Yao Bang nodded and took Oliver's hand. "I promise you, son."

It was the first time his future father-in-law had ever called him son.

"What about my mother?" Ursula interrupted.

"Let me handle your mother," Ursula's father promised. "I'll find a way to tell her if it ever becomes necessary." Then he brushed some dirt particles off his tuxedo. "And now, I think it's time to get on with this wedding or your mother is going to have a fit."

Oliver chuckled. "I'd better get cleaned up a little."

Ursula giggled. "I've got *vampire* all over my dress." She pointed to the dust on her skirt.

Their gazes met and heated in an instant. In a few short hours she would have *vampire* all over her body. Her naked body.

13

From his vantage point on the small podium in the tent, Oliver looked down the aisle. He couldn't see Ursula, but he knew she was standing at the French doors to the living room, ready to walk along the covered walkway into the tent. He'd made sure that nothing else would happen now. Zane and Cain had volunteered to remain in the living room with her and her father until they were safely inside the tent. And once they were married, Oliver would blood-bond her as soon as possible. Only then would she truly be safe. Because only then would they be able to communicate telepathically with each other. And Oliver would always immediately sense when she was in danger.

He tried to relax and watched as Isabelle walked down the middle of the aisle, carrying the little pillow with the rings in her hands. Delilah coached her from the sidelines, making sure she didn't stop midway, but walked all the way to the front.

When he got his first glimpse of Ursula walking on her father's arm, coming closer with each step, he held his breath. During the fight and the few moments afterwards, he hadn't had a chance to admire her and take in how truly beautiful she looked. He'd never thought that she could look more glorious in a red wedding dress than any other woman in a white one. As graceful as a princess, she walked toward him, her eyes focused on him. All fear and panic was wiped from her face.

His heart started to thunder and he feared that everybody in the tent could hear how wildly it beat. Because it beat for her. And because of her.

When Ursula and her father finally stopped at the podium, he exchanged a brief look with Yao Bang. A contented smile played around the older man's lips. Even though Oliver didn't know his father-in-law very well, he grew fonder of him by the minute. To be accepted by Ursula's father so wholeheartedly warmed his heart. His gaze drifted over the guests. Quinn sat near the podium. His sire looked at him as proudly as any father would, and behind him, Samson beamed with a happy smile. He'd been the first to see potential in him and had offered him a chance for a new life. Without Samson and Quinn he wouldn't be here today.

He tore his look from them and smiled at Ursula. Their gazes fused.

Oliver barely heard the words of the minister as he spoke an introductory prayer and Yao Bang answered him when asked who was giving this woman to this man. Then he took his seat next to his wife.

Seconds turned into minutes as they exchanged traditional vows. The only thing they had changed was the ending. They'd replaced "till death do us part" with more suitable words.

" . . . for eternity," Oliver now said and felt tears rise into his eyes when he saw the wet sheen covering Ursula's irises.

"The rings," the minister prompted and looked at Blake.

His best man crouched down to Isabelle and nodded at her, giving her a sign that it was her turn, and the toddler staggered toward the minister, holding the pillow with the rings in front of her. She glanced sideways as if to seek approval from her mother, when she tripped and fell forward. But the little hybrid's reflexes were as sharp as those of a vampire, and she braced her fall with her hands before her knees could hit the floorboards, though she dropped the pillow in the process.

A collective gasp raced through the guests, but Isabelle lifted her head with a wide smile, looking almost apologetic. Two tiny fangs flashed from her open mouth.

Oliver had never seen anything more adorable. He and Ursula had never spoken about children, but he knew that eventually they would have some. Once they were both ready.

It appeared the minister had seen Isabelle's fangs, because his forehead pulled together and he leaned toward the toddler.

"Isabelle!" Blake chastised under his breath, and she seemed to understand him and quickly pressed her lips together again. She reached for the pillow that had fallen from her hands, and with Blake's help, she was back on her feet within seconds. "That a girl," Blake praised, winking at Oliver.

Oliver suppressed a chuckle.

The minister took the rings and blessed them before handing one to Ursula and one to him.

When Ursula repeated the minister's words, Oliver's heart expanded, filling with love and pride, with joy and happiness.

"With this ring, I thee wed." Ursula slid the ring onto his finger.

Oliver didn't wait for the minister to prompt him, impatient for Ursula to be his wife. "With this ring, I thee wed."

Nor did he wait for the minister to tell him that he could kiss the bride. He simply pulled Ursula into his arms and kissed her.

"I now pronounce you man and wife." He heard the minister's words somewhere in the distance.

"I love you," he whispered against his bride's lips only for her to hear, though he knew that the vampires in the tent would be able to pick up his words. And maybe even the humans, for it was a feeling he couldn't hide from anybody. Nor did he intend to.

14

They had danced. They had cut the cake. They had toasted to their guests, listened to speeches, and accepted well-wishes, while secretly wishing they could escape and be alone.

Somebody finally had mercy on them and announced that it was time the bride and groom withdrew, while the rest of the guests could continue to celebrate. That somebody was Quinn.

Holding Ursula's hand, Oliver now walked to the door of the gym which was located in the basement in one corner of the large garage, still thinking about Quinn's words that their wedding present would be down there and the subsequent sparkle in Rose's eyes. As if they had set up a prank.

He knew all about wedding pranks: toilet-paper-wrapped furniture, shaving-cream-decorated cars, confetti-littered beds, the things that your best friends did to the apartment while the couple was still dancing at the wedding reception. Oliver couldn't care less what prank they'd set up, because nothing could erase the relief he felt knowing Ursula was safe now. He'd almost lost her tonight, and he needed to wipe out those memories by making new ones with her.

Oliver turned the doorknob and pushed the door inward. Then he froze, not in shock, but in wonder.

Next to him, Ursula sucked in a breath. "Oh my god!"

The gym equipment was gone.

"It's beautiful," she whispered.

He could only echo her words. This was the best wedding gift Quinn and Rose could have ever given them: a place to consummate their blood-bond away from any curious eyes and ears. A place just for them.

In the center of the small room stood a large bed draped with soft sheets, a canopy of sheer material over it. The fabric that flowed all the way to the floor, covered with plush rugs, turned the bed into a cocoon. Along the walls, sconces with candles had been installed, and the subdued light made the room glow as if a fireplace were burning. It looked like a dream.

Oliver tore his gaze from the bed and looked at his wife. The word still felt so new, but it felt right.

"There were moments when I thought this would never happen," he said, his hand reaching up to stroke his knuckles over the elegant curve of Ursula's neck.

"I was scared," she confessed.

"I'll make sure you'll never be scared again." He leaned in to brush his lips over her cheek.

Ursula's arms slid around his neck, pulling him against her body. "I missed you."

"Not as much as I missed you." The last few days had been hell. Finally they were past them. "This week I thought I would have to break into my own house just so I could feel you in my arms."

She laughed softly. "Break in? Maybe I would have opened the door for you."

"Maybe?" he growled, dropping his lips to her neck and nibbling there.

"If you'd asked nicely."

He loved it how Ursula teased him, how she seduced him with her sinful voice while she rubbed her tantalizing body against his. "How nicely?" He pressed his hard-on against her soft stomach, letting her feel what she did to him.

"Oh," she murmured. "As nicely as you're asking now." Her hand slid to his backside, squeezing him through his tuxedo.

Oliver lifted his head. "I'm glad we're speaking the same language."

"I am too. But were you planning on talking all night, or would you rather we do something else?" She tilted her head toward the bed.

"Well, since you're asking so nicely . . . "

Oliver slid his mouth over hers and kissed her. He stroked his tongue over the seam of her lips and felt them part under light pressure. Without haste, he drove his tongue into her mouth and explored her. No matter how often he'd kissed her in the last few months, it was different now. Tonight she had become his wife, and in a few moments she would become his blood-bonded mate. This kiss was the kiss that would start the rest of their lives. He had no intention of rushing this.

This would be the memory they'd always cherish, the one that would help them overcome any obstacle in the future, any quarrels they might find themselves in, any disagreements or misunderstandings that might arise between them. It would make them stronger as a couple. Their union would be unbreakable. And last longer than one lifetime. Their love would last an eternity.

"I love you," Oliver murmured, briefly breaking the kiss before capturing her mouth again and pouring every ounce of passion and love he felt for Ursula into the kiss.

They undressed each other slowly. Layer by layer of clothing fell to the floor, first his tuxedo jacket and shirt, then her wedding dress. Finally his pants, until they stood in front of each other only in their underwear.

Ursula's strapless bra and panties were as red as her dress, but there was a different color he noticed. He slid his finger under the blue garter she wore around one of her thighs.

"Something blue," he whispered, smiling. "I wanted to incorporate some Western traditions too. You were so accommodating in accepting everything Asian my parents threw at you. I wanted to thank you."

Oliver licked his lips. "I like the way you think."

She pointed to her ankle, making him look down. "Something borrowed."

Oliver spotted the diamond ankle bracelet she wore. "Whose?"

"Nina lent it to me."

"I like it. I think I should buy you one of your own."

She smiled. "I think you should."

"How about something old?" he asked.

Ursula reached to the back of her head and took out the sparkling comb that held up her hair. The red comb was decorated with gold Chinese symbols. "It was my grandmother's. My mother wore it for her wedding."

"It's beautiful." Then he looked into her eyes. "But nothing can ever be as beautiful as you." He kissed her, pulling her against the curve of his body, feeling her soft skin against his. Instantly, his entire body was in flames.

"Don't you want to know what's new?" Ursula asked, pulling back slightly.

"Later." Impatiently he tore at her bra, unhooking it and sliding it off her.

He put his palms over her small but firm breasts, squeezing them. Ursula moaned softly.

Gently, he urged her to take a few steps back, directing her toward the bed. When the back of her legs hit the mattress, he lowered her onto it. She looked perfect on the white sheets, like a present he didn't deserve. His eyes ran over her body, drinking her in.

He braced himself on the bed with one knee and one hand, hovering over her, while his other hand caressed her silken skin, reacquainting himself with her body. A week of not touching her had been too long.

His fingers trailed down the valley between her breasts and crossed her flat stomach until they reached the red silk of her panties. He slid underneath it, combing through her thatch of hair, and felt her spread her legs wider.

The scent of her arousal wafted to him, and he soaked it in, allowing it to drug him. Then his finger slipped lower and touched her moist cleft.

A hitched breath came from Ursula, then another one as he traveled along her slit and bathed his fingers in her wetness. Her flesh quivered. He loved how receptive she was whenever he touched her. And he loved arousing her. And making her surrender in his arms. Just as he was going to do now. With his hands and his mouth.

Oliver used both his hands to pull her panties down and free her from them, but when he looked at her naked body, he noticed something different. He lifted his head to stare at her. She met his gaze.

"Something new," she whispered.

He dropped his gaze back to the small tattoo that sat just above the left edge of her pubic hair: a Chinese symbol and within it, the initials U and O were intertwined.

"It means forever," she said.

"I love it."

He lowered his lips onto the tattoo and kissed it. Then he shifted on the bed and took his place between her spread legs, bringing his mouth to her weeping pussy. His tongue swiped along her moist folds, gathering the wetness that coated them, tasting her sweet essence. Her soft moans and sighs provided the background music to his caresses, and her hands drove into his hair, making him shiver with pleasure. As she spread her thighs wider, offering herself to him, he slid his hands under her backside and tilted her sex, giving him better access. His tongue drove into her inviting slit, then moved higher to brush over the tiny organ at the base of her curls.

Ursula writhed underneath him, and he tightened his hold on her, shifting his hands to the front of her thighs to hold her down as he licked and sucked her with more intensity. He tried to ignore his aching cock that was still confined within his boxer briefs. He knew he couldn't yet free himself of the last piece of clothing, or he would attack her like the hungry beast he was. Because tasting Ursula and making love to her brought out everything primal in him. Civility was pushed into the background, humanity obliterated. All that was left inside him was pure vampire: ravenous, insatiable, intense.

The urge to make her his was stronger now. The vampire inside him knew that this was the night of their blood-bond, that tonight they would become one. And the vampire was impatient.

His hips jerked against the mattress, moving back and forth to grant his cock some measure of relief. To no avail. Oliver knew that there was only one way he could get relief: inside of Ursula's body.

Growling, he licked her clit faster and harder. Ursula thrashed, her body so close to release he could almost taste it. Sweat dripped from his face and neck, and to his horror he could feel his hands turn into claws, his fingernails sharpen to spiky barbs.

"Oh God!" Ursula called out.

Then a shudder raced through her body, visibly shaking her as her orgasm claimed her.

The vampire inside him broke to the surface, unleashed by the call from his mate. His claws sliced through his boxer briefs, freeing him at last. Cool air blasted against his burning cock, but only for a second. Faster than ever before, he thrust into her, seating himself to the hilt. A choked breath escaped her throat as her interior muscles imprisoned him, still quivering from her orgasm.

Unable to hold himself back, Oliver pulled halfway out of her tight sheath then plunged back inside. And again. His vampire side went wild, fucking her hard and fast.

"I'm sorry!" he cried out. "I don't want to hurt you!"

He'd always thought the bonding would be a tender affair, a slow merging of bodies, a gentle lovemaking. He hadn't counted on his vampire side taking over so completely and giving him no choice in the matter.

He watched as his claw sliced into his own shoulder to create a small bleeding wound, before he lowered it to her face.

"Drink from me!" he demanded, his voice gruff and barely recognizable.

Ursula should reject him, afraid of what he would do to her, yet she did nothing of the sort. Instead, she placed her lips over the incision and licked it, lapping up the blood that oozed from it.

His entire body shuddered.

"Oh God!" he murmured.

He'd never felt anything like it. It was like the most sensual caress. The most tender embrace. The movements of his body slowed, becoming more gentle and tender. Then his eyes zoomed in on the throbbing vein at her neck, how it beckoned to him, called to him to take her.

In slow motion, he lowered his lips to it, feeling her shiver when he connected with her skin. Without haste, he opened his mouth and grazed her with the tips of his fangs. Slowly, they pierced her skin, descending into her flesh.

He drew on her vein. Blood rushed into his mouth and cascaded down his throat. He'd drunk from her many times before, but his time was different. This time she drank from him too. It created a circle, an unbreakable bond between them.

Ursula's hand slid to his nape and pressed him to her.

Take me, all of me, he heard her thoughts drift to him and knew their bond had been established.

The knowledge that they were one now catapulted him over the edge. His climax blasted through his body like a tsunami, unstoppable and uncontrollable.

Ursula's muscles spasmed and he could now feel her orgasm as it traveled through her in waves, just like she would be able to sense his climax and experience it as if she were inhabiting his body.

So beautiful, he thought.

Will it always be this way? she asked, continuing to drink his blood, just as he still sucked at her vein.

Yes, always.

Because he would make sure that they would always be as happy as they were now. Whatever it took. Because she was his life, just as he was hers.

THE END

About Tina Folsom

Tina Folsom is a New York Times and USA Today Bestselling Author. She's always been self-published and has found tremendous success with her paranormal series, Scanguards Vampires, Venice Vampyr, and Out of Olympus, selling more than 1.5 million copies of her 50 titles (which includes titles in German, French, and Spanish) in almost 4 years.

Tina writes about hot alpha heroes, bad boys, and kick-ass heroines. Fast-paced plots and steamy scenes are her specialty. She loves vampires and the concept of immortality.

Tina is a one-women-enterprise. She writes constantly, translates her own books into German, her native language, and manages all aspects of her publishing empire. Her books are available in ebook format, as paperbacks, as audio books, and in foreign languages. She doesn't plan on stopping there and is constantly working on new and innovative ways to bring her books to more readers worldwide.

For more about Tina Folsom:

http://www.tinawritesromance.com

http://www.twitter.com/Tina_Folsom

http://www.facebook.com/TinaFolsomFans

Sign up for Tina's email newsletter!

You can also email her at tina@tinawritesromance.com

Tina is a member of the Indie Voice, a group of 10 New York Times bestselling indie authors who love recommending indie books. If you want to receive **information on great books and bargains**, and be entered in the **Indie Voice's monthly raffle (gift cards, e-readers, and other great prizes)**, please sign up for our newsletter on our website: http://theindievoice.com/

Also from Tina Folsom

Tina's books are available in English, German, French, Spanish, as well as in audio.

English

Samson's Lovely Mortal (Scanguards Vampires #1)
Amaury's Hellion (Scanguards Vampires #2)
Gabriel's Mate (Scanguards Vampires #3)
Yvette's Haven (Scanguards Vampires #4)
Zane's Redemption (Scanguards Vampires #5)
Quinn's Undying Rose (Scanguards Vampires #6)
Oliver's Hunger (Scanguards Vampires #7)
Thomas's Choice (Scanguards Vampires #8)
A Touch of Greek (Out of Olympus #1)
A Scent of Greek (Out of Olympus #2)
A Taste of Greek (Out of Olympus #3)
Lover Uncloaked (Stealth Guardians #1)
Venice Vampyr #1
Venice Vampyr #2 Final Affair
Venice Vampyr #3 Sinful Treasure
Venice Vampyr #4 Sensual Danger
Lawful Escort
Lawful Lover
Lawful Wife
The Wrong Suitor
Steal Me
Captured to Breed

Sign up for the 1001 Dark Nights Newsletter
and be entered to win a Tiffany Key necklace.

There's a contest every month!

Go to www.DarkNights.com to subscribe.

As a bonus, all subscribers will receive a free
1001 Dark Nights story
The First Night
by Lexi Blake & M.J. Rose

Turn the page for a full list of the
1001 Dark Nights fabulous novellas...

1001 Dark Nights

WICKED WOLF by Carrie Ann Ryan
A Redwood Pack Novella

WHEN IRISH EYES ARE HAUNTING by Heather Graham
A Krewe of Hunters Novella

EASY WITH YOU by Kristen Proby
A With Me In Seattle Novella

MASTER OF FREEDOM by Cherise Sinclair
A Mountain Masters Novella

CARESS OF PLEASURE by Julie Kenner
A Dark Pleasures Novella

ADORED by Lexi Blake
A Masters and Mercenaries Novella

HADES by Larissa Ione
A Demonica Novella

RAVAGED by Elisabeth Naughton
An Eternal Guardians Novella

DREAM OF YOU by Jennifer L. Armentrout
A Wait For You Novella

STRIPPED DOWN by Lorelei James
A Blacktop Cowboys ® Novella

RAGE/KILLIAN by Alexandra Ivy/Laura Wright
Bayou Heat Novellas

DRAGON KING by Donna Grant
A Dark Kings Novella

PURE WICKED by Shayla Black
A Wicked Lovers Novella

HARD AS STEEL by Laura Kaye
A Hard Ink/Raven Riders Crossover

STROKE OF MIDNIGHT by Lara Adrian
A Midnight Breed Novella

ALL HALLOWS EVE by Heather Graham
A Krewe of Hunters Novella

KISS THE FLAME by Christopher Rice
A Desire Exchange Novella

DARING HER LOVE by Melissa Foster
A Bradens Novella

TEASED by Rebecca Zanetti
A Dark Protectors Novella

THE PROMISE OF SURRENDER by Liliana Hart
A MacKenzie Family Novella

FOREVER WICKED by Shayla Black
A Wicked Lovers Novella

CRIMSON TWILIGHT by Heather Graham
A Krewe of Hunters Novella

CAPTURED IN SURRENDER by Liliana Hart
A MacKenzie Family Novella

SILENT BITE: A SCANGUARDS WEDDING by Tina Folsom
A Scanguards Vampire Novella

DUNGEON GAMES by Lexi Blake
A Masters and Mercenaries Novella

AZAGOTH by Larissa Ione
A Demonica Novella

NEED YOU NOW by Lisa Renee Jones
A Shattered Promises Series Prelude

SHOW ME, BABY by Cherise Sinclair
A Masters of the Shadowlands Novella

ROPED IN by Lorelei James
A Blacktop Cowboys ® Novella

TEMPTED BY MIDNIGHT by Lara Adrian
A Midnight Breed Novella

THE FLAME by Christopher Rice
A Desire Exchange Novella

On behalf of 1001 Dark Nights,

Liz Berry and M.J. Rose would like to thank ~

Steve Berry

Doug Scofield

Kim Guidroz

Jillian Stein

Dan Slater

Asha Hossain

Chris Graham

Pamela Jamison

Jessica Johns

Richard Blake

BookTrib After Dark

and Simon Lipskar

9 781682 305706